A WEB OF LIES

A WEB OF LIES

BRITT VAN DEN ELZEN

NEW DAM PUBLISHING

This is a work of fiction. Names, characters, places, and incidents either are the product of the author's imagination or are used fictitiously. Any resemblance to actual persons, living or dead, events, or locales is entirely coincidental.

Copyright © 2024 Britt van den Elzen

All rights reserved. No part of this book may be reproduced or used in any manner without written permission of the copyright owner except for the use of quotations in a book review.

Second edition

Cover Design by Seventhstar Art
Map created by Fred Kroner of Stardust Book Services

ISBN 978-9-0833-6063-8 (hardback)
ISBN 978-9-0833-6062-1 (paperback)
ISBN 978-9-0833-6061-4 (ebook/kindle)

Published by New Dam Publishing
www.brittvandenelzen.com

Ever said, "My professional success is more important than my happiness"?

This one's for you.

ASHAR

Ashtior ("The Upper City")
Domain of the Cardinal

Angeli (have wings), including
the Archangel and *the Seraphim*

Ashium ("Shard City")
Domain of the Prime

Ethereal (have advanced speed)
Lupine (have advanced strength)
Pisces (have fins underwater)
Humans (...)

Ashrior ("The Undercity")
Domain of the Supreme

Sanguis (have fangs)
Daemon (have advanced eyesight),
including *the Supreme*

Trias Politica

Legislative Power = The Cardinal *(Seraphim)*
Executive Power = The Prime *(Archangel)*
Judicial Power = The Supreme *(Supreme)*

PROLOGUE

The man had been waiting at the door for well over an hour, but no one dared to urge him inside or hasten him. His eyes were red-rimmed, the stubble on his face neglected for a day or two, wings limp behind him.

Forgotten.

When he finally moved, he reached for the door handle with trembling hands, hesitating. He moved his hand higher, refusing to give into this game of wills, and splayed it flush against the heavy doors, leaning his head against the cold wood as a sob threatened to break free from him. The man rocked his head from side to side as if convincing himself nothing of this was happening, that nothing beyond that door was real.

His hand balled into a fist, causing the wood underneath his fingers to groan under the pressure he exerted, and he let out a quivering sigh as he tightened his jaw and straightened. With reluctance, he opened the door slowly and stepped inside. He spun around, directing his attention towards the door as he closed it, unable to endure the sight of what awaited him. Every inch of his body shuddered as he tried to keep breathing.

Inhaling a large quantity of air, he turned around achingly slowly, his gaze fixed on the middle of the room, where a large stone altar protruded from the ground. A pattern of beautiful, intricate carvings marked the stone slab—the only decoration in the otherwise cold, stark room.

Positioned on the altar was a woman, her wings a pale, slightly off-white hue, the markings of an Angeli not yet of age. At first glance, she might have appeared to be resting, but the man's eyes clouded with tears, shielding her features from view, and it was the only reason he dared to step closer.

But the more he blinked, the more his sight cleared, and the horrifying reality came crashing back down on him. His legs buckled, no longer supporting him as he broke down, sinking to his knees. He had been there when she died—had witnessed her last breath, had been the recipient of her last heartbreaking smile. He had watched as the light left her eyes, that precious life moving on to another place.

Away from him.

And still, he had held the hope it was all a misunderstanding. A cruel, cosmic joke—*a nightmare*. But being here, facing her lifeless body… It broke his already shattered heart all over again.

Carefully, he clasped her small, slender hand between his own with fervor. He blew warm air into the hold, willing her hand to warm back up.

It did not.

"*Coranima*," he whispered, caressing the skin of her hand as he pressed her palm to his cheek. *She was too pale.* "You can't leave me here."

The Angeli pushed himself back to his feet but never let go of her hand. He kissed the back of it, moving his gaze to her face—the face he knew better than any other. Inching closer, he gently stroked a hand through her blonde hair, running a strand between his index finger and thumb before carefully placing it back beside her.

"How am I supposed to live without you?" he asked, voice breaking on the last words.

His hand grazed the top of her wings. She had never gotten to use them. It had been something she had looked forward to so much. Her feathery lashes brushed against her cheeks, cheeks that had blushed from the faintest compliment. It was as though she could open her eyes at any moment. Even in death, she was the most beautiful woman he had ever laid eyes on.

Someone like her was meant to *live*, to build a life. She was one of the good ones.

It seemed the gods did not care, and he cursed them for it.

"I can't do this," he choked out, shaking his head. "This can't be the end."

Tears stained his cheeks as he got lost in the memories they had shared. "We were supposed to live this life together. You were supposed to move in with me." He pulled something from his pocket—a thin, golden chain with a pendant shaped like a key—and studied it hard. "We would have gotten married, had children. Three, like you wanted."

He swallowed with effort and had to close his eyes to continue. "But not three boys that look like me. We would have a girl, too, resembling you." A trembling breath escaped him, but his lips curved into a smile as he pictured it. "We would have the evenings to ourselves, going on dates in Shard City—like you always dreamt of. And then we'd come home, end the night in each other's arms, and try to sleep in, only to be woken by our kids early the next morning."

His chin trembled as he delicately traced his knuckles over her cheek. "We would have been so happy."

He looked at the necklace again and put it back in his pocket. "I will keep this safe for you, as I promised. It will go wherever I go."

With a sharp inhale, he rubbed his fingers across his eyes and swept a hand over his nose. He swallowed and looked at the ceiling, a hand still holding hers. "Your brother… I know you worry about him." His gaze landed back on her. "But don't feel guilty. Okay? There's nothing to feel guilty about."

She didn't respond; *of course she did not*. The anguish and harsh reality of it carved a frown between his brows. "I don't know how much I can do to get him out, but I will do my best. I promise—I will ensure *all* of them are looked after."

Another shuddering breath left him. "And I won't take more from them than they've already lost, so our reunion might take some time, *Coranima*. I hope you will wait for me beyond the veil."

Nodding to himself, the Angeli let go of her hand and tucked it safely beside her body. He held onto her face with both hands and pressed a last kiss to her lips. Clearing his throat, he rose, sealing off his emotions and hardening his expression behind a mask of unbridled nothingness.

Gazing at her once more, for the last time, he already felt less: less anguish, less hurt, less grief. In mere moments, nothing but dust would remain of her. And all that remained for him to feel was rage—a fury unparalleled by anything he had ever experienced. It was the only way for him to move forward.

The only way for him to survive.

PART ONE

Our worth used to be judged by magic and established within a society dominated by it. Obsessed with it. Where people now need to rely on advanced technology to solve problems, magic used to do it for us.

It has become a rare commodity in this world. We slowly lost touch with universal forces and succumbed to logic to make sense of the world instead. Declining rapidly with each passing year, magic has been proclaimed nearly extinct. And if people indeed possess it, it is all but a spark—to light a candle, control droplets of sweat, or move a strand of hair.

Useless.

But it has always been among us. It never left. Powerful magic lays dormant. I sense its tendrils everywhere I go and can feel the threads seeking me out—all but a few sources left scattered throughout the world. Those powers are in slumber, waiting for their masters to call on them, need them, claim them.

Wield them.

Such power is not an easy burden to bear, and it will never be.

The scale has been broken for too long, with the balance tipping in favor of surrendering to the darkness. Although the traces of magic are faint, it instills hope within me. We overcame once, which means we can triumph again. There is no other option. <u>They</u> are waiting.

And yet, no one believes.

But I have seen them, fought them, defeated them.

I know.

— The Magnum Iter, A.M.

CHAPTER ONE

Leyla
100 years later

My ears were still buzzing from the loud music of Supernova, the club I'd visited with my best friend, Dana, for my twenty-fifth birthday.

Despite Dana's efforts to convince me to prolong the night, the sweet poisons I'd been drinking were overpowering my senses. She had made me vow to take a cab back home, but everyone knew you couldn't swear a Daemon into submission. We were skilled in the art of manipulation, deception, and conning—at least, according to others.

I ran my fingers through my black hair and strutted down the bustling streets in my high heels. The long, ebony coat I wore covered most of my bare skin, but with only a short dress underneath, the chill lapping at my legs still made me shiver. Even though it was late summer, the cold that descended these nights was vicious.

The click-clacking of my heels echoed through the street, attracting fewer eyes as I left the buzzing clubbing area behind. Every stare remained on me for longer, anticipating what I would do if I noticed them—or what they might do if I didn't.

Alleyways came and went beside me, sometimes occupied by people, other times just darkness filling them. But the neon lights of the restaurants and shops burned brightly, reflecting in my leather trench coat.

Most people would call me stupid, world-weary, and naïve—an adrenaline junkie who loved living on the edge. Who, in their right mind, would walk home alone, *tipsy*, in Shard City, the city center of Ashar, where crime and death rates were rising steadily with each passing day?

Unlike the many tourists from all over Celestia, I didn't let the bright colors of the city center fool me. The only thing they did was disrupt my innate ability to see in the dark, courtesy of my Daemon heritage.

It was hysterical how romantic those lights had seemed to my younger self.

Someone whistled. "What're you hiding underneath that coat, gorgeous?" The small group across the street from me was laughing, but I didn't pay them any mind. Clearly, one of their egos had become inflated beyond sense and thought it was amusing to harass a passerby. Most of them were all bark and no bite, anyway, though part of me always hoped they would attempt something.

The shadow trailing me patiently followed my every move. He would intervene if anyone dared to approach me. Yet, apart from a few chuckles, the group carried on.

On my side of the street, I encountered a stooped silhouette—human by the looks of it—rummaging through the restaurant containers in search of her next meal. I slowed down, swaying on my heels a little as I opened my purse and took out some *shards*, enough for her to buy a proper meal with come morning. I approached the homeless individual and paused before her hunched posture, still occupied with scouring the container.

Whenever I did something like this, I could almost perceive a faint hissing emanating from the shadows. My shadow, at least, thought me stupid; no doubt he was reporting back to his master, telling him all about my nightly outings and charity like the good lap dog he was.

He could do how he pleased. It did not matter to me.

"Here," I said, my voice hoarse from the singing and yelling I'd done in the club. Holding out my hand, the shimmering coins were impossible to miss with the bright lights reflecting on them.

The woman's head whipped up, her bloodshot eyes focusing on the coins in my hand. I could see her deciding to take them from me, but then her gaze moved to mine, and she recoiled like prey—flinching at the sight of me. Daemons had incredible sight at night, but our eyes were also beacons, shining like the inherent predators we were once born to be. Our reputation was far from stellar.

"Take them." I moved my hand closer to her, but she inched back like my touch could harm her. While my intention wasn't to hurt her, a fraction of me entertained the idea of flinging the coins at her out of sheer exasperation.

With a sigh, I bent down and dropped the coins on the ground, indifferent to whether their clinking sound would draw any unwanted attention. Life wasn't fair—I learned that a long time ago. This was a survival of the fittest, and if she declined my money in her desperate state, perhaps she was one of the weak. I retracted my hands into my pockets and left her alone, although I could hear the human scraping her loot from the cold pavement the moment I departed.

I didn't sympathize with the homeless; I felt indifferent to who they were. What I cared about were the issues they caused and the reasons they were on the street in the first place. It was degrading to watch a person be desperate for something that I could provide without a care in the world. I wouldn't miss the money; I had plenty of it—enough to last me at least ten lifetimes. And it wasn't like I was doing world-altering things with it, anyway.

The number of homeless people I encountered grew as I approached my street. More and more people lined up outside with every passing year. I paused in front of three of them, huddled in fabrics to shield them from the chilly night. *Fuck it*—I was in a giving mood tonight. I didn't wake them; instead, I took the remaining *shards* from my purse and placed the coins close to them, ensuring they remained invisible.

I wasn't foolish enough to think they would all spend it on food or shelter. But it was better than nothing. They could experience a moment of bliss with it, however they preferred. I didn't do it as an act of penance for my sins or to clear my conscience. There were no rainbows and sunshine in the cards for me. I was born from sin itself. My blood ran thick with it.

But I loved this city, and that, to me, was enough.

I finally arrived at my apartment, the street dark, and opened the lock on my door near the mailbox, saying L. C.

Leyla Cuprum.

A girl that didn't exist. *Replaceable.* At least he'd let me keep my first name. Still, nobody knew who I was.

Not truly.

I hoped he hated his job as much as I hated him following me. I tossed my head sideways, scanning the darkness behind me, and said, "Goodnight." Loud enough for him to hear, no doubt. Then I slammed the door without locking it.

No one could get in, anyway.

Hours later, I woke up from the bright light that entered my bedroom through the open curtains I'd forgotten to close that night. I turned around in bed and groaned into my pillow. The sun didn't fucking help with my raging headache.

What a way to start my twenty-fifth year.

I took my phone from where I'd left it on the nightstand, nearly knocking off the small potted cactus Dana had given me to *liven up the place*. The motion unveiled my new serpent tattoo, coiling around my arm. I unlocked the screen and looked at my unread messages. Even though I lacked online profiles and a large social circle, there were still a handful of texts.

Josiah: *Happy birthday, Leyla.*

I arched an eyebrow. Dana must have told him.

Dad: *Enjoy your day.*

My father had wired money into my account—something I neither needed nor wanted from him.

Me: *When can I visit?*

Dad: *Patience, Cara. We will meet soon.*

It was his nickname for me, meaning something akin to *dear* or *sweetheart*.

I refrained from replying, feeling a surge of frustration in my body. He was busy, but that didn't mean I appreciated being hidden from view. As if I were nothing more than the young girl I once was that had needed his protection.

Several weeks had elapsed since I last saw my father and

my life had trudged along. I was ready to be useful and work for him, but he kept pushing me away with excuses about not being ready yet. Deep down, I knew my father wanted what was best for me, and I respected him. But I wanted to prove myself worthy of his trust and show him I could handle whatever tasks he threw at me—no matter how difficult or dangerous.

No more coddling. I wanted to be respected. And to earn his respect, I needed to show him that all those years of living in Shard City and attending college hadn't been in vain.

He had always been protective of me, and I was aware of his apprehension about including me in the organization he administered. But I'd seen what it was like living a life of luxury and comfort, and it had gone stale. Now, I wanted to prove that I could handle the pressure of being a part of something bigger than myself. To make a change.

I looked at my other texts.

Z: *Awake?*

I zeroed in on his text and promptly typed back: *Affirmative.*

A couple seconds later, his caller ID lit up my screen and I bit my lip as I answered. "Hi."

"Congrats, Ley," his low voice sounded.

"Thank you," I replied, a grin forming on my face.

A low chuckle, then, "Did you have fun last night?"

I nodded, even though he couldn't see. "I did."

"Not too much fun, I hope?"

My blood heated at his tone. "Perfectly moderate."

"Smart ass."

"When will I see you?"

"Soon," was all he said.

I bit back my disappointment. "Okay."

"Enjoy your day."

Resting my head back against the cushion, I repressed a sigh. "I will."

It was my birthday, after all.

"Think of me?"

Rolling my eyes, I said, "No."

He disconnected the call with another soft chuckle, but the aftermath of hearing his voice was short-lived as I noticed the next text.

Dana: *I'm on my way.*

My brows furrowed. On her way? How long ago did she send that?

Shit.

I rolled out of bed and stumbled into my bathroom, ignoring my growling belly. *Stupid. Stupid. Stupid.* I knew better than to drink on an empty stomach. I peered into the mirror and groaned.

My rundown, smokey eyes made me look like a train wreck. I opened my drawer and took out the expensive cleansing milk and tonics I should have used the night before. While stepping into the shower, I made a mental note to have my sheets cleaned, too. If I were to have any possibility of demonstrating my worth, I had to, at the very least, get my personal life together.

I rinsed my body, ridding myself of every dried-up drop of sweat, dirt, and alcohol from last night. By the time I was drying my hair, the doorbell rang, and I walked over to the intercom, buzzing Dana in. I didn't even bother to verify if it was truly her. If they weren't on my list of trusted people, they wouldn't be able to ring the bell.

I looked outside in search of the Daemon trailing me, but

to no avail. You'd think it would be easier during the day. I had always wondered when that jerk slept. Or maybe multiple of them alternated shifts? I didn't know; I had never actually seen them, which was the point—but I knew he was there, I sensed his presence. Besides, I was well acquainted with my father, who would not allow me to live in Shard City without adequate protection.

The door swung open, and Dana entered my apartment.

"Congratulations again!" She walked over to me, kissing me on the cheek before draping herself over my brown leather couch as if she owned the place. As an Ethereal, every move she made was graceful. They were known for their elegance and refined beauty, and everything suited her—even her new hair color. A few weeks ago, she had painted it a bright fuchsia instead of her own color, which was a medium brown.

Bright colors matched her personality. Where she was bubbly, I was not. When she lit up a room, I seemed to get people on edge. We were different sides of the same coin—a perfect duality.

"You really should put better locks on your doors."

"Hmm," I agreed vaguely. We had this exchange each time she dropped by.

Dana rolled her eyes. "By the light, you're impossible."

"Don't worry about me. I'm fine."

We had known each other since high school, going to the same boarding school. On several occasions, I had contemplated revealing the truth about myself to Dana, but my father had refused every time I asked. He had expressed that any breach could be dangerous. If anyone knew his daughter lived in Shard City, they would try to hurt him through me. Especially people like Dana's parents. Her mother, for one, was a well-known Ethereal in Ashar. Knowing everything Dana has told me about her mother, she was a real bitch. The woman pushed the city's segregation to a boiling point, potentially leading to the isolation of certain areas, the Daemon Domain being one of them.

"Yeah—for now," she grunted.

I was applying some fresh makeup when I leaned back to show her my feigned indignation.

"Hurry." She waved a hand my way dismissively. "We need to go."

With a shake of my head, I chuckled at my own reflection. "Alright, how about you call me beforehand next time so you actually know I'm awake and I have time to prep myself?"

"I get mad ungrateful vibes from you right now. I've planned an entire day full of surprises, you know! The least you could do is show some gratitude." There was no mistaking the mock humor in her voice.

"Aw, you remembered how much I just love surprises," I crooned, walking back into my living room.

Dana smirked with self-satisfaction, knowing full well that I decidedly did *not*. "Thank me later."

CHAPTER TWO

Dominic

"Funding for the public park in the Sanguis domain has been secured," Asa said.

I loosely balanced a weighted silver pen between my fingers, dragging it over the empty paper in front of me in lazy strokes, scribbling down some unintelligible nonsense. "Excellent."

"Adding some green down there definitely wouldn't hurt," Nathan joked. The Ethereal Domain's representative was one of my most trusted friends. He leaned back, neatly rolling the sleeves of his navy dress shirt, and rubbed his meticulously groomed stubble.

The representative of the Sanguis Domain, Asa, let out a chuckle, revealing the sharp points of her fangs. Despite her calm demeanor, the smile she displayed bore more resemblance to a sneer. And next to Nathan's dark complexion, her pale face seemed almost translucent.

"When does construction start?" I asked her.

Asa shrugged. "We haven't made plans for it yet, but we want to have it ready before the start of the ACC next season."

Marking the busiest season in town all year, the Ashar

City Cup was currently a highly discussed event. It took place during *fall reborn*, the last of the fall seasons, as it brought forth an abundance of meteorite showers. The game of Starball revolved around catching these 'falling stars'. With a nod, I entwined my fingers and relaxed in my seat, observing the table to see if anyone had other matters to raise.

"Any word from the Cardinal regarding the status of the renovations for the lift to Ashrior in the Human Domain?" Rakelsh, representative of the Daemon Domain, asked. She brushed her hands through her platinum hair and idly touched her neck, trailing her fingertips over the red scar spanning from ear to ear. "Ever since some lunatic dismantled it, they've been throwing garbage down to Ashrior, and the Daemons living there are this close to taking matters into their own hands." With that, she looked at Serena, the only human at the table.

I tensed and spoke up before the two representatives could get into it—again. "I've sent word about it but will raise the matter again when I speak with the Cardinal in person. You have my word."

Rakelsh nodded stiffly, but her dark, glistening eyes returned to Serena. "And what are you going to do about it in the meantime, *humano*?"

Serena's auburn hair was neatly secured in a tight ponytail, emphasizing her naturally defined cheekbones. I've witnessed this argument unfold in countless manners, and the representative of the Human Domain was anything but a pushover. "What are you going to do about the human trafficking in Ashrior? Does the Undercity ever help any of them?" She clucked her tongue when Rakelsh rolled her eyes. "I didn't think so."

"That's enough," I said, scrutinizing both of them with a warning expression, prompting them to seal their lips. "Both issues are on my radar." I looked at Serena, who straightened in her seat and brushed her hair over her shoulders. "You know we're working on that. So is Rakelsh—despite how much she likes to push your buttons. There is no need to add fuel to the fire."

Before anyone could utter another word, the door opened, and Fredo, my personal assistant, walked into the room with a coffee tray.

Thank the light.

"Prime," he said reverently as he moved through the space. It was the largest boardroom on the highest floor of the Town Hall, which I redesigned upon becoming Prime of the city. It was large enough to fly in if I wanted to. Fredo offered me a cup brimming with hot liquid before attending to the seven representatives.

It was a strange title. Prime: one of the highest ranks in Ashar. Assigned to me by chance. I had told Fredo more than once that he wasn't obligated to use my formal title or address me as Archangel—which was the reason I had gotten the job—but he insisted.

"Thank you, Fredo," I said before he left the room again. He was a man of morals and principles, and I let him be just that. Whatever brought him joy. It was a rare commodity in this world as it was.

I peered through the floor-to-ceiling windows where the sun's rays reflected off the Shard City skyline, swiping a hand through my shoulder-length, slicked-back curls and asked, "What did your domains vote for regarding the cultural budgets?"

Nathan sighed. "Most of the Ethereals voted against. They want the increase to be added to the science and tech budgets."

"Well, we weren't voting for the science and technology budget," Paplos quipped, who was representative of the Pisces domain.

Asa rubbed her temples.

"What about the rest?" I looked at the other people at the table: Inesa, representative of the Angeli domain, and Heller, of the Lupine domain. I knew the Angeli were pro-cultural budgets, and the Lupine didn't really care.

In the end, the cultural budget was approved for an increase, and I had once more regained hope for the population of Ashar City. I stood up from the chair, adjusted the jacket of my light grey pin-striped suit, and shook hands with the representatives before they left.

Once they were gone, I stretched my wing muscles and sighed at the relief it brought me. They grew restless when I was locked up in the office all day, not having one moment to spread my wings wide and let myself take off into the sky.

I grabbed my phone from my suit jacket, and checked it for any new messages.

Eliza: *Any time to meet this week?*

I accessed my calendar. Later today, I had a meeting with the minister of education. Tomorrow, I had back-to-back meetings about the next ACC tournament. The day after that... Time would always be a problem, and I wanted to maintain clear boundaries. I switched back to the chat with Eliza.

Me: *Thursday?*

Eliza: *I'll arrange your table at Moby's.*

Shard City had the best restaurants in Ashar, especially Moby's on 44th Street. It had earned several accolades from around the world and won prizes every year. The chef, a female Lupine, had built the place from the ground up. Rumor had it she hunted some of the meat she served herself outside of Ashar's borders.

The restaurant was fully booked for months; however, I had a designated table as an investor. And Eliza thrived on the attention I received and the admiration that came from being seen with me. It was the validation she craved. My wings were bound to attract attention, and somehow, people always seemed to have the energy to care about who I was with or what I was doing.

Eliza didn't notice my indifference or didn't care, but I indulged her. I had no energy for anything else. To me, this relationship was purely transactional. She understood that and seemed content with the arrangement as long as it meant we were seen together.

Me: *OK.*
Eliza: *See you there.*

"When are you going to cut her loose?" Inesa stepped into my peripheral and made me look up from the screen. The white feathers of her wings and the white dress she wore starkly contrasted with her long, black hair. Alongside Nathan, she was one of my closest friends.

I pocketed my phone. "We get what we want from each other."

I always laid out the terms from the start, without exception. A little blunt, but realistic. I promised nothing. We had a mutually beneficial agreement. An exchange. They never went home with me, I never went home with them, and we didn't catch feelings. So fucking what?

Inesa arched one of her brows.

"I am aware that I am not a saint," I stated. Hadn't been for a while, anyway.

"Dom, you deserve something real." Inesa's voice was almost pleading, but it did not fool me. I could see the pity in her dark brown eyes. It made my stomach turn, and I clamped down on my response.

"Don't worry about me, Inesa. I know what I'm doing."

"If you say so," she whispered before Nathan made his way towards us, and she nodded at him in acknowledgment. "But you must know that Em—"

My attention snapped back to her like a bowstring as anger flared through me. "Don't," I bit out, barely keeping my voice steady.

When Nathan arrived, he reached out to Inesa and put a hand on her shoulder, but she rolled her eyes. "Relax, man," he said. Inesa's gaze returned to me. "Sure, Dominic, I see there's absolutely nothing to worry about when it comes to you." She pulled away from Nathan's grip and marched out of the room.

Nathan watched her go, then turned to me with equal amounts of disappointment and frustration. "She wants the best for you, Dom. You shouldn't push her away like that." My inhale was sharp. I knew he was right. "She was our friend, too," he continued. "You're not the only one with wounds. She's allowed to talk about her."

"Gods, *I know*." I looked Nathan straight in the eye, showing him my remorse. The hurt in my friend's eyes was enough to make me feel like the asshole I was nowadays. I couldn't manage to rid myself of him; he had become part of me as if he were a second skin.

Nathan stood his ground and locked eyes with me, but his gaze softened. "Then stop acting like you're all alone in this."

"I'm sorry," I said.

He nodded towards the door Inesa had just left through and gave me a meaningful look. "Tell *her* that." Without another word, he squeezed my shoulder and left the room, leaving me with a heavy guilt settling on my chest.

I had a few seconds to regain a grip on the raging storm brewing inside me before Fredo arrived to walk me to my next appointment.

It was one of those days where all I wanted to do was to run away and never look back. Nothing I did seemed to benefit anyone. Contrary to my efforts to keep this city afloat, I felt like I was slipping into an endless downward spiral.

I took a deep breath and turned around.

Yet another hour.

The rain had been pouring all evening—a dull, relentless patter that mirrored the heavy weight of my mood. I had been wandering the deserted streets of Ashar for some time after the workday had concluded, striving to blend in with the shadows and remain unseen.

I kept my hands folded inside my pockets and my wings tucked in tight. Night was the only time I could wander the streets and remain semi-anonymous. In this part of town, there were no lights to reflect the golden glimmer of my wings and, with the rain, no people outside to recognize me.

I withdrew my hands from the coat and gazed skyward. The rain had slowed to a steady drizzle, and the clouds were an inky black against the night sky. The moon was barely visible, as if it, too, was mourning my losses. I heaved a sigh, feeling a deep loneliness settle around me. While knowing it would be best if I went back home and tried to get some sleep, I continued wandering through the streets. As I walked past the shuttered storefronts, my reflection stared back at me from their windows: a dark silhouette, golden wings barely grazing the ground.

The loneliness looming in my heart was tangible. It threatened to consume me if I stopped ignoring it. The abandoned streets around me only made it worse—nothing stirred except for the occasional gust of wind and the relentless patter of raindrops against the pavement.

I remembered her laughter, how she had looked at me with a warmth that had made my heart swell with fucking *joy*. And then she was gone, leaving an unbearable void in the shape of her.

A void no one would ever be able to fill.

CHAPTER THREE

Leyla

My father invited me to Ashrior a week after my birthday.

Ashar City was akin to a small country, and Ashium, the middle layer, was vast. The city was divided into three layers, each with its own infrastructure and rules. I had to travel underground to Ashrior to reach the Daemon Domain from Shard City, where I lived. There were two ways to get there—well, *three*, but the third was only available to the Angeli. You could travel by aircab or use one of the many lifts scattered throughout Ashium. I always opted for an elevator down, as it was the most discreet option. Daemons widely disliked aircabs, as they were used mainly by tourists and frequently the cause of various construction problems. Given the anthill-like construction of Ashrior, there weren't many places for them to land properly, which caused a number of problems.

As I entered the elevator and the doors closed, my shadow was nowhere in sight. He probably called to whatever Daemon would wait downstairs to take over. I never had a moment alone if it was up to my dad unless I was inside somewhere.

The doors opened after a few minutes, and a soft light entered the metal shaft. The daylight in Ashrior was much kinder to my Daemon eyes than the bright sunlight above the ground. Tall buildings rose from all around me, similar to Shard City, but lacked its brightness. The mismatch of buildings looked out of place together.

The longer I stayed away from here, the more out of sorts I felt when I visited. Despite residing in Shard City, this place had shaped my identity. Ashrior was where I'd grown up, my *home*, but all I ever dreamed of when I was younger was living up there. My wish had been answered, but the price I had to pay for it had left its scars.

At last, I caught sight of the tall gates of my childhood home. With extensive grounds surrounding the home, it was clear my father was wealthy. In Ashrior, everything was so tightly packed that even having a small patch of ground around your house was deemed a luxury. And my dad owned nearly an entire Starball field.

The building was filled with countless memories. I had lived here until my father sent me away to Shard City, and since then, I've spent more time walking under the sun than below the ground. I rang the intercom and waited until the gates opened wide enough to enter. The unfamiliar guards positioned at the inner gates scrutinized me from head to toe, wearing smirks but remaining silent. One of them patted me down for any weapons while the other inspected the contents of my bag. The guard that had plundered it held it out to me, and I practically snatched it from his grip as the other gestured for me to continue. They exchanged amused glances, and I could guess what they were thinking because I had heard guards whisper to each other more than once.

My childhood had been a lonely one. Growing up, my dad kept me hidden from the world beyond his property. He had deemed it best to protect me from the prying eyes of outsiders, those he couldn't trust. My interactions had been limited to our close-knit family, and although it had been a quiet upbringing, I'd been content in that small corner—blissfully ignorant and shielded from the dangers of the outside world.

For a while, anyway.

To keep me as safe as possible, my dad eventually sent me to a highly guarded boarding school in Ashium. It had been easier for him that way. Here, I met Dana—another wish granted. She was the best thing ever happening to me and sparkled light on a dark place in my life. My father disapproved of our friendship, but let me have it. It was a win for both of us; he didn't have to worry about me, and I wasn't so lonely anymore.

"Hey," Ulverin said as I made my way into the house. "Long time no see, kid."

The familiar, copper-haired Daemon lifted her chin. She scarcely smiled, yet her eyes softened slightly as she looked at me. There were several knives and a gun strapped to her pants. Being one of my father's most trusted associates, she was even more dangerous than she was pretty. Having known me since birth, Ulverin was among the few who knew my true identity. And growing up, I had aspired to be like her in many ways.

I smiled. "Where is he?"

"Xanon will come to the living room in a couple of minutes," she said and then continued, leaving the house.

My hands started fidgeting with my coat. I wouldn't say I was ever desperate for recognition and inclusion in my father's life, but I yearned to be a part of something. To be trusted and respected—especially by him.

I strolled into the living room, and the ever-present scent of leather and cigar smoke that perpetually lingered in the room welcomed me. Sunlight sparsely streamed in through the shutters, casting a glow on the older wooden furniture. The subdued browns contrasted with the rich burgundy of the walls. This room remained unchanged, just as it had been for as long as I could remember.

The moment my father entered the room, I knew. I didn't hear him, but the hairs on my neck raised with a prickling sensation that I was being watched… His presence exuded immense power. *"Leyla Illiath Naan,"* his low, familiar voice sounded behind me.

I turned around, my expression blank as I looked at him, disregarding the man who never strayed too far behind him.

"Look at you." He advanced towards me, kissing my cheek. "Twenty-five suits you, *Cara*."

"Thank you."

My father's brow curled with amusement as he observed my expression. "What's bothering you, daughter?"

"It's been a long time since I've heard that name."

"It's your name, is it not?"

The man behind him emitted a snort, but I kept ignoring him.

"Can you not meet me without your doting sidekick?" I asked my father instead.

"Play nice, Leyla," Zade said from behind him, prompting me to cluck my tongue.

One day, my father brought Zade home with him after a devastating time for the organization. His parents and little sister, among others, were murdered by a rival Sanguis gang. He had been outside when it happened, and upon returning from work that day, Zade had been the one to find them.

I had fallen in love with him at first sight. He was handsome in a heartbreaking way, with short black hair, light skin, and piercing blue eyes that told stories of everything wrong with the world. Those sad eyes were contrasted by the tattoos that decorated his entire body. He was a bit older than me, but that was part of the appeal when I was younger.

After our first meeting and my piss-poor attempt at flirting with him, Zade had called me a *spoiled princess who knew nothing about the real world*. He told me to stay away from him. It wasn't anything I hadn't heard before. And instead of feeling hurt, I felt anger—the urge to prove him and my father wrong. I wasn't the naïve, sheltered girl they made me out to be. I was daring and intelligent, unafraid of getting my hands dirty.

The rest of the house grew silent. Not even the clock on the wall made a sound. I folded my arms together. "Is it?"

"What?"

I raised a brow. "My name?" I had changed it for him, after all.

My father clamped his large hands on my shoulders. "Don't be like this, *Cara*." His black hair was graying a little, showing his age; old, for a Daemon.

My nostrils flared as I clamped my lips shut.

"You remind me of your mother when you're this stubborn."

He had been an older father. He told me he didn't know he wanted children until he met my mother. Ironically, she passed away shortly after my birth. That's why he was so adamant about keeping me safe. But I wasn't a child anymore and refused to be hidden away. I was determined to carve out my own place in the world—to show everyone I was capable of *more*. I wanted to be someone my father could be proud of.

"What prevents you from giving me a chance? Do you not trust me?"

He bared his teeth, a gesture between a smile and a frown. "It's not about trust. You are invaluable to me. I want you to live without a threat hanging above your every move. This is how I make sure of that."

"I can decide for myself—I'm not a child anymore."

A gentle look appeared in his eyes. "Of course. But understand you will always be a child to me."

"Let me prove myself."

He clasped a hand around his throat, assessing me. "You really want this?"

My pulse quickened. "*Yes*."

"Very well." My father cast his eyes downward in contemplation while my focus shifted beyond him to Zade. Our eyes crossed, his blue ones dark with promise as he held them.

I attended college once I completed high school, despite my father's reservations. I didn't come home often during that time. Part of me—call it pride—refused to visit when Zade was around. But soon after graduation, our paths crossed again. The first thing I did was scowl at him, and he had caved in like a house of cards. Clearly, he had been expecting another version of me, a younger, clueless one full of wide-eyed innocence. That wasn't what he got. Heated gazes and secret touches suddenly replaced those stinging remarks and firm boundaries from before.

And my foolish crush had turned into pure lust.

Nobody knew about us. Not Ulverin, nor Dana, and certainly not my father.

When I heard about the things Zade got to do, I started

yearning for *more*. The desire to be involved in something greater than myself, rather than being a mere spectator, was reignited. I longed to experience what he and my father had: something they dedicated their lives to.

We broke eye contact as my father's head rose again. "I have been hesitant to tell you this, but I see you're growing impatient—not one of my traits. There is something of immense value to me within reach, and with your help, I might be able to get it. You are well-suited for the role it demands. However, it will not be a simple task."

"I'm not interested in easy," I said immediately.

My father chuckled darkly as he walked closer. "*That* is something you do have from me."

"Well?"

Clutching the railing of the couch, he shook his head dismissively. "You'll hear about it once I've determined a course of action."

I wanted to argue, but I swallowed my frustration. Clearing my throat, I pivoted. "There is something else I would like to discuss."

"Yes?" My father turned his head, eyes narrowing slightly, but the rest of his features weren't malicious.

"The person shadowing me—"

"No." He was shaking his head again.

"You didn't even listen to what I had to say."

"Tell me you weren't trying to have him dismissed."

My mouth popped open. "But—"

"That's what I thought."

I pushed away from where I was standing and brushed past him, but before I could, he laid a hand on my shoulder to stop me. "*Leyla*," he warned.

I ground my molars. Behind him, Zade merely shook his head in disapproval as if saying *stop acting like this*, and I felt myself getting frustrated. How was I ever meant to prove my strength if they continuously treated me as if I were fragile?

"The only thing you're showing with this behavior is that you're not ready."

In a way, he was right. I had to quit acting like a child if I wanted them to stop thinking I needed protection.

"I'm sorry," I uttered through clenched teeth.

"You never have to apologize to me, *Cara*." My father's eyes crinkled. "Patience is a virtue, but know that you won't have to wait long."

I nodded, though my jaw did not relax.

He looked at his watch as he dropped his hand from my shoulder and said, "I need to go now." He turned around and focused his attention on Zade behind him. "See my daughter out, will you, Zade?"

"Yes, Sir."

"Thank you for coming." My father kissed my cheek, and as his retreating form disappeared, my eyes finally drifted to the man I had been left with.

"*Such a good boy*," I purred.

Zade chuckled darkly as he approached. "I love how you roll those green eyes at me without expecting punishment."

He focused his full attention on me, but it had already been mine for the last ten minutes. "Care to share anything about the part my father wants me to play?"

He trailed his fingers over my bare arms, a static feeling following his trail. "Does it matter?"

"So that's also a no?"

"Xanon doesn't share all his plans with me. I had never

heard about it until now."

My father meant well. He's been there for me my whole life, ensuring I had everything I needed. But I only wanted his appreciation. I shouldn't have asked him for something he didn't offer. First, I had to show him I was ready and prove I could handle it—whatever he wanted me to do.

All I could do was show him.

"I have to go."

Zade snatched my arm before I could bolt. "When can I see you?"

I shrugged. "I'm sure you'll find time. And if not, don't be upset if I find pleasure elsewhere in the meantime."

"Ouch," he said, eyes flashing as he put a hand on his chest, grinning. "*Ice cold*, Ley."

I gave him a sly wink before leaving the house, with Zade trailing my steps. Outside, I encountered Ulverin, who lifted a single condemning eyebrow at us.

Well, scratch that. I guess nobody *besides* Ulverin knew about us.

CHAPTER FOUR

Dominic

The annual Ashar City Award show had always been mundane, but the past few years were particularly draining. Every time, I was surrounded by flashing cameras and fake smiles. The halls hadn't changed for decades, and even the people attending looked the same, like carbon copies of each other. Even the women approaching me had become boringly predictable.

I moved through the crowd, posing for photos with people desperate for a minute of my time, and flowed through conversations on autopilot: *We have to see.* Smile. *Good to hear. How's the family?* Try to sound genuinely interested. *Really?*

I disliked the person I became in public—disliked portraying myself as someone I wasn't. But I couldn't let the expectations, the stress, and the constant reminders of my titles impede the fact that this was a job. I had to be the Prime of Ashar instead of Dominic Venetia, though people didn't see the difference.

According to the people of Ashar, I never said enough, didn't prioritize the right things, and dated around too much. They demanded I did the impossible: doing everything right and pleasing everyone.

It was up to me to draw the boundaries.

Tonight marked my 88th time attending to watch the same old routine. I would watch as innovative citizens received awards, and listened to speeches I couldn't care less about, but had to appear interested in what they had to say. The amount of shit I would get from the press just wasn't worth dropping the mask.

It was all so... trivial. Especially considering it was the same show on repeat. Every. Damned. Year. And I was still young for an Archangel.

Not that I didn't applaud progress; I, too, wanted this city to prosper and evolve into something better. Obviously, we need rulebreakers and rebels to fire the first shot—people who deviate from the norm and who think outside the box... They are the ones to guide us into the future, and it's up to the rest of us to follow. But they aren't getting the awards. These awards are given out to the people who do well *within* the standards we have set. Which makes the innovation portion of the award seem like a fucking joke. Pointless.

"You look exceptional tonight," a soft voice said behind me.

I turned around to take in the Angeli I knew would be there. "Eliza." Her tanned face seemed sprinkled with golden dust, and her dark brown hair fell in waves over her shoulder. "As do you."

"Generous as always, Dominic." She smiled shyly, casting her eyes down, but no blood crawled into her cheeks. Eliza was too seasoned a lover for that.

I nodded politely, my eyes fixating longingly on a passing tray with champagne just beyond my grasp. Eliza gently placed her hand on my arm with a smooth efficiency to recapture my attention.

"Any plans after?"

I blinked down at her. "I'll be working all night."

Eliza and I clearly defined our relationship: no mixing pleasure and business. However, her disappointment was still evident. "Of course."

The last guests gradually entered the hall, prompting me to make my entrance into the theater. I covered her hand with my own and squeezed it passionlessly. "Excuse me."

She briefly closed her eyes, her long lashes cast down like they had been when we'd first met, but I couldn't recall why I had found that so captivating. It seemed fabricated. "Talk later?"

"Sure," I answered, already distracted. My eyes focused on the path toward the staircase leading me to the private balcony overlooking the theater. I grabbed a flute of champagne that floated past on my way there and swallowed it down in one gulp, desperately in need of something stronger.

Fortunately, the show raced by, and I found myself exiting the theater in no time, proceeding straight to the afterparty hosted in the Town Hall. I had to attend, given that I was the Prime of Ashar and Shard City fell under my jurisdiction.

The room that served as the venue for the afterparty was expansive, adorned with sizable chandeliers dangling from the overhead ceiling and multiple tables strategically positioned around the perimeter. A live band accompanied the thrum of conversation and laughter while people moved around in their finery, drinks in hand.

I navigated through the space, wearing a polite smile as the crowd parted around me. Moving closer to the bar, I caught sight of Inesa. She wore a flowy white dress, and her black hair was pinned back in an elegant bun. As if she sensed my presence, she turned around, and her eyes lit up with recognition when she noticed me. I made my way towards her, my shoulders slightly tensing as I remembered our last interaction. Inesa met me halfway and grabbed my elbow, saving me from being approached by anyone else as she steered us to one of the hall's quieter corners.

"How are you?" she asked me over the music, holding onto my arm as we made our way through the throng of people.

"Listen," I started when we were out of earshot of any people. "I want to apologize for the other day."

Inesa shrugged, but the warmth in her smile was genuine. "It's still delicate. Trust me, I get it. I shouldn't have pressed."

I put my hands in the pockets of my dark blue suit. "My reaction could have been better."

Suddenly, Nathan was on my other side, slinging his arm over Inesa's shoulders. "You rescue *him* but not me?" he asked, kissing her cheek.

With a dramatic sigh, Inesa readjusted the necklace adorning her neck—a present from her mate, Leon, no doubt. "Enjoyed the show?"

I groaned. "You have *no* idea."

Nathan took a sip of his drink. "Who dictated we are required to be here as representatives again?"

"And be here alone?" I chuckled. "Nah, I'd rather drag you two with me through the trenches."

"I bet." Nathan rubbed his chin. "Don't we have such a

selfless leader, Ness?"

"Hm hm." Inesa's focus was elsewhere.

Without effort, I shoved him, causing Nathan to nearly spill his drink as he thundered a laugh. It reminded me of when we were younger. I had met Nathan in college, both taking political science classes. There was no instant click between us. He'd appeared quite arrogant, but after being forced on a joint assignment, our friendship had taken off like we had known each other since birth. My friendship with Nathan was effortless. We understood each other on a soul level.

Inesa let out a low whistle. "I don't think I've ever seen him here."

I followed her gaze, settling on an unmistakably tall figure across the room. An unexpected presence.

Nitas, the Supreme of Ashar, seemed wholly out of place. He wore his usual all-black, making him stand out among the colorful array of extravagantly clothed people. His jet-black eyes seemed to pierce through me as our gazes crossed, the only warmth coming from his tanned skin. Nitas rarely left the Undercity, so his presence set off a flurry of whispers, and even the music seemed to falter as the musicians tried to see who or what caused the disturbance.

While I was the Prime of Ashium, he was the Supreme of Ashrior, the bottom layer of the city. Together with the Cardinal—a group of eleven Seraphim who ruled Ashtior, the highest level—we formed the *Trias Politica*.

The Daemon's eyes brimmed with urgency as he discreetly nodded at me. Then he directed his attention towards greeting certain attendees who tried to grab it—resulting in his mouth forming a tight line and his shoulders tensing.

"What is he doing here?" Nathan asked me as if I knew the answer.

I furrowed my brows. "Guess I'm about to find out." I stepped away from my friends, again passing through the crowd. Nitas hadn't come all this way to enjoy a party. He never bothered with these events, and it wasn't just because he hated the large number of people—he rarely left Ashrior at all. Even from a distance, I could see his brows knitting together as if irritated with every single person talking to him. Nitas was indifferent to his reputation and somehow always evaded consequences for his callous behavior. People got the message when he moved away from them, following me to one of the standing tables positioned to the side.

This was an unsuitable moment and location for more than a hushed conversation, but he spoke once we were out of earshot from others. "Something serious is stirring up the Undercity. Samples of some new drug in early production were given out."

I raised a brow. Drugs in the Undercity weren't surprising. Drugs *anywhere*, for that matter. "What type of drug?"

Nitas shook his head. "It doesn't have a name yet." He paused, choosing his words carefully. "All I heard is that it is unlike anything out there right now."

"You're sure?"

The Daemon nodded and rubbed a thumb over his bottom lip, concealing his mouth. "Xanon's name is written all over it."

"*What?*" My body froze in place. "You've got to be kidding me."

The mere mention of his name caused an instant headache. Years of silence had enveloped Xanon Naan, and I'd harbored the hope he finally retired, but this sounded far from it. The man was corrupt. He caused disorder in the Undercity, deliberately aggravating the hardships faced by every living being in Ashar to amass wealth. And the bastard was cunning enough to bend the rules, so he never got caught—redirecting every arrow that pointed his way with deliberate precision.

I clung to the hope that Xanon would make a mistake, and then we would strike.

Nitas' eyes had gone even darker, as if anger clouded his vision. We were alike, Nitas and I, both our souls slightly beyond salvation. We had a primal longing that seemed to drive us forward, to push at the boundaries of justice, to wipe the scum walking this earth, or underneath it, from all of Celestia.

The crowd shifted again, and when it parted, a familiar head of reddish curls appeared. Wearing a bright smile, Vaphoryn immediately came our way. She wore an elegant blue robe with intricate embroidery up the sleeves, a variation of her regular Cardinal uniform. Usually, she wore her hair in elaborate braids, as was expected from Seraphim—members of the Cardinal—but Vaphoryn had opted to wear her long hair loose tonight. Daring. She moved gracefully toward us, the crowd parting around her reverently, turning many heads as she went.

"*Divinitas*. What a surprise," she said to Nitas as she arrived, her nose wrinkling as the smile reached her eyes.

Next to me, Nitas had gone still. "Vaphoryn."

The Seraphim smiled and moved her eyes to me. "Dominic."

"Thank you for coming." I didn't kiss her cheek or shake her hand. Nobody was supposed to touch a member of the Cardinal. Her white wings were bound to her back, permanently withdrawn. The sight of it always made my wings itch in a suffocating manner. I knew that joining the Cardinal was a voluntary choice, but at times it felt like a sentence, and I couldn't fathom why someone so full of life would choose it.

Nitas, who remained silent, appeared fixated, his unwavering gaze locked on her. He seemed powerless to look away, a crease forming between his eyes.

Her gaze moved between us, a smile forming on her full lips. "Well?" she said. "Is anyone going to tell me what's going on?"

Nitas snapped from his trance and put his hands in his pockets before explaining the problem to her. Vaphoryn served as one of the eleven Seraphim in the Cardinal, meaning she had to communicate what she heard. Though she took some liberties with that. When she joined the Cardinal twenty years ago, she was by far its youngest member and the easiest to talk to. The three of us came together now and then and shared information we didn't want to go through the official channels. Since the Head Cardinal rarely came down from Ashtior anymore, Vaphoryn came as a sort of delegate.

"I see…" Vaphoryn inhaled deeply, lost in thought. "The Head Cardinal seems somewhat aware of the unrest in Ashrior. I overheard her discussing it with Balan, but she hadn't sounded concerned."

Rubbing my jaw, I said, "I wonder why Rakelsh hasn't mentioned anything. She must not be aware."

"Or she's landed in Xanon's pocket." Vaphoryn wrapped her hands together.

I gave my head a shake. "Rakelsh might be reckless, but she would never support him." *Too much of his destruction had touched her life.*

"True," Nitas said, surveying the room before redirecting his gaze to us. "And with that, I will take my leave."

I huffed a breath. "You just got here."

His eyes crinkled a little. "Good night, Dominic. Vaphoryn." And in the same abrupt manner that he had arrived, the Supreme Daemon departed from the Town Hall.

Vaphoryn sighed as she stared after him. "At times, when I witness a sliver of his humanity, he promptly shuts himself off and reverts back to his shell."

"If I hadn't had Nathan and Inesa during the darkest moment in my life, I might have given up," I said, looking at my friends laughing together on the other side of the room. "I might as well have ended up like him, alone, not caring about anything."

The Seraphim smiled. "You are very lucky to have people like that, Dominic. I hope you treasure them."

"I do my best."

Vaphoryn looked up at me. "Life would be boring if we had nothing left to learn. But it rarely gives you second chances if you do not heed its lessons."

"Who said that?"

"Me." She smirked.

I chuckled. "Sounds wise."

As if Nathan sensed my attention, he glanced at me with concern and gestured to ask if everything was alright. Always looking out for me. I nodded and conveyed, *later*, which he accepted.

Vaphoryn was right. I was very lucky.

Then she said, "He came here to warn you."

"What?" I redirected my attention to her.

"Nitas—he came here to tell you. *He cares.*"

"You can be done with life but still care about the living."

Vaphoryn pinched her mouth. "Sounds to me like you're not done living, then."

She winked, and her cloak brushed past me as she made her way into the room, immediately capturing the attention of those present and conversed with them.

Sounds to me like you're not done living, then.

But I wasn't so sure about that.

CHAPTER FIVE

Leyla

There was a blockage in the sewer. A group of teenagers in the Sanguis Domain had been up to some bad shit, intentionally clogging several pipes with garbage, and the unbearable smell lingering on the streets of Shard City made it impossible to ignore.

Dana and I entered the little chocolatier with scrunched noses and sat down at the corner table, looking out onto the city. People dressed in business attire sped across the street, their faces filled with varying looks of disgust at the smell. They only entered the shop to get some coffee before going to work.

Had I known the amount of hours I would waste waiting for my father to let me work for him, I might have invested in an actual career like these people. Going somewhere with co-workers to talk to and doing something straightforward with your life sounded tempting. College had always been a way to fill my time and satiate my thirst for knowledge while waiting to be awarded a role in my dad's organization.

After graduating, the City Development Master program at Shard City University briefly caught my eye. It combined many of my interests and fondness for the city, but the significant time investment held me back. I had been afraid that my father would never give me a chance to prove myself or take me seriously if he thought I had other aspirations.

But by now, I could have graduated from that program years ago.

Instead, my 'career' was fabricated from lies—Dana thought I had a low-profile logistics job in Ashrior. When our careers came up, I usually stirred the conversation back to her.

She hadn't gone on to further studies, either. She had always dreamed of becoming a fashion designer, and her fingers had been itching to get to work after getting our undergraduate degrees. Dana's sense of fashion surpassed that of anyone I had ever encountered. She put things together no one ever thought of, and after, I'd see more people mimicking her ideas. In contrast, my style was rather simplistic; monochrome and silver, with the occasional out-of-character pop of color. *Part of my aesthetic*, as Dana often pointed out.

"But seriously, Ley," Dana said, snapping me out of my thoughts. "Why won't you give the guy a chance?"

I stirred the hot chocolate before me, casually brushing my lengthy hair aside to keep it from brushing the cup. She meant Josiah Eden, the popular Ethereal Starball player. "We flirt a little over text."

"You're not hooking up—there's a difference."

"And we won't." I lifted my hands and wiggled my fingers, inspecting my manicure. Dana loved playing matchmaker, but I couldn't tell her why the golden boy of Starball and I would never work.

My best friend sighed. "There'd better be a *why* following that statement." She perked up, extracting the vibrating phone from her pocket. She dropped the tiny spoon she held and it clinked against the mug as she pressed the phone against her ear. "Tommy. How are you?"

I lifted my eyebrows in surprise. Really? Tommy, as in Starball-playing-Ethereal-fuckboy-Tommy?

Are you serious? I mouthed, giving her a judgmental look. That guy was a first-class dick. I seriously never understood why Dana wouldn't just go for Josiah herself. Compared to Tommy, Josiah was a saint. But she'd once told me he gave her sibling vibes, of which neither of us had any, so she might be mistaken.

"Me too," she responded to the phone, biting her lip. "How about this: you, me, Josiah, and Leyla? Tonight?"

"Dana!" I hissed, turning my voice down when several people in the little shop glanced our way. I rubbed my hands over my face in exasperation. How would I ever get it through her thick skull that I didn't want to date him? *Or anyone.* I'd lost count of how many men she had tried to match me up with over the years.

Dana winked at me and said, "Alright, see you tonight."

She and I couldn't be more different. We didn't even like each other when we first met at a party in boarding school. Back then, her hair had been her natural brown instead of the bright fuchsia it was now, and I had worn predominately black and wanted to be anywhere but there. We had our assumptions about each other, coming from different backgrounds.

We were never supposed to be friends, but when we both saw a freshman get dunked in a tank, our paths collided.

"Dude, what the fuck is your problem?" I said as I advanced on the tall Ethereal keeping the head of a young Lupine server underwater, his

soaked arms clawing at the arms that held him down.

The guy pointed to his stained white blouse. "He spilled a drink."

"Hey!" a girl called out, stomping over in a short pink dress. "Knock it off, Greyman."

I recognized her immediately because Lodana Fivaldor was a big deal with the Ethereals at school. The guy, Greyman, had looked between us as if we'd been his wet dream come true and completely forgot about the sputtering Lupine drowning by his hands. Lodana had noticed, too, and she shoved him aside with much more punch than she looked able to pack.

I reached the guy and pulled him away from the tank, getting my face close to his, and bared my teeth like the predator I was. "Feel like a big guy taking on people half your size?"

"You Daemons are fucking hypocrites," he sneered as he shoved me off and staggered away, rubbing his neck as he growled at the people surrounding us. Lodana helped the young Lupine out of the tank and nudged him toward the bathroom. "Fun is over, people," she yelled to the other people still looking at us, and the crowd gradually dispersed. I followed them to the bathroom, grabbing some dry clothes from the bench near the jacuzzi. Somebody shouted, but I didn't care whose clothes I'd grabbed. I bet the Lupine needed them more.

The kid was shaking when I got to the bathroom, hot water already running and steaming up the mirror.

"Here," I said, handing him the clothes. He looked at them with a frown. "You might wanna go out the front door if you don't want them to catch you wearing that."

He wouldn't meet my eyes, cheeks pinking a little, but nodded his thanks either way. Lodana handed him some money for a cab as I stepped back out of the bathroom again. She quickly followed, murmuring some soft words to him before closing the door behind her.

For a moment, neither of us said anything as we stood on either side of the door.

"I thought Daemons only preyed on the weak." She looked at me from the side, one corner of her mouth pulling up.

I inspected my nails and bit my cheek not to smile back instantly. "I thought Ethereals only cared about themselves."

We had been inseparable ever since, though Dana doesn't know I've been keeping my real identity from her all these years. I don't doubt her love for me or her loyalty. She wasn't even quick to judge. But I always had this little voice in my head saying that if she ever found out the truth about me and realized who I truly was, she would drop me without a second thought. The thought was so painful that my body tensed up.

Losing her wouldn't be worth it.

So I locked away the part of me who wanted to tell her and threw away the key.

Dana and I were the first to arrive at the café, and we took in the atmosphere: Dana loved it, whereas I struggled to keep the frown off my face. Neon words lit up the walls, saying things like *easy breezy* and *cozy up* and other cringy lines. The lights assaulted my eyes everywhere I looked. It was too bright, colorful, and loud, just how Dana liked it.

A server led us to a corner booth tucked away in the back. Oblivious to my unease, Dana settled in, taking in the details of her surroundings with delight. She was wearing all green today—her favorite color and the exact shade of my eyes. It was one of the first things she liked about me. She had said it was how she knew I was meant to be her best friend. *My fucking eye color.*

I chuckled to myself, and Dana narrowed her eyes at me.

"What?"

"Nothing." I gave a little shake of my head.

We knew the moment our dates had arrived because their entrance caused quite a stir through the place. Both Ethereals were famous, especially now that the City Cup was right around the corner. The tall, broad forms of Tommy and Josiah emerged from the front, and I kept my eyes from rolling out of my head at the commotion, but Tommy's smug smile made it really damn hard. Instead, I focused on Josiah, who took the edge off a little. The pro-baller was good-looking in a timeless way. His eyes were a deep shade of blue—darker than Zade's—and he wore a wide, infectious smile with dimples and everything.

I bet he wanted the perfect wife to fit his perfect life. Add some perfect children to the mix, and Josiah Eden would be *perfectly* content. It was the description of a life that would bore me to death. However, he was a genuinely good guy, which was why he should stay away from me. I didn't want to burn him.

Tommy, on the other hand…

I nudged Dana, jolting her out of scrolling on her phone. She gave Tommy a look of obvious admiration, even though he had done nothing to earn it. We all stood, greeting each other, and settled in the booth. The only thing keeping me in my seat was picturing Dana's disappointment if I left.

"How was practice?" Dana asked, leaning her chin on her hand. Tommy told her about their afternoon and how pumped their team was for the Ashar City Cup. Meanwhile, I was busy counting all the silly little potted plants in the café.

"Are we boring you?"

I turned to my right, amused by Josiah's bluntness. "More

like this place is overwhelming my senses. I'm still taking it all in."

"It's... something." One of his dimples appeared again.

"Dana has been very adamant about getting us together."

His other dimple joined in, and he draped one of his arms on the backrest behind me. "I noticed."

Josiah was half-Ethereal. His parents were still together, despite his father being full Ethereal and his mother human—sad if you dwelled on their lifespans for too long. But being half-Ethereal in Ashar meant he had to work twice as hard to prove himself before being considered for the Starball team, even with his last name; his father was a retired player. So him being the captain of the Ethereal team said something.

Honestly, his persistence was kind of hot.

"Why did you agree to this *date*?" I asked him.

Josiah's eyes found mine. "I was bored."

I arched a brow. "Bored?"

"Let's just say you're a pleasant change of scenery compared to the women that I'm usually around."

I bit my tongue, surprised by his answer. There was no harm in a little flirting, but... Josiah was intelligent. He must realize we weren't a good match. We met each other enough times to know we orbited two very different planets.

"Why did *you* come?"

Shrugging, I said, "Honestly? Mostly to humor Dana."

Josiah looked amused. "Give it to me straight, why don't you?"

"You just called me a *change of scenery*."

"I meant a challenge."

"This one's a little too complicated, *Eden*. We're too different."

"That's half the appeal."

"And we want different things out of life," I added.

"So what? I'm not asking you to marry me."

He bumped his elbow into my arm, and I looked away, smiling. "Get it out of your head. We're not happening."

"You're not very convincing, though."

To be honest, if I had been anyone else, if I came from somewhere different and had a normal home situation, I might've given him a chance. He was good-looking, smart, and actually interested in me. I had a feeling he was a generous lover, too.

Dana and Tommy were cracking up at something, and Tommy casually brushed her hair behind her ear.

Nauseating.

I focused on Josiah, who looked unaffected by my earlier comment. "I don't understand why you don't just pursue Dana."

He took a sip from his drink. "There are several reasons. For one, she's not my type. Another obvious one would be that Tommy's with her."

"He's not good for her."

"I mean, he's not perfect, but he really likes her."

I groaned. It was something Dana could have said. Since when did 'not perfect' translate into sticking your dick in every girl that showed interest?

Tommy said something that pulled Josiah into their conversation at the same time that dinner was served. It smelled delicious, and the bottle of wine that accompanied the food I had ordered was especially good—a small consolation.

My mind wandered to Zade, imagining what he would do when I told him I'd gone on a double date. The last time I'd told him Josiah Eden was texting me, Zade had spanked me so hard during sex that I had still felt the burn of his hand the next day. *Gods*. The thought alone made me fidgety.

As the meal drew to a close, I couldn't help but think about what would have happened if I was another girl, someone fitting for a guy like Josiah. I tried to picture that life as he leaned back in the seat next to me, his hair falling in his eyes as a server came to take our plates away. The Ethereal noticed my eyes on him, and he dropped his hand from the backrest, brushing my back on the way down. Leaning closer, he said, "When you look at me like that, Leyla, you don't even seem convinced yourself."

Josiah was called the golden boy of the competition for a reason. He obviously knew how to work his charm.

"I would eat you alive."

His pupils flared, and his tongue flicked over his bottom lip. "You're right—I don't date cannibals."

I barked a laugh. I couldn't help myself. And even though he was smiling, too, I could see him pulling back, and part of me was disappointed by the loss of his undivided attention.

It made me say, "Okay."

Josiah looked at me from the corner of his eye—pleased. "Okay, what?"

"One date."

His lopsided grin was sure. "You won't regret it."

CHAPTER SIX

Dominic

If it weren't for Fredo's diligent schedule management, I would have forgotten about my dinner plans with Eliza in Shard City at Moby's. The cozy restaurant was hidden on a quiet street, but it was the busiest spot in town this season.

I had been just in time, barely waiting inside for a few minutes before Eliza arrived. She looked perfect, as always. However, after living for more than a century, perfection began to lose its appeal.

The day had been filled with back-to-back meetings about city affairs, and the never-ending influx of emails had left me drained. I made a mental note to ask Fredo to get an assistant to take over my email. I only wanted to know about the emails from people who had business emailing me. Somehow, they always figured out what my address was and flooded my inbox. It was a complete waste of my time.

As Eliza walked in, her eyes locked onto me with an intention that was hard to miss. She had never been shy about touching me, laying her claim in public, and I didn't care. A server led us to our table—well, *my* table—and Eliza sat down across from me. She began discussing the happenings at the

Angeli council, where she worked, assuming I would be interested in hearing even more about work when all I wanted was to get my mind off it. There was no need for her to prove she was intelligent. I knew she was, but I just wasn't into that part of her, to put it bluntly.

I tried to focus on our conversation, trying my best to act interested, but I couldn't wait for the food to arrive, be done with this 'date', and go to the hotel. To do what we actually came here for.

It was like the gods heard my prayers because the servers arrived with our first course. With more courses to come, I could already feel my battery fluttering as it tried to stay alive, but I found solace in the fact that the food tasted exquisite. Our conversation stalled as we admired the meals, basking in the warm smells of garlic and herbs. Moby's *never* disappointed. A plate of their food was pure satisfaction.

I could feel Eliza's eyes on me, and I looked back, unable to force a smile, as I picked up my glass of wine to take a sip and swallow a groan.

My legs were suddenly restless, and the muscles in my wings strained from disuse. An urge to shove my chair back and stand, hit me. One of my knees collided with the table, causing the plates and glasses to clatter loudly.

I needed to *move*.

But something demanded me to stay put. I apologized to Eliza and neatly folded my napkin when something white in my peripheral caught my attention.

A woman entered the restaurant, and my restlessness immediately eased. She shrugged out of her dark brown trench coat, revealing more of the long, white dress underneath. Her dark hair cascaded over one shoulder, the rest disappearing down her back like a silk waterfall, catching the light. Her long legs, outlined through the shiny fabric, hypnotized me with each step she took. Confidence exuded from her.

Each breath I took echoed like a storm in my ears.

Now, I *couldn't* move, my eyes following her as someone pointed her to the bar. She swung her hair over one shoulder and combed her hands through the curls, showing off her tattooed arm. A dark serpent curled around it, its face pointing to a slender hand. From the back, the dress she wore revealed a section of her bare back to me. The fabric was a startling white, with a silver chain wrapped around her waist that looked like it was made for her. Her curves were accentuated, forming a perfect *S* from the side as she leaned closer to the bar, and her deep brown skin seemed to glow in the subdued lighting of Moby's as if she had just finished a workout.

My heart thumped as she gripped the bar, asking for something I couldn't make out, and then she turned around. The woman tilted her chin to take in the restaurant, leaning back on those high heels. Her eyes swept across the room before finally locking with mine.

Time seemed suspended as our gazes locked, a look of surprise flickering in her vibrant green eyes before quickly glancing back down to the bar as a drink was put in front of her.

She was undeniably a Daemon.

"Dominic?"

I looked back at the Angeli opposite me and swallowed. It had been a long time since someone had distracted me like that. "Yes?" It was impossible to explain what had just happened.

Eliza's lips curved into a gentle smile, and she reached out to touch my hand. "You must have a lot on your mind," she said, her voice full of understanding and compassion.

I nodded slowly, still feeling the pull of the Daemon woman's presence in the restaurant. "Forgive me. What were you saying?"

"Just that the Draconis have no idea that…"

My mind trailed off again as my eyes searched for the mystery Daemon. She was still standing at the bar, silently sipping from her drink. And, as if on cue, the restaurant doors opened again, revealing someone else. The man who entered immediately walked over to the woman and kissed her cheek, his hand firmly on her waist in a possessive gesture. He said something to her that elicited a playful eye-roll. She seemed glad to see him.

I cleared my throat.

"Because how else would we know, right?"

I watched Eliza cut her food. "Right," I responded.

A server walked the pair to a table in the front, a colder spot closer to the entrance, and the guy—an Ethereal I vaguely recognized now that I could see him better—pulled up her chair before they both sat down.

She didn't seem like a woman who needed help.

As she sat closer to the table, her eyes flicked up to meet mine from across the restaurant. Her stare was blatantly inquisitive as she cocked her head somewhat. Her black hair slipped over her shoulder with the gesture before she peered back at the table. She moistened her lips as she unfolded her napkin.

Taking a breath, I tore my eyes away from her to refocus my attention on Eliza and our conversation. I discarded any thought or diversion that hindered my ability to be here and enjoy the evening with her fully.

"This course is absolutely delicious," Eliza said, biting her bottom lip. She kept looking at me from underneath her lashes, taking deliberate, slow bites from her quiche and licking her lips after she'd swallowed them down. As usual, Eliza's flirtatious behavior became more and more apparent as the night went on.

If it weren't for the constant distraction of the Daemon woman in the front, she would have successfully captured my attention. I might not think with my dick, but I was still a man.

Attentive green eyes focused on the guy before her, lips pursed as she listened to him.

I couldn't take my eyes off her.

Who is she?

I pushed the thought down as Eliza shifted in her seat and cleared her throat, arching an eyebrow as she looked at me. She seemed to sense my distraction and finally started showing her frustration. "Dominic, are we going to do this or not?"

As I brushed a hand over my eyes, trying to ward off fatigue, I listened to the steady thrum of conversation surrounding us. This was all just a result of insomnia. My sleep cycle had been in a sorry state for quite some time. When I faced her again, I gave a slight shake of my head. "I think not. It's been too long a day."

Eliza nodded, slowly, before offering me a softer smile, one full of fake understanding, her blue eyes frozen into chunks of ice. "Another time then," she said and arranged her cutlery on her plate before stealing a quick glance back towards the restaurant's entrance.

Despite the heavenly taste of my dessert, I chose not to

finish it in this uncomfortable silence. I informed a passing server we had finished eating and requested them to charge the bill on my card. Eliza took a moment to wipe her mouth with a napkin before getting up from her seat and grabbing her purse.

I left a tip on the table and buttoned my suit jacket. "Ready to go?"

With an absent smile on her lips, she nodded.

I had been an asshole. I was well aware of the fact. I simply didn't care.

We walked to the front of the restaurant, where someone was already waiting with our coats. However, my attention was drawn back to the Daemon in the front, who spoke while holding her hands beneath her chin.

As I passed their table, I was surprised to hear, "Archangel Venetia?"

I turned, looking at the Ethereal—her date—who had risen from his seat and had put a hand to his chest. "I'm Josiah Eden. My father used to tell me many stories of your Starball rivalry."

Recognition slowly dawned on me. "Gustav Eden?"

He nodded. "My father would want me to pass on his greetings, I'm sure."

Gustav Eden had been an incredible player in his time; already at the end of his career by the time I had come around the corner, but had still been just as fierce as at the beginning. "Weren't you made captain this year?"

"I was."

I didn't want to like this guy, but his godsdamned smile was filled with so much light it nearly blinded me. "Congrats. I'll be seeing you on the field then."

"Thank you, Sir."

I looked at his date for another split second. With a mask of indifference, she studied the plate in front of her, digging into the food with her fork—as if I wasn't even there.

"Dominic, are you coming?"

Upon hearing that, the girl raised her head, briefly making eye contact with Eliza, but swiftly averted her gaze.

I shook the guy's hand and guided Eliza out of the restaurant with my hand on her back. Something about the woman made me want to know her. The sensation was akin to an itch, but the speed at which the press would report any interaction of mine was staggering. And then I would realize it wasn't worth it.

It never was.

The highlight of Inesa's office was the wall of floor-to-ceiling windows that brought in plenty of sunlight and offered a view of the Ashtior skyline. Inesa and Nathan were already inside as I walked in that afternoon. Nathan tilted his head playfully while Inesa gestured with her hands. She had always been an animated talker.

I couldn't help but crack a smile watching them.

"Dominic!" Inesa cried out when she saw me. She got up and gave me a kiss on the cheek. "We already started without you."

Inesa becoming the Angeli domain rep sparked this tradition of drinking together on Friday afternoons. We saw each other all the time at work, but that was *work*. I held the time with my friends sacred.

"It's good to see you, man," Nathan said. I put my hand

on my friend's shoulder, and he passed me a bottle when I sat down next to him.

I slumped into the seat and rubbed my temple, feeling a thousand years old. "It's been a busy week."

Inesa leaned forward with a concerned smile. "Just busy, or did shit hit the fan?"

I let out a deep sigh, relaxing a little now I was with only them before I said, "Remember Nitas at the Ashar Awards afterparty?"

Nathan's demeanor turned serious as he sat up, and Inesa stopped drinking.

"He told me something about a new drug circulating the streets. According to him, it's something we haven't seen before."

Nathan and Inesa exchanged a concerned glance. "What has he heard?"

I shrugged. "Only that Xanon's supposedly behind it, and he's made the stuff stronger than any other drug out there right now."

"That fucking asshole." Inesa shook her head as she processed my words. "Do you know when he's dropping it? Can we do anything to stop it?"

Nathan let out a frustrated growl as he looked out the office window. "That's going to cost us," he muttered. "With the ACC just around the corner... *Fucking hell.*"

Xanon was cunning. How else has he remained under the radar for this long? The Ashar City Cup was the biggest event of the year in our city and brought in all kinds of people: tourists, fans—people from the Undercity looking to make a quick buck. The launch of this new drug was far from random; Xanon would surely capitalize on this opportunity.

The drug economy was an invisible one, with all transactions done in cash. If anyone were stupid enough to create a traceable virtual transaction, our law enforcers would be upon them before they could draw their next breath. Sadly, most of them weren't that stupid, which made it hard to get a grip on the Undercity's dealings and gave criminals like Xanon an advantage when it came to trafficking drugs. Nitas and I had been working hard, trying to build relationships with key players to get information about what was going on in the streets, but so far, we had had little luck. People were either too scared or too loyal.

We couldn't do anything except wait for Xanon to make a move and hope the damage would be minimal. None of this was ideal, but it was the only choice we had when dealing with the criminal Undercity.

"We've dealt with worse," Inesa said softly.

I let out a noncommittal sound that fell somewhere between amusement and frustration, causing us all to fall into silence.

The sun cast a golden hue over Ashtior's cityscape, highlighting every bit of marble and reflecting on every piece of metal. I smiled as Nathan removed his blazer and rolled up his sleeves. Inesa's mouth tensed as she poured another glass of wine. A thought struck me as I looked at my friends—Inesa nervously twirling her glass in her hand and Nathan leaning back, deep in thought. We loved this city because it was *home*.

Hell would freeze over before I'd ever let them be in danger. I wouldn't let anyone be taken from me again.

We stayed longer than usual and drank a little more, but we needed the relief. Nathan and I even managed to remain silent when Inesa received a call from Leon, putting him on speaker. He'd asked her if she would eat at home, and she started babbling some nonsense that Leon would definitely blame Nathan and me for. After she'd ended the call, we laughed until we could hardly breathe—until we forgot all about the dark clouds closing in overhead.

No matter what happened, I knew that Inesa and Nathan would be by my side. Our bond was unbreakable. They meant everything to me.

They were my family.

CHAPTER SEVEN

Leyla

"What's up?" Dana answered my call with her usual cheer after only a couple rings.

I sank back into the couch with the ghost of a smile. "Nothing much. Just finished work for the day and wanted to catch up. How was your day?" The lie rolled off my tongue like it was second nature, which might just be the case right about now. Maybe I should take up acting. At least then, I'd have something going for me. Contrary to Dana, I was going nowhere—fast. She put her talent for fashion design to good use, and her early career was already off to a head start. I did not doubt that her success would come in no time, and it had nothing to do with where she came from. No, she'd done it all on her own.

Dana sighed. "It's been… *interesting*. The morning sucked, but the afternoon was way better."

"What happened?" I lived vicariously through her.

"The new intern misplaced the swatches, but hey, what's a little stress at this point, am I right?" She chuckled. "My boss would've freaked if he found out."

I pulled my legs closer to my body. "No way you had taken

the blame for that."

"Then you haven't met my boss."

Dana had to work crazy hours, and her boss was one of the most demanding—and successful—Ethereal designers. The entire city was filled with his designs. Dana showed she had what it takes and got promoted to junior designer in no time. Although, in the beginning, we'd often go out after her work so she could have a few drinks and unwind.

"What about you, Ley?" she asked. "How was your date with Josiah?"

I'd been expecting this. "*Ugh*, Dana…"

"Tell. Me."

"He took me to Moby's," I began, but a knock sounded on my door. "Hold on." I stood from the couch, clutching my phone against my ear, as I looked through the peephole, drawing back a few steps in panic as I spotted my father.

Fuck.

"Everything alright?"

I put the phone back to my ear. "I'll have to call you back, Dana."

"I was just about to get the juice!"

"There's no juice. And my dad's here."

"Okay," she responded. "You better call me back." Of course, Dana didn't know who my father was, but she knew my relationship with him was… complicated. Dana never asked questions. She trusted me.

Another knock.

I got up from the couch and walked to the door. "I will."

My father appraised me for a moment after I opened the door, his stare so heavy I hadn't even noticed Zade standing behind him, both their eyes darker above ground. I wasn't sure what to do. Why the hell were they here? There had to be something if my father felt inclined to come all the way to Shard City. It sure as hell wasn't just to see me. He never showed up here. "What's going on?"

He stepped inside. "We need to talk. Sit down."

Zade followed him in before I closed the door swiftly. As much as I faulted others for mindlessly obeying my father, it was me, this time, who sat down at his command without hesitation. It made me want to cringe, but I only wrapped my hands together in my lap.

My father sat down opposite me, and only now did I notice the folder he was holding. I glanced back and forth between the folder and his face. What did it say? What was important enough to come here for? My friendship with Dana? The date with Josiah? They were harmless, even if their families were high profile.

"If this is about—"

"No." My father shook his head and leaned back in the chair, crossing an ankle over his thigh as if he knew exactly what I was about to ask. His greying hair was slicked back more meticulously than usual, forming a sharp contrast with his light brown skin and hardened features. He was an imposing man, and if I hadn't known him my entire life—wasn't confident he wouldn't hurt a hair upon my head or even risk a strand—I would probably feel intimidated. Any survival instinct I had would surely kick in.

"I am here because I grant my promises," he began, and the words made me instantly sit up taller. My father handed me the folder. "A place in my organization."

I remained silent, overwhelmed with excitement as I realized what he was saying. But then why did Zade look so uneasy about it? When I opened the folder, the first thing I saw was a photo.

"Recognize him?"

Part of me wanted to burst out laughing. The picture showed one of the most famous people in Ashar: Dominic Venetia, Archangel and Prime of Shard City, our mayor and safe keeper. He commanded the city's outward protective dome and controlled the weather inside it. The picture I looked at was of him entering the Town Hall, those enormous golden wings folded against his broad back, his half-long light brown curls a little disheveled as if he had just landed.

Who fucking wouldn't recognize him? He was *everywhere*.

I looked up from the photo. "What does he have to do with it?"

"He's your assignment. Your mark. It's vital you get close to him."

Looking away from the photo, I frowned at my father. What did he want with the Archangel? "Close, how?"

"*Personal.*"

My mouth popped open, and my throat closed up. Zade's eyes were burning a hole in my face. "You want me to seduce him."

My father quirked a brow. "He needs to trust you. I don't care how you do it."

"Why?" I asked him.

"He possesses something I require."

Not good enough. "What does he have?"

"I will tell you when the time is right."

My father got up from his seat and walked to the window, giving me a chance to glance at Zade. A fire ignited in my gut as I noticed the angry set of his jaw. Something about the way his eyes locked with mine didn't sit right. It must be something really special if they were this adamant for me to get close to *the Archangel*.

"You're a beautiful girl," my father said. "Got most of your looks from your mother—thank the light—who was considered one of the beauties of her time."

"Is this task solely given to me because of how I look?"

"Leyla," he warned, turning back around. "Drop the attitude. You *know* why you are given this task. Looks only get you so far; they're just a tool to get his attention. You'll find a way to keep it with intelligence."

Sure. We're only talking about one of the most powerful men in the world, after all. What's the big *fucking* deal?

As if he could still sense my apprehension, he said, "Everyone in Ashar will benefit from your success, *especially* Ashrior. Remember what I always told you?"

I looked at him. "The world is not a fair place." There was a divide between the different levels of the city, especially the one between Ashium and Ashrior—Shard City, and the Undercity.

"You know wealth is not distributed equally. Ashtior flourishes, Ashium plucks the rewards, and Ashrior is left with scraps."

I clamped my lips tightly shut.

"Think about it, Leyla. You can finally get vengeance." He pressed one finger to his temple as he looked at me. "He may not be the culprit, but he's certainly the one who buried the crime."

Memories threatened to unravel, and I willed them to stay put. My hands fisted as I bit down so hard the tears wouldn't come.

"Ashari like him—" My father pressed his finger into Prime Venetia's photo "—have had the final say for too long. Their self-interest is their only priority." He dropped the folder on the side table. "All you need to know is in that folder. Look into it. Zade will reach out to get things started."

In other words, *don't be impatient and get in touch first.*

I nodded and watched him leave as suddenly as he arrived. Zade lingered in my living room, his throat working up and down, dark eyes brewing with a storm inside.

"Tell me you didn't know." I rose from the couch.

He rubbed a hand over his mouth. "It sure as hell wasn't my decision."

"But you swallowed it anyway."

Zade's eyes turned even darker. I didn't care. I made my way to the door and held it open for him. It felt like he had handed me over to the Archangel without so much as a blink. "Go on, Zade. Get out. Chase after your master."

A dark glint in his expression caught my eye—sharp as a knife, as he stalked closer, getting into my face. "Don't forget that this assignment will serve all of us in the end, Leyla. You're part of something bigger now."

With gritted teeth, I observed Zade disappear down the hallway stairs. I slammed the door shut, causing the frames on my wall to tremble and I leaned back against it.

Yesterday, right before Josiah made his entrance, someone had caught me off-guard. As if I'd felt him, I peered into the restaurant and noticed a pair of eyes already fixed on me. The sight of Dominic Venetia had been startling—unexpected. To learn he had been watching me only added to the surprise. His image was all over town, in newspapers, on TV, online... but seeing him in real life was like a punch to the gut.

As I looked away from him, I noticed the golden feathers visible behind his head, with his hair bound back and his beard perfectly tailored. His brows had been drawn, and his wings were folded, but they still looked mighty behind him. The sight of him had seemed impossible, a figment of my imagination.

He hadn't changed at all.

The Archangel had worn a wine-red suit, his white blouse underneath unbuttoned to show some of his tan skin. His shoulders were broad, and his hand fisted on the table as if he was itching for something.

He had come especially close when Josiah addressed him on his way out. His body had carried a warmth with it so strong it even smelled good, sweet with a hint of spice. Once again, I could feel his golden brown eyes on me—as they had been all night. If I were anyone else, I would have taken it as unabashed interest. He had been there with his current fling, and despite her using his name so casually, I'd been unable to gauge the depth of their relationship. Considering the amount of times he glanced my way in the restaurant, it had to be *platonic*.

My plan had been put in motion before I was ready to begin. Many questions were answered, and variables were solved that night. The Archangel had noticed me, and his gaze had been searing. But the man was overwhelming, and I had the feeling that with him, you always bit off a little too much. Getting close to him would be like diving into a deep ocean with no hope of resurfacing.

It had been a pure coincidence that the Archangel had been there. But a lucky one, at that. There was no doubt that Josiah had used his connections to score that table at Moby's, and I appreciated his effort.

Josiah picked up our conversation once the Archangel had left the restaurant. "Sorry for that." He laughed, rubbing a hand over his chest. "He was a very impressive player."

I sipped from my wine. "Your father played against the Archangel?"

Josiah had nodded. "Apparently, they'd had an infamous rivalry between them, all in good sport, of course. My dad always speaks highly of him, as a player and as our Prime."

My smile had slipped. "I hadn't known Prime Venetia was such a good player."

Or Prime.

"He was the best of his time, actually. Especially after my father retired."

I raised my brows. "The best? Really?"

"Yeah. Only the gods know what he could've been if his wings hadn't turned golden. He would've gotten worldwide fame."

I let out a snort. "Well, I think he has that."

"What about you?" Josiah asked, sporting his signature lopsided smile. "What are your aspirations?"

Taken aback by his question, I had rambled off some vague answer about being in search of a path I wanted to commit myself to. Something to pour all of myself into, like Josiah had Starball and Dana fashion. *Like my father had his cause.*

Josiah had been excellent all night. He flirted at the right times, made me laugh more than once—which was a feat in itself—and every answer he gave me had been sincere. He hadn't been shy about his interest in me, and I couldn't get myself to tell him there was no future for us. I made myself enjoy the evening, pretending I was someone else on an actual date with the Ethereal Starball team's captain.

In the end, despite it being very tempting, I hadn't taken Josiah up on his offer to go home with him. It had nothing to do with Zade—we weren't exclusive. Seeing the Archangel had thrown me off. I wasn't in the mood for lighthearted, fun sex after a knot full of conflicting emotions had formed, despite how good Josiah undoubtedly was in bed.

He deserved better; his hands were too clean for me to soil them.

Now that my father had finally given me an assignment with which I could prove myself—something I had been begging for—my life had to change. Casual dating was out of the picture. I would do anything to make my father proud, to right the wrongs that were made.

And if that meant getting close to the Archangel, so be it.

CHAPTER EIGHT

13 years ago

"Where is my favorite girl?"

The familiar low, thundering voice vibrating through the house made me perk up from where I was reading on the couch. "Uncle Bohrod!"

I wasn't blood-related to the Daemon, but it felt like that. He and my father were business partners, but their relationship was almost brotherly, and Bohrod treated me like family.

His greying brown beard was longer than when I last saw him before his trip outside of Ashar and his pale skin had a little tan. I hugged him tightly, and he put one of his broad hands on my head. "Happy belated birthday, darling."

I inhaled his scent, grinning as I looked up at him. "Please tell me what it was like, what you have seen, who you spoke to." I was always extremely curious when he returned from a trip.

Bohrod flicked my nose as he chuckled. "I will, but not before I've given you your present." He took an envelope from his pocket and handed it to me. "Don't think I forgot about you."

With eager hands, I grabbed the envelope and opened it,

taking out two cards. *Tickets*. "What…" I looked up at him with big eyes.

"I'm taking you to see a performance of *The Magic Lake* in the Shard City theater."

"Shard City? You're taking me *up there*?" Excitement spilled from me in waves. Going to Ashium for the night was a dream come true. I hadn't been there often but had soaked up every glimpse I'd gotten.

He nodded. "We're going to see a ballet show, thought you'd appreciate that, seeing as you're always dancing around the house."

I looked from the tickets to him. "I love it!" I hugged him again. "Thank you."

"You are welcome, Leyla."

"Father was okay with it?" I put the tickets between the pages of the book I was reading and stuffed it under the pillow.

Bohrod rolled up his sleeves, baring his tattooed arms to me. I had always been fascinated with his tattoos. "I'll talk to him about it. Don't worry, it'll be fine. He knows you are safe with me."

I grinned. "I cannot wait! It's the best birthday present ever!" The sound of children laughing outside caught my attention, and I walked to the window, looking out at the playground near the house. With longing, I watched as they chased each other, big smiles on their faces.

It must be nice to have friends.

"Take your coat," Bohrod said from behind me.

I turned around. "What?"

His smile was visible through his beard. "You want to hear about my adventures or not? Because if you do, you must come outside with me. Let's take a walk."

He wouldn't have to tell me twice. I seized every chance to go outside. For days, I was inside this house, within the barrier of the grounds, but not free to roam beyond the fences—not like the other kids. My father thought it was too dangerous.

But with Bohrod, I could. He would keep me safe.

I ran into the hallway, taking my coat and scarf, and met him at the open door. With his hand on my shoulder, the guards opened the gates, and we walked into Ashrior together.

"I'm glad you're back," I told him.

He squeezed my shoulder before letting go. "Me too, darling."

The prospect of going to the ballet in Shard City, visiting the city, and hearing about Bohrod's adventures made me giddy. It was physically impossible to keep the smile from my face. I hadn't felt this light in a *long* time.

Bohrod told me about the underwater Sanguis clans, who had a network a hundred times as big as the underwater palace in Ashar. He described the regions outside the protective dome, where they built extensive underground structures, similar to Ashrior, to protect the people living there against falling stars during fall reborn. How he had been forced to take shelter there one night when the meteorites' numbers were a little too high.

I had only witnessed the phenomenon from the Ashrior hole, never above ground. It must be a magical sight.

We walked past a dark oak tree, the sort that grew with little sunlight, and I lowered on my haunches to collect a few acorns. I collected things from outside in a small box, and I sometimes went through it just to imagine I was out there again; that I was some other girl, free to do as she pleased.

"Are the trees different from here?" I asked him, picking

up another acorn and showing it to him.

He smiled at the small nut and nodded. "Some grow twice as tall."

"*Twice?*" I exclaimed, looking up at the trees surrounding us. "They would be so much fun to climb."

"Not if you're afraid of heights," Bohrod said, raising a brow at me.

I wrapped my arms together. "We'll see about that." My eyes roamed over the acorns in my hand again. "You think I will see them someday?"

His eyes softened. "You will. I promise, one day I—" Suddenly, he perked his head to the side, eyes moving from left to right as he scanned the perimeter.

"What is it?"

Bohrod signaled for me to be quiet as he continued to listen to something I couldn't hear. His mood shifted as his eyes widened, and he cocked his head my way, scanning our surroundings in rapid succession. I was trembling by the time he took my head between his big hands. "Leyla, listen very carefully. You need to run and hide. Not too far, or they'll hear your steps and find you. Be as still as possible. Can you do that?"

"What do you mean? Who will hear me?"

"There is no time, darling. You have to hide and be dead silent. Please tell me you understand."

I nodded again. "Yes—yes, I understand."

He brushed a lock of hair from my face with his thumb and smiled reassuringly, but I knew it was solely for my benefit. "Go, now."

"But—"

With force, he shook my head. "*Now*, Leyla."

I turned around and ran while my eyes filled with tears. Something was wrong. Very, very wrong if he would send me away to hide. My steps skidded on the stone as I found a bush nearby to crawl into, not too far, not too close. Despite the time of year, most of the plant's leaves remained, allowing me to glimpse Uncle Bohrod's face as he stared directly at the spot he had been fixated on.

Then, I heard the voices. A group of individuals dressed in black entered the street, and one of them whistled. *"Bohrod Teller."* The man who spoke had a chiseled face and blonde hair. His facial characteristics appeared almost unnaturally sharp and I noticed his fangs. *Sanguis.*

"What do you want?"

The blonde guy shrugged. "Only your head."

"You're making a grave mistake." My uncle's words held a warning in them.

"I'll take my chances." The man pointed to the other people surrounding my uncle. "The odds, as you may notice, are very much stacked against you."

As one, they moved.

I looked away and clamped my trembling hands over my mouth as I froze. Bohrod was strong, and he held his ground for a few beats, but the sounds of my uncle's fight quickly transformed into pained grunts as his assailers overpowered him and attacked repeatedly until only the sound of slashes filled the surroundings.

I couldn't even bring myself to shield my ears from the wet gurgles that reverberated.

It didn't take long until the leader of the group spoke again. "Bring me his head."

I nearly choked on the bile rising in my throat.

"Fane, we need to go."

"Not before I get my trophy. He would look good on my mantle."

I suppressed the nausea threatening to consume me. Someone started the process, and I dug my fingers into my scalp, clenching my jaw. The sounds of it filled my ears—I would never get it out of my head again—when something disturbed them.

"Leave him, then," the man said. "Let's go."

The sound of footsteps fading away coincided with the ticking of water droplets on the leaves surrounding me. A slow drizzle of rain seeped through the bush I was sitting in. I dropped my trembling hands from my mouth and covered my eyes with them, catching the silent tears that fell at the realization of what had just happened.

The rain got louder as it swallowed my muffled cries.

Uncle Bohrod was dead. He'd been brutally murdered. *Slaughtered.*

I sensed the urgency to check on him, unsure if he could still be saved, but my heart knew the truth.

Footsteps sounded on the pavement. Someone was here. There was a faint voice—a woman's—and moments later, a loud bang rumbled through the street. I dropped my hands to look for the source. Golden wings folded together as they revealed a man. *Angeli.* Strands of his hair stuck to his neck as he stalked forward to the woman already looking down. She was also drained from head to toe, her light blonde hair dripping on her leather coat.

"It's him," she said.

They shared a look, and the Angeli lowered on his haunches.

"Please tell me he is as dead as he looks," the woman said again, voice trembling a little, afraid, as if she couldn't quite believe what she was seeing.

The Angeli with the golden wings rose as he looked at her. "Very much so."

The woman nodded to herself as she looked down, transfixed by the sight. "What happened, you think?"

"A rival organization. The half-severed neck and dozens of stabbing wounds are a dead giveaway."

The woman snorted humorlessly as tears welled over my cheeks. My head was starting to hurt from the cold, the rain, and what had happened.

"We should leave him here. Let the vultures pick his body."

The man shook his head. "It would only make him a martyr."

Not much later, big lights filled the street, and people dressed in white took my uncle's lifeless body from the pavement. One of his bloodied arms fell from the stretcher. I stopped looking as they carded him in the vehicle like he was trash. As if he didn't leave behind people who loved him.

As if he was *nothing*.

First, he was robbed of his life, and then we were robbed of our final goodbyes. Of justice.

Night descended upon Ashrior as the woman and the Angeli exchanged more hushed words before departing, taking the bright lights with them.

My tears kept streaming until I had none left in my body. The salt trails they had left on my cheeks felt like ropes tightening on my skin, tugging painfully as every limb in my body grew sore from the cold.

I did not know how much time had passed before sound

other than the rain filled my ears again.

"Leyla?" someone yelled. *Familiar.* I opened my eyes and willed my frozen, stiff limbs to rise. "Leyla!"

I stood from the bush and watched as Ulverin scoured the place, hovering over a dark red spot on the stone in the middle. When she noticed me, she immediately ran over and lowered, bringing her face level with mine while gripping my chin to ensure it remained raised. "Are you okay, kid?"

I couldn't tell her. I didn't even know myself.

She swallowed and glanced down at me, nodding to herself as she took off her jacket and wrapped it around me. "You're safe now, Leyla. You hear me? Everything's going to be okay."

How could she say that when Bohrod had just been killed?

"*You're okay,*" she said again.

The return trip home was swift, and as soon as I entered the deserted courtyard, a wave of shame engulfed me. I had done nothing to help him. I had hidden while they killed Bohrod, like a coward.

When we entered the house, my father immediately walked into the hallway, his concerned eyes focused on me. "Get some towels—*now*,"

I winced.

Ulverin let go of me, and my father's eyes softened. "I apologize, *Cara.*"

He was only worried about me.

When the red-haired Daemon returned with a fresh stack of towels, my father asked, "Why was she outside?"

"Bohrod must have taken her out."

"He was telling me about his adventures," I said, my croaking voice hoarse. I sniffled. "And then he suddenly told me to hide and—and..."

My father took a towel and dried my hair, brushing over my arms to get me to warm back up. "It's okay, Leyla. Take your time. What happened then?"

My chin trembled. "There were many people, all Sanguis from what I saw. One of them, the leader... they called him Fane. They told Bohrod they wanted to kill him. And then they did. Dad, they—" I choked on the words. "They killed him. Uncle Bohrod is dead."

"There was a lot of blood," Ulverin told my father as she crouched before me. "Are you sure he is dead? They didn't take him?"

I nodded, my nostrils flaring. "They said his head—his head—" I hiccuped. "The people who killed him wanted to take it after they had stabbed him so many times I can still hear it." I clutched my head with both hands and closed my eyes as I sobbed. "They fled and left him when they heard other people coming."

"Who took his body?"

"There was a woman with blonde hair and a man with golden wings. They—I didn't understand. They didn't want to leave him, and they took him. Like *trash*," I growled, brushing at the tears running down my face.

My father and Ulverin shared a look.

"You are sure the man's wings were golden?"

I nodded.

"There is only one person with golden wings," my father told me as he brushed away some of my stray tears. "Listen well, *Cara*, so you'll never forget. The Archangel doesn't care about us. None of them up there do. They let us rot here like the dirt underneath their boots."

I swallowed.

"They are going to act like Uncle Bohrod never existed because they wished it to be true—just like they wish us dead, too. They don't care, and they never will."

"We can't even say goodbye to him?"

"No," my father said. "They robbed him of a worthy farewell, and they robbed him from us, his family. And you know why? It's because they are scared."

"Scared?"

He took my hand, warming it in his. "They have left us down here for so long they no longer know what we're capable of. We could change this city for the better, and we *will*." With a kiss on my forehead, he said, "Get some rest now, *Cara*."

He looked at Ulverin, telling her to get me warm and cleaned up before putting me to bed. "Let's go, kid. Sorry your day had to end like this."

A month later, my father sent me to boarding school in Shard City for my safety because the individuals who had harmed Bohrod would not hesitate to harm me too. He wanted to keep me far away from his organization—to protect me.

But I wasn't a kid anymore. And I no longer needed his protection.

CHAPTER NINE

Dominic

I found myself standing precisely in the bustling heart of the atrium at the newly constructed rehab center of Shard City Hospital. The hallways were packed with patrons and supporters of the cause, as well as the press, all waiting for my speech. I felt a sense of satisfaction as I looked around the space. The walls were painted in calming blues and greens, and the furniture was modern yet practical. The team made good use of the funds for this ward, and I was hopeful about how many people would benefit from it. Especially now that help might be crucial. Drugs in Ashrior were already wreaking havoc, and with this new one hitting the streets…

Cameras shuttered as I entered the small dais set up for me. "I want to thank everyone for being here and supporting a worthwhile cause."

It was one of the few projects that actually mattered to me. The number of people with addictions was staggering, not to mention the progressively younger age at which they started using. There weren't many places they could turn to when they wanted to heal from their disease—not any most could afford.

"We stand here with a common goal: to create a safe and supportive environment for those in need. To ensure that everyone who needs our help can get it," I said. "I cannot emphasize enough the significance of a center like this, aimed at better understanding addiction and striving to diminish the stigma surrounding it. Every day, people fall prey to addictions, and every day, we also mourn loved ones lost to them.

"There has been a gap in care facilities for people who want to change their life but don't know where to begin, people who want to end their self-destructive behavior, and rarely have the resources to do it. We are talking about people who still have a shot at life, things to contribute and ideas our society could benefit from. We aim to give everyone a fair shot at life, so this will be the first of many rehabilitation centers across Ashar." My eyes roamed the crowd, eyes lingering on individuals.

"We all have a responsibility to look after each other, and this new center will be a place where we can do just that. Here, we can provide help and guidance to those who need it. Offer advice and support to those who care for them or anyone who wants to make this city a little safer." I bowed my head to the crowd. "Thank you."

The first reporter raised her voice. "Prime Venetia, what would you say has contributed to the exponential rise of addiction in Ashar?"

I looked at the woman in front of me, who gave me a self-assured smile as if she thought it did anything for me. She was beautiful; there was no question about that, but contrary to what people believed, my brain did all the thinking. For one, it warned me to stay away from the green-eyed Daemon I'd seen at Moby's. No matter how intriguing she was, my brain recognized trouble when he saw it. "The problem is the Ashrior drug circuit itself, the invisible cash flow, and the blatant disrespect for the law we try to uphold."

"Would you say Xanon Naan belongs to that category?" Another reporter asked, eliciting some stunned whispers from the audience. "Should he feel addressed?"

Wonderful. News had the habit of traveling fast.

"I'd say anyone involved in the trade is part of the problem. Our mission is to dismantle every cog in the machine." I knew it would require drastic measures for that bastard to leave the deep belly of the Undercity.

Several more questions came up after that, but I walked away from the stand towards Fredo, who was already holding out a bottle of water. The audience quickly applauded me before I started touring the facility. I had visited the location a few times during construction, but seeing the final result was different. They escorted me to the therapy rooms, where I could observe firsthand the impactful work being done to support patients. The amount of care and attention given to each person surprised me, as well as the wide range of activities and therapies available.

Next, we visited the dormitories, and I had the chance to meet recovering patients and see their progress firsthand. I counted the empty beds, haunted by visions of the near future. How long before this place would flood with more patients than they could manage?

I also made sure to stop by the children's ward of the hospital whenever I visited. According to a nurse, the children were filled with excitement for weeks after one of my visits, which compelled me to ensure I continued doing so when I was around. I exchanged fist-pumps with the few bold kids and even received a hug from a young Angeli boy.

I stayed longer with one child in isolation—even let her touch my feathers. As an Archangel, I was immune to illness, but anyone else who wanted to approach her had to wear a hazmat suit. Her parents had expressed their gratitude, because they were unable to get close to their daughter without wearing it. It was worth the complete purifying process afterward.

At the end of my visit, they showed me the different programs the center had set up, ranging from physical activities to art therapy. The staff's dedication was inspiring, and their relentless pursuit of creating a center for healing and growth, admirable. I knew from experience that anything good had the habit of being tainted by the ugliness of this world. Nonetheless, I remained determined to continue this work to ensure it had a lasting impact so that it would eviscerate this new drug in Ashrior before it affected the city.

Fredo was waiting for me outside the hospital's back exit, holding the car door open. Press approached me and bombarded me with questions, but I brushed them off—leisurely unbuttoning my suit jacket before getting into the car.

The drive to my next appointment, the Modern Art Society, was short, but I wouldn't walk these streets with all the press swarming them. The worst part of my job was people tripping over themselves for comments and pictures and then twisting them to fit their narratives.

The Society comprised curators and art collectors who were eager to show me some of their most prolific works. I was searching for artwork for this season's kick-off gala and an upcoming auction. The artworks donated for the auction were astonishing. I paused to appreciate every detail and admire the creators' expertise, coming from all over Celestia, varying in style and origin. I tried to understand the history and themes of each one, as a story added depth to something that was simply beautiful.

Often, the things the eye couldn't see made it worth viewing the most.

My eyes lingered on a painting depicting stunning mountains and valleys somewhere in Celestia, with a backdrop of falling stars. I was sure this year's auction would end up with a staggering amount of donations and that this year's gala would be the best yet.

Fall reborn was my favorite season of the year. Not only because I loved Starball but because the view of those burning stars against a backdrop of the night sky was mesmerizing.

When one curator asked after my private collection, I politely told them about some of the work I had back home but spun the conversation around by expressing my admiration for the pieces of art they had been able to collect. Art was one of my life's pleasures; it made me feel like the man I used to be, and that was too personal.

My phone rang, and I dragged it out with reluctance to check who it was. Eliza's caller ID lit up my screen. I put the phone back into my pocket, ignoring it. Being surrounded by art like this was a privilege I could hardly afford anymore, and I wanted to enjoy it uninterruptedly.

After accepting a tour through the Society and looking at some other pieces up for sale, I expressed my gratitude for their hospitality. They had closed the establishment while I was inside, granting me some privacy.

I left soon after taking one last stroll through their exposition and bathed in the bright sunlight as its warmth washed over me. The reflective light on the car was so blinding that I had to squint on my way there. Filling my lungs with a deep breath of crisp, clean air, I made my way into the car.

My wings yearned to fly.

Many people, even at night, flew to Ashtior by aircab. They were filled with tourists from outside of Ashar and Ashari without wings who were visiting the Upper City or going back home. I strolled through the bustling streets of Shard City, disregarding the people snapping pictures of me or calling my name. It was all white noise to me.

On my first day as the Archangel of Ashar, I went to Shard City for my inauguration and had been overwhelmed by all the attention. It took a year before I became accustomed to the constant buzz of people around me. Thankfully, my height allowed me to disregard them for the most part.

Taking off, I aimed for the hole in the middle of Ashtior, but it was too busy with aircabs. I even noticed one flying over my home—as close as the protective field allowed. Its power rippled, communicating with me directly about what it detected. Feeling no inclination to go there whatsoever, I chose to land on a quiet street on the outer edge of Ashtior. I combed my fingers through my hair and straightened my clothing, which had been tailored to fit my wings and made to accommodate flying.

I walked down the narrow street, folding my wings tightly to avoid reflecting light and drawing attention. As I reached the end of the street, I crossed a large square and continued without a second thought. Most Angeli that lived in Ashtior had seen me pass throughout the century. This was my home.

The Ashari living in Ashrior—Daemons and Sanguis—didn't care about me either; hate would be closer to the feeling they harbored. But the Ashium tourists, especially Ashari from Shard City... They were a pain in the ass. Too excited, too loud, too... much.

When I first became Prime, I was young and didn't know how to handle all the attention. I had taken countless photos with people, chatted with them, and let them flirt. But I quickly learned to set my boundaries and to not let anybody fucking cross them.

After going through this for a century, there was no space left to care about their opinions. I didn't have time for bullshit anymore.

I stopped in my tracks as I heard the silent trickle of water and looked up.

This square...

My attempts to steer clear of this place proved futile as my distracted thoughts and traitorous feet unconsciously guided me here.

After crushing my Starball practice, I felt famished and desperately craved fresh fruit from the market. As I walked across the square, my attention was drawn to an anomaly in the bustling crowd: a subtle discoloration amidst the sea of white wings. Most wings were pure white, but the wings of younger Angeli were slightly darker, their feathers not yet strong enough to support them in flight.

It was easy to spot them.

Since the square belonged to the common Angeli and not the aristocratic, it was not unusual to witness a young female, who was not yet of age, venturing out on the street. Even so, the sight of her, visible behind the fountain, made my heart clench. Something about this Angeli was different. It tugged at me. Maybe it was the music to her steps or the way her blonde hair moved in the breeze, but—

She turned, and I could finally see her face. The girl was almost of age and breathtaking. Her peachy cheeks were visible from a distance as she smiled at a merchant. The complexion of her skin was light, pale even, as if she spent too much of her time indoors. Her blonde hair hung just below her wing muscles, the tips curving inwards and bouncing as she conversed with people behind the stalls.

Her smile attracted attention. I noticed many people around her gravitating towards her, just like I had been. The girl did not fit in—a ripple in the current.

I began walking towards her, trying to get closer, see her better, but then she turned around and spotted me, too. Her eyes grew wide as she looked at me. We both froze, locked in this moment, our eyes meeting. The people on the market had no clue what was happening and went on with their lives.

But we were caught in the eye of the storm.

With a fierce blush rising in her cheeks, she turned her face away and smiled at the ground, gripping her bag tighter. Then she turned around and started walking the other way. I cleared my head and followed her, the speed of my strides outpacing hers. She glanced up as if she sensed me walking beside her.

"Hey," I said. Up close, she was even more beautiful. Freckles dotted her nose and upper arms.

"Hi."

"Would you like me to help you with that?" I pointed to the bag hanging from her shoulder.

"No need, but thank you." The beginning of a smile formed on her face again; seeing it was addicting. When I kept walking next to her, she halted, her eyes amused as she turned them on me. "What are you doing?"

My mouth opened as I turned to her fully, focusing on keeping my wings from flexing like a schoolboy. They longed to burst open and carry her away into the sky. Irrational. "Who are you?" *I asked her instead.*

"I can't say." *She smiled that smile again—the one that had my heart palpitating in my throat, made me feel short of breath.*

"Tell me your name, at least."

I couldn't just let her go without knowing her name. But she kept her lips sealed, her eyes shy as she looked away from me.

"Is there somewhere I can call on you?" *I tried.*

"You don't even know me."

"Exactly," *I laughed.* "That's what I'm trying to fix."

"I'm sorry," *she said hoarsely.* "I'm afraid that's not possible." *She turned around and started walking again.*

She moved resolutely, seemingly unfazed, yet I had never been more serious. "Can you tell me something at least?" *I called after her, pulling a hand through my hair.*

The girl turned around, her blonde hair moving in the soft breeze. "My favorite flowers are the ones that belong to the sun."

I remained frozen in the alley, defying my instincts, watching her until she vanished. I paced back and forth in the street until I couldn't help myself and ran after her, but she was nowhere to be seen.

I found myself back in the square, the exact same one where I first saw her.

The memories attached to this place hurt, but there was no rain to fall—no storm was brewing in the soft white clouds that specked the night sky. And maybe, for the first time, I experienced some peace being here in her absence.

Turning back time wasn't an option. If I could, I'd do it in a heartbeat. I would do anything to get her back. But the memory felt more and more like a distant dream from another life, another me. The hurt didn't slice as deep or grate the bone as it used to. The edges had been blunted.

I fiddled with a cigarette, took it from my pocket, and lit it between my lips, gazing upwards into the night sky as I took a deep drag.

Yes. I exhaled a cloud of smoke. The stabbing pain I expected to feel was absent.

Something I never expected to be possible.

CHAPTER TEN

Leyla

As I ran, the morning air was still chilly, marking the seasonal change from summer to fall. I had been trying to clear my mind, but the humid air seemed to short-circuit my thoughts, running in circles and circles. My assignment was a big question mark. No matter how much I thought about it, the solutions and scenarios seemed too complicated, more so than I had initially thought.

I had stared at the file for hours after my father and Zade left my apartment, my heart a steady drum in my ears. For months, *years*, I'd been waiting for an assignment. And now, I had finally gotten one, but I didn't know what to do with myself.

My focus had been locked on the picture of Dominic Venetia—the man who had played an antagonistic part on the worst day of my life. He had turned a blind eye when I had needed him to see. *To help.*

Dominic Venetia was our *fucking* Prime; people mentioned him in casual conversation and headlines. Everyone knew who he was, but what did they truly know?

With his golden wings and deep golden brown eyes, he

was undeniably handsome. The Archangel's straight nose and strong, slightly square jawline matched his other chiseled characteristics. His brown curls, somewhat coppery in color, fell to his shoulders. The rigid slant of his lips parted in a smile, but I couldn't see who or what he was smiling at. Even the devil was supposed to be charming, right?

I had opened the folder to the first page, glancing over the contents. The file contained details about Dominic's personal life, ranging from childhood to adulthood, but with gaps in the timeline. It included information about his parents, education, accomplishments, and connections. There were even records of his travels, the places he frequented, and his interactions with other important people in Celestia, as well as some information about his position. Only one Archangel could reside in a city or region for an extended period to maintain a power balance, and his ability to stabilize the magnetic field kept Ashtior afloat in the sky.

The folder also contained information on his role as Prime. Dominic Venetia was a powerful figure in the *Trias Politica*. Ashar's political system had three main branches, each with its own distinct power structure and purpose. Being Archangel, he automatically gained the title of Prime, the executive power. He ruled Ashium, the main layer of the city, including Shard City. There were two other entities next to him. Up in Ashtior, you had the Cardinal, a group of eleven special Angeli called *Seraphim*. They were the legislative power. And last, in the Undercity, Ashrior, we had the Supreme, a powerful Daemon holding the judicial power in the city.

Prime Venetia mostly worked with the representatives from each domain. He was particularly close to those from the Angeli and Ethereal Domains: Inesa von Hoes and Nathanial Farcroft.

I continued reading, gathering information about his life. The file revealed that Dominic's mother had died during childbirth and that he had spent his childhood as an only child in Ashtior with his father. He was sent away to a private school, where his path had crossed with Nathanial Farcroft. He went on to study theoretical physics and mathematics at university until his father's passing. After that, he dropped out and went to play for the Angeli Starball team. Dominic had been one of the best players in the league before being appointed Prime when his wings had turned golden.

The file also mentioned his dating history. He had a reputation for consistently having a different woman by his side, rotating with the seasons. The woman he was last seen with was a brunette—the high-stationed Angeli he'd been with at the restaurant. He hadn't appeared overly fond of her. If the Archangel had any inclination toward settling down, it wasn't with her, which made things easier for me.

I had a good understanding of Dominic Venetia, in theory. But reading this file felt like reading a resume. Outside of business dealings and romantic trysts, there wasn't a lot of information available about how the Archangel spent his free time or what he was like. It told me nothing about the person behind the public persona.

I didn't care, not truly. If I could stay far away from him, I would, but it was now my job to know. And there was only one way to find out.

I might have been sheltered during my childhood, as my father and Zade always pointed out, but they underestimated what I was capable of now that I finally had a chance to show both men how resourceful I was and how I could benefit the cause.

A loud honk startled me from my run. I stopped myself from crossing the street that went through the park in the Lupine Domain and watched as a car raced past me with loud music.

By the light.

Taking a deep breath, I continued into the park. Usually, running cleared my mind, but now, all I could think about was how the Archangel had looked at me in the restaurant, trying to decipher the look in his eyes. It had been more than just curiosity. The way his eyes had perused my body when I'd been standing at the bar clearly translated into blatant interest.

Dominic Venetia had been looking straight through me with his golden eyes. His stolen glances at Moby's had affected me in no way, but I would be a liar to say he didn't do it for me physically. He was handsome, there was no other way to put it.

Too bad he had treated Bohrod like he was nothing.

And dealing with his wrath when he found out I fucked him over in whatever way my father planned? That was something I looked forward to.

Sweat trickled down my temple. How was it so hot this time of year? I looked up at the sun above, a bright spot in the clear blue sky. Besides the Angeli domain in Ashtior, the Lupine and Ethereal Domains got most of the sunlight. Shard City frequently experienced shade throughout the day.

My phone started ringing just as I reached the edge of the Lupine Domain. I slowed to a walk and looked at who it was, not expecting to see my father's number on the screen. It was rare for him to call, even more so in the morning.

I answered the phone. "Yes?"

"Where are you?" he asked without preamble.

I paused and took a deep breath, reminding myself that arguing would be pointless. "Isn't it your shadow's job to report that?"

"Leyla."

"I'm in the Lupine Domain," I said calmly, looking for a way out of the park that wasn't lined with tourists.

My father was momentarily silent before finally saying, "You made a promise."

He didn't need to say anything else—I knew what he was referring to. Upon moving to Shard City, I promised to avoid the Lupine Domain as much as possible. Being the law enforcers in Ashar, my father didn't trust them. I didn't get the hassle; my father seemed to have no trouble so far, but he had been really adamant about it.

"I know." I mustered some guilt for not keeping my word to him. "No one knows me, and if they did recognize me, it would have happened already. Besides, I'm in a park. It's hardly dangerous."

He sighed. "Just be careful." *You know better than this.* I could practically hear him say it, but then he changed the subject.

Irritation grated on my nerves. "Is this how you monitor all employees?"

"Only the ones that matter."

My shoulders loosened a little. I moved out of the park, shouldering through the throng of tourists surrounding a statue.

"Let this serve as a reminder that we have much to gain from your efforts."

I crossed the street to walk under the trees on a more shaded sidewalk. "There's no part of me that doesn't take this seriously."

"Don't doubt my faith in you, *Cara*. And don't mistake it for anything but concern. There's no one I trust more than you to carry out this assignment. You are my blood."

"Then trust me when I say that I'll tell you if there's anything worthwhile to know."

A gruff chuckle sounded on the other line. "Color me impressed."

Going out in the middle of the work week had been an impromptu idea, but Dana had needed a respite from work. They had passed her up for promotion, and thus, I, too, needed a distraction from wanting to strangle her backstabbing, sore-loser boss.

"I swear, starting my own line is starting to sound like a better option than staying in this job." The queue we were waiting in to enter *Isla Dela* shuffled forward.

"He just doesn't want anyone else in your position because you are too good at what you do."

She took a swig from the bottle she'd been carrying down the street. "Or he is afraid of me surpassing him. Which I could, *by the way*."

I chuckled. "It's not me you have to convince. Either demand a promotion or a hefty fucking raise to fund your own business. And if they don't give you either, you take the jump immediately. You have the skills and the connections for it to take off. I would help you; you can even live with me if rent is too much."

She had styled her fuchsia hair into two top knots, with silver glitter adorning her roots. "If I leave now, he will end my line before it has even launched. He is cold-blooded."

"And you're Lodana fucking Fivaldor. There's no one able to mess with you. And if they try, they haven't met your best friend yet." I hit my chest with my fist in a display of unity.

Dana burst out laughing, but I was dead serious. She wasn't the only one with strings to pull. There were few things I wouldn't do for her.

We arrived at the end of the row, where the bouncer eyed the alcohol Dana was clutching. "Leave that here." He pointed to the bin.

Dana pouted. "I need it."

"Buy your drinks inside."

"But—"

I tore the bottle from her grip, discarding it in the bin next to the bouncer, and then dragged Dana into the club. The music was so loud that it vibrated through my bones. The lights were spinning me out as we stood in the doorway, taking in the scene.

Dana beamed with excitement, already forgetting about her confiscated bottle. "Yes!" she groaned. "This is exactly what I need! No more work-talk. Let's fucking go!"

Now, *she* was dragging *me* through the club, passing people who were dancing, talking, or making out. The club was huge, with a vast dance floor, a bar in the center, and several VIP areas hidden away in the back.

We headed towards the center of the room. My heart thumped in my chest, a mixture of excitement coursing through me as I moved my body to the beat of the music. Hands frequented my body, but I kept them off by merely glancing their way. In the dark, my eyes always burned the brightest, which most took as a warning not to mess with me.

Once we had reached the bar, Dana gestured to the bartender. He gave her a wink, and she rested her head on her hands, pushing her breasts towards him. I couldn't help but laugh.

At least her thoughts weren't with Tommy.

"What do you want? I'm buying," she said to me.

"I'll take a Shardpolitan."

"Too fancy." Dana eyed the bartender again. "We'd like two Dirty Subs."

Leaning back on the bar, I smirked at her. "You know, there is a reason they're called *dirty*."

The bartender returned with two large glasses filled with see-through alcohol and a deep red liquid dripping inside it like it was water mixed with blood. The sweet smell made me scrunch my nose.

"Here," the bartender said, pushing a napkin across the bar to Dana. "You gorgeous ladies in for a treat?"

"Depends…" Dana drawled, lazily sipping from her drink. She lifted the napkin and checked what was underneath. "What is it?"

"A sample of something new."

I frowned. A new drug? That didn't sound like a *treat* at all. I could know. My gaze flicked to the barman, whose eyes were half-mast, mind on a different plane as he smiled at Dana.

Yeah, no.

Before Dana could take the vial filled with an orangy powder, I pressed her hand back down with mine. "*Nah*, thanks," I told the guy, shoving the napkin back to him, eyeing him with caution. "We're good."

He just shrugged as if to say 'your loss', and Dana clutched my arm. "*Leyla*."

"We're not just sniffing anything up our brains," I hissed. Especially not from some high-as-a-kite bartender.

"I'll take it." Someone beside Dana gestured to the bartender, who pushed it his way. Before the blonde Lupine walked off, he sneered at us and said, "Only prissy bitches pass up on free drugs."

Dana rolled her eyes at me and laughed. "*Oh, come on,*" she said. "We're those people now?"

My response was a head shake. Both of us had lots of experience experimenting with drugs, but Dana took things too far sometimes. It was only through sheer luck she hadn't ever found herself in the ER. "Regular drugs are *just* bad, Dana. New, unknown drugs are plain dangerous."

"You need to loosen up," Dana said, her voice teasing, before she ordered a round of shots from the bartender.

I let the comment slip and took the shots with her before we made our way onto the dance floor. We seamlessly merged with the crowd, and in no time, we were dancing with our arms raised in the air. As we moved, the music seemed to engulf our bodies, lifting us up and away, while the alcohol made me feel weightless. The assignment that was hanging over my head slipped my mind as I danced with some random guy, closing my eyes and imagining he had a certain eye color.

The night went on like this for hours, the two of us laughing and dancing until my limbs grew sore and my feet cramped from the high heels I wore. As the night came to an end, exhaustion washed over me. I glanced over at Dana, who was still going strong, and I was just about to ask her if she was ready to go home when a loud shriek pierced through the music.

We turned around to the sound of a loud crash, people

screaming, and the crowd parting.

"What the hell?" Someone behind me cursed as the music turned off abruptly. Before we understood what was happening, we were herded towards the exit, passing some girls who were crying. One of them cradled her arm in her hand, the bone bent at a weird angle, and another had a hand pressed to her head, blood smeared through her hair.

What the fuck happened?

People looked increasingly distraught as they watched others huddle around something on the ground. When we got closer, I caught glimpses of someone between the moving crowd hurrying out of the club. Some guy lay on the ground, blood pooling around his head, staining his blonde hair. His eyes were wide open, fixed on the ceiling.

It was that Lupine who had taken the drugs from the bartender.

"What's going on?" Dana asked, but I shook my head, unable to tear my eyes away from his motionless body.

Another person responded instead. "Someone jumped from one of the balconies."

A medical team entered the premises and shouldered through the crowd toward where the man lay lifeless on the ground, but they wouldn't be able to help him.

He was dead.

CHAPTER ELEVEN

Dominic

The *Curia* in Ashtior was located close to my home. The building, made from a massive rock formation, was enormous, and the roof was a large marble dome built on top of the gigantic round structure. It cast a large contrast with the hyper-modern architecture of Shard City and the other domains in Ashium.

Because of the sunny weather, numerous Angeli were outside. Children played on the square in front of the steps leading up to the building, and people enjoyed their meals on several terraces. I walked up the steps to the building, passing through the carefully crafted, invisible dome surrounding it to keep out anyone not allowed to enter.

The inside was immaculate; they spared no expense when decorating it. Goldleaf and stones I didn't know the names of adorned the curved walls. Instead of separate rooms, there was only a vast, echoing hall. A hole in the middle of the curved roof let the sunlight in, illuminating the building in an almost dreamlike way.

I approached the round table in the center of the room, which also had a hole in the middle, mimicking the gap in

Ashtior's city layer. The floor was flecked with rays of sunlight seeping through the ornamentally carved openings in the Curia's roof, creating a beautiful pattern that moved with the sun.

I sat down among the eleven already-seated Seraphim—the Cardinal. A group of eleven women who had each volunteered at Ascension; the age at which Angeli officially matured. Their wings would have been clipped in the past, but now, the act was considered too brutal. The Seraphim today had them bound at Ascension as they bound their hair. Depending on their duration of service, the ropes used were either silver or golden, with their wings tied securely to their backs in intricate knots. They were granted power in exchange for never using them and pledging loyalty to the city.

Being an uneven number of Seraphim, they formed an entity, voting on everything democratically. The Cardinal was the legislative power in Ashar. They decided things. I just acted it out.

Head Cardinal Kemalgda wrapped her hands together where she sat in the main seat. The other ten Seraphim lined up next to her in an even tie—Vaphoryn included. She sat on my right. As the youngest in the group, she sat farthest from the Head Cardinal.

I faced Seraphim Kemalgda to close the circle with an even number and nodded at her. She reciprocated the gesture.

"Prime Venetia, what is the state below?" Balan, the Seraphim on Kemalgda's left side, was again the first to raise a question. She referred to everything except Ashtior, which left Nitas' and my territories.

I leaned back in the chair, feigning a mask of indifference. Nitas, the Supreme of Ashrior—the Undercity—rarely visited the Cardinal to report. He barely left Ashrior at all. Most information passed through me. "Ashium is doing fine, but I have received news about some unrest stirring Ashrior."

Vaphoryn cocked her head, her gaze as blank as mine. "Concerning what?"

No member of the Cardinal knew we were well acquainted. She was often shoved to public events in Ashium or Ashrior that none of the other Seraphim wanted to attend, and that's how we met. Years ago, Vaphoryn had told me she loved coming to the city but couldn't let it show too much, or Seraphim Kemalgda would take those visitations from her. The old Seraphim liked to be in control a little too much.

"There is a new drug on the market." I had even heard some rumors about it circulating the city now. Somehow, vermin knew how to seep through the cracks undetected, but people always talked.

Head Cardinal Kemalgda kept her robed arms motionless as she raised her chin. "Then what is causing the unrest?"

All heads turned from her to me.

"From what Supreme Somnos has gathered, the consequences of taking the drug are dangerous. There have been three victims that resulted in death so far, with two of them collateral. And the drug is still in demo."

At once, *the trio* opened their mouths, chirping like birds. "There must be something we could do," Clothos started. Lachesis, who often had a hard time keeping a straight face, had paled visibly. "What do you mean, *collateral?*"

Atropos said, "I think he means they weren't the ones taking the drugs."

"Could we consider visiting Ashrior and conversing with the locals?" Clothos proposed. Atropos rolled her eyes. "And go there by aircab? No, thanks." Lachesis looked up at me with wide eyes and tilted her head back a little. "Three deaths? How did we only hear about this now?"

I opened my mouth, but Head Cardinal Kemalgda answered for me, cutting off their verbal avalanche. "It's not the Prime's doing. It's because Divinitas holds the leash on his part of the city too loosely." The Head Cardinal's face remained impassive, but her eyes turned sharp.

The atmosphere grew tense, and a wave of pent-up energy accumulated on my right. Vaphoryn's long, red braid moved so abruptly with the movement of her head that the strand of hair tucked behind her ear sprung free. Her expression was tight, and she pressed her lips together as if trying to restrain herself from saying something. She was blinking furiously, and I cleared my throat to get her attention. The air grew heavy and still as she slowly shifted her gaze away from the Head Cardinal and fixed her eyes on me. Although we exchanged no words, a silent understanding passed between us.

Head Cardinal Kemalgda and Nitas Somnos had never seen eye to eye. The old Seraphim was far too controlling for Nitas' tastes, and their history was full of animosity and clashing personalities. I knew Vaphoryn was fond of Nitas, considering him a friend. But her reaction had been almost primal—so different from the wise woman who had talked about him some nights ago. It was something the rest of the Cardinal probably shouldn't be prone to.

Vaphoryn quickly regained her composure, seemingly annoyed by her loss of control. She shifted in her seat, uncomfortable yet still determined to set aside personal differences for the sake of helping those affected by this new drug. "Either way," she said, "we must act fast before this drug reaches the public. There must be a way to warn people about its dangers or limit the spread."

Head Cardinal Kemalgda nodded slowly, those observant eyes carefully gliding over the rest of the Seraphim. "Indeed. It's crucial to find the individuals responsible for producing and distributing this rumored substance to our citizens."

"We already know who's behind it," I said.

Balan raised her brows as she leaned closer. "Oh?"

The room froze as my next words echoed in the silence. "Xanon Naan."

Vaphoryn shifted in her seat, clenching her hands, and said, "The man behind several assassinations of political figures in the city, and the collapse of one of Shard City's biggest banks?" She scanned the room, exaggerating her words—precisely what she had promised she would do. "Not to mention all the drugs he already has in circulation. What's next? He's going to rule Ashar?"

Atropos crossed her arms over her chest and curled her lip disdainfully. "Nonetheless, there is no evidence to support any of those claims."

"These aren't mere rumors," Clotho interjected, taking a deep breath. "It's all tied to him. We've known this."

"Of course," Atropos said a little impatiently. "However, evidence has consistently been either limited or fraught with deficiencies. We are unable to take any action regarding him."

Head Cardinal Kemalgda nodded slowly, her perceptive gaze sweeping over the rest of the Cardinal before returning to me. "Do we have proof now?"

"Not yet."

She nodded. "I propose we tackle one problem at a time, beginning with the drug."

Vaphoryn and I exchanged knowing glances, silently

acknowledging our resolve before we both refocused on the rest of the group. We couldn't take any more action against Xanon without more information, but the mention of his name was enough to shake everyone awake. The ball was rolling.

I looked straight at the Head Cardinal. "Where do you propose we start?"

From above, I watched Ashrior through the windows of my top-floor office in the Town Hall. The Undercity was visible through the hole bordering Shard City and formed an imposing part of the city, attracting many tourists. There were several ways to get down, but the lifts scattered throughout the city were the most popular, which was why they malfunctioned a lot and gave me headaches almost every season. Repairs for the lift in the Human Domain had finally started, and it was crucial that they had. First, because it needed to be a functioning way to get to the official ACC stadium located in the domain. And second, to keep Rakelsh and Serena from killing each other over it.

A shadow drifted over the streets below, and I tilted my head up. The sky remained clear except for a few clouds that occasionally obstructed the sun. The trees below turned a slightly richer shade of green in the shade, reminding me of the woman from the restaurant. Her eyes had been almost that exact color—the color I kept seeing everywhere.

Movement in the reflection of the glass windows caught my eye. Fredo knocked on the door and walked inside, reminding me of his presence. Sometimes, I wondered what he did in Town Hall to fill his time.

"Is there anything you need, Sir?"

I shook my head and waved a hand. "I am sorry I have kept you here for so long, Fredo. The day is over. You can go home."

He bowed his head. "Sir."

My attention returned to the view, and I observed a gust of wind passing through the city, forcing all airborne Angeli simultaneously a little to the left in the sky.

I can't wait to fly.

The sudden words echoed through my head, their sound conjuring an image of *her*: the way her eyes had sparked and her lips curled into a smile. The sight of her ached. Slivers of *before*—a time when I had been happy—flashed through my head. Distant memories banged on my mental walls. I was free back then.

Alive.

And yet, I had detected a faint trace of those familiar emotions when I had watched the woman in the restaurant. Her presence had stirred a slumbering part deep within me.

I looked at the gleaming white stone of the Courthouse far below, visible through the hole in the ground, and drowned myself in distant, painful memories. The same thing I felt when anyone spoke her name.

Closing my eyes, I took a deep breath and focused on the sun's warmth on my skin, the whisper of her voice still ringing in my ears.

All too real.

CHAPTER TWELVE

Leyla

The auction for Ashar's orphans had been scheduled a year ahead, and with Prime Venetia as the special guest, it provided a perfect opportunity to observe his interactions and devise a plan. Seeing as our paths had already crossed at *Moby's*, and his interest that evening had been evident, I had to be a little creative in my approach. Though his prolonged gazes made me confident he would recognize me when he saw me.

The taxi dropped me off at the beginning of the street, across from the red carpet. I bypassed the alternative entrance and walked straight into *the Shard*. No one knew my true identity, and I planned to keep it that way for as long as possible.

The click-clack of my heels echoed through the lobby, the polished marble floor gleaming and mirroring the wall's lighting. I had been here before, but it was completely rearranged to pose as a receiving hall for the auction tonight. The event itself was held in the opulent, sweeping ballroom of the hotel. The expansive room was a spectacle, with its gleaming silk, gold-trimmed details, and lush blue velvet fabrics. Paired with the glittering chandeliers, everyone bathed in a warm, golden light that gave the auction an air of luxury.

A stage stood in the back of the room, ready for the auctioneer to take their place. There were rows of chairs before the stage, filled with guests eager to start bidding on the offered items. I found an empty chair along the aisle and sat down. From my position, I could survey the entire crowd, and noticed the rich and famous represented all domains almost equally.

I had considered inviting Dana tonight, but any attempt at explaining what I was doing here would have made things complicated between us. She would have had a million questions about why I was here and why I was bidding on art pieces I had never mentioned to her. I mean, she knew I liked art and that my family had some money, but to go to auctions and bid more money than she thought I made in a year was stretching it. Her inevitable prodding had been the only thing stopping me from inviting her.

I was tired of lying to her about my "job", my family, Zade… But this assignment was too important to get distracted by my conscience. People depend on me.

The table on stage was being prepared with the initial auction items; I recognized several from the program I had studied last night at home. The list consisted mostly of heirlooms, expensive jewelry, and paintings. The former items were useless to me, but paintings were a different story—one I had some knowledge of.

Eventually, the doors closed, and the audience silenced as the lights dimmed. The auctioneer appeared on the stage, welcoming everyone. He described the first items at an excruciatingly slow pace, giving the audience ample time to bid. Because of the charity element, the bidding for each item lasted longer than it normally would. I watched as item after item was sold, feeling a blend of nerves and anticipation as the items I wanted to bid on slowly approached.

I had researched the Archangel's items thoroughly and was sure about my decision to wait with bidding until his items were present. My father had given me access to a bank account that had plenty of money in it to do something like this as long as it benefited the cause.

The auctioneer sold a vintage emerald ring that once belonged to a renowned singer before moving on to the items I was waiting for. "In light of tonight's auction and the cause, Prime Venetia has generously donated a curated collection of paintings."

The crowd erupted in cheers and applause as the auctioneer signaled towards the Archangel, who gracefully stepped onto the stage.

He was the same, yet... different. His hair had been bound back in the same way as when I'd seen him at Moby's. The suit he wore was similar, except for the color. His smile seemed effortless but practiced, and his eyes didn't crinkle in the corners as I had seen them do in some photos. Dominic Venetia's golden wings were completely still, appearing relaxed, but his shoulders visibly tensed. He wore a look of indifference, but I sensed something else beneath the surface.

Unease.

The atmosphere shifted as he started speaking. "Good evening, everyone."

His voice was the same as I remembered: soft, deep, and a little throaty. "I have curated a small collection of astonishing works of art that have been made by talented artists throughout Celestia, who gracefully donated them to this great cause. I hope you see their worth as I do, as well as the difference these proceedings could make for the orphanages throughout Ashar."

I understood why people fell for his do-gooder act. He was very convincing—seemed almost sincere.

Four people walked onto the stage, each carrying a display with the first pieces: four small canvases. With a camera, they filmed closeups of each one, which were projected on the large screens lining the room. I had already examined the items in the auction's booklet, which provided close-up details and additional context on the paintings.

The art history modules I had taken in college finally proved useful. Although I wasn't as knowledgeable about it as Dominic Venetia, my interest could challenge his. I loved art, going to museums, and just staring at paintings for minutes on end. And when I saw the Archangel's curated collection in partnership with the Modern Art Society, I immediately knew which one I wanted to go for.

The third one, the smallest of the four. It was a painting of a raging storm, capturing misery and despair in such a simple yet profound way that it evoked emotions from deep within me.

If anything, art's purpose was to make you feel.

The first painting sold for twenty-five thousand *shards*, and the second sold for twenty-one thousand. No doubt both buyers were trying to accomplish the same as me: to impress the Archangel.

The man himself knew he was an effective marketing tool, nodding and smiling at the people who won the auctions. Everyone wanted to bask in the light of his approval.

They moved the third one to the front—my turn.

"Bidding starts at four thousand *shards*," the auctioneer announced.

The first paddle rose. "Four thousand."

"Four thousand five hundred."

I waited for the perfect moment, allowing the same five interested individuals to place bids. Occasionally, an unexpected bid turned up, but its sole purpose was to increase the price. I had to say; it was an exciting thing to witness.

"Seventeen thousand."

The bidding was stalling at eighteen thousand, less than what the other two paintings had earned but proportionate to its size. It might not have as much detail or be as romantic, yet still… the painting had character—feeling.

"Going once, going twice…"

I raised my paddle, jumping in when no one expected it.

"Thirty thousand," I said. Perhaps a bit dramatic, *excessive*, but certainly noteworthy. It was money my father didn't blink an eye at, and I wanted to make a point—attract a certain pair of eyes.

The audience buzzed, some people turning around to see who had said it, but no one raised another paddle to go over my bid. The auctioneer started wrapping up: *going once, going twice…* Sold!" he cheered. "To that lovely lady in the middle for *thirty thousand shards*. Another generous sum to support the cause."

I smiled and lowered my paddle as people turned around to look at me. Dominic Venetia looked into the crowd, too, and even in the dimly lit room, his eyes found mine. His brows furrowed in confusion at the sight of me, and a faint smile touched his lips. It was the only genuine expression on his face all night.

My heart raced in my throat when I realized he recognized me. The sudden attention was uncomfortable, but I maintained eye contact with him, barely suppressing the urge to look away.

Dominic Venetia's answering smile was pleased.

His attention on me was so overwhelming that I felt a blush spread. I silently scolded myself for getting affected at all, but I was used to being in the background. The unfamiliar feeling twisting in my stomach was just as foreign. I finally looked away, brushing at the folds of my dress as I wondered what the hell was going on with me. I took time to collect myself while the rest of the art was auctioned off. When the final pieces were carried from the stage, Dominic Venetia remained standing, looking out onto the crowd with an impassive face—nothing like the way he had looked at me earlier. Then, the Archangel bowed closer to the auctioneer and said something to him.

The auctioneer grabbed the microphone again, scrambling with his cards. "We are concluding this night with a surprise auction: a date with Prime Venetia!"

The audience erupted, and I shifted in my seat uncomfortably as the bidding began. Dominic Venetia looked through the crowd, grinning and winking at the people who were bidding, eliciting cheers from those present in the room. Though his eyes always seemed to find their way back to me, amusement lingering there. The room was dark, so people couldn't discern where he was looking at exactly, but I knew.

The weight of his gaze was monumental.

"Prime Venetia is by far the most eligible bachelor in town," a woman next to me told her friend.

The friend responded with a snort. "Wasn't he dating that

Angeli? Eliza *whatshername*?"

"I'm not sure. Maybe it was more casual than she'd let on? I sure wouldn't like my man to go out with someone else. Even if it was for charity."

"Here, here."

The bids grew higher and higher, and the tension in the room seemed to thicken. I'd be so uncomfortable if I were in his position, but Prime Venetia stood there confidently as the audience vied for his attention. I watched him intently, taking in every detail of his non-verbal communication.

Conversations faded as the bidding reached its peak. Some contenders were going at it like feral animals, their cheeks flushed and bid paddles permanently in the air. It seemed like even the auctioneer couldn't keep up with what was going on. It was an amusing sight.

I went back to watching Dominic and froze as I found his gaze lingering on me once more. The look in his eyes changed, and I swore my Daemon sight noticed the slight twitch of his brow as he silently dared me to join in the bidding. The smile on my face turned saccharine as I bit my cheek.

He must be really arrogant to think I would participate.

I didn't raise my arm. Not when the Archangel's eyes grew more intense with every second that trickled by, and not when the auctioneer announced the last bet. Not even when I lost his attention to a gorgeous Sanguis woman who won the date at a whopping seventy-eight thousand *shards*, and he tilted his head, moving his attention to the woman, not once looking back at me.

I watched him smile at her, clapping with the crowd as it erupted in applause. Something ugly stirred beneath my skin as he descended from the stage to approach the woman in the front row, planting a gentle kiss on the back of her hand before uttering a few words. After flashing another winning smile at her, he waved to the crowd and departed from the stage.

The man clearly knew the game he was playing.

It made me hate him even more.

As the room slowly dispersed, I checked my phone for the first time that night, finding a message from Zade.

Z: *How are things going?*

I typed back a quick text, already standing from my seat to leave for the reception hall, determined to find a solid, cold drink.

Me: *Fine.*

Swallowing to relieve the dryness in my throat, I put my phone away, feeling a tinge of irritation. It felt as if the roles were reversed—that he was now playing a game with me. I had momentarily overlooked his seasoned politician status, but now I was firmly back in touch with reality.

He had almost an entire century over me. I shouldn't underestimate him. Dominic Venetia was no mere man I had to get close to. He was the Prime of Ashar.

The Archangel.

It was something I would not lose sight of again.

CHAPTER THIRTEEN

Dominic

The auction ended, and the crowd slowly entered the hall for drinks. I made my way backstage through a private hallway with stairs leading to a room overlooking the hotel's grand hall, providing me with a moment of reprieve.

"Impressive turnout," Inesa said, entering the private room. Fredo showed her in and shut the door. Jewelry adorned her ears and neck, similar to some items that had been auctioned.

I kissed her cheek. "Thank you for coming."

She smiled at me, her dark eyes and black hair contrasting sharply with her white wings and suit. "Watching you sell yourself off to the highest bidder is hardly a chore. I promised Nathan to take pictures."

A groan escaped from me. The date wasn't my idea, and I hadn't wanted to put myself up for auction. I had lost a bet to Nathan over the Angeli Starball team selections. And gods, I was rarely mistaken… but also a man of my word. When I told the auctioneer what I wanted to do, the man had turned bright red, which was more than sole indignation.

Through the windows, I observed the crowd of people below. My eyes flicked back and forth over the people inside, searching—

"What's on your mind?"

I cleared my throat, adjusted my suit, and refocused on Inesa, who looked curious with raised eyebrows and questioning eyes. I shifted my weight, feet pivoting on the smooth marble, and ran a hand through my hair. "Nothing."

My eyes flicked back to the room.

"You're not fooling me. Who are you looking for?"

I raised an eyebrow at her.

Inesa approached the windows with a way too eager smile as she peered down. "Who is it, Dom?"

Turning my head back, I rubbed a hand over my neck. "She's not there yet."

"I knew it!"

"You know nothing," I snorted.

The Daemon had been an interesting surprise. After seeing the number on her paddle, I had been tempted to ask the register for her name and address. To buy any art piece, she had to list them. But that meant crossing a boundary, one too high when it came to mere interest, even for me.

Especially for me.

"Drop the indifference act," Inesa said. "I'm not buying it, Dom. Not when you have that look in your eyes."

I pushed my tongue into my cheek and gave her a different look altogether. "I'm not acting."

She rolled her eyes. "I know you don't want to hear this, but there's no point in always being the toughest guy in the crowd."

"Didn't we just have that conversation about boundaries? How you should mind my business *less*?"

"Dom, look," she said, touching my arm, her face softening. "If she could bring you even a sliver of happiness—*care*."

I moistened my lips. "She caught my eye, that's all. Stop making it more than it is."

"At least find out. Go down there, look for her."

I cast a sidelong glance at her from the corner of my eyes.

Inesa threw her arms in the air and sighed. "*Gods*, you're impossible! I'll see you downstairs, you fool."

I spent an extra fifteen minutes in the room, ignoring the crowd, to make a statement to myself and Inesa.

I didn't care.

And I never would.

A cacophony of voices and laughter filled my ears when I entered the room. People moved in different directions, guided by the multitude of reactions my presence elicited. I saw smiles and nods from people in my direction wherever I looked. My brain wanted to evict itself from my head after repeatedly experiencing the same moments at every event.

My eyes roamed the room, skimming past the Sanguis woman who won the date with me, and then stopped.

On *her*.

I hadn't intended to search for her, but by the light, how could I not? She was breathtaking.

The last person I had expected to see at the auction was the green-eyed Daemon. I hadn't known she was there until she started bidding on the painting. It had been my favorite of the entire collection, and there was no way she could have known that. I had refrained from publicly voicing my opinions.

Just like days before, she stood out among the crowd. Her black hair was done in a tight updo, not a hair out of place, and she bared her slender neck to me. It practically begged for interference. The light shining on her hair formed a halo on her head. A simple black dress hugged her frame, and a thin, see-through scarf wrapped around her arms—but the simplicity only enhanced her beauty.

The air around me was charged. I felt a strong, irrational urge to check my surroundings for potential threats. But I remained motionless by the entrance, unable to look away from her. Some people approached me, and although they tried very hard to engage me in conversation, my attention always found its way back to her. Her presence was palpable from across the room, as if an invisible tether connected us.

I felt a familiar presence as someone brushed past me and whispered, "She *is* pretty."

I glared at Inesa and turned to get a drink. Reaching the bar, I ordered *something strong*. My mind went over the reasons I shouldn't approach her, trying to convince myself of them. And just as I put the glass to my lips, sealing the silent promise to myself with a drink, my eyes moved back to her involuntarily.

From the bustling crowd, a man emerged and made his way towards her.

My muscles tightened.

The tall Lupine had an unfamiliar face, indicating his lack of importance. It wasn't like I knew everyone in the city or even longed to, but something about this guy raised immediate questions.

Who was he? *Did he know her?*

As if sensing my stare, she turned to look at me. This time, it was her daring me. She raised one of her brows while the man kept speaking to her, unbothered by her straying eyes—or unaware if he wasn't looking there.

I stood there, clenching my jaw, swirling the liquid in my glass. I wanted to turn away and not care, but I forced my fists to relax, put down the glass, and began wading through the throng of people. Gradually, I walked across the room until I stood before them.

Up close, she was even more mesmerizing. The combination of dark lashes and liner made her green eyes look captivating. My pulse quickened.

As her eyes landed on me, a rush of blood pumped through my veins. For a moment, it felt as though no one else was in the room with us—only her and I. It had been a while since someone evoked such a vivid reaction from me. A little too intriguing; *dangerous*, if anything. It didn't, however, stop me from addressing her.

"Just the woman I was looking for."

I looked only at her, ignoring the Lupine, making it clear he could leave. He must know his efforts were wasted. Casting another look at her, he mumbled, "I'll see you around."

Her eyes moved to me, and she shrugged her shoulder indifferently, like she didn't care either way—like she wouldn't even blink if he dropped dead on the spot. And the Lupine finally got the message.

The woman gave me a knowing smile. A spark of *something* lit her eyes as she raised her other brow. "Efficient," she drawled. There was a slight hoarseness in her voice. I liked it—a lot.

"Wouldn't want your boyfriend to get the wrong idea," I said. Josiah Eden, who had been with her last week, was absent tonight. "Where is he, by the way?"

One corner of her mouth curved, but her eyes darted back to the crowd as she crossed her heeled ankles. "Josiah is not my boyfriend."

"*Ah*," I said. "So that can't be your excuse for not bidding on the date."

Her smile blossomed, those sensual lips pulling into the barest curve. "I usually don't have to pay men to go on dates with me. And seventy-eight thousand *shards* is a little overpriced—even for the Archangel of Ashar."

"Ouch." I pressed a hand over my heart. "You really know how to crush a man's ego."

"I doubt it," she snorted.

I reached out a hand. "Dominic."

She looked at my hand before shaking it. Her throat bobbed. "Leyla."

Leyla—the answer to a question I had been pondering on for days.

"What brings you here, Leyla?" I ran my thumb across my chin.

Those green eyes roamed over my body. "I'm actually here on behalf of someone else—business, not pleasure." Her lips curved into a more monitored smile.

"Funny how things always seem to work themselves out," I said, my eyes falling to her lips as if a magnetic force pulled them there.

Leyla pursed them. "It certainly is something."

Intrigued by everything about her, I asked, "Tell me… What made you bid on that painting at the auction?" I feigned casual nonchalance, but the balance within me was tipping, and I didn't understand why.

Her gaze was guarded as she said, "It was simply beautiful."

I remained silent, waiting for her to elaborate. She wouldn't be so easily let off the hook. *Tell me why*, I wanted to demand. There's nothing *simple* about art.

She swallowed again as she realized I was waiting for her to continue. Her voice filled with hesitation as she said, "The painting was dark, angry—a whirlwind of conflicting emotions. Everyone has a part of something dark within them, I believe. That piece spoke to that part—" She cut herself off.

Of me, she had wanted to say. I could hear the words echoing in the silence.

Yes, I would have responded.

Her cheeks darkened a little, almost invisibly, but I noticed. For the first time in a while, I felt my lips curl, baring my teeth in a full-fledged smile. "Exactly."

I wanted those eyes, recognizing the dark, focused solely on me. I wanted that mouth, validating my inner feelings with mere words, all over me. My throat turned bone dry. I wanted to relish in her.

Dangerous, a voice whispered inside me again. When feelings came out to play, so did hurt.

She was far more than just stunning. I should tread carefully around her, as I had always done. Women like her knew how to wind men around their fingers and play with them.

Something grabbed her attention, prompting her to pull out her phone from her purse. Whatever she saw on the screen made her frown. "If you'll excuse me. I have to take this, so—"

Business, not pleasure.

"Please do," I said, but felt reluctance. Because what I

wanted to say was, *not yet*.

Before she walked off, though, she seemed to hesitate, too. Holding the phone in one hand, she looked at me, lips drawn open to say something. Though all she did was close them again, nod, and walk away. I stared after her disappearing form, trying to piece together what had just happened.

At least this time, I had gotten more than just glances.

A name.

Leyla.

CHAPTER FOURTEEN

Leyla

"Why did it take you so long to answer?" Zade asked.

My phone had been buzzing relentlessly before I'd finally taken it from my purse in front of the Archangel. "I was busy." I didn't know why I was so frustrated with him, but his texts and missed calls struck the wrong cord. He knew I was working.

He was silent for a moment. "Doing what? The auction was three hours ago."

"It only ended one hour ago." As I left the hotel, the doorman hailed a taxi for me.

"And what did you do after that?" Zade muttered something under his breath. "I don't fucking like this, Leyla."

"I played my part." I stepped into the car and told the driver where to drop me off. "Tell my father it's going great."

Zade exhaled. "Your father isn't behind this call."

"Then stop wasting my time and get to the point."

"I wanted to check if you were home."

My first inclination was to tell him a firm *no*. My life was becoming complicated as hell. But then I recalled how Dominic Venetia had glanced at me, confidently approaching without concern for onlookers. He was the Archangel of Ashar, one of the most powerful Ashari in the city, and his eyes had been locked on me. I refused to even think about the way his eyes had seen right through me as I told him about the painting...

Lost in our conversation, for a brief second, I'd forgotten that the assignment had driven me to him in the first place. The vibration of my phone had snapped me back to reality. I didn't like it. Not one bit.

I swallowed and felt my cheeks burn. It was what made me say, "I'll be home in ten." Before I disconnected the call.

I needed a damned release.

A knock sounded on my door not even five minutes after I returned home. I opened the door, and Zade stepped inside, smelling of leather and rain.

I remembered the moment I fell in love with him. He had looked similar to how he looked right now, wearing all black, his hoodie pulled over his head, obscuring most of his face except for his eyes. Those sad, blue eyes that now flickered in the darkness.

Zade pushed his hoodie back, revealing his black hair and the scar on his cheek. "Hey," he said but didn't smile. His eyes roamed over me from head to toe, looking at the clothes I had worn to the auction, and the hunger in them stalked closer to the surface. "Listen—"

"I don't want to hear it." I wove my hands in his hair and tugged on it to get him closer before slamming my lips to his.

Zade stepped inside, one of his arms curling around my waist, moving me with him, and slammed the door shut with a loud bang. He shrugged out of his leather jacket as I stepped out of my heels, kicking them into a corner of the living room. Zade resumed kissing me even deeper, his tong sweeping in and out of my mouth with bold, languid strokes.

We stumbled through the hallway, but instead of letting him lead me to the bedroom, I pushed him into the bathroom as we frantically undressed each other. I only broke the kiss to turn on the shower. He leaned his back on the wall and raised his brows.

This was precisely what I craved right now.

"I need a shower," I said. How could I explain? I wanted the Archangel's scent *gone*. It was too intense—too overwhelming. The path his eyes had trailed over my body, the way his presence had wrapped around me. It was all too much. There was too fucking much of him lingering.

The mirrors were already steaming up. Zade stepped under the shower, his tattoos burning in my vision; I knew every line of ink by heart. I discarded the rest of my clothing until my bare feet hit the cold, dark tiles. Walking around to one of the open sides of the shower, I stepped inside.

The moment I let my hands graze his body, he captured them and turned around. He wasn't stupid enough to ask me why I didn't want to talk. We shared a silent understanding.

I bit my lip and let my hands roam over his muscled chest. "I want you to take me, Zade," I told him breathlessly and moved closer to his ear. "*Hard.*"

He expelled a breath as I let my hands trail further south, and he crushed his mouth once again to mine, pulling me flush against him and making me feel how hard he was. I wrapped my arms around his neck and drew him even closer. He grabbed my ass with his large hands, lifting me off the floor and squeezing firmly.

I hoped his fingers would leave red marks the next morning.

It made me ache for release, and we hadn't even done anything yet.

"Did he touch you?"

Water clung to my lashes and splattered on my chest as I looked at him. I pushed away the invading thoughts of the golden-winged Archangel. "You're not jealous, are you?" I asked teasingly against his lips.

He chuckled, biting my bottom lip. "Out of my mind." And recaptured my mouth, our tongues wrestling for dominance.

I wanted him to be. I wanted him to feel so damn bad that he couldn't sleep at night.

He pushed me against the shower wall, his blue eyes boring into mine. "Did he?"

Almost invisibly, I shook my head. "Dominic was a perfect gentleman."

"You better remember what name to scream when I make you come, Leyla," he warned.

"Then stop fucking talking about him."

The water flow ceased, and I chuckled as Zade carried me from behind the murky glass and blindly grabbed a towel from the rack. His erection pressed against my back, hot and demanding, as he brushed the fabric over my pebbled nipples and the rest of my body, cupping me with it, and I let my head fall back to rest on his chest as he dried me off.

Yes. I needed this.

Zade pulled the towel to his nose, sniffing it, and I turned around to see his nostrils and pupils flare—the Daemon in him waking up. He pulled the towel heedlessly over his hair and the rest of his body while looking at me. My body felt electric, especially with the water dripping from my hair onto my back, setting my nerves ablaze.

Zade stepped closer, and I stepped back, a tiny smirk playing around my lips. But he wasn't in the mood for games as he shot forward swiftly, his speed getting the upper hand. He grabbed the back of my neck and crushed me against him, angling my chin, and walked me back to the bedroom. He dropped me back on my feet, and I wanted to come up to kiss him again, but he only let me graze his lips before he pushed me back around, lowering me on the bed so my front pressed into the soft, thick sheets as he lined himself up with my entrance and dragged his length over me.

He played me like this for a while, pulling every string he knew that would make me sing until I was begging him to finish the song.

I pushed my hips back as he entered me in one swift thrust, demanding more, more, more, while I whimpered for him in pleasure. He pushed me further into the mattress, and I clawed at the sheets to find purchase as he pulled in and out of me with relentless repetition.

"You feel so fucking good, Leyla," he said, and I moaned in response. The beginning of an orgasm was building inside me, but his thrusts slowed, and he pulled out of me, leaving me dripping and aching wet.

I turned around and hoisted myself further onto the bed while he entered it, eyes devouring me. I lay back down, my eyelids lowering, and parted my legs, inviting him in again. He trailed kisses over my legs, up, up, up, before turning his mouth to my tattooed arm and biting the serpent curling around it. Zade lowered to my chest, taking my nipples between his lips one after the other as he pushed back into me. I clawed at his back, his neck, his face—pushing mine up so our lips could meet again.

He pushed my arms down and held our hands together above my head, immobilizing me. "I love you," he murmured in my ear as he fucked me slowly.

Tenderly.

"I love you too," I murmured back, closing my eyes in bliss, squeezing the hands he held me captive with.

I loved him so much that I'd tear out my heart rather than be forced apart. I would stab out my eyes before I had to give up seeing him—would cut off my ears if it meant I didn't have to stop hearing his voice.

His hips rolled between my legs at an achingly slow pace, but his thrusts were deep. Claiming.

I opened my eyes again and found golden ones staring back at me, a halo of feathers spreading above him, shielding us from the world. His eyes were so full of love that there was no doubt of his feelings for me. He would die for me as I would for him. He moved back a bit so I could see him better.

I felt him swell inside me as he upped his pace, and I bit my lips as my release started climbing.

Finally, he caught my lips as I came up to meet his, and I fell off the cliff—moaning into his mouth as he, too, slammed into me and finished.

I blinked, my throat constricting as Zade groaned my name. I pushed up to capture it on his lips, sweeping my tongue inside as I found my release.

Disorientated, I let my head fall back and stared at a point on the ceiling as Zade nuzzled my neck and slowly pulled out.

I inhaled deeply as if coming up for air, and blinked. "I'm going to clean up," I told him as he lay back on the bed with contentment etched in the lines of his face. Walking to the bathroom, I felt wobbly, as if I was standing on a ship in the middle of a storm. I stepped back under the shower, letting the water wash away any remnant of the sex. As if in a daze, I walked to the sink and brushed my hair, drying it a little with a towel. I didn't dare meet my reflection. Swallowing thickly, I blinked, and blinked again.

Confused was the best way to describe how I felt. I squeezed my eyes shut and forced myself to swallow. Something was inexplicably wrong. Because if I wasn't losing my mind, I had been imagining having sex with Dominic Venetia instead of Zade just now. His face, the voice... It had undeniably been him.

I finished cleaning myself and grabbed my discarded clothes from the bathroom floor with trembling hands. As I dressed, I looked around the room as if searching for something to help me get out of this mess. I eventually stepped back into the bedroom, bile rising in my throat. Zade lay on the bed with the sheets just up to his stomach, eyes closed.

I cleared my throat. "You need to go," I said firmly.

My words hung heavy in the air, and Zade slowly pushed himself onto his elbows, looking puzzled. "What did you say?"

"I want you to go," I repeated.

He swung his legs off the mattress and ran a hand through his hair—arm and leg muscles flexing. His blue eyes blazed as he searched my face for answers. "What is going on, Leyla?"

I couldn't meet his gaze, so I just bit my cheek. "Nothing."

Zade tipped up my chin, those blue eyes steeling. "You want me to go?"

Part of me didn't want him to leave; that part wanted him to demand me to drop the assignment and stay far away from the Archangel. It wanted him to tell me I was the one for whom he would risk it all—even my father's wrath.

But that part of me was younger. I wasn't her anymore. The part of the woman I had become felt bitter. Bitter at fate for weaving together such a cruel path, for spoiling *everything*. That part made me nod at Zade.

He gently brushed his knuckles across my neck. "Don't tell me this assignment is already messing with you."

The unspoken meaning hung heavily in the air between us. "I'm just tired and have an early day tomorrow."

"You should tell your father if it's too much, Leyla."

"*It isn't*," I bit out. It was the worst thing he could have said, and I suddenly wanted nothing more than for him to leave.

He lingered briefly, his gaze weighing on me, before he moved away and quietly dressed. His movements were methodical and slow as he grabbed the scattered clothes off the ground. The tension in the apartment intensified as he put on his leather jacket last, his posture straight and unbending.

Zade sighed, the sound heavy and labored. "Call me if you need anything."

I stayed still, only managing a brief nod. His footsteps resonated through the hallway, leaving me with the sound of the door closing. I convinced myself that I was *fine*, that everything was *okay*. Just imagining having sex with Dominic Venetia had probably happened to most people in Ashar.

It was nothing to be worried about—yet the thought rang hollow in my mind.

CHAPTER FIFTEEN

Dominic

Days blurred together in an endless stream of meetings, answering emails, and visiting different domains. What little free time I had, I usually spent with Nathan and Inesa once a week, twice at most. And between a date with the Sanguis woman from the auction and filling the rest of my free time with piss-poor attempts at relaxation, I had no interest in contacting Eliza.

So far, she hadn't been a demanding lover, and she knew full well that when pushed too far, I would inevitably pull back. But she'd insisted on meeting me since our last dinner at *Moby's*, the night I had left early. I needed the relief and would have welcomed it, but I declined almost every invitation from her in favor of my own hand.

My thoughts circled back to Leyla. *Ley-la*. I'd tasted her name on my tongue more than once in the past few days, testing it out. The sound of it was right.

During a meeting about safety measures for the Ashar City Cup, my mind wandered to the moment I spotted her in the auction's audience. The memory had been so vivid I altogether forgot where I was. I had agreed mindlessly when the Starball committee spoke about the protocols they had improved since last year, and I approved the drawings for the new field design without even a second glance.

After the meeting was over, I loosened my tie and splashed some cold water on my face. Every year, I had something to remark on the field. Starball was my forte, and the ACC my favorite time of year. But my mind had been preoccupied; all I could think about was how her lips tugged in that little smile or the way the light caught her dark locks. How that black dress had clung to every curve, and the way her tattoo seemed to make sense on her.

She would look amazing between my sheets.

A distraction, that's what she was.

After changing into a fresh suit, I flew down from Ashtior in the setting sun. Streaks of pastel pinks, purples, and blues painted the sky. Passing an aircab on my flight down, the people inside yelled my name and banged on the windows. My preferred mode of transportation would always be flying with my own wings, but it garnered more attention than I wanted. If you searched for my name online, many photos of me in the sky would pop up.

Or so I was told.

I landed on a quiet side street and stretched my wing muscles, relieving them of any tension, before I folded them neatly against my back. I straightened my jacket and pulled a hand through my hair before being welcomed by a private server at the back door of *Lumia*, a bar downtown.

Fredo reserved a room here earlier and let them know I would be visiting. Heller was one of the investors and had brought me here a few times; the Lupine representative had excellent taste. The owners valued privacy and treated me like a normal person, so I started bringing my own guests here. It helped that the space looked like it stemmed from the Gilded Age—an aesthetic I admittedly veered to.

A server led me through a hallway in the back of the building, saving me a trip through the main area. Eliza's continuous communication led me to invite her here because I couldn't keep avoiding her and string her along. As I entered the room and checked my watch, I prayed she would be here on time. I had plans to meet Nathan and Inesa for dinner later, so I wanted to wrap this up quickly.

Laughter reverberated through the thick walls from the main area, but the sound was muffled. A soft melody played in the background, and the dark blue room was decorated with wine-red and custard-yellow details. Just as I was reaching for my phone in my pocket to message Nathan about my impending delay, the door swung open once more. Eliza entered, accompanied by a server who promptly exited.

She stilled, her gaze fixed on me as she wrapped her lips together, not saying anything. A heavy silence hung between us. Things had cooled down quickly, it seemed.

I approached anyway and leaned forward to kiss her cheek. "Elizabeth," I said, her full name foreign to my tongue.

"Dominic." She acknowledged me with a pointed look as she gracefully settled in the seat opposite of me. "I'm relieved you could find some time for me in your busy schedule." Her eyes narrowed slightly, though her face remained carefully composed. Her blue-painted nails ticked lightly on the tabletop. It seemed she had an inkling of why she was here, and I was glad for it. It would save me some time.

"I am the Prime, Eliza," I said firmly, emphasizing each word. "I never have time to spare."

Her eyes narrowed further, and her lips curled into a sneer. She drew in a sharp breath, her chest rising and falling with the force of her—

"You're such a hypocrite."

—anger?

A tense silence enveloped us as we locked eyes, neither willing to back down. Eventually, Eliza diverted her gaze away from me and sighed heavily in defeat. She crossed her arms and angled her body, communicating her reluctance to be there. "Well?" she asked.

Her frustration was palpable, but I ignored it. "I never kept alive any illusion that this was a long-term thing," I said bluntly, not wanting to sugarcoat the matter. I didn't understand why she was upset about it.

Eliza's expression shifted from anger to mock humor. Rolling her eyes, she said, "My friends warned me about you, you know? They said you were a walking red flag. I only saw a man in need of some compassion."

"Don't make me out to be someone I am not." It was a warning. She had no place coming at me like this. I never gave her the impression that I desired more or that she could provide it.

Eliza's expression shifted. When our eyes locked, she slowly shook her head. "You're a toxic man, Dominic Venetia." She let go of a shuddering breath, her voice dripping with disappointment. "I should have known better than to get involved with you. I guess it's my fault for not listening to the warnings of those who care about me."

I didn't reply; what could I say? She was right, to some degree. But I had promised her nothing. Our 'relationship' had been on an expiry date from the start.

"I never pretended to be anything I'm not, Eliza."

Her eyes flicked up at me, hurt brimming in them as she tried to keep her composure. Eliza cleared her throat before speaking again. "I hope you meet someone who can thaw your icy heart, Dominic, but I doubt the day will come."

Something ironic bubbled up inside me. It would indeed be unlikely. "You and me both," I said, but a flash of dark hair wound tightly around my fist clouded my vision, making my blood sing. Green eyes looked up at me in surprise, gasping— breaths mingling.

I swallowed and moistened my lips.

Eliza stood abruptly, her chair skidding back on the wooden flooring with a loud screech that echoed through the room. With her white wings tucked back rigidly, she departed through the open door. A servant swiftly walked over to close it again, but not before I watched Eliza's retreating form disappear into the bar, a hand touching her cheek.

She had forgotten her bag, which lay discarded on the table. I picked it up and handed it to the server stationed outside the room, giving him a one-hundred-shard bill. "I'm afraid it was a brief stay this time, Michael. Will you make sure she gets this back?"

"Of course, Sir."

Handing him the bag, I turned around, brushing my hands over my suit pants.

I felt lighter than I'd had in days.

Toxic, indeed.

The Starball Stadium in the Human Domain, known more commonly as Shard Stadium, loomed across the river in the distance. Its glass walls reflected the setting sun's fading rays, creating a bright contrast with the surrounding buildings.

It was magnificent—by my design.

I approached the gigantic building, experiencing a familiar sensation. My magic recognized me as I zipped through the invisible barrier around the stadium. With a quick burst of bright blue light, the air seemed to ripple as I went by.

Being an archangel, I had an incredibly large well of power. Our purpose was to preserve the equilibrium and oversee our designated territories. There hadn't been an archangel in Ashar for decades before I had manifested my golden wings and accompanying power. That power now wrapped around the entire city, keeping Ashtior afloat, my home protected, and buildings like the Shard Stadium secure. Those tasks had previously been outsourced to wielders outside the city, which had cost Ashar a lot.

I also controlled the weather inside our city's dome, which was, simply put, a bonus. It did nothing besides react to some of my mood shifts.

Soaring through the airspace above the stadium's field, a smile tugged at my lips. My wings were working hard as I raced through the windless air. I dove deeply and landed in the middle of the field, glancing around. The setting sun cast fading rays of light on one side of the bleachers while stars began to appear in the sky.

I hadn't been at the Shard Stadium for an entire year. Normally, I had trouble being on the field—it reminded me too much of times past. But tonight, something about the melancholy had turned into sentiment. When there was only silence around me, it felt almost peaceful here. This wasn't just a place for games or entertainment; it was also a sanctuary for those who sought refuge from everything else. For those who needed to be reminded that life could also be fun, and light, and exciting.

With my feet firmly on the ground, wings ready to launch into the sky, I could almost taste the smoky odor of meteorites scorching through the sky. Could practically hear the crowds roaring and feel their cheers reverberate.

I had always dreamed of being a professional Starball player. After achieving it, I'd imagined being a player for my entire career instead of only a decade going down in history as one of my previous jobs. It was a shame. I had been fucking good at it.

These days, it always seemed like I couldn't get it right, no matter what I did.

Life had been simpler back then because it had been filled with *more*. It had slipped through my fingers over a century ago, and I would never get it back.

I breathed in the earthy scent and exhaled, clearing my mind before focusing on reality—to get back to where I was and not to remain where I had once been.

I looked up at the sky just in time for one star to turn a bright blue, gone in a blink—a preview of what was to come during fall reborn. The stars had been here to witness it all. They knew, as well as I did, that those times were long gone, replaced by a world of fighting and strife.

Even so, I couldn't stop longing for them. To get them back. Just for a brief moment.

CHAPTER SIXTEEN

Leyla

I had isolated myself since the night of the auction. I was ignoring Zade's texts because I didn't know how to respond to him, and I had turned down any attempt by Dana to get together. Being alone allowed me to regain focus. My thoughts had been all over the place following the auction and my hookup with Zade.

I only left the house after my father sent a card with a location and time. He was, after all, my boss. It came with a cloak and mask to hide my identity, which meant I was invited to a larger meeting than just the two of us.

At the designated time after midnight, I arrived at a building in one of Ashrior's sketchier neighborhoods, a street I had never been to before. My father had never allowed me to go this deep into the domain. The large warehouse was pushed away into the deepest, darkest corner of the Undercity. The lack of street lamps cast shadows, making the tall, windowless structure blend in. Its concrete walls made it look more like a construction site than an actual building.

The entrance seemed unguarded as I approached, but two individuals in dark cloaks and masks like mine went inside. I checked the number on the summoning card again. It was the right place. Closer, I heard hushed voices coming from inside and saw a faint light flickering behind a single metal door. I stepped inside, where a guard was collecting the summoning cards at the actual entrance. The guard's brown eyes glowed brightly behind his mask, and I quickly cast my eyes down. Green wasn't a common eye color, and I didn't want people to recognize me, even if they were working for my father.

After being let through, I walked a long corridor that bled into a large room filled with dark-cloaked figures, all wearing the same disguise. Only a few were quietly murmuring, but the rest kept to themselves. Most stood together, waiting as metal rosters clanged, while others continued to find a spot in the room in one of the three rows. I entered the first row, passing on the metal stairs that would make it much harder to flee if needed. A large pit was created in the center of the room, complete with draw-gates and sand—almost like a fighting pit. But summoned here only for a fight? Not my father's style.

Anticipation filled the air as everyone waited for something to happen. I scanned the room, searching for my father as I walked to the middle of the row. A few figures were as tall as him, but it was impossible to discern who they were.

Someone seized my wrist and dragged me towards them in the row. I grabbed onto the metal railing to avoid tripping and causing a scene. Extracting my wrist from the stranger's grasp, I was about to tell them to *fuck off*, until I glimpsed two familiar blue eyes peering down at me.

Zade.

My throat turned dry, equal parts unhappy about the

stunt he pulled and thoughts of that night. I shifted my gaze toward the pit, turning my body to the center. "You know why we're here?" I whispered.

"Suddenly tired of ignoring me?"

Feeling his intense gaze, I glanced back at him without blinking. "Well, do you?"

His eyes moved down, perusing my cloaked figure before looking away. "Yes."

The room was illuminated only by a handful of exit lights and the faint glow emanating from the sandbox, causing eerie green reflections to dance on the walls. The room was occupied mainly by Daemons, who didn't require light to see. However, the few eyes that didn't burn behind the masks likely struggled to make out any details.

"What is it?"

"You'll see."

My irritation simmered beneath the surface. Zade had a history of withholding information from me, acting holier-than-thou regarding my father's trust. Didn't stop him from fucking his daughter behind his back, though. *Loyal, my ass.*

The room was filled with the sound of feet tapping on metal stairs and rosters as everyone took their places inside the mock-shift arena before the doors closed. Another door opened, and we all looked at a large plateau protruding from the wall above the stairs: a private balcony. Two cloaked figures stepped out. My father was unmistakably one of them. The height, the vibrant green eyes—there was no doubt.

Clapping, humming, stomping feet on shaking rosters, and hollering filled the air as my father's presence transformed these people into caged animals. The other cloaked figure beside him raised a hand, hushing the room. "Welcome, everyone," a female's voice thundered through the warehouse.

Ulverin. It had to be, although her voice was a little distorted.

She walked forward on the balcony, arms splayed wide. No strand of red hair or pale skin showed through the disguise. "We've invited you here, dear friends and associates, for a special occasion."

People pressed closer to the railing in anticipation as the doors opened. Six cloaked figures stepped into the room with us, two for each row, handing out items that produced low clinking sounds. One of them approached me and offered a basket filled with tiny glass vials containing copper-colored powder.

I hesitated. It looked… It looked like the powder from that night out with Dana. *Something new,* the bartender had said.

Something new.

Was this it? The memory of a limp body with eyes staring at the ceiling flashed before my eyes, and my blood heated. The person holding the basket hissed, so I swiftly took a vial before I hesitated for too long. I didn't look at it again as I slipped it inside my cloak.

"I've seen this before."

Zade promptly turned his face to mine. "Did you take it?"

There was a hint of concern in those words. "No."

I watched his head bob with silent confirmation that he had heard me.

I felt a tingling sensation and glanced up at the plateau. My father was looking at me. How had he found me among a hundred people? I straightened and met his stare until Ulverin spoke again.

"We introduce our newest product, Ambrosia. Day and night, our experts have worked to improve it, and our alpha and beta tests have yielded positive results."

Successful? Were they fucking kidding? The only time I had ever seen it in action, it had immediately resulted in catastrophe.

Did they even know?

"And thus, we wanted you to be the first to witness the end product in action."

An excited current leaped through the room like we were vultures spotting our next big, meaty prey. Instead of the anticipated flesh, a gaunt-looking man crawled out to the center from one of the pit's gates.

"This colleague of yours was noble enough to volunteer for the test. He had a daily hit for a whole week, except for seventy-two hours ago, when he stopped getting any."

The man was dragging his tongue over the ground, sniffing and salivating.

A week? My eyes widened, and I looked up at my father again, whose eyes were trained on the pit below. "He's about to get his first hit in days," Ulverin said. "Watch closely."

She threw a vial down to the ground as if he were a dog playing fetch. The glass stayed intact long enough for the man to latch onto it immediately and crush it with his fist, making drops of blood appear on the sand. He sniffed the ground, inhaling the coppery powder, not caring as glass and sand went with it. Wheezing, the man licked the ground for any remaining powder, coughing up what wasn't it.

Nothing happened for a moment. He leaned back on the ground, gazing up with a blissful expression.

The people who grew restless, exchanging disappointed

looks and shaking their heads, weren't the ones paying attention. My sharp sight registered the man's pupils widening, his back that seemed to straighten, and the saliva that stopped dripping from his chin as his chest rumbled.

This wasn't a regular drug, and this wasn't a normal reaction.

Ulverin spoke again. "Every one of us has a magic well inside of us, but by far, most of us have nothing in it. Ambrosia fills this well for some time, granting the feeling of having magic and being powerful—without the actual powers. The user will be Ethereal-fast and as strong as any Lupine." She motioned her hand downwards. "Or it will substitute the powers already there and nullify them, rendering the wielder powerless even longer."

The crowd hissed with excitement as the man in the pit clawed at the walls.

"We have never been closer to a collapse of the power dynamics in Ashar, of having the upper hand," my father's voice echoed, and my gaze flew up. "Until now," he said as he stepped forward. "With this invention, the *Trias Politica* will have no more sway over us. They will no longer be exalted because of their powers. We can start building our own army and govern ourselves. We are no less powerful."

Once again, the crowd began banging on the railings.

A draw-gate opened inside the pit, and a mountain cat entered. It was a stealthy, cunning beast, circling the man as if he were looking at his next meal. My forehead creased as I prepared for the onslaught I was about to witness. How could they be excited about this? All I saw was discord, the opposite of what we wanted to achieve. There must be alternative methods to overthrow a government and bring about change.

The man remained unmovable until the mountain cat attacked. What followed was a rapid and intense display of violence. The beast tried to bite him, but the man grabbed the mountain cat's jaws in a sudden movement, defending himself with supernatural strength. Before the cat could withdraw, the man had ripped open its mouth, tearing his jaw straight off as he used every bit of his strength to overpower the animal until it dropped dead on the ground, blood spreading through the sand like an ink stain.

The crowd cheered in awe as the man rose, victorious and clueless. He had just won against an animal far more powerful than him, and he didn't even realize it.

I looked on in horror.

"How long until they're hooked?" a woman asked from the crowd.

"The average Ashari gets addicted within the first two vials, which contain two to three hits," Ulverin said. "The effect from one hit lasts an hour, and the withdrawals are strong. They need the next hit to stay on that high."

Exciting murmurs filled the room. *The possibilities. The money. The power.*

It was like an anvil dropped onto my chest as I looked around me. Why the fuck did no one see the destruction this drug would cause in our city? To our own people?

The blood rushed into my ears as I refused to look up at my father. "Who will deal with the consequences?" I asked, loud enough for everyone to hear.

Zade grabbed my cloak and tugged hard in warning, but I clamped my hands down on the bar in front of me and remained unmoving.

Ulverin turned to me, her stance indicating recognition.

"Consequences?"

"Children walk these streets, and if addicts like *that* run loose, they won't be safe. The Lupine already do fuck-all in Ashrior, so I don't see how we would manage a situation like that."

Some people chuckled, but others seemed intent on hearing the answer, too. Zade pulled at the fabric of my cloak again and nearly growled, "*Stop.*"

"Let the Lupine figure it out!" someone yelled, but Ulverin raised a hand again, stepping closer in my direction. "You raise a valid question," she said. "But don't worry, we have weighed our options extensively. Withdrawals don't last long, not longer than of that garbage the Sanguis brought on the market, anyway. That being said, there's danger around every corner. It has always been a manner of wrong time, wrong place."

I clenched my jaws. "But—"

"How much per vial?" someone else asked.

"A hundred *shards*."

"It'll never sell."

Ulverin chuckled hollowly. "Then get the fuck out, Benzo."

People laughed and cheered, ticking their rings against the metal bars, but my father remained unmoving as he looked down at me.

Zade shook his head. "You're making a fool of yourself."

"By raising valid concerns?"

He turned to me. "By questioning *him*."

I cast my eyes down. I wasn't ready for my father or Zade to see the hesitation or disappointment. This was fucked-up, even for my father's cause. The man in front of us had displayed desperation so severe, so inhumane, that it was nothing but bad news. If this were the effect the drug could have in a few weeks, I didn't dare think about the effect it had in months. How could my father believe this drug would solve anything? It would only destroy.

What Zade had said was true.

I questioned my father's decision for the first time in my life.

I left Ashrior almost immediately, disappearing into the crowd before Zade could stop me again. I didn't want to speak to him. I didn't want to talk to my father or anyone else, either.

The way home was a blur, but as I entered the apartment, I immediately forced the vial's powdery contents into the toilet and flushed them. Wanting to be rid of any trace, I threw away the glass vial in the containers outside and watched as the black cloak and mask burned to dust in my hearth. My anxiety slowly simmered underneath the layer of fatigue. I couldn't shake the feeling the Ambrosia demonstration had cast over me. The Archangel was nothing compared to this.

The feeling lingered, and nothing stopped it from following me into my dreams.

This dream, this nightmare, starred three bodies. Three too-small bodies. Their faces were so blue they looked almost purple, with reddish-blue lines all over them, as if veins had burst beneath their skin. Their bodies were twisted, and their eyes bloodshot. Actual streaks of blood leaked from their corners.

I was crying. The tears had come as soon as the bodies appeared. Closing my eyes didn't help, and turning around only made the room spin with me. There was no escaping their lifeless forms. They were always there, hovering in my mind like a festering wound. No matter what I did, they wouldn't go away. It was as if they demanded my attention, urging me to look at them and do something.

That insistent fear eased a little when someone joined me—*found me*—and I was no longer alone. I couldn't see who they were, but they were there, trying to console me while all I wanted was to be left walloping in my anguish.

I wasn't sure what had happened, but I knew it was on me. *I* had let it get this far. *I* had created this.

And I didn't want to hurt them, too.

I wanted to be left alone in the dark without solace or comfort. So I stayed there until eventually they went away and took the bodies with them. Until the night passed and a new day began.

Only then did I wake up.

I lay in bed, eyes fixed on the ceiling of my room. The shadows that played against it danced to a slow and sinister rhythm, stirring up unease in my stomach as I thought about the demonstration. The dream felt like a bad omen after what I'd witnessed, but what could I do to prevent that drug from being distributed? My father's convictions for this venture were clear, and I did not know how to convince him otherwise. I had never felt the need to change his mind before.

The desperation of the man in the pit as he fought for his life, the havoc he could wreak on anyone—*that panic*—matched that lingering feeling from my dream. More people, *children*, could get hurt because of this drug. And there was nothing they could do to stop it.

CHAPTER SEVENTEEN

Dominic

The moments I shared with my friends were priceless. It was the rare instance I could inhale without restriction.

Night had fallen in Ashtior, and the streets had long since been deserted. I looked at the dark sky from the balcony of Inesa's large mansion, where she lived together with her mate, Leonardo Zemya. It was close to my home.

Light pollution from Shard City reached up through the fog, but stars sparked high above, where the light couldn't reach. I was undeterred by the gentle drizzle of rain and made no attempt to halt it, instead only feeling a strange sense of stillness.

I touched the pack of cigarettes in my pocket and plucked one out. Lighting it, I took a long drag. The smoke infiltrated my lungs, and I held it for a few seconds, savoring the poison before exhaling. The rain dissipated the smoke just as my body expelled it from within, leaving the air as unaffected as my lungs.

I extinguished the cigarette after taking one final inhale before discarding it, barely smoked, into the damp ashtray. Inside, I walked over to Nathan. His dark curls had been cropped short since the last time I saw him, and he was wearing a casual shirt with loose-fitting pants instead of his usual grey and green suits.

Nathan shot me a look and raised his eyebrows. "I'm not going to say it again, you know."

I joined him on the couch. "By all means—don't."

With a tray in hand, Inesa returned to the room, our wine glasses refilled. She set them down on the coffee table between us. A moment of silence followed as she wrinkled her nose. "You should really quit smoking, Dom," she said in an almost scolding tone. "The scent is foul."

Nathan snickered. I rolled my eyes in response. *By the light.* It seemed everyone thought they could tell me what to do these days.

"We just want to ensure you're taking care of yourself." Inesa smiled at me as she crossed her legs.

There was no need for them to be concerned. Smoking didn't hurt me as an archangel, I couldn't get sick. I'd never even had another running nose a day in my life since getting into my full powers.

Nathan nodded in agreement. "I also want to remind you that you're the Archangel and that you can control the weather. I repeat: Control. The. weather." He put his hands together in prayer. "Please stop making it rain so much, Dom. It's getting tiring."

I chuckled, drinking some of my wine. Being the Archangel of the city, I controlled some of the weather in Ashar inside the dome. Most of it was regulated by the seasons, but I influenced it. It wasn't like I could change the climate with a flick of my wrist; it was more like a dance. The weather responded to my inner emotions as if we were bonded.

"You think I'm joking, but I'm not," Nathan said. "Even Asa complained about it, and the Sanguis Domain is in Ashrior. You know, below the ground?"

Inesa nodded with a laugh. "That's true. She asked, no, begged us to talk to you."

"That sounds like Asa." The representative of the Sanguis domain was touchy. "No word from Rakelsh, though?"

"You know she likes discourse. Seems to thrive in bad weather, too." Inesa raised her shoulders.

I shook my head but looked at Nathan. "Well, it's either that or smoking. Changing two major things at once would require too much effort."

He glared at me. "Lazy motherfucker."

I wiggled my eyebrows at him.

We had barely spent an hour together when my phone buzzed in my pocket. I forgot to silence it and checked to see the sender was Nitas.

N.S.: *We need to talk.*

He rarely texted.

Me: *Now?*

N.S.: *Preferably.*

I glanced back at Inesa and Nathan. Tonight was supposed to be our night off, but Nitas, who was practically nocturnal, never reached out at a time like this.

Inesa met my eyes with a knowing expression. "Everything okay?"

Nathan seemed to sense the sudden change in the atmosphere and straightened.

I rose from the couch. "It's Nitas. He's asking me to meet him." Well, *asking* was a big stretch.

Inesa and Nathan shared a worried look before turning

their attention back to me. "Do you need us to come with you?" Inesa asked, already on her feet and approaching me.

I touched her arm lightly in reassurance and grinned. "I think I'll be able to manage."

Nathan nodded in understanding, though he didn't seem pleased at all.

"I'm sorry for cutting tonight short," I said.

They followed me to the front door of the house. The sound of rain tapping on the glass roof in the hallway was louder. "Shoot us an update, okay?" Nathan asked as I hugged him, and he put his hands in his pockets.

I kissed Inesa's cheek. "I will."

The rain was coming down a little harder now, but Inesa didn't care as she stepped out with me. Her courtyard hid her and Leon's old-fashioned house from any prying eyes. A layer of my magic protected it, keeping out anyone with malicious intent, just as it did for Nathan's home in the Ethereal domain.

Inesa took one of my hands. "You know you can always ask us for help, right? No matter what."

"I know." I squeezed her hand, the rain dampening my hair. Glancing back at Nathan, I waved and began walking down the driveway until they vanished inside. The streets of Ashtior were still quiet despite the now-pouring rain. I turned a corner, veering towards the edge of the floating city, and pulled up the collar of my jacket.

I stilled at the edge and climbed up the railing. Looking down, I saw the twinkling abyss open up to Shard City; its lights were hazy in the falling rain. I tucked in my wings before leaping off the edge, allowing my body to slice through the air with my arms firmly at my sides. I broke through the fog and saw the sprawling metropolis below, clearer now.

Descending further, I could make out the hole to Ashrior in the fading light, and I dove straight through—into the dark Undercity.

The streets on my way toward Nitas' home were dark. I had been there a handful of times since becoming Prime. During those first decades, we barely had contact. Nitas Somnos had avoided me like he still did the Cardinal. It seemed as if he was Supreme in name only. Our first decent conversation had been three decades into my run as Prime. When I had investigated a human trafficking case that led me to Ashrior, the Undercity, our paths had crossed. He had been looking into the same case, and we have worked together ever since.

The few stars visible through the cracks were distant specks of light. I wondered what this was about. Nitas wasn't the type to overreact when something went wrong, yet it had troubled him enough to ask me to come.

I arrived at his place: a charming little house with an arched, metal porch adorned by dark Ashrior-native flowers, their petals dark and stems thick. It looked like nothing, but the protective layer surrounding the building was palpable the moment I passed through it. Nitas was powerful, but no one knew the exact extent of his powers. The Daemon was secretive and not only about his magic.

I knocked on the door and heard a mechanical latch unlocking before it swung open, revealing a built-in elevator. Layer upon layer upon layer—impenetrable—just like the Daemon himself. The doors shut after I entered, taking me further below ground.

The doors to his underground office opened. Bookshelves

lined all four walls and were filled with texts, both new and ancient. The space even included a living area. With a stony expression, Nitas sat behind his desk, his dark eyes focused on the paper in front of him. He only looked up when I stepped into the room.

"I like what you've done with the place," I said. "New paint color?"

He motioned for me to sit down opposite him and wrapped his hands together, but there was a hint of a smile on his face. "Thank you for coming."

I sat down. "Do you ever work from your office at the Courthouse?"

"No." His black eyes glimmered with amusement. He looked at me again, face suddenly unreadable, though some of that humor lingered.

"What?"

"Something about you is different."

I raised my brows. "Meaning what?"

He looked at me for a moment longer, cocking his head. "There is something you must see," he said. His voice was steady and matter-of-fact, skipping my question, straight to business. He turned the screen on his desk my way. "Xanon officially released the drug. It's called Ambrosia."

Nitas pressed play, and a video started playing. It showed a large room with a lit center, some sort of sandbox. Cloaked figures were lined up in rows around it. I heard nothing of what was being said but watched as the figures moved and slammed the railings. Then it cut to a man getting something from the ground, face pressed against the sand of the pit, eventually killing some kind of feline animal. That sick crowd was rowdy, excited by the cruelty of what he had done.

The cowards were dressed in cloaks for a reason. They were leeches benefitting from others instead of creating their own way in the world.

"Where did you get this?"

"An opportunity arose, and I took it." Nitas' face betrayed nothing.

"You have an inside source, don't you?" I leaned forward. We had been attempting to snare one for quite a while. "The person who gave you this video?"

"Possibly."

"What did they want?" They always wanted something in return. People rarely did things from the goodness of their hearts—especially people entangled with Xanon Naan.

"Not something I can disclose." He turned the screen back to face him. "I already have someone working on figuring out the location."

"The source didn't say?"

Nitas kept quiet.

I sighed. "We also need to find out where they produce and store this stuff. We could consider implementing high penalties for anyone involved with this drug, including buyers caught with it. It will make people hesitate or even altogether refrain from buying."

"Then we should hurry, because it's already in circulation," Nitas said. "I've seen clips of someone foaming at the mouth, thrashing dumpsters in some alleyway at the Sanguis Domain. The behavior was similar to what we could see in the video."

I cursed. *Fucking Xanon.*

"It's only been a few hours since the first batches hit the streets, but the situation is already spiraling out of control," he continued. "Even if we act quickly, I doubt we'll contain it before it spreads too far."

Our gazes met, and understanding passed. We both knew this was a wildfire. Untamable. Xanon was a blight on the world, a plague that withered everything it touched. His name had become synonymous with malice and evil. It would be even more so after this night was over.

Nitas ran his hands through his hair and leaned back in his chair. "The last thing Xanon Naan should get is more power."

"We'll do what we can," I said, but wasn't reassured. Not by a long shot.

As Prime, I had faced many situations before, but this... If it affected everyone, like the person in the video, this would be far from a walk in the park. We had to find a way to stop Ambrosia from wreaking chaos in our city. We needed to stop Xanon.

CHAPTER EIGHTEEN

Leyla

Ambrosia tugged at my mind the days after the demonstration in Ashrior. I had to discuss it with my father. It felt all wrong, and I wasn't waiting until he asked me to come over.

The Daemon guarding my father's gates nodded at me, expressionless. I had never seen him before, but he opened the gates and gestured for me to enter as though he knew who I was. I crossed the threshold, the cool fall air greeting me in a gust. The familiar courtyard was filled with unfamiliar Daemons, even more so than the last time. Their eyes fixed on me as I passed. Ignoring them, I raised my chin and walked until I reached the manor entrance.

After quickly stepping inside, I passed Zade in the hallway. He looked at me, brows lowering, and stopped walking. "Leyla?"

"Zade." Brushing past him, I opened the office door ahead of me, and my father looked up as I walked inside, catching my father's confused and slightly irritated expression.

"What are you doing here?" he asked, voice clipped. As if I couldn't just visit him or the home I'd grown up in. As if I needed a valid reason to stop by, and it should have been one granted by him. It pissed me off.

Ulverin was in his office, too, leaning on a side table, one foot dangling in the air. The sight of them together mimicked that of a teacher and principal who had been waiting to reprimand a student.

"I need to talk to you," I said to my father, my throat suddenly dry. "It's important."

His eyes, like two laser beams, seared through mine. It felt like an eternity as he studied me in silence. Finally, he beckoned me closer with a wave of his hand. "What is it?" he asked, his eyes narrowing.

As I moved nearer, my eyes darted between them. "Don't tell me you're seriously planning to sell that stuff."

They shared a look, and Ulverin said, "I told you."

My father let go of a sigh and leaned back in his chair. "You've been very sheltered, Leyla. And perhaps that is on me."

"No." I was shaking my head. "You always do this. Don't turn this around. It's not like I don't know suffering or haven't faced the ugly parts of humanity." He made me out to be like some naïve kid.

Ulverin pushed away from the table and brushed past me. "I'll be outside." She closed the door behind her as she left the office.

"You don't want me to treat you as a child," my father said, "but now you're acting like one. You got what you wanted—you're in. What more do you need? You want me to stop selling drugs? *Futile*," he spat, opening his palms in an expansive gesture. "There is a supply and demand. If they don't buy from me, they'll buy from someone else."

I stepped forward. "People aren't aware how harmful

Ambrosia is."

My father rubbed a hand over his eyes. "You are right, to an extent. It differs from what's already out there, and if anything, I want you as far away from it as possible."

"Doesn't that tell you everything about the product you're selling?"

He suddenly stood, hands splaying on his desk. "Do you not drink alcohol? Have you never done drugs, Leyla? Just because things are bad doesn't mean there isn't a demand for it."

My shoulders dropped, but I kept my voice steady. "This is different." *And he knew it.*

"Sometimes, we must dabble a little in the dark to let out the light. We don't have the upper hand here, but we could. This is the way." His wooden desk groaned as his index finger pressed into it.

I remained silent as he stepped from behind the desk and stalked closer. "Why do you question the person who has done nothing but provide for you? Who gave you anything you wanted?" His tone had a dangerous edge, but his hands came down on my shoulders.

"I just fear this drug might do more harm than we've bargained for," I said, looking up at him, eyes pleading. "Crime rates will rise. With this inhumane strength, the number of murders will climb—Ashar will become unsafe—"

"Ashar is *already* unsafe," he thundered, arms dropping to his sides. "But that's something you don't see because I have always been here to keep you safe. I made sure you didn't have to deal with such things."

I stared at my father. Really looked at him. My thoughts were completely uncertain—a mess. I loved Ashar. I loved Ashrior—it was my home, and he was my family. But he had never given me a reason to doubt him before.

"You still don't have to. I can assure you your assignment does not involve Ambrosia, but working for my company means you need to know what's going on within it. If you can't cope with that, say so now. There are plenty of other jobs in Ashar for you to occupy your time with. But once you're out, you're out. There's no going back."

The disappointment was evident on his face. He looked at me as if I had already failed, as if he could sense weakness. As if I had solidified every preconception he had of me. He didn't think I would do it. I had failed to meet his expectations thus far.

I steeled my spine. "It has nothing to do with the assignment," I said.

"Then why question me?"

Gritting my teeth, I glanced to the side.

"If the Archangel is too big of a challenge…"

"I can do it."

"Are you sure?"

"*Yes*." I swallowed.

His expression completely changed, appearing pleased once more. The rope around my chest loosened. For the first time since getting down here, he smiled, and it was the exact smile I longed for as a child. He looked proud that I was his daughter, his blood. It was like feeling the sun on my face, so I remained silent to feel its rays a little while longer.

"I'm glad, *Cara*."

I needed to redirect my thoughts away from Ambrosia for the night. Desperately. Maybe my father was right, and I couldn't see it from the right perspective. Perhaps I lacked the strength to do what was required. Either way, I didn't want to think about it anymore, especially after the quizzical look Zade had given me on my way out.

Burying it all underneath a pile of reality shows and getting takeout with Dana at her place turned out to be the perfect diversion. Her apartment in the Ethereal Domain was stylish and decorated impeccably. Even though it wasn't large, Dana was completely independent. Contrary to me, she had paid for everything herself.

Tonight, we were going to the Shard City stadium in the Human Domain for the Ashar City Cup team presentation. I had never been—had never taken part in the previous years at all, so this would be my first time. Dana typically attended the Ethereal games during the actual tournament, but because she was still fucking around with Tommy, and Josiah was somehow still interested in me, they invited us. Since her family received invitations to almost every high-profile event related to it, she typically avoided such occasions, but this year we would attend together—because fuck that. We were going to have fun.

Prime Venetia's heavy involvement may have also played a role in my decision to go. I would welcome any opportunity to cover grounds on this assignment.

I had a point to make.

"Something about Tommy... I don't know, Ley. He just doesn't understand me. So many of our arguments get lost in translation."

I snorted. *No shit.* "That's because you're not in the same league."

"Stop gloating, Miss Independent." She rolled her eyes.

"Or should I say miss no-man-will-ever-be-good-enough?"

"That would have hurt me if I actually had a heart," I said.

My thoughts jumped to the Archangel. The man had the habit of dominating every room he entered, and he made no effort to hide his attraction to me. He wanted me to know. According to the tabloids, which I now followed closely, he hadn't been spotted with another woman since cutting ties with that Angeli. Apparently.

From the moment I first saw him years ago, I've had a feeling about him. It's almost like I could sense him when he was near or looked at me. His presence had me on edge, a result of the traumatic memories in my mind, no doubt.

Dana settled back into her couch. "I'm unsure if we should go tonight."

"To the stadium?"

She grunted.

"Oh, we're going," I said immediately.

With renewed interest in the situation, she perked up and narrowed her eyes. "Why?"

"I've never been."

"Bullshit," she deadpanned. "That's not the reason."

"Can't I be curious?"

"It's not one of your common traits."

"You're such a pain in the ass sometimes."

"Well, well, well. Isn't this intriguing?" Dana said, clucking her tongue. "You've persuaded me." She pushed off the couch and strode into the hallway. "Let me get dressed into something fabulous so Tommy will see what he's about to get no more of. And don't think I won't figure the real reason you want to go!"

We arrived at the stadium, which was filled with influential people and players' families. Stars and celebrities were everywhere I looked. It was quite an experience.

"Oh shit," Dana screeched as she squeezed my arm. "There's Miranda Lesley! You know how much I love her editorial eye. And holy shit—*Wanda*? Hold on, I'm going over there for photos. I'll be right back."

"Sure," I responded, but she had already left. Chuckling to myself, I weaved through the crowd until I found a spot by the railing, away from most people. A stage was assembled on the grass, and the press was gathered around, arranging their equipment for the ACC team presentation and player line-up. Only the press and players had permission to be on the field. The rest of us would be watching from the first ring.

Turning around slowly, I scanned the crowd, but the anticipated golden wings were nowhere to be found.

I attempted to conceal my impatience and redirected my attention to the field. The least I could do was enjoy my night, regardless of how it unfolded. I hadn't lied to Dana; this was a new experience for me. Even the small, uncorrupted part of me found some indulgence in it.

The lights dimmed, and music started playing as they began to introduce the Lupine team. Dana was still in the audience, chatting with different people. Unlike me, she effortlessly made contact, but I didn't mind being alone. The crowd cheered as each player was called on stage. One of them even received boos, but my lack of knowledge about the game left me clueless. Regardless, I laughed when the player flipped them off.

Then, it was the Ethereals' turn. It felt like every eye in the room was glued to the stage. Despite my limited knowledge, I knew the Ethereals were in the running for the title. Both Dana and Josiah had told me about it. With a frown, Tommy approached the podium, his gaze fixed on the crowd. As I followed it, I saw Dana touch the arm of a Pisces.

I chuckled to myself. *Served him right.*

However, the atmosphere shifted when they finally called out Josiah's name. He got a loud applause, and I even joined in. I knew he was a talented player, not only because Dana hadn't shut up about it. I might have done a quick search on him once or twice. He took the stage, grinning brightly. Golden boy, indeed.

A tingling feeling traveled up my spine, settling at the base of my neck. I had to swallow down the urge to turn, aware of my surroundings but glad I was on the crowd's outer side.

He was here. Close. I could feel him.

Gold caught my eye as the Archangel exchanged handshakes amid the crowd with representatives from other domains. His towering figure stood out, and the Archangel met my eyes even from a distance.

Slowly, I turned my gaze back to the field, feeling my heart race. Dana was nowhere to be seen, but so wasn't that Pisces guy she'd been flirting with. Or could her absence be connected to her parents? I had spotted them in the crowd along with other Ethereals.

A hand leaned on the railing next to me not a minute later. The Prime of Shard City gazed out onto the field, a tight smile once again gracing his lips.

Josiah waved to the crowd before the team left. I applauded again. He kept texting me every few days after the date, but I delayed my responses and replied with short messages. Part of me felt bad about it because he was a great guy, but no part would have dated him the way he wanted, and now that I was working on the assignment... I had to keep my distance.

The situation with Zade was already tiring to deal with, and we weren't even exclusive.

"I thought he wasn't your boyfriend," the Archangel said, inclining his head toward the field.

That was the first thing he said? "I don't know what else to tell you. He isn't."

Dominic Venetia turned his entire body toward me. "Alright, Leyla. You have my attention."

I looked up at him in surprise and noticed heads turning our way.

"What do you want?" he clarified, looking at me like he could look past all of it and uncover my deepest, darkest secrets.

I met his gaze again with a steady one of my own. His eyes remained inscrutable, but there was an added depth that simultaneously drew me in and made me wary. "What do you mean?"

"What do you want *from me*?"

He asked it so casually, assuming I would ask for something because that was the norm with everyone else. That was his problem, right there—the obvious lack of empathy. He had gotten so big he couldn't understand he was just another person, like the rest of us. His position and titles didn't make him superior to us. We didn't all *want* something from him.

"Why do you assume I want anything?" I lifted a shoulder in an unconcerned gesture. "It's you who keeps approaching me."

Dominic narrowed his eyes, seemingly taken aback by my

comment, and for a moment, I thought I had made a mistake. I had to play my cards right. If this would drive him away, I needed to crush my pride and do some damage control.

He licked his lips and smiled. "I suppose you're right. But pray tell, why are you here?"

"My friend Lodana was invited and asked me to come." It wasn't a lie, per se.

"Hm," he said, nodding to himself as he leaned against the railing, looking out onto the field where another team was standing. "Does that imply that you're not in a relationship?" His expression had softened a tad, though his golden eyes still searched my face, trying to uncover the truth. I could tell he didn't fully trust me. And why would he? I didn't trust him, either.

"It might."

He looked at me for a few more moments before breaking eye contact and running a hand through his unbound hair. Then he turned back to me with a mischievous smirk on his lips that made my chest tighten. "It seems something has led our paths to cross again. Other than business, of course."

At that moment, Dana appeared on the other side of the balcony and looked at me with wide eyes, completely ignoring the person talking to her. It seemed as if she wanted to scream: *this is why you wanted to come?* And she seemed far too excited about it.

"I don't believe in fate," I said, telling him a truth as if it untangled the web of lies I had begun to spin.

Dominic raised one of his brows. "I guess I don't either," he responded with a smirk, seemingly amused by my declaration for a reason that made me feel exposed.

I watched Dana retreat in the back of the room, trying to

hide from her parents' eyes. Her form disappeared through the exit, and Dominic followed my gaze. "You should go after your friend." He motioned towards the back of the stadium with a jut of his chin. "I'm sure we'll meet again."

"Yes," I mumbled, grabbing my purse tighter. "It was nice seeing you again."

He grinned at me, shaking his head a little. "Sure. *Nice*."

Then I went after my friend, cringing internally at the way I had choked. It felt like I was now in on some secret no one else knew about. Something that, in time, would be hard to ignore.

CHAPTER NINETEEN

Dominic

Fall reborn was approaching, and with it came an increasing workload on top of the drug situation we were trying to contain. I met with multiple representatives to discuss the ACC and visited numerous locations to monitor the progress. I was preoccupied with safety measures for the Human Domain, preparations for the gala's location, checking the protective wards around the city, and all the other things that demanded my attention.

And still, my brain kept returning to Leyla.

I don't believe in fate.

The previous version of myself had believed in fate. I crossed paths three times with an attractive woman I had never seen before. The idea that it was a coincidence became increasingly unbelievable, but time had turned me into a skeptic.

She didn't seem to exist online. I looked through public records but came up empty-handed. Her name hadn't been registered in any public file work I had legal access to. There seemed to be no trace of her, and it was maddening.

The desire to find out more about her without overstepping was challenged over the week that followed. Let's say that finding someone's last name wasn't as easy as it sounded, and there were only so many legal ways to find out. As Prime, it was my responsibility to enforce the law, and having double standards would be highly hypocritical. Thankfully, my better judgment won out in the end, and I had let it rest.

For now.

At least the weather had been good. The sky was a clear blue, the sun rising high and burning even in fall, reflecting off the beautifully decorated *Curia*. Rays managed to slip through the roof's carvings, illuminating a white marble carving of the old gods.

I took my place among the eleven Seraphim, and Balan went straight to business. "How are the preparations for the ACC coming along?"

I looked at the older Seraphim. "We are on schedule. Every domain is chipping in. Our focus has mostly been on monitoring the black market in Ashrior, though we don't have all the data yet." I looked at Head Cardinal Kemalgda, who nodded at me. "We're also making sure we have adequate security measures in place and enough resources to provide food and shelter for those who will attend from outside the city."

The other Seraphim hummed in agreement. They seemed confident that all would be sorted with the ACC, but they weren't thinking of how bad a season could get if something like this rampant drug took over.

The Cardinal exchanged glances, and Balan cleared her throat. "I hope Supreme Somnos has everything under control in Ashrior?"

Kemalgda tipped her head up to the ceiling. "I'm unsure

how long we can tolerate Divinitas' free rein. Nitas Somnos doesn't care about Ashar. He only wants the power that comes with the title."

Vaphoryn straightened. "That's not a fair judgment of his character," she said as he looked at the rest of the Cardinal. "I've known Divinitas for some time, and although his morals aren't always the purest, he never strayed over the edge. His seclusion does not make him self-centered or corrupt."

Head Cardinal Kemalgda looked at her. Not irritatedly or sternly, but as if she saw the young Seraphim in a new light. I nodded in agreement with Vaphoryn's words, but doubt still lingered on most of the Seraphim's faces. "Supreme Somnos has Ashar's best interests at heart. The information about the drug came from his hand first."

"Alas." Balan waved a hand. "All that is important is that he has his domain under control."

"As long as Xanon Naan influences the Undercity, there's no one in control," I said truthfully. The *Trias Politica* encountered a challenge with Xanon Naan because of legal restrictions on punishment. We were limited in how far we could go within our boundaries of upholding the law.

Head Cardinal Kemalgda nodded, her brows furrowed. "Indeed."

"Which leads me to another pressing matter," Clotho said as Lachesis and Atropos glanced at me with matching smiles on their crinkled faces. Although the latter looked more like she was humoring the other two. "What's the status of your love life, Prime Venetia?"

"I have a pretty niece who I'd love to introduce you to," Lachesis chimed in.

I smiled, observing the other Seraphim—many of whom

were also laughing.

"*By the light*," Head Cardinal Kemalgda said. "Why you three are on this council will haunt me for the rest of my life."

Kemalgda's disdain wasn't enough to shut Clotho up. "Is it true you broke up with the lovely Elizabeth?"

"*Lovely?*" Atropos scoffed.

Lachesis let out a sigh while gazing at me. "His babies will be so pretty."

All three nodded as if it was indeed the most pressing matter.

I raised my brows at Vaphoryn on my right. A tiny smile teased the edges of her mouth. She pressed her fist against it to force the curve of her lips back into place and keep others from seeing her glee.

Head Cardinal Kemalgda sighed and rubbed her forehead with a hand, sighing in exasperation. But even Balan couldn't hide her amusement. "As much as I enjoy this digression," Kemalgda said, her voice weary, "I think it's time to get back to discussing matters of import. How we should handle the lack of control in the Undercity, for one."

Balan nodded her agreement. "It'd be best if we handled this quickly."

The Cardinal continued their conversation, but I focused on the golden signet ring I wore on my pinky, bearing my archangel crest. Following an additional hour of discussion, they decided all preparations would be ready for the start of the ACC next week.

I rose from my seat, thanking the Cardinal, and excused myself from the *Curia*, leaving the Seraphim to their work while I made my way out into the bright afternoon sun. The rays already streamed through the roof's carvings and burned a path across the marble floor as I walked towards the exit.

The sun outside momentarily blinded me, and I removed my suit jacket. With my sleeves rolled up, I spread my wings to absorb the sunlight while descending the steps from the *Curia*.

"Wait, Dominic."

Vaphoryn followed me in her ornate robes, the embroidered silk rustling softly as she moved. Each fold created a whisper as she approached, and her reddish hair billowed around her like flames in the wind.

I waited. My wing muscles felt heavy from having rested on a chair for so long. If flying inside the *Curia* was allowed, I would have flown through the large hole and into the sky half an hour ago. Feeling a slight thrill as the wind ruffled my feathers, I itched at the idea of finally launching off into the sky.

Vaphoryn stopped a few steps away from me, shielding her eyes from the sun, "Are you alright?"

"Why wouldn't I be?"

Her brown eyes crisscrossed my face before they stilled. "I thought I felt…" She paused as if weighing her words. "Never mind."

At the bottom of the steps, children were playing with some kites, shouting in excitement.

"I was sorry to hear about Eliza."

I looked back at her, glad she hadn't opted for 'you deserve to be happy'. I had grown so tired of hearing that sentence. "It was never meant to last."

Some of the other Seraphim exited the building, laughing and enjoying the sun as we stood silently. Balan said something to some of them, and they all nodded. Head Cardinal Kemalgda was nowhere to be seen.

"You know us cardinals swear secrecy when we join the council," Vaphoryn said suddenly, her tone hushed. "Like the priests of old, the magic binding us is real. Everything that is said to the Cardinal belongs to the Cardinal." She stepped closer, swallowing. "Some of us are sharing about our dreams, most of them filled with sinister forces hiding in shadows and an ancient evil rising again."

"Is there truth in them?"

Vaphoryn let out a soft sigh. "I cannot say for sure. Sometimes, they are metaphors, telling us something else. Sometimes, they're to be taken literally. But more and more I get the ominous feeling bad things are happening. Things we can't see." She was so close now her robes brushed me, and I looked in her hazel eyes—such a contrast to her pale, freckled skin. "I had a dream the other day. Of eyes turning from happy to sad, an atmosphere changing from hot to cold, eyes that shut forever, like a blink, never to open again." Her nostrils flared. "It was *suffocating*."

Her words settled between us. "What are you trying to say?"

"I felt you there." Vaphoryn glanced around, making sure nobody was within earshot. "Things are not as they seem, Dominic. I've felt it for a while."

"What things?"

"People, things—surrounding you. The specifics are unclear to me."

"Things are not as they seem?" I repeated dubiously. "Isn't that just politics?"

Vaphoryn's smile was tinged with sadness. "We're required to speak our dreams in the circle, but I didn't tell anyone about this one—nor will I. Just… just be careful, okay?" She then turned and walked back up the steps of the *Curia*.

Things are not as they seem.

What did she mean when she said I should be careful? What the hell was I supposed to do with this information? Vaphoryn wasn't usually one for dramatics.

I looked up at the sun again, its warmth caressing my face. It was a beautiful start of the season, the last burst of summer forcing its rays onto Ashar, and despite my conflicted feelings—despite Vaphoryn's warning—just maybe, I played a part in that, too.

CHAPTER TWENTY

Leyla

"I am obsessed," Dana said, falling back on the bed, her fuchsia hair spilling over the edge. "You and the Archangel... *Ahh*, I can't get over how perfect you looked together."

I rolled my eyes and kept flipping through the magazine on the carpet. Dana had drilled me after the team presentation like a general on the hunt for blood. There hadn't been much to say, or at least not much I could tell her honestly. I settled for the truth anyway, telling her about our unplanned first encounter and his blatant interest while we'd been on different dates.

She raised her arms to the ceiling. "He will be there, too, you know? At the kick-off gala."

"I figured. Given that he is the Prime."

"We need to get you a dress he won't be able to look away from, and I've found the perfect boutique in the Pisces domain." Dana clucked her tongue. "You're so lucky to have a friend like me."

I honestly had forgotten about the gala. Dana had invited me months before the assignment had been on my radar. I supposed things had a strange way of figuring themselves out.

The last week messed with my mind. I was still reeling from the Ambrosia demonstration, feeling utterly powerless. I didn't want to pressure my father again since he wasn't receptive to my concerns the first time. He had made up his mind.

"Earth to Leyla?" Dana said, rolling onto her stomach. "We're going, right?"

"Right," I said, clearing my throat. "Yes, of course." It would be an important night—another opportunity to see the Archangel.

Dana whistled under her breath. "Why were you excited about the team presentation but make the gala sound like a chore? It's one of the most popular events in Ashar, and you get to go! With *me*, no less."

"I'm aware." I chuckled, shaking my head. "And you wonder why I sound so reluctant..."

She shoved my leg off the bed. "When shall we shop for dresses, then? This week would give us ample time to find something before the event."

"You schedule it, and I'll show up."

My best friend studied my face with a sly grin. "What has your panties in a twist, Ley? Is it the Archangel? Cause he even has me clenching my thighs."

Dana made me laugh out loud as she rose to her knees on the bed, putting her bright pink hair into a top bun and making her freckles pop even more. She leaned back on the cushions, wrapping her arms together, and curved an eyebrow.

With a smile, I looked back at the magazine, turning another page.

"Spill it, Leyla Cuprum," she said.

I inwardly cringed at the name, so I told her another truth—something I hadn't acknowledged since it happened.

"I had a sex dream about the Archangel." *While I had been sleeping with the man whose text messages I was still ignoring.*

"And?" she pressed, leaning forward. "Throw me a bone, girl."

"It was a very real dream. I don't know what to say; far from any sex dream I experienced before."

"Yeah, but how was it?"

My cheeks heated. "Real, Dana. It was real."

"You're killing me here!" she groaned. "Real *what?* Real hot? Real hard? Real tender?"

I tried not to think about it.

"Why didn't you ask for his number at the stadium?"

"And then what? Booty call the Prime? It was just a dream."

"Yeah, but that eye-fucking had been pretty real."

What was she talking about?

Dana shrugged. "Listen—there's no shame in it. Everyone on the planet has dreamt of the guy," she said. "The man's practically a god. I bet you he even is one in the bedroom."

I cast a look in her direction.

Shaking her head, Dana straightened to a sitting position again. "I don't buy it, Ley. Not the way you just looked away ten times while I talked about him. There's something there. You and Josiah… yeah, you would have been great together. But the Archangel and you… Holy shit, you would be out-of-this-world, mind-blowing amazing."

Swallowing, I leaned my head back on the carpet in front of her bed. "He isn't the type to settle down. Nor am I."

"Not yet," Dana corrected me, standing from the bed. "But there's a first time for everything." She took her phone from her pocket, ticking away at it furiously. "How about we go out tonight? Blow off some steam?"

I thought about it. Maybe it would get my mind off this entire ordeal—the drug, the Archangel, the fact that I was continuously lying to my friend. "Why not?"

Dana clapped her hands. "Yay!" She opened the doors to her closet. "Then let's get dressed, my friend."

To my surprise, Dana took me to Ashrior to go clubbing this time. I hadn't been back to the Undercity since the Ambrosia demonstration, and I didn't know if what we were doing was harmless fun or possibly very dangerous. The sight of the packed elevators with partygoers eased my concerns slightly. If it were genuinely unsafe, there wouldn't be this many people skipping off into Ashrior's nightlife.

We entered a club in the Daemon Domain I didn't know the name of, and I immediately felt the music's pulse thump through my bones. We *did* have the best music. The loud bass and dancing people filled me with such crackling energy I didn't have the space to think anymore.

It was bliss.

My long black hair cascaded over my silver, sparkling dress in straight locks. I curved my lips into a faint smile as I brushed away a stray strand that had escaped to the front. I yearned for a night like this after the last couple of weeks.

"Let's hit the dance floor!" Dana shouted over the noise, her eyes glittering. We passed the bar and seating areas filled with smoke and the strong odor of booze.

When we were pulled into the dancing crowd, my guard finally started slipping. Before we left Dana's apartment to go down, we had already taken a couple of shots each, so the heady feeling in my brain offered a warm blanket as we danced. With my elbows close to my ribcage and hands raised in the air, I moved to the beat, each moment resonating through me as hands skimmed me, touched me, and people bumped into me.

The music built up to a crescendo, the beat getting ready to drop again. I closed my eyes, tipping my head up as I smiled, really savoring it. My shoulders and hips moved in different directions as I rolled my body, head swaying to the music. I opened my eyes again as the lights in the room flashed to the beat, and Dana and I joined the rhythm of the rest of the dance floor.

Dana was dancing with some Sanguis guy who had come behind her. I smiled at her and turned around, getting my bearings and looking for the bar. The mix of alcohol and music was the perfect concoction to help me forget who I was for a minute, and I wanted *more*.

As I peered over the crowd a flash of gold grabbed my attention. It was so fast that I initially thought it originated from the wildly flashing lights. But no—

I paused on the dance floor as I caught sight of gold once more in the back of the club.

There he was, sitting in the VIP section—the Prime of Ashar, *Dominic Venetia*. With my cunning Daemon vision, every detail of him was vivid. He wore his brown curls down for once, framing his aristocratic face. His golden eyes shone in the dim lights, matching his wings.

"What's up?" Dana peered over my shoulder, looking in the same direction as I was. "*There* he is!"

"I haven't had enough drinks for this," I said, but there was no way she could hear me over the music. *Wait*—I turned around to a smirking Dana, her eyes glittering with amusement.

No way.

"You so set me up."

She shrugged. "Perhaps I had been reading *A-sham* at the exact right time, and *perhaps* they wrote about a certain archangel who had been spotted in a nightclub in Ashrior. And there might not have been tickets left for tonight anywhere, but luckily, I have connections in the right places."

I closed my eyes. "I hate you." Why on earth was Dominic Venetia here, of all places? Based on my research, I knew he didn't often go out in public.

"Sure you do. At least you weren't lying when you told me he noticed you. It's as if you're magnetic."

I turned around again. "What do you me—"

People moved around me, but none of it registered. Dominic was looking straight at me. Those golden eyes focused on where I stood on the dance floor. I couldn't look away from him. The pull between us was palpable, even though we had never spoken more than a few sentences. The music seemed to fade into nothingness, leaving me trapped in his gaze—was confident and sure.

He was eyeing me up like I was his next meal.

I shivered, and he smirked like he knew exactly what was going on.

This was all happening too fast. Unscheduled—not according to plan. That was one time too many now. I didn't even have time to catch my breath. I was the first to look away, suddenly remembering I had been searching for the bar.

"Come on," Dana said, grabbing my arm. I allowed her to pull me away, grateful for my best friend's intervention. "Where are we going?"

"The VIP area, of course."

Pulling free from her hold, I said, "*What?* No."

Dana shook her head like she didn't understand. "He sent someone over to invite us. Didn't you notice?"

"Clearly not."

"Well, we are going over there right now. *Together*," she emphasized. No room for argument. "This is a once-in-a-lifetime opportunity, Ley, let's fucking milk it."

I followed Dana through the crowd and couldn't help but be cautious. Dominic was the Archangel, Prime of the fucking city, and I still hadn't covered all my ground with him. The man was dangerous. He wouldn't be in his position if he weren't. I needed to remind myself that he was an apex predator underneath the charismatic facade. He was more skilled at wrapping me around his finger than vice versa. And he'd probably succeed if I didn't already loathe him.

With reluctance, I focused on Dana as she navigated through the club, and Dominic Venetia came back into view. I sensed the moment we shifted through the invisible barricade upheld by his magic. He looked over at us, his golden eyes darker now. As we approached him, the music appeared to decrease, intensifying the sound of my pounding heart. He looked big, sitting on that couch with his arms splayed wide and his ankle crossed carelessly over his knee.

The smile he directed at me was too intimate—as if we were the only two people in the room. Again.

Lightness, save me.

Dana immediately walked over and thanked him for inviting us while blood still rushed through my ears. Then she tugged me closer before making herself scarce and started chatting with other people in the secluded area. Honestly?

Fuck. Her.

"It's almost as if you're stalking me," Dominic Venetia said as he rose from his seat.

I forced my lips to remain neutral. "How so? This is my domain."

"Right," he said, stepping closer, his eyes never straying from my face. "Just a coincidence, then?"

I don't believe in fate.

I guess I don't either.

"Or a best friend who is acting like a meddlesome teenager." My eyes flicked back to Dana, who gave me a thumbs-up.

Dominic chuckled. He flicked a thumb over his bottom lip. "What did you tell her?"

My throat bobbed as I tried to block out the intensity of his gaze. "Only that our paths had crossed."

He made a guttural sound, his lips pursing a little. His golden gaze seared through me, tracing a path from my head, lingering on my lips, down to the rest of my body.

"Stop looking at me like that," I said. The combination with my intoxicated blood made my head spin, but the Archangel's eyes pinned me in place.

A shiver ran down my spine as he held my gaze before finally asking, "Like what?"

"Like that." I inclined my head at him.

He looked past me and stroked his jaw in thought. "What's wrong with the way I look at you?"

Nothing. Everything about it seemed right, which was the problem. "Just stop."

"You can't order me around."

"Well, you can't look at me," I exclaimed in exasperation.

He raised an amused eyebrow, a smirk tugging at the

corner of his lips. "Oh?"

Confusion swirled low in my gut. The man was driving me off a cliff.

He moved closer, his height towering over me as he inspected my face. His hand reached forward as if in slow motion and took a strand of my black hair between his fingers, looking at it before tucking it back behind my ear. I held my breath as I let him, and I had no idea why. We had never been this close.

I was supposed to be the one in control.

"I'm seeing someone," I breathed, cursing myself inwardly. That was about the stupidest thing I could have said—for multiple reasons.

But he just smiled down at me, baring his straight teeth. "Are you, Leyla?"

A hand landed on Dominic's shoulder, and he turned around to look at the man standing behind him. Our little bubble burst as the atmosphere changed in a heartbeat.

"Nitas," he said by way of greeting but it sounded as if he were asking what the hell the Supreme wanted.

I recognized him. Divinitas. Nitas Somnos, the Supreme of Ashar. Our higher judicial power and the supreme judge of Ashar's courthouse. I had heard the tales about the Daemon that painted him a god, like Dominic, but darker.

He wore all black, a natural fit for someone who seemed to blend with the shadows. His skin was a light, golden brown, and his hair was black, his eyes just as dark. Their light was faint, but I noticed his Daemon heritage shining through. Now, they were focused on me, unmoving, unblinking, and all I could do was look. My heartbeat slowed down for the first time since coming here, making me a little lightheaded. The tall Daemon stepped in front of the Archangel, brushing past his wings, his attention entirely on me now, perusing me in a way that made me nervous.

Dominic's eyes narrowed, boring a hole into his skull.

Nitas Somnos took a step closer, his eyes moving in a languid motion. "Have we met before?"

I took a step back, locking him out of my personal space. "No."

He didn't mind. Instead, he said, "A Daemon I have never seen before attracted the attention of Dominic Venetia…"

"Not the first one, I'm sure."

"Hm," he murmured non-committally, then he whispered, "Jealousy seems to be a new emotion to him." His voice was low and suave.

I blinked more than once. "What?"

"Your archangel, *Amica*. He wants you all to himself."

I stole a glance at Dominic, briefly averting my eyes from the Supreme.

"He is not my anything," I responded.

"Ah," Nitas chuckled, his eyes assessing. "Unfamiliar emotions in you, too."

Sweat broke out in the small of my back.

He cocked his head in interest, and I didn't dare look at anyone but him—holding my ground. The Supreme shrugged, amusement lining his emotionless face. "There's more, isn't there?"

"I have no clue what you're talking about," I said, my voice low and threatening.

He clucked his tongue, pressing his index fingers to his pursing mouth. His powers reached out, and a trail of shivers broke out in my neck, at odds with the warm club. I didn't move. "You're good."

My eyes narrowed while the corners of his mouth widened. What game was this man playing?

Did I show him my hand?

Nitas turned, facing Dominic, and all I could see was a twitch of the Supreme's lips before he put his hands in his pockets and left.

CHAPTER TWENTY-ONE

Dominic

Irritation swirled in my gut as I watched Nitas retreat through the crowd. He had a brand of humor no one was subscribed to, so I felt like pushing his face through a wall after seeing his amused expression when he finished talking to Leyla.

The only reason Nitas and I were here was because we were trying to discover more about the circulation of Ambrosia in Ashrior. The Undercity's nightlife was the epicenter of illegal trade, and if there were any traces of the drug, they would be found here. Nitas had told me he would check out other, darker clubs, where they only let in Daemons and Sanguis. This was not that kind of club, though.

"Talking to the Prime *and* the Supreme—in one night, no less. I'm a lucky girl."

I met Leyla's gaze, her expression filled with the same sarcasm as her voice, but there was an edge to it. Her eyes darted through the club as if searching for something.

"Pay him no mind."

She cocked her head. "Pretty hard to do, you know? He's one of the most powerful people in Ashar. Not someone you just ignore."

Leyla looked away, lowering her eyelids, and a sliver of illuminated irises peeked through dark lashes, making her usual color pop even more. The woman was a mystery, but she was one I'd like to solve.

"What's the Prime of Ashar doing here anyway?" she asked, her voice low and husky, those piercing green eyes assessing me.

"I'm off the clock," I said. "Just a regular Angeli enjoying his night out."

She licked her lips, rolling her shoulders. The silver dress she wore hugged her in all the right places, showing just enough to leave you wanting more. "I don't think that's how it works."

I stepped closer, forcing her chin to rise. "It works how I say it works."

"Right… *Prime.*"

I bellowed a laugh. Her Daemon side came out more down here than it had in Shard City. One second, she seemed uninterested, and at other times, she seemed downright seducing. I didn't know how to figure her out. There was more to her than what met the eye, but what met the eye was fucking good.

Another person called her name, and she turned around. Her friend, Lodana Fivaldor, daughter of well-known socialite Evelyn Fivaldor, was sitting at a table with one of Nitas' watchdogs. She had him smiling at her as she sat on his lap. He was supposed to be vigilant for any transactions, but the guy was wound so tightly around her fingers that he didn't notice anything but the Ethereal.

She was waving over with a wide smile. "Come sit!" Though the music was still loud, my warped layer of protection allowed me to adjust the sound to my preferences.

Leyla angled her head towards me, pursing her lips. She tilted her chin a notch and raised her brow in a silent question, though it seemed more like a dare. In response, I opened my palm in a gesture for her to lead the way. My shoulder brushed hers as I sat down next to her. The electric current between us was unmistakable. It charged the air and made my heart beat faster.

It made me feel alive.

She kept an impenetrable composure as she looked at me, but the question in her eyes reflected mine. Both of us were treading water, neither of us crossing the line.

And yet…

I let her play her game for now. My patience would eventually wear thin. There was only so much time and space I could give her before I would give her a choice to move this any further or not.

Lodana Fivaldor looked at Leyla with a gleeful expression and waved her arm around the room. "Fun, right?"

"It's definitely… something," she answered with a smirk, but Lodana was distracted by the nonsense the Daemon whispered into her ears. Leyla chuckled, but I leveled a stern look at him. When he noticed my expression, he straightened a little.

I adjusted my legs underneath the table, brushing her knee, and she quickly pulled it back. A smile stretched my lips. The surge of power I felt when her pupils dilated as I recaptured her attention exhilarated me. I leaned back, bathing in that little triumph as she glanced away. This game of back-and-forth she was playing wasn't one I would lose. "What's wrong?" I asked, my voice low and teasing. "Don't like the way I'm looking at you?"

She shifted in her seat, and I could nearly see the thoughts racing through her head. "I don't like people looking at all."

"Perhaps," I drawled, "you should learn how to stop caring." My tone was soft, daring her to show her true colors.

For some reason, she didn't want to hand over any control. The women I dated usually wanted me to take the first steps and be in control. They had all preferred me to take the lead... Even—

"Does it hurt?" She pointed to my wings, and I snapped back to the present moment. "To sit with them?"

I turned my head to take in the sight of my golden wings, surprised by her random question. "No. They're very flexible. If they weren't, harsh winds would snap them in half before we even took flight." They had ample room to drape over the backseat, but I felt some of my feathers more than others as I leaned back in my seat. Angel wings had a sensitive nervous system interconnecting every feather. Tucking them in merely made them less prone to touch.

Leyla furrowed her brow. "So, it isn't uncomfortable?" She seemed unconvinced. "At all?"

"Does it look uncomfortable?"

"A little."

I shrugged. "It's all I've ever known."

Leyla nodded as her gaze lingered on my wings, examining the golden feathers.

"Want to touch them?"

A hundred years ago, I might as well have asked her if she wanted to sleep with me. But times changed, and so did people.

She bit her lip, shifting her weight in her seat, eyes locking with mine. I could see a spark of curiosity in them as she hesitated, but I was suddenly desperate for her touch. "Many people do."

Her lips formed a thin line. "They touch them?" A waitress delivered some drinks, and Leyla took one, pushing it closer to her on the table.

I chuckled, trying to picture anyone attempting to touch my wings. You didn't come near an Angeli's wings without their consent—least of all, an archangel's. It was a very private and intimate thing, saved for loved ones. "They want to, I mean."

"And you let them?" She stared at me like she couldn't picture it.

My chest rumbled with laughter. "Of course not, Leyla."

Her mouth twisted in a grimace as her fingertips slowly traced the rim of the glass. The serpent tattoo on her arm curled as she moved.

"But you may touch them if you want," I said. "This one time."

Leyla's green eyes took in the wing beside her again before looking back into the club at the crowd below and surrounding us. She swallowed. "People will see."

That was the whole point. If there were any effective way to mark my territory, this would be it. "So?"

"Don't you care about your reputation?"

"Do *you* care about my reputation?" I asked. I was playing dirty. "If I'd care, I wouldn't bother leaving the house."

Folding her lips in contemplation, her curiosity won out, and she reached out a hand, albeit tentatively. She let her fingers graze the feathers on the edge of the wing closest to her. Her throat bobbed.

Shivers erupted over my back as her featherlight touches moved over me. I resisted the urge to close my eyes. As her hand threatened to go higher, I clasped my hand over hers. Those vibrant eyes looked up at me as I guided her hand back down over the wing instead and let her feel the warmth and strength that radiated from them.

"They're so soft," she said, as if it surprised her.

"They are."

She pulled back her hand and looked at it, amazed. "Not one shimmer."

I smirked and pictured myself sprawled in my bed, with her between my arms, my wings wrapped around us like a cocoon.

Leyla closed her hand into a fist, and we held each other's gaze, neither of us speaking. I could only guess her thoughts.

My phone buzzed, interrupting the moment. She cleared her throat and averted her gaze. I took it from my pocket, glancing at the text.

N.S.: *I have a lead.*

"Everything okay?" Leyla asked.

I ran my tongue over my teeth. "I need to go."

A slight smile tugged at her lips. "Work, huh?"

"Something like that." The hand holding my phone drifted back to my breast pocket, but I halted the movement. "Can I have your number?"

Leyla's eyelashes fluttered as she blinked in surprise—thick, dark, and captivating. Her lips parted. "Okay."

I handed her the phone, watching intently as she put in her number with those slender fingers. The screen lit up her face and dulled the vibrancy of her eyes a little. A few moments later, her contact information was saved.

I pushed my chair back and rose from the table. "Alright," I said. "Until next time."

The promise was deliberate.

She nodded and gestured to her friend, Lodana, was still making small talk with the Daemon. "We'll be at the gala." The corners of her lips curled up and sent my mind spinning, imagining several scenarios.

"*Good.*" I dipped my chin and winked before turning on my heel and walking away from her.

I had to. Otherwise, I would never leave. Coaxing reactions from her was thrilling, but having her full attention had me downright addicted. Leyla stirred a side of me I had kept firmly behind lock and key, and it was desperate to come out.

We had danced this dance long enough. It was about time I took this somewhere.

CHAPTER TWENTY-TWO

Leyla

As a child, I was completely captivated by the Pisces Domain. They had the ability to shapeshift and explore the entire sea, with most of their domain being underwater. It seemed like such freedom, especially for someone who couldn't go outside alone and lived underground. And perhaps Colberto Manvil, one of the hottest movie actors at the time who was a Pisces, had fueled my dreams of having fins.

I had begged my father to take me to the domain, but he didn't like being out in public like that, so he instead took me to one of Ashrior's caves with a private natural spring that posed as a pool. There had been no one there that day, and the water was cold, but he had allowed me to stay there for as long as I wanted, which turned out to be all day. My father stayed with me, teaching me how to swim while telling me all he knew about the Pisces Domain. Even though I quickly moved past my Pisces phase, it was still one of my favorite days.

Since then, I have visited the domain dozens of times, mainly with Dana because she loves their fashion and also dated a Pisces or two. It had been a while since my last visit, and my dreams of living there as a child, marrying a Pisces—preferably the gorgeous movie star Colberto—had long gone out the window. But *my*, it was breathtaking every single time.

The metal columns supporting the foundation against the seawall reflected a coppery hue and held up the large glass windows looking out into the sea. Fish were swimming by, and if you looked closely, you could even spot some larger gleaming metallic fins that belonged to a Pisces. I had never seen a Pisces transform in real life, but I had once looked it up online and had been equally disturbed and interested as their legs wove together and turned scaly.

"He was obviously interested in you at the team presentation, but you didn't tell me *how* interested. He's fucking into you, Ley! Like knee-deep into you. Why do you keep brushing it off like it's nothing?"

"Because it isn't." The Archangel and I had quickly become Dana's favorite topic of conversation, and I was getting worse at trying to divert her attention. I didn't want to talk about it because I didn't want to be forced to lie to her, which meant I had to keep firmly behind my preset boundary.

"I don't believe you," she said, raising her voice. "Prime Venetia—"

I shushed her. People were looking our way, and the last thing I needed was some magazine spreading rumors to the mix. Quieter this time, she said, "Prime Venetia being into you, *not a big deal?*"

"By the light, Dana."

Before she could say anything else, Dana had stopped walking. "Fuck."

I turned my head to my best friend and saw that she was frozen in place. "What is it?" I asked, following her gaze.

"My mother," she bit out with effort. Her eyes were shooting daggers, and her hands clenched at her sides. The woman in question hadn't noticed us yet, but I spotted her immediately. She was a well-known socialite who pushed conservative ideologies. My first time coming home with Dana had made an unforgettable impression on me. I didn't have to see the Ethereal often to recognize her. No matter how regularly she changed her hairstyles or facial features, the sneer on her stony face remained the same.

A daughter befriending anyone from the Undercity was no daughter of hers—that was as much as she'd implied the moment she met me.

You know better than to mingle with Daemons, Lodana.

Dana had turned to me and said: *Feel free to ignore my mother, she's used to it from father, anyway.*

I had barely retained a startled gasp.

Declining an arranged marriage at nineteen to a stuck-up prick from the Ethereal Domain had finally severed the ties between mother and daughter irrevocably. Too much had happened over the years. Dana's mother had done her best to make her daughter feel as miserable as she did herself, and Dana would not succumb to a life like that. On the day she left her childhood home for good, we moved into our college dorms and made a pinky promise to stick together. We would be in each other's corner, having each other's back—*always.*

I hooked my arm through Dana's and tried to get her to move, but then the Ethereal we wanted to avoid noticed us, and her jaw set. She had her hair in long, brown waves and looked only slightly older than us. Ethereals aged slowly, so it was usual for them to look eternally young. The woman licked her lips, raised her brows as high as possible without creasing her forehead, and approached us. She hadn't yet looked at me, laser-focused on her daughter. Her steps were careful but deliberate, the high heels click-clacking on the marble floor, and her white-knuckled hands clutched around the shopping bags she carried.

Dana said nothing, though her stance spoke of contempt. If I were Evelyn, I wouldn't have dared come up to her in this state. You didn't want to be on Dana's wrong side.

"Lodana," her mother said stiffly as she stopped in front of us.

Dana nodded curtly. "Evelyn." It had been a long time since she had called her 'mother' or referred to her as such.

The woman swallowed. "How are you?"

I couldn't tell if the question was sincere or not. The rest of her seemed entirely unbothered, face carefully void of emotions, though the eyes betrayed her. They roamed over her daughter, and Evelyn blinked more than once, more than she had done the entire culmination of moments I'd ever seen her.

"You remember Leyla, right?" Dana asked instead with a voice like crunching ice.

Evelyn Fivaldor nodded, but the only recognition she gave me was a twitch of her eyes, moving them to me and back to Dana again. I kept my face neutral, no longer feeling anger at the blatant dismissal. I did not care about her at all.

"I'm shopping," she said suddenly, answering a question neither of us had asked. Evelyn clutched her belly, a clear outline visible beneath her lilac coat. "I was in need of some new clothes that would fit me better."

Dana's body went rigid beside me, her gaze pointed at the swell underneath her mother's hand in disbelief. "You're pregnant?" she ground out between clenched teeth, the shock on her face quickly turning to rage. A hiss of venom escaped her lips. "Fucking up with one kid wasn't enough?"

"I think we need to go," I jumped in. "We're already late for our appointment." Evelyn latched her eyes onto mine, disdain seeping through the cracks of her facade. "Goodbye, Mrs. Fivaldor," I said and dragged a seething Dana away from her with effort.

We walked through the busy halls of the Pisces Domain, passing rows of stone pillars and splashing fountains, when she finally exploded. "How *dare* she!"

"She wanted to rattle you, Dana, you know that. It's what she does," I said calmly.

Dana fumed, her nostrils flaring. Rage rolled off my friend in violent waves. "They're going to put another child through that wretched childhood I endured?"

"Nothing to do about that now," I said.

She stopped walking abruptly, grabbing my arms. "That baby will be my brother or sister, Leyla!" Her eyes flashed with panic. "I need to do something about that."

I swallowed, but I nodded, taking her hands in mine and squeezing them. "We'll do something together when they get here," I promised her. "But not now. Now we're going shopping."

"I swear you're going to melt on the spot," Dana exclaimed from inside her stall, and I chuckled in response. "I would happily die wearing it."

She had calmed down a bit after our encounter with her mother. Being surrounded by clothes was her comfort zone.

It made her happy.

The whole boutique had items to sell a limb for—all worthy of being worn by royalty. When the shop assistant walked up to Dana's stall with more options in her size, I took my phone from my pocket and read the text Dominic had sent me. He had been texting me since we parted ways at the club last night, and I had done a double-take when I read his first message.

Considering he was one of the most famous people in Ashar, our entire conversation was almost normal. There was the occasional back-and-forth flirting, but significantly less than I'd expected from him. Discovering the man had depth was slightly disappointing to me. It made me enjoy the conversation a little too much.

I constantly reminded myself of Bohrod for that exact reason. Swallowing, I pushed the thought away and turned my attention back to my phone.

Me: *Hard at work again today?*

Dominic: *It never ends, as you well know. You?*

Me: *I have to, shamefully, admit I'm not. Dana and I are shopping for the gala.*

"Tada!" Dana walked out of the fitting room, arms splayed wide. She wore an olive green taffeta dress with a tight bodice resembling a corset. It fanned out into a long, wide-flowing skirt. The fabric appeared slightly wrinkled, but it accentuated the bright pink sheen, perfectly matching her hair color.

I smiled. "That is, without a doubt, your dress."

Dana regarded herself in the hundred eighty-degree mirrors and nodded. "It is indeed."

"You'll be the belle of the ball," I said with an accent, bowing my head at her.

She was a natural beauty with a small, upturned nose and delicate features. Dana pressed her hands into her skirt as she turned around. "Now you try on the dress I picked out for you. It's the entire reason we're even here."

"You picked out a dress for me?"

"Oh yes," she said, deadly serious—as always when it came to fashion. "I saw it in a magazine the other day, from two decades ago, and I immediately pictured you in it. I called around to see if any of the stores had a vintage piece, and here they had one left in your exact size."

The shop assistant strode over to us with a clothing bag swung over her arm. She gave me a friendly smile before hanging the cover into an empty dressing room, gesturing for me to enter.

"I also noticed a beautiful—" *simple, classy, not too remarkable* "—dress at the entrance," I told Dana.

"All black?" she guessed.

I shrugged. "So what?"

She rolled her eyes. "*Ba-ba-boring.* You're too predictable, Ley. I promise you, this dress will blow your mind—as well as the Archangel's."

Stepping into the stall, I said, "I'll try it on, if only to please you."

"Whatever. You'll thank me later."

I opened the bag, took out the dress and gloves, and hung them on the clothing rack.

If Dana's dress had been hot, then this one was scorching. Wearing it should be illegal. It looked like one ticket straight to hell because this piece was made to sin. I had the chance to try it on and wear it, and I couldn't help myself. Dana had been right.

I stepped into the garment, being careful with the delicate fabric. It fit me like a glove, clinging to every curve and angle of my figure, stopping just below the calves in a plume of black feathery tassels that caressed the skin of my bare ankles. It began with the same, though smaller, feathers on the swell of my breasts, accentuating the comfortable yet tight top. The black body melted from orange into a fiery red sprinkled with different shades of yellow and gold.

It was the spitting image of a falling star.

When I took out my phone to take a picture so I could look back on it whenever I wanted—or make it my screensaver, *who knew*—I noticed Dominic's new text.

Dominic: *How's the shopping coming along? Any success?*

I began to smile but quickly stopped, looking at the dress before texting back.

Me: *Who's asking?*

He answered a couple seconds later.

Dominic: *A man that should be focusing on his meeting.*

Me: *Then don't tell him I found the perfect outfit for the gala.*

Dominic: *Too late. He's thoroughly distracted.*

I grinned, putting on the black see-through gloves that stopped at my upper arm and took a photo of the black plumes above my breasts. I sent it to him with my hand covering my chest to block out any colors.

"Are you in your dress yet?" Dana's voice came from the other side of the door.

I pushed against the wall, righting myself. "Yes." My voice was hoarse from disuse. "I'm coming."

Putting away my phone and brushing my hands through my hair, I counted to ten and pushed open the stall.

Dana applauded in excitement. "Ha! I knew it. I'm a

genius!"

"You are," I admitted, grinning at her. "Ever thought about starting for yourself?"

She stuck out her tongue as I stepped back into the stall, still laughing, and checked Dominic's reply.

Dominic: *I hope you know what you just started, Leyla.*

CHAPTER TWENTY-THREE

Dominic

The Pisces Domain was a peculiar place. Only a third of the domain was visible above water; the structure was built like a fortress at the sea's edge and continued underwater, with interconnecting structures. Pisces loved the water like a second home. They belonged in the seas as I belonged in the sky. So, naturally, each floor had its own sea entry points, equipped with air-lock chambers that would fill with water when someone wanted to enter, and drain afterward.

Being the Prime of the city, I had to make periodic visits to all domains, but this one always filled me with dread. I disliked being underground in Ashrior but *hated* being in a place where I couldn't even see the sky. It was unnatural—it made me feel like a caged bird. The sensation heightened with each level I went down until I was at the bottom, where the higher Pisces officials were located. My ears began to ring from the depth pressure at this level. Barely any sunlight reached here. The air grew colder, and the decorations more elaborate. It would be charming if not for the murky, dark green water visible through the large glass panels.

Paplos' office was filled with paintings of the sea throughout the different seasons—his art the only bearable thing about the domain. I tried to focus on my favorite, of water reflecting the falling stars of fall reborn, but near the end of the meeting, I was getting a little too lightheaded.

I needed fresh oxygen.

With relief and some black and white spots dancing in my vision, I thanked Paplos and pressed the elevator button to get going. I entered, leaning against the side, closing my eyes to focus on breathing and regain my bearings in the small space. The elevator climbed at an excruciatingly slow pace. With every few levels up, more and more Pisces entered the elevator, saying things I responded to with incoherent grunts. Some people inside even frowned at me as if I owed them pleasantries.

When the elevator stopped for the eighth time, I couldn't stand it anymore and barged outside, shouldering my way out of the elevator. The floor was brightly lit, with crisper air and less pressure. I was close to the surface. It had to be one of the higher floors, *thank the light.*

I closed my eyes and rubbed my brow to soothe the aching that had been building there. Sounds flooded my ears. It was especially busy in the Pisces domain today. I was glad I wouldn't need to return here for another few months. Maybe asking Paplos to meet somewhere higher above the ground would be a good idea. The depths never treated me well, even after coming here for decades.

"Dominic?"

I turned around to the sound of the familiar voice, and— Leyla? The sight of her surprised expression had me stunned for a moment.

"Are you alright?" she asked, looking at me as she walked closer.

I smoothened my light grey suit jacket and forced a smile on my face, though that wasn't so hard with her as the recipient. I cleared my throat. "Being below sea level messes with me."

"Ah, yes," she said, looking at the large glass panels separating us from the water. Then her eyes flicked back to mine. "You were born for the sky."

The way she said it set off a fuse inside my brain, and I stared at her, unblinking. Leyla's lips parted, looking just as startled by her own comment as I was. "You didn't mention you were in the Pisces domain," I said instead, gripping my neck.

She raised an eyebrow. "Neither did you."

"Yes, well." I swallowed. "If I had known..." But alas, here we were, meeting again, by *coincidence* and off schedule.

She cleared her throat and angled her head to her friend, Lodana Fivaldor—who, even though her fuchsia hair was hard to miss, I only now noticed. Her arms were crossed in front of her chest, fingers tapping, and she waved at me with a knowing smirk.

My eyes moved to the bag in Leyla's hand. "You bought it?"

"I did." Leyla looked again at Lodana. "She dragged me here, had the perfect dress picked out and everything."

The Ethereal in question inched closer, looking only at me. "And what a good deed that was. She looks smoking in it, if I do say so myself." I laughed as Leyla rolled her eyes and nudged her friend with her elbow. "You'll see." Lodana winked at me before leaving me and Leyla alone again.

"Ignore her," she said, echoing what I had said about Nitas, and her answering smirk was just for me. We were drawing attention. I watched Leyla grow aware of the stares, shooting glares left and right. Part of me respected how she didn't want to be seen with me, but the other part wanted to know why the hell *not*.

"I'm looking forward to it."

Those emerald green eyes shot back to mine. "What?" she asked distractedly.

"Seeing you in that dress." *To peel it off her.*

Her lips parted, blood rushing to her cheeks again. She looked back at her friend scrolling on her phone a few paces away, clearly a little uneasy, before turning back to me. "I think we should go. I may not be born for the sky, but I'm definitely not born for the water either."

I put my hands in my pockets. "I will let you go then."

"Yes," Leyla agreed, but a second later, neither of us had moved. She bit her cheek, trying to hide a smile, before saying goodbye and walking over to her friend. I watched her go all the way up the stairs. She quickly glanced back at me at the top, and the small gesture made me ruffle my feathers like a pleased fucking dog.

As I stepped out of the tall entrance of the Pisces Domain minutes later, a gust of wind caressed my wings. I inhaled deeply, taking in the salty scent of the fresh sea air—realizing that for a moment inside, being close to Leyla, I'd almost forgotten I'd still been underwater.

Leyla drew me in and captivated me with her mere presence—this afternoon and every other time we met proved it. I wanted to learn more about her, but nothing could be found, and all she handed me were mere scraps. If I was taking this somewhere, I needed to know more about her before I did.

After the team presentation, I had tasked Fredo to do a background check. It was the bare minimum I did before considering dating someone, but with Leyla, even that had brought me next to nothing. All he'd found was her home address and some Ashrior-based company she used to work for that I'd never heard of. I knew she worked for someone who had her going to an auction to buy art, but that was all I had to go by. There wasn't any public record of relatives or family. Nothing. It certainly raised alarm bells, but the desire to know drowned them out.

I had let it rest for a day. *It didn't matter; I was a great people reader*—and all that bullshit. But the previous night had spurred me on to hire a professional to investigate Leyla the moment I left. It was more like a deeper background check. Just in case. To be sure. I had a hard time trusting people, with good reason, and after meeting her in the Pisces Domain today, I wanted it all to move the fuck along.

A long-abandoned part of my brain had become obsessed with her. No one had a life that empty. Leyla was deliberately keeping her past hidden, or at least parts of it.

She was a riddle I wanted to solve.

When I got home after work, the private investigator sent me a clip of Leyla walking the streets late last night. He'd already sent me a folder with diplomas, information, fines, and other things he could find on her. Nothing had surprised me except for the video. I didn't know he would have someone film her like a godsdamned stalker, but here she was, crossing the streets like it was a normal thing to do alone at night.

I watched her every move as she walked down the pavement, a surge of protectiveness washing over me as she paused in front of some hunched figures in dark corners, doing... What on earth was she doing?

As I kept watching, I slowly understood. The times the homeless people got a glimpse of her, they shrunk back at the sight of her eyes. Daemons were regarded as predators along with the Sanguis, so it wasn't anything new. But watching her give them things—coins, by the looks of it—made my gut clench.

Why was Leyla out there at night? She was alone the entire time, but nothing seemed to faze her. She didn't seem scared at all. Her behavior surprised me. Not that she gave the impression of being uncaring. I hadn't thought of her as a person who concerned herself with other's problems at all. It had nothing to do with her being a Daemon—it was the type of people she surrounded herself with, the clubbing, the way she dressed.

But her actions revealed a side that I had not seen at first.

Shard City at night wasn't a place for anyone to walk alone. I watched as she passed a few blocks and eventually reached her home. The video ended. Despite my confusion about her roaming the city alone at night, I also felt a rush of something else.

Why do you assume I want anything?

Maybe she had been speaking the truth, after all.

CHAPTER TWENTY-FOUR

Leyla

Zade rang me for the second time that night. I looked at my phone as it buzzed. He rarely called—even when we'd been on good terms. I ignored it again, continuing to eat, but still read his text as it flashed on my screen.

Z: *Pick up, Leyla.*

When his number flashed on my screen for the third time, I rolled my eyes. "What?"

"I just spoke to Ulverin, and there's something you should know."

"Business. Of course. I should've known."

Zade clucked his tongue on the other line. "Someone has been following you."

I slowly chewed the last few bites of my dinner and placed my fork on the table. My gaze focused on the far wall. "Isn't there always?"

The Daemon on the other line groaned. "It was a private investigator."

I froze. "How do you know?" I gathered my plate and

brought it to the counter.

"She wasn't as stealthy as she believed herself to be. The Archangel hired her."

My eyes widened, and my body shook with simmering anger as I realized what he was saying. I put down my glass with a little too much force, the sound ringing through the small kitchen. "What?" Dominic had someone following me?

"Apparently you've piqued his interest," Zade said.

"So it seems," I bit out, trying to regulate my breathing.

"You got to work on getting him to trust you."

"Well, thanks for transferring the message properly and with a bow. Your boss must be proud. Bye now."

"*Fucking light.*" A crash sounded on the other end of the line. "Just be careful around him, alright? You hear me, Ley?"

"What's it to you?"

"Don't be so fucking stubborn. You know I'm looking out for you." He sighed. "And stop giving out money to those people again. It's like giving our product away for free."

"Whatever." I ended the call. Heat crawled up my cheeks. Having someone following me on my father's orders was one thing, but *Dominic*? Hell no.

That was not the way this game would be played.

I was crazy for going to Ashtior at this time—absolutely out of my mind as I haphazardly threw on a coat and some gloves before barging out of my front door and taking an aircab. But a handful of things were supposed to be conveyed face to face, my privacy being one of them. I knew I had no right to be this pissed, but I couldn't let it slide. I had to stop this before he dug too deep.

As I approached Dominic's house, I felt the thrill of anticipation. I had never been to his home and rarely visited Ashtior at all. Barging outside and straight into an aircab without thinking left me no room to go back into my apartment and look up his address in the folder, but apparently, everyone knew where the Archangel lived. One search online had gotten me the full address.

I tried very hard not to be captivated by the grandeur of his home, but failed. I'd grown up in an estate, but Ashtior was a world away from the Undercity. His gates were made of wrought iron, elaborately designed, and polished to a fine sheen. Two marble statues guarded the entranceway, their faces stern and unyielding. The perfectly laid cobblestone path of the driveway had grass joints. It screamed of generational wealth, though I had no idea if the man actually came from money.

I couldn't let myself be distracted. I was supposed to do a job—supposed not to care whether Dominic Venetia sent someone to spy on me other than that it could blow my cover. And yet, I couldn't shake the indignation, which was more than a little ironic.

His enormous front door had a doorknocker, but I opted to beat the wood with my gloved fist, waiting for someone to answer. An older Angeli opened the door, her hair almost as white as her wings. If she was surprised to see me, a stranger, she didn't show it.

"Hello, can I help you?" she asked, her voice warm. The lines on her face told me she had seen much during her lifetime.

I opened my mouth and closed it again like a fish on dry land. I cleared my throat. "I'm here to see Dominic." The hour was late, but the Angeli nodded and said, "Of course, come in."

My mind raced. I hesitated on the threshold. "No need to know who I am?"

She smiled, even though my question had been blunt. "If you made it this far to the door, Dominic would want you to enter."

That caught me off guard. I hadn't felt any wards when I entered his grounds, but my anger might have clouded my senses.

He trusted me?

What a conflicting revelation.

I caught the older Angeli glancing at me. "I'm Amy, by the way. The housekeeper."

"Leyla." Not sure what to say, I awkwardly kept it to that.

Amy nodded. "I'll tell him you're here if he doesn't already know. Please don't hesitate to let me know if you need anything." She gestured to the comfortable-looking sofa before disappearing through another door.

I ran a hand over the seat and marveled at the soft fabric before sitting down, looking around the large living room with a second floor, which split the enormous space in half. The house was a mix of two worlds; the stairs, balustrades, and furniture were all modern, yet the painted ceiling and carved walls gave the house an old feel. It stemmed from the Golden Age, no doubt. I distracted myself by taking in all the details, but the longer I sat there, the more my mind spun with possibilities unraveling in front of me.

Eventually, the large doors overlooking the gardens opened, and a windblown Dominic strolled into the house, taking a gush of chill wind with him. He buttoned his suit jacket as he focused on me and closed the doors. It was clear he had flown here. A curl had escaped from his bound-back hair, and he brushed it behind his ear with a cocky smile, moving with confidence and grace. Every bit the Archangel.

"Leyla," he said. "What a pleasant surprise."

I rose from the couch, suddenly restless after I had waited in silence for what felt like too fucking long. "Why do you have someone following me?"

To his credit, he didn't deny it. "Define following." He gestured back to the couch, but I kept standing as he sat down anyway and crossed his long legs.

It irritated the living hell out of me. "Did you order someone to investigate me?"

He flexed his fingers. "You have to understand I don't just let everyone into my life on a whim."

That had my mind going in all kinds of conflicted places. "So you resort to stalking? Have I passed your entry requirements, then? Did I pass the fucking test?"

"Don't be ridiculous."

"Don't fucking gaslight me." My nostrils flared. "Why not ask me directly like a normal person?"

He still didn't apologize or even look remorseful but said on a softer note, "People have the tendency to lie in my face when there's something they want."

"I already told you." *It's you who keeps approaching me.*

"So you did," he said. His gaze was inquisitive. "I won't apologize for being cautious. I had never seen you before in my life. Trust me, I would have remembered. And now, *suddenly*, you are everywhere." Dominic's eyes pierced mine. "How did you find out?"

Goosebumps covered my entire body, and nausea seemed

to swirl through my stomach. He had valid reasons to be cautious. "Does it matter?"

His eye ticked, but before he could answer, Amy, the housekeeper, decided to re-enter the room, her face lighting up as she noticed Dominic. She brought a tray full of treats with her, and I didn't have the nerve to tell her I was only there for a brief visit, so I dropped down on the couch next to Dominic.

The way he treated her caught my attention. Amy was polite and warm, but Dominic was equally as respectful and kind. They addressed each other by their first names. He thanked her for the tray and offered her the rest of the night off, obviously making sure she was well taken care of. I couldn't help but compare him to my father, who had never treated his staff with this level of... familiarity.

When she left, Dominic's gaze hardened a little. "You have no business going out so late at night."

"Excuse me?" I shot back, stirring my tea aggressively with the little golden spoon. It was as if he'd brushed away our previous conversation and started over from a different angle.

Something flashed in his eyes. "The streets are not safe right now, Leyla. This is not the time to fuck around with people like that. There's a reason crime rates have risen exponentially."

"I know!" I shocked myself by saying. "That's why I want to help." It was the first time I had raised my voice at him—at anyone, in a long time—and I immediately understood my mistake. I was just so tired of people talking down to me.

"What do you mean, you know?"

I recovered quickly. "I may live in Shard City, but I'm not naïve. I'm aware of some stuff that goes on in Ashrior."

"Specifically?"

"That there's a new drug." Ambrosia's chaos was evident to those who knew what to watch out for. It had been creating turmoil wherever it went.

He appraised me before saying, "News travels fast then." And I swallowed my relief.

"The drug does, too. It was offered to me and Dana at a club some weeks ago. We passed on it, but some other guy ended up taking it. He had a bad trip and died."

Dominic cursed. "At *Isla Dela*? You were there that night?"

I nodded.

"Did anyone hurt you?"

"No."

"Try to keep away from those clubs, okay? It's likely more of those incidents will occur."

I nodded and moved my arm to brush a long strand of hair over my shoulder. Dominic's eyes caught on the movement, locking on my skin, eyes narrowing a little.

I froze my movement as he gestured his head toward my arm. "Can I see?" he asked, and I nodded. Dominic took hold of my arm and moved closer, the sofa dipping lower from his weight. I had to tighten my core to keep sitting upright. He bowed his head, moving up my sleeve to reveal more of the serpent tattoo coiling around my arm, and brushed a finger over it.

"It's beautiful."

Carefully, I suppressed a shiver and pulled back my arm from his grip. "Do you have any?"

He turned his head my way, that curl once again loose, hanging in front of his eyes. "Tattoos?"

I nodded.

"I do."

"Of what?"

Dominic's eyes turned distant, and he retreated, looking out into the night through the windows. "Old angelic mourning bands."

Angelic mourning bands? "I've never heard of them." But I could guess what they were.

He straightened his back, opening a button of his white blouse with deft fingers. His large hand curled around the fabric and pulled it down an inch, showing black markings that curled low beneath his neck. "They go from my neck to my upper legs, winding around my left, symbolling the forever tie you have with a person who has passed."

"Who did you lose?" My voice had turned quieter. I knew he had lost his parents.

He looked anywhere but to me. Seemingly lost for words, Dominic rubbed his jaw. But finally, he responded.

"My mate."

My face moved sharply to his, eyes widening. I pushed down the turmoil building within me. I clenched and unclenched my hands. Mate? He had lost his *mate*? Dominic Venetia, Archangel and Prime of Ashar, had lost the love of his life. Why wasn't that public knowledge?

"I'm…" I croaked.

With a sinister twitch of his lips, he closed the button again and put on the suit jacket he had draped over the couch. I lay a hand on his arm, stopping his movements. "I'm sorry for your loss."

"It happened a long time ago."

"That doesn't make it any less painful."

My words were sincere.

His golden brown eyes found mine as he finished buttoning his shirt. Vulnerable—he looked so vulnerable in that moment that it filled me with sorrow. "You're right, it doesn't."

I squeezed his arm as his throat moved.

There was a moment between us, and I could have sworn it was one of understanding.

A dangerous thing.

"You should go home," Dominic said when the moment stretched too long. He rubbed his hands over his face and inhaled deeply.

Foreign refusal was on my tongue, but I caught myself. "I think you're right."

His eyes flicked up and down my body, an indecipherable expression on his face. "I will take you."

"No, thank you. I'll take an aircab."

The corner of his mouth raised. "You're not serious."

"No need to make it sound so dirty." I smirked. "It's fine, really."

"Why? Afraid to fly?"

"I told you I'm not born for the sky, and I meant it."

"How could you know? Have you been there?"

A jolt went through my body. "I'm afraid of heights," I confessed.

"No." He was shaking his head in clear dismissal. "You're afraid of falling—but I won't let you fall, Leyla."

Goosebumps lined my arms in a phantom caress. I held his gaze for a long moment, getting lost in those swirling depths. There was so much to see in them—that he let me see. "Next time," he said, breaking the silence, his voice a little hoarse. "You'll let me fly you."

I stood. "We will see about that."

In the end, Dominic got me a private cab to dock in front of his gate. This one was smaller than most, bringing people closer to home instead of the usual stations. He spoke with the pilot before walking to one of the doors and opening it for me. He held out a hand, and although I could easily climb in by myself, I accepted his help—ever the chivalrous Archangel.

When I sat down, Dominic visibly hesitated before letting go of my hand, his thumb brushing over my fingers as he let go. He looked into my eyes and beyond, straight into my soul. "Can I trust you, Leyla?"

I stopped breathing. Everything about him had heightened. I was painfully aware of the shimmering gold of his wings, the emotions lingering on his face, the whisper of a promise in his eyes. There wasn't a hint of humor in my reply, which came automatically. "Yes."

My expression must have looked as grave as I felt, because he nodded, his gaze dipping to my lips before slowly coming back up, peeling away my defenses layer by layer. "Sleep well."

I held his gaze with matching intensity, the tension building between us. "You too."

Dominic closed the door and signaled for the pilot to go by knocking on the roof. I turned around in the cab, looking back through the rear window as we went. Dominic put his hands in his pockets and stared into the sky. The look on his face was void, fit for a painting that portrayed feelings so complex his expression seemed utterly blank.

Staring at him until he disappeared from view, I couldn't help but feel as if I now shouldered some of his loss. And I had no right to—none whatsoever. I was already too busy bearing the weight of the suffering I was going to cause him.

I leaned back in the seat, staring out the window at the flickering stars. Over the course of a few weeks, my perception of Dominic Venetia had altered dramatically. All while I'd been holding a grudge against him for years.

And despite my best efforts to avoid it, I found myself trapped in a web of lies of my own making.

CHAPTER TWENTY-FIVE

Leyla

I felt like an avalanche, tumbling down a steep slope with no control over how fast I moved. My feelings, thoughts, and actions were all one big, confusing jumble.

Can I trust you, Leyla?

He couldn't. I had felt the truth of it deep down. And not for the first time did I long for things to be different. With him, with Dana... My whole life seemed fabricated, and the lies were getting threadbare and worn out.

Entering my home, I swung the door closed, threw my key on the tray next to it, and looked at myself in the mirror above it. My cheeks were flushed, and my eyes sparkled with something that shouldn't be in them. I looked away. Couldn't stomach the sight right now.

I was in way over my head. Things were getting serious. Stabbing Prime Venetia in the back had been on the menu since we first met, but seeing how he looked at me... I would twist the knife lodged in him, and it would fucking hurt.

Suddenly, everything about it felt wrong.

My stomach twisted into a tight knot as I braced myself for the inevitable, a million 'what-ifs' clouding my thoughts and holding me captive. All I could do was grip onto what shreds of hope remained and prepare for the worst. It was only a matter of time before reality caught up with me.

I removed the leftover makeup from my face and changed into more comfortable clothes. But instead of lying down in bed, I sat on the couch and put on some bullshit reality programs. There was no way I could sleep yet. I was too restless.

I had seen the true depth beneath his public persona. Imagining the things he had gone through before becoming the Archangel of Ashar... He'd had a life, a future, dreams—someone to live them out with. A mate whom he lost so early in his life. I didn't know how he'd lost her or who she was, but I found myself wanting to know.

Jealous of a dead woman. How pathetic.

I had even tried searching for her online on my way home, but she was never mentioned. No one had even heard so much as a rumor.

Unlocking my phone again, I looked at the picture I had found during my search. I rested my head on a cushion, tracing his golden wings that were on full display in the photo as he landed somewhere in Shard City. I didn't know if I would ever stop being awed by the vastness of his wings. The image came from an article about his dating life. Apparently, it was common knowledge Angeli were peculiar about their wings. My chest heated as I read how he let nobody close to his wings. Not even his lovers.

A journalist wrote: *The lucky woman who will change his ways must be incredibly rare indeed, but even then, Dominic Venetia is not known for his exceptions. When asked about his love life, the Archangel of Ashar had ruefully kept his lips sealed... Don't we all adore a mysterious man? Add tall, dark, and handsome to it, and you describe the most eligible bachelor in Ashar.*

Dominic rarely moved his wings more than an inch and didn't like people, strangers, being near them. He told me as much in the club.

But he had let *me* touch them.

I put down my phone, pressing it to my chest as my gaze moved to the ceiling, and I closed my eyes.

Was I the exception?

The following morning, I stepped out of the lifts, my breath fogging in the cold air. Ashrior was silent as the few early rays of the sun crawled up the buildings. Most people were still sleeping, but I had been unable to close my eyes for longer than an hour after the evening I spent at Dominic's.

My father had asked me to come to Ashrior, and I could only guess what he wanted to discuss. I had no choice other than to go, so I went as soon as I saw the text; my head completely scrambled, and I was glad I finally had some way to put myself to use.

I made my way through the narrow streets of Ashrior, following the path I knew by heart. Every step I took towards my father's house made air leak from my lungs. When I finally arrived, I was met by the many guards still lining my father's home. I passed multiple Daemons I'd never seen before reaching the entrance and going straight to my father's office.

His face was set into a stern expression.

Zade walked in after me, closing the door. I hadn't noticed him when I walked into the house and looked at him as he took a place in one of the room's corners, leaning against the wall as if this bored him. The only telltale sign stating otherwise was his inability to meet my eyes.

My father motioned for me to sit in the chair before him. "What happened at the Archangel's home last night?"

Of course. My shadow hadn't been able to follow me through Dominic's invisible barrier. I fidgeted in my seat. "I needed to talk to him."

He looked at me, eyes alert and assessing. "About what?"

"Zade mentioned he had a person keeping tabs on me."

My father glanced at Zade, who nodded at him. "So?" His eyes slitted as they regarded me again.

"I went to him for an explanation."

The silence stretched between us like an impenetrable fog, heavy and suffocating.

"Did you blow your cover?"

Shaking my head, I said, "Of course not." *On the contrary.* But that wasn't something I wished to share.

My father closed the book before him and placed one hand on the leather cover. "I think it's time I tell you the purpose of all this." He searched my eyes, taking my silence as a sign to continue. The dimly lit room illuminated his face as his brows knitted together, and he paused before asking, "Have you ever heard of The Magnum Iter, Leyla?" I made a face as I stared at the thick tome he pushed my way. "There's an old text about it," he explained, tapping his finger on the cover as if to emphasize his point.

The pages were yellowed with age, and the title was barely legible. "Magnum Iter?" I repeated aloud. Where was he going with this?

He opened the book to a particular page, and I ran my finger over lines of text, not really paying attention to the words on the page as my father continued, "This contains lore on The Magnum Iter, *the great journey*. It references a legendary sword—one that is extremely powerful, according to the stories inside." He pointed at a particular passage. "That's exactly why you've been getting close to the Archangel."

I observed the text with confusion. "Where does Dominic fit into all of this?"

"*Dominic?*" He shook his head, green eyes narrowed on me, the smile on his lips straining. "It's not his' if that's what you're thinking. This text is far older than the Archangel. He was, however, appointed warden of the sword."

Wait—*what?* This was about some magical sword? Such objects belonged to children's stories and history lessons, not real life. It would have been hysterical if my father didn't take this so seriously. My eyes shifted from him to Zade. "And what? You want me to locate it?"

"I want you to get it for me," my father said, his face grave. "He likely keeps it in a vault somewhere in his home, given the tight wards surrounding it."

The wards I'd had no trouble entering.

"You want me to steal that sword from him?" I asked again. It sounded ludicrous.

"I do."

Pointing to the Daemon in the corner, I asked, "Your guys aren't adept enough?"

"They can't get in."

And now my father knew I could. Last night was proof of that.

The realization dawned on me as my heart raced. He was serious about this, and I had just given him an opening, though I severely lacked the skill to do it. I'd assumed my role was merely to serve as a distraction. "What does it even look like?"

He sat back in his large chair. "A sword, I suppose." A chuckle. "All I know is that he has it in his possession."

"How?"

"Reliable sources," he said simply.

My foot was tapping on the floor. "Who?" I pressed.

"I fail to see how that's important."

That had me pausing. "You don't trust me." It wasn't a question.

"It has nothing to do with trust, *Cara*, and everything with integrity. I don't tell that person you are the one trying to steal the sword from him, now, do I?"

I inhaled deeply, looking away, but felt Zade's eyes still on me.

"Did you see anything suspicious yesterday?" My father asked instead. "Anything he wanted to hide?"

I had looked nowhere but at the Archangel. I didn't want to like the man, but I did. He was the only thing occupying my mind these days and all I had noticed was how beautiful his home had been. But I hadn't seen a lot of it. *Yet.* "I've only been in his living room, and nothing appeared unusual."

My father rubbed his chin in thought. "Ah. Yes. It's probably somewhere more... private."

I blinked. It was true I had been focusing on getting closer to Dominic, precisely what my father wanted me to do, but something about the way Zade now studied me made me uncomfortable. It was as if he had caught me doing something I couldn't understand myself.

"Can you get it for me?"

I couldn't breathe as I pictured how it would all unfold, and Zade remained eerily still.

"Leyla?"
"Yes," I said. "I can get it."

PART TWO

It was decided long ago that it should never be used again. The days of glory have long since passed. Wielding this sword is like a dance. It was as much an entity as the Wielder, two sides of the same coin.

A duality.

The sword could see one's intentions as clearly as we can see each other. Yet, it has been blinded. It can no longer discern whether someone is shrouded in darkness or purged from malice. Its Wielder died along with the rest of them. Another might yet open its eyes.

Until then, anyone can participate in its thrall. Good or bad. The eye cleaves through every shadow and cuts through any bone. It cleaves any barrier, thick or thin. It traverses anything in its way—making it the most powerful blade in history.

See how this could be dangerous? Understand why it must be laid to rest?

Or are you blinded by possibilities? Do you have ideas on leveraging it to advance yourself and your cause?

I hope it is the latter, for I will be there, waiting. My eyes are wide open. I am still watching.

I would have destroyed it if I could. But as I mentioned, there is no obstacle in its way it can't defeat.

Just like there is none in the way of mine.

— *The Magnum Iter, A.M.*

CHAPTER TWENTY-SIX

Dominic

The ACC kick-off gala took place at the Museum of Modern Art in Shard City, just like every year. A line of black cars dropped off high-profile guests who entered over a red carpet, surrounded by paparazzi and fans. The event kicked off both the ACC season and fall reborn.

It was the city's most profitable season because of the influx of tourists from all over Celestia visiting to watch the unique weather phenomenon. The season would officially begin tonight at midnight, and a large crowd had gathered at the museum.

I looked around, scanning the people ahead on the red carpet in search for my friends. They were probably already inside. The occasional white wings caught my attention but didn't belong to Inesa.

"No date tonight, Prime Venetia?" someone from the press yelled as I walked the red carpet. Light flashed in my face, but I only smiled at the cameras and waved a hand in greeting. *No*, I thought, *I don't have a date tonight. But there's someone at this gala that I'd very much like to see.*

Once inside, away from the cameras, I checked our message thread from a few days ago.

Leyla: *I'm sorry for showing up at your house like that.*
Me: *I shouldn't have sent someone after you.*
Leyla: *No, you shouldn't have.*
Me: *I hope it didn't change your mind about coming to the gala.*
Leyla: *And let that dress go to waste? Never.*
Me: *Save me a dance.*
Leyla: *If you ask nicely.*

I wasn't fond of texting, but I looked forward to each of Leyla's texts with an enthusiasm that alarmed me. I wanted to do this the right way. Having publicity so early in our relationship could be toxic. Thank the light, the press wasn't allowed inside. Guests were also prohibited from taking pictures of anything inside. Although I knew it was impossible to prevent *everyone* from taking photos, they still faced fines and future event bans—which most didn't want to risk.

The lighting inside the museum was dimmed. Instead of the typical art pieces, the exhibition showcased themed artworks featuring falling stars, the highlight of this season. They always tried to curate a brand new, exclusive collection for this night, inviting familiar and up-and-coming artists to take part and win a spot in the museum. It was a fantastic opportunity. Guests could, tonight only, bid on pieces and take them home in the end.

I walked through the halls, too restless to take my time with any of the pieces yet. I usually bought some of the art to hang in my home or the Town Hall and sometimes to give away as gifts. But now, I had more pressing matters occupying my thoughts.

The main hall was lavishly decorated with art, from paintings to sculptures and ceramics. The sprawling room was large enough to fit the entire wealth of a small country. A sparkling marble dancefloor occupied the center, and the couples who had already taken to its surface danced in perfect harmony with the soft string music that filled the air.

I scanned the crowd, my eyes settling on Inesa and Leon. Upon spotting the pair, I immediately made a beeline for them, effectively dismissing anyone who tried to approach me. Leon wore a sharp suit, the blue color contrasting with Inesa, who looked wonderful in a soft yellow dress. Her radiant smile balanced his thundercloud expression.

"Finally," I murmured, shaking Leon's hand and kissing Inesa's cheeks. From her mate's expression, I gathered it was best to avoid going plural in the future.

The man really did not like me for some unknown reason.

"Inesa von Hoes!" A random Sanguis clasped her arm before Inesa had even uttered her first words to me. The newcomer's dress was revealing, and her blonde curls bounced as she looked up at my friend. "It's been such a long time! How are you?"

"Oh?" Inesa said way less enthusiastically. "Do we know each other?"

"College," the girl said immediately, but still Inesa didn't recognize her. She had gone to college at an older age; some parents hadn't allowed their Angeli daughters to study—especially if they could get a husband instead of pursuing academics. But not Inesa. She had refused even to consider marriage before she had earned her degree. She had rejected every suitor her parents had presented to her. Eventually, they relented and let her attend college, where she met Nathan and me. She had made school more accessible for Angeli women when few had been allowed to think independently.

The Sanguis girl flicked her attention to me. Her eyes were lucid, calculating, as she feigned surprise. "Prime Venetia!" she said, stepping closer to me and holding out her hand. "What a pleasure."

"Is it?" I asked, not bothering to hide my indifference. I had no idea who this girl was or what she wanted, but she sure as hell would not get it from me.

"Did you come alone?" she purred, not picking up on it.

I curved a brow. "I'm not interested."

The girl was beautiful, almost boringly so. If it had been a few months earlier, I wouldn't have cared and might have taken her up on her eventual offer.

Inesa's eyes nearly rolled out of her head, telling me what I already guessed: she didn't know the girl. It had been a way for her to get close to me. Same old, same old. I had lost count of the number of acquaintances I'd had in common with the women who had tried to get into my bed. I always respected the few who walked up to me and told me they wanted to sleep with me, getting straight to business. It was much more effective. They were also the ones who could take a *no* and left me alone when I dropped them a hint.

I spotted Nathan in the crowd, his tall frame filling the entrance with the same look on his face as I must've had in search of familiar faces. His eyes reached us, and I tipped up my chin in a silent hello. He walked up to our group and greeted us. Leon didn't seem to mind Nathan as much as he did me, which frustrated me. What the hell did I ever do to him?

"I'll make it worth your while." The Sanguis girl was still there, laying a hand on my arm, and I did not know why she thought she could touch me.

My answer evaporated on my tongue as I sensed a now familiar presence. With my forehead tensed, I turned my face towards the woman who had me under her spell.

The Sanguis' fingers tightened on my arm, trying to regain my attention, and I shrugged her off.

I could hear Inesa's voice from a distance. "He said he's not interested." Waving her hands dismissively, she added, "*Shoo.*" Inesa was incredibly kind, so you had really crossed a line if her bitchy side came out.

I was unaware and uninterested in what happened next. All my attention was fixed on Leyla Cuprum.

The dress she had on began with a fitted sleeveless top that hugged the curve of her breasts. The black fabric bled into different shades of red, yellow, and gold. My eyes followed the pattern down, the effect of the skin-tight dress much like fire. She wore gloves made of a sheer, black fabric, darkening the skin underneath. Her black hair cascaded over her back in straight locks, and her ears were adorned with golden earrings that reached her bare shoulders like tiny, shimmering waterfalls, caressing the bare skin there as fingers would.

Her black open sandals had sky-high heels, but as I looked at her, my mind was consumed with thoughts of stripping her of it all.

She looked perfect.

I noticed her friend, Lodana, next to her, but they parted ways when she spotted someone and left Leyla on her own after sharing a few words, both of them smiling at the other. My eyes remained on the Daemon, keeping her in my line of sight. I even blocked out Josiah Eden, who went over to her and started chatting. There was no reality in which they ended up together. Though judging by the way he was studying her, he hadn't gotten the memo yet.

The laugh she gave him had to be forced because she wasn't the smiley type. Just right for me, since I wasn't either. She had rough edges and was unafraid to speak her mind. Mature, sophisticated, controlled—matching the man I was in every sense.

When he finally left, Leyla's smile disappeared, and she walked away. I let go of a breath, chest constricting because I was right. Her dress and golden earrings shimmered in the light as she turned. Clasping her hands together in front of her, she walked along the art pieces, from time to time cocking her head in thought at the displays. I wanted to know what she was thinking and feeling as she looked at them.

One of the servers came up to her and offered something to drink. She took a glass and offered a tight-lipped smile. The shield she was wearing made my head spin. I wanted to break her composure and see those lips stretch as far and wide as they could go in earnest. Not because she forced them to.

Leyla put her lips to the rim of the glass, sipping a little, lost in thought. She continued, arriving at the winding gallery with paintings that circled the museum. Sometimes, she stopped, leaning closer to inspect a painting in detail. Other times, someone made her pause by addressing her. Every conversation was brief, and they always ended with her turning her attention back to the art. She didn't even notice the eyes trailing over her, following her, either for her outfit or for *her*. Everything in me longed to shield her from those eyes. I wanted to keep her all to myself.

The sight of her had me so captivated that it took her disappearing around the corner for the spell to break. Only then did I realize Nathan had been speaking to me.

"Dominic?" he asked, as if repeating himself.

I lay a hand on his shoulder, briefly glancing his way, barely seeing anything at all. "I'm sorry, brother. Hold that thought. I'll be right back."

And then I went after her.

CHAPTER TWENTY-SEVEN

Leyla

It was my first time at the kick-off gala. Dana had received tickets months ago via Tommy, now her ex, and her parents wouldn't attend, so it was a neutral playing ground for us tonight. When Tommy invited her, she offered me her 'plus-one' ticket, but I knew it was Josiah's; the players only got one to hand out. Prior to everything happening, I already knew it was an exciting event and had agreed to come. It was like getting a free ticket to the zoo to view near-extinct species.

When Dana had seen some familiar faces in the room, she had taken off, but only after I reassured her it was okay. She told me to find my archangel, but I didn't dare glance around the room. I was too aware of myself. Thankfully, Josiah had approached me soon after she was gone.

"You look amazing, Leyla."

I smiled at him. "Thanks for the invite."

The Ethereal flashed a lopsided grin. "You're welcome." His focus shifted to another part of the room almost immediately, clearing his throat. "I'll have to excuse myself—talk to sponsors and such. Save me a dance?"

"It's the least I could do," I promised him, and he touched my arm before walking off.

Not knowing what to do with myself after that, I turned to the art pieces. I needed time to prepare myself before searching the room for my... *mark*.

Practically speaking, I could fill a lot of time by studying each piece in the museum without looking awkward. But the more pieces I saw, the more captivated I became. The art depicting the fall reborn season, along with the falling stars that were linked so closely to the ACC, had been captured in many ways and mediums. None were disappointing or dull, but only one painting had me in its thrall. I couldn't take my eyes off it.

It was a bright painting depicting Shard City from above; the colorful city center lit up in different hues. Ashar's skyline reflected fall reborn's stars as the balls of fire cascaded down at night. The painting had an almost surrealistic aspect to it, as if the artist made it through a different lens, catching things we couldn't perceive with our own eyes.

"Stunning, no?" a voice said from behind me, startling me from my thoughts. I nearly spilled my drink despite my steady hands as the intruder's warm breath caressed my ear.

Looking forward, Dominic stepped up next to me and gestured to the painting. "Tell me what you think." One of his hands had disappeared in the pocket of his all-black suit, the non-color making the gold of his wings pop. I could see his tan skin under the unbuttoned white blouse, and his brown curls were neatly styled back.

"It's breathtaking," I confessed.

His eyes flicked over to me. "Indeed," he murmured in

agreement, but the word was an almost guttural sound. My legs clenched together underneath my dress, but his eyes didn't stray from mine, those golden wings rustling a little as he rolled his shoulders back.

My breathing turned uneven. "You love art." It was the first coherent thought that popped up in my head.

"I do." One corner of his mouth hooked up at the random statement.

I turned fully to him. "It was your idea, wasn't it? To showcase this art and these different artists this way?"

He turned his body toward the wall, rubbing a hand over his jaw. "I might have brought it up once, but it was truly the museum's initiative."

I looked back at the painting and said, "Well, it's wonderful."

Dominic bowed his head and held his arm out to the rest of the hallway. "Shall I show you around? Tell you about the pieces and some of their artists?"

My fingers touched the hollow beneath my throat, and his eyes followed the movement. "I would like that."

Passionate—that is how I would describe Dominic when it came to art. He spoke animatedly, pointing out details in certain pieces and techniques I did not know, and talked in length about different origins. It was true that the more you learned about a piece, the more it came alive. There was more to appreciate that way.

It was the same with people, really. You formed an opinion on someone with the limited context, knowledge, and experience you had. But when you got to know someone and understand their complexities, the origin of their flaws, and the hurdles they had had to overcome… your opinions slowly adjusted, morphing into another person entirely.

That's how I felt about Dominic Venetia. The more I learned about the Prime of Ashar, the more I began to see him in his entirety, through all his layers and titles. He was someone who knew what it was to love and lose, be vulnerable, and carry the pressure that weighed on his shoulders every single day. He cared—more than I had ever imagined. The image I had created in my head did not translate to the man I'd met.

Still, some people were incredibly skilled in the art of deception. They could craft their image in the exact way they wanted to be perceived.

When we had made a full circle and returned to the main hall, the music greeted us in a lovely swirl of different instruments. A live band was playing, and more people danced, but nothing like you would in a nightclub. This style of movement was more sophisticated. Couples held each other, talked, and twirled around, all doing whatever they wanted, but somehow in the same rhythm.

"Come," Dominic said, taking my hand in his palm and pulling me after him. He guided me onto the dancefloor before I could protest.

"That wasn't a question," I reminded him softly as he laid a hand on my waist and pulled me closer to him.

He smirked down at me. The feeling of his broad hand on the small of my back was doing weird things to my brain. "Will you dance with me, Leyla?"

I smiled, because we were already dancing. Putting my hand on his shoulder, I looked around the room for the first time. Many eyes were on us as we moved, but none of it did anything to me. The blatant stares were nothing compared to the feeling of being in Dominic's arms—of feeling his strength and the warmth of his body seep into me through his clothes. I caught Dana's eye from across the dancefloor, and all she did was wink at me with a big grin plastered on her face. She looked terrific with her fuchsia hair in straight locks down her back.

The music slowed until only heartbreaking snares threaded together in a soft, swaying song. Dana got swept away by a player I recognized from the Lupine team, someone she talked to because it irritated Tommy, the douchebag who was now glowering at them from the sidelines. I smiled, glad my best friend was having a great time. She deserved nothing less. She deserved nothing less. My eyes found Josiah standing next to him, his focus on me as he raised his glass.

Dominic's fingers curled around my hand as he pulled me closer, nearly flush with his chest. Goosebumps prickled on my arms. I placed my free hand on his shoulder and focused on the smooth expanse of skin visible above his blouse, his angelic mourning bands curling around the edges, before lifting my chin and looking into his eyes.

"You look beautiful tonight."

My eyes jumped between his own, and I felt a fucking blush rising to my cheeks. "This is the dress Dana chose for me in the Pisces Domain."

"She picked well." Dominic nodded like he meant it, looking away with a smile before turning his gaze back to me. "But I wasn't referring to the dress."

Oh. "Well," I said. "I—thank you." Not knowing what else to say, I opted for a hoarse chuckle. My father would likely die of mortification if he saw me like this.

The Archangel twirled me around in his arms and caught

me, his strong hand planted firmly on the crease of my waist. The large room glittered around us, the lights, people, and clothing mirroring the magic of the coming season.

Dominic didn't look at me as he said, "It has nothing to do with what you wear." His jaw clenched. Everyone around us seemed to disappear as my eyes moved to his lips, determined to hear what he said next. "You awaken something in me that has been dormant for a while. It makes me gravitate towards you. It's what made me notice you the first time I saw you at *Moby's*, and what made me sense you the moment you walked into this hall."

"Dominic…"

He squeezed the hand he was holding. "Dom."

"*Dom*," I repeated. "You can't—" I inhaled, my breath hitching a little. "You can't say things like that."

"I can't, or you don't want me to?" he whispered, bowing his head a little so he could look me straight in the eye.

Gods. I wanted him to. I truly, truly did. It was exactly what I wanted to hear. But it wasn't something I could let myself have. When the curtains fell, the light was not supposed to hurt. No part of me could fall for him while simultaneously screwing him over.

"There is no difference," I breathed.

"There is, though." His lips thinned as he moved closer. "Leyla, take a good look at my face and tell me if you see a man who's easily deterred."

I faltered, stepping back a little, halting our dancing midstep. How we must have looked: pressed together, heads close, a blush on my cheeks, softly murmuring things to each other… "You're the Archangel, the Prime," I pleaded. "I'm…" *A liar.* "Me."

"Good thing it is *you* I want, then."

I tried to swallow my shock, but it clogged my throat. Dominic looked at something over my shoulder as the couples kept dancing around us. His gaze moved back to mine, stepping closer. "Break it off with the Ethereal. Cut off all other men that think they have a chance while you're at it." Dominic bowed closer to my ear and murmured, "I want you all to myself. And when there's something I desire, I usually get it."

Nodding faintly, he let his fingers trail my arm with an appreciative murmur. He let me go, kissing the back of my limp hand before walking away from me—his golden wings disappearing from view like he hadn't just turned my world on its axis.

I got his message. *Loud and clear.* He wasn't messing around anymore. This was no joke. Stunned by his blunt confession, I left the dancefloor and looked straight into familiar blue eyes.

Zade stood in the back of the room, leaning against the wall, wearing a tux with a bow tie and everything. He stared at me with narrowed eyes.

My breath came in faster. I turned around, deciding to go the other way. Why was he here? This assignment was complicated enough without his presence in the room. I didn't need anyone telling my father I was faltering or losing my grip. Gripping my ribcage, I tugged at the fabric there. The dress didn't leave me enough room to breathe, so I went straight to the bar and ordered some champagne.

While I waited for my drink, I kept an eye out for the Daemon that wasn't supposed to be there. He was nowhere to be seen, but I did find Dominic on the dancefloor with Inesa von Hoes in his arms. With her long black hair and the fluffiest white wings I had ever seen, she was truly stunning. I watched as something she said made him laugh.

Whereas I only brought destruction to his life.

Many people looked at them as they swirled around, and I felt something twitch in my gut—akin to the knife I was supposed to bury in Dominic's back. With a scowl, I turned around and grabbed my champagne flute from the bar.

Some moments later—my head a little light from the oxygen I was sorely lacking—a familiar presence approached me. I quickly looked around for Josiah. After all, I had promised him a dance, and now would be the perfect moment for him to cash it in. Though, maybe he wanted to keep his distance from me after the Archangel's public marking.

"Tough night?" Zade asked me, leaning down on the bar. "Or was it the conversation?"

I clenched the glass in my hands. "What the fuck are you doing here?"

Zade inhaled, ordering something I couldn't hear over the blood rushing through my ears. "Your babysitter wasn't allowed in, so your father pulled some strings to get me inside and check up on you."

"Keep your distance. We can't be seen together here. I have everything under control."

"Yeah," he drawled. "You have him wrapped around your finger, don't you?"

"I'm just doing what I'm told, same as you." *False.*

"Difference is, I think you're enjoying it a little too much." There was an edge to his voice, but it was nothing compared to the edge I was on.

I chugged back to champagne and slammed the glass back on the bar, stepping close to him. "What do you want me to do, Zade? Huh? Want me to tell my father you can't deal with it—that you're succumbing to jealousy and don't want to share me with someone else? Or will you choose the coward's way out and tell him my acting skills need some brushing up?"

His eyes turned dark. "Leyla, I don't—"

"Shut up!" I dragged a hand through my hair. "Just shut the fuck up and back off." People looked at us with surprised expressions.

I was surprised my brain had not exploded yet.

Zade followed me and grabbed my arm as soon as the bar was behind us. "It's the doubting, Leyla. Your questioning, the sudden moral compass. It's creating a rift between us—between you and your father—and it's all the Archangel's doing. He fills your ears with nonsense. I shared this with your father, and he ignored it, but he didn't see the way you looked at *him* just now."

Is that what he believed? That the Archangel affected how I felt about Ambrosia? The whole concept had been crooked from the start! "I can think for myself. I am not some dimwit, naïve child." Zade was shaking his head. "And you have *no* business going to my father behind my back like that."

"Don't sleep with him," he pleaded. It was not a pretty look.

My mouth popped open, but I kept my voice low. "You're kidding, right?" Because this truly was a ridiculous fucking joke. "You have no claim on me. *None*."

Zade merely responded by clenching his jaw, and I decided I was not doing this tonight. I didn't like how he thought he could boss me around. Approach me at an event like this! He jeopardized my assignment, my cover, my life... "Go home, Zade," I said.

It looked like he had something else to say but slipped

away without uttering another word.

"Leyla?" I turned around to see Josiah, still wearing his perfectly fitting green suit. His eyes were on Zade's retreating form. "Everything alright?"

Swallowing, I nodded. "Nothing I can't handle."

"Want to talk about it?"

"No."

He swallowed. "How about a dance?"

I smiled, taking his offered hand, and he grinned back at me as he spun me in his arms. We were silent as my mind went a thousand miles an hour. When I passed Dana on the dancefloor, she reached out a hand. "You good?" she asked, looking between me and Josiah.

"Yes." I smiled. "I'm good."

She squeezed my hand before letting go, moving to the upbeat music that was playing.

Josiah let me be quiet, and I was grateful for that. I unconsciously looked for golden wings in the crowd, but Dominic had disappeared. I spotted Inesa von Hoes and Nathanial Farcroft standing side by side, staring at me. Nathanial was saying something, to which she nodded—a weary look in her eyes as they paused on me before continuing through the crowd and murmuring something back to him.

Did they catch my interaction with Zade? His godsdamned stunt could blow everything to pieces.

My phone vibrated, but I ignored it while dancing with Josiah. After the dance ended, I went to the restroom and checked the two messages I received.

Z: *I will tell him it's all going according to plan. I am sorry.*

Dominic: *Remember what I said, Leyla. I'm serious about you.*

II put away my phone, drowning in the conflicting feelings

that erupted all over my skin upon reading the last message. Back inside, Dana shot me a concerned look, but I smiled at her, even though I was dying a little on the inside.

Everything wasn't going according to plan.

Not even close.

CHAPTER TWENTY-EIGHT

Dominic

I buried my hands deep in the pockets of my suit, looking at Shard City below. I had shown my face at the gala, which was sufficient. There was no need for me to stay until the end. My departure happened shortly after my interaction with Leyla. Being in her presence was like a game of wills. I couldn't take it to the level I desired. Not yet.

So I returned home, yet I hadn't moved since landing in my garden fifteen minutes ago.

My name was called. When I turned around, Amy was coming towards me. "How long have you been standing here?"

Amy Stuart was the closest thing to a parental figure I had left. She'd been there through it all. When she first approached me for a job, she had a black eye and felt the need to apologize, as if it would upset me. I realized what was going on from the start and demanded his identity in return for a job. Let's just say she hadn't been bothered by her now ex-husband ever since.

I shrugged. "Go visit your grandkids, Amy." My words were kind but commanding. I would never lose my patience with this woman, least of all my temper.

"I went there after dinner. They're asleep now. Have been for hours." Amy walked closer, unfazed by the thundercloud hanging over us, and lay a reassuring hand on my arm. "What's troubling you?"

Releasing a sigh, I said, "I never compared women to Emiliana. There was no point. But I can't—" I took a shuddering inhale "—I can't help but compare her to Leyla."

Emiliana was my mate. *Leyla Cuprum was nothing to me*, I reminded myself, *nothing compared to her*.

The thought rang so hollow it frightened me.

Amy's eyes turned sympathetic, and she approached me in silence. I had spent an entire month locked up in my house, dealing with the aftermath of Emiliana's trial and trying to cope with the fact that she wasn't here anymore. I drank every mind-numbing concoction I could get my hands on to last me long enough until I finally fell asleep at night. Nobody was allowed to enter, and I'd cast a power shield around my house to keep everyone out. But as soon as my wards had weakened because of my pathetic state, Amy had barged through it and started taking care of me, helping me get back on my feet.

The emptiness was especially suffocating during the first decades. But as the years trickled by, I learned to give it a place. I focused on anything but her: I willed my powers to grow stronger, my knowledge to sharpen, and I gathered political alliances like they were the weapons I needed in battle. All to get me into a position that solidified my control.

With the support of Amy and my friends, I tried. If it hadn't been for them picking up the pieces, I would have likely ended myself long ago. Something kept me going, pushing forward through the endless sludge, the dread, the hardship.

"What about it makes you so sad?" Amy asked softly.

I put a hand on the balustrade but didn't turn to look at her. The shame of my feelings was overpowering. "I'm not sure."

Leyla was beautiful, strong, but her features delicate. She looked like she was made of steel instead of flesh and bone. So different from the fragile beauty of Emiliana.

The man I'd been when I was with Emiliana had changed, as well. He had been gone for a long time. A much stronger, hardened version had taken his place. And perhaps that was okay. Maybe that was how it was supposed to be.

Thoughts about it being time to move on made me shake my head and curl my lip. That was not in the cards for me, ever. I had lost Emiliana and would never get her back. No one could replace her. I was a fool for even thinking otherwise.

"There is something about that girl," Amy said. "Something good."

I turned to the side. "What do you mean?"

"There's a sense of *fatis* surrounding her."

Fatis roughly translates to 'fated' from the old angelic tongue. It was used to describe things that were supposed to be a certain way, that belonged in your life. Events that weren't coincidental.

A low growl escaped my throat, warning the older Angeli not to cross that line.

"Dominic," she said, shaking her head. "You're not dead, but sometimes you do act like it."

"Part of me died the moment Emiliana was torn from my

life." Her name was a heavy weight on my chest that I'd been carrying for over a century.

She clucked her tongue. "There is no rule saying we only get one shot at happiness."

I recognized the truth in her words. I had felt it again—what it was to be alive. The moments I spent with Leyla had felt like something finally clicking after you'd thought about it a million times; it was expected, somehow, while part of it remained equally unreal.

It felt like being woken from a slumber that had begun with a storm, only to be greeted with sunshine upon opening my eyes.

But the light would dim eventually. It always did.

"You're not sure about her?"

A sarcastic chuckle slipped out. "She's intelligent, beautiful, and more caring than she admits—but extremely guarded. I can't help but question where she popped up from all of a sudden."

"You're over-analyzing something that should be felt," Amy responded curtly.

"Maybe," I said, feeling one corner of my mouth lift. But perhaps not. I'd jumped off that cliff once already. I wouldn't do so again. There were already too many feelings for the girl, which was messing with my head. I almost lost it when I saw Josiah Eden, Ethereal's golden boy, looking at her from across the room while she was in *my* arms.

Amy nodded, accepting my answer. "You really will be fine on your own?" she asked. "I can stay if you want me to."

"No, I'm sure." I took a cigarette from my inner breast pocket. "Take the night off."

"You know where to find me." She gave me a last, lingering look before turning on her heel and walking away. I neatly tucked my wings away and walked into my home with one last backward glance at the city. I purchased this house for Emiliana. It was supposed to be *our* place. Which it had never been. Would never be.

Inside, the warm light shining through the doorway's etched glass greeted me. Memories lingered in every corner, like ghosts that refused to move on. Everywhere my eyes roamed reminded me of Emiliana and her vibrant presence—her favorite books, paintings she had picked to adorn the walls, our first time together... Even the air was heavy with her absence. And despite all my efforts to push her to the back of my mind, I couldn't get myself to erase her from this place. As much as I wanted to stay sane, she lingered on the edge of my awareness.

The cigarette between my lips remained unlit. Emiliana hated cigarettes.

I smiled ruefully.

With a heavy sigh and a flick of my wrist, I made my way toward the kitchen, where I found a bottle of whiskey waiting for me on the countertop. Pouring a glass, I lifted it in a silent salute before taking a long swig. A small amount of time went by before I finally acknowledged the root of this suffering within me.

No matter how hard I tried, she would always be there—part of who I was, part of my story. But there was someone else who I might continue writing it with.

The Ethereal Domain was beautiful no matter what season you visited. Everywhere I looked, lush green plants and trees lined the clean, nearly spotless streets. The air was crisp and free of any vapors. Even the sounds were different here. There wasn't a construction site in sight.

As representatives, Nathan and Inesa had to keep their domains under control. I oversaw Ashium as a whole, but they handled the day-to-day business of their regions. When I became Prime of Ashar, I immediately placed my friends in positions near me. The public's opinion on the matter did not affect me. I needed people I could trust, and there were no people I confided in more than them.

Nathan's long-time secretary, Eni, greeted me with a warm smile before I entered his office. In the center of the room was a large desk filled with stacks of books and folders. He loved antiquity and collected every old tome he could get his hands on. He'd even covered the walls with ancient tapestries depicting scenes from Ethereal history.

"Dominic." Nathan smiled as he gestured for me to sit in one of the plush chairs as he finished writing. When he put down his pen, he said, "Rumors about you falling for a new girl are circulating town. Word goes her emerald green eyes lured you in." He raised his eyebrows. "Correct me if I'm wrong, but… Didn't the Daemon you danced with at the gala have green eyes?"

I sat back and shrugged. "No idea. I hardly even looked at her."

Nathan's eyes were cunning. "Anyone can see that she's beautiful, Dom."

"You make me sound shallow, brother."

"Please enlighten me, then. Because all I see is my best friend dragging himself from affair to affair with the most gorgeous women he comes across. How's this one different?"

I looked at the tapestries, debating what to tell him. "There's something about her." The wood of my chair groaned as I unhooked my legs. "I don't know what exactly, but it pulls me in. I haven't felt anything close to that in…" I exhaled. "A long time."

Nathan's brows knitted together as his mouth flattened, eyes changing from skeptical to pitying.

"Don't look at me like that," I said through gritted teeth.

"Honestly," he said, shaking his head as he scratched his stubbled chin. "I don't get your obsession with her."

That comment ticked me off. "There is nothing for you to *get*."

"Really? She was flirting with all these other men at the gala while you were drooling at the sight of her. I don't know what she did to crawl into your head like this, Dom, but get her the fuck out."

"Look, man. I know you want the best for me, but you're treading a thin line." I gripped the chair in warning.

He assessed me. "As long as you know what you're doing…"

I glared at him.

His hands went up in surrender. "I'm just looking out for you. I don't want you to become the mess you were after losing Emiliana."

If Inesa were here, she would have told Nathan to back off. But she wasn't, and I wasn't the bigger person. I wanted to hit him back right where he hit me. I would not take this lying down. "If only you were this frank about Apolo. When was the last time you even *thought* about visiting Blackport Penitentiary?"

Nathan stood, the wooden legs of his chair screeching over the floor as it skidded back, anger overtaking his features.

"You know what, Dominic? Sometimes, I'm fucking tired of being your friend. You cut us off when we speak about Emiliana, and now you do the same when I mention anything *remotely* bad about Leyla Cuprum—someone you've known for three fucking minutes." He claps his hands, a dark chuckle escaping from his chest. "*Hell*—why not prioritize her over friends who have been with you for a century?"

I remained seated. "Are you kidding me? Don't blame my grief for your weakness, Nathan. Get a fucking life."

He rolled his eyes. "*Sure*, because your three-minute fling counts as a life."

"I don't have the energy or patience for this." I rubbed a hand over my face. "Let's get over the domain status so I can get the fuck out of here."

"No need," he said, his voice full of indifference as his eyes moved to the folder before him. "Everything's in here. You can go now. I wouldn't want to hold you up."

Nathan shoved the folder my way, and I felt my anger simmer to a boiling point. We never fought like this, but at that moment, I couldn't give two shits about it. I rose with a strained 'thanks' and turned on my heel to walk out, my mind whirling with conflicting thoughts and emotions. I pushed open the heavy doors with more force than necessary, and Eni pointedly looked at the screen in front of her.

What a start to my fucking day.

CHAPTER TWENTY-NINE

Leyla

I spent hours engrossed in the media's account of Dominic's life history. While most of the facts were in my father's folder, I eagerly consumed the rest of the gossip online like it was essential to my assignment—fueling an addiction I never asked for. I reached a low point and even searched the web for information on Dominic's late mate when Dana texted.

Dana: *Are you watching the news?*

I pushed my feet closer to me on the couch as I grabbed hold of my phone with both hands.

Me: *No, why? What's going on?*

Dana: *It's about this new drug. Looks like the powder we got offered in the club.*

A sudden uneasiness slithered around in my chest, and creeping dread wrapped around me as I turned on the television, pulling up the leading news channels.

They were reporting on Ambrosia, the drug my father had been working on. He had released it. Even its name was out there now. All the news channels I zapped through went on and on about how it had been increasing the number of users in the city, starting in Ashrior. Especially Ashrior. Crime was rising at an alarming rate. Ashar appeared to be adopting caution, announcing that the drug's influence would soon spread to Shard City, predicting the havoc it would bring.

It was spreading much faster than I had expected.

Every channel was saturated with incidents surrounding the drug from the last days. Prime Venetia had opened havens and urgent care facilities, one of which I recognized close to my apartment. Once again, I found myself questioning the consequences of my father's actions and my part in it.

Unlike what my father believed, these means did not justify the end. His willingness to uproot the system had been haunting me ever since the demonstration. He was powerful, his ambition without bounds. I had known that. Yet, to see it play out, every vicious detail so carefully orchestrated... I felt powerless. Guilty.

Dana: *A friend took it last night, had a bad trip, and was brought to the ER to get her stomach pumped. Someone she was with died. And apparently, he isn't the only one.*

Me: *I'm watching now. It's appalling.*

I meant it. My ties to Ambrosia weighed me down, cutting deep into my treacherous skin.

The news changed to a reporter standing in Shard City before a nightclub that was barricaded by police and cordoned off with tape, lights flashing. "Rumors are suggesting Ambrosia was released by an organization in Ashrior that is well-known to law enforcement," the reporter began. "Seeing as they have been historically tied to the drug circuit, they could well be founded in truth." It was followed by clips of ambulances driving off and hospital ERs being swarmed.

I stared at the screen. What information did they have? And how long before it would be linked to my father's organization? As far as I knew, he had never been arrested, so he had ways of staying off the radar, but was it naïve to think he would remain unscathed through this, too?

The reporter continued, "As the police search for answers, one thing is certain: the city's drug problem has reached a tipping point. The question now is, where do we go from here?" Chaotic images of the club they cordoned off tonight, the man who had died some weeks ago by jumping down from the VIP area—how my father's associate had killed that mountain cat without flinching… They all flashed through my mind.

I relived the sense of foreboding I had felt the night of the demonstration. Something was wrong. This drug was slowly seeping into Ashium and I had done nothing to stop it. Trying to change my father's mind was futile.

Me: *Steer clear from it, okay?*
Dana: *I will. You as well.*

The two boulders weighing on me made it impossible to calm down, one tugging at my loyalty to my father and the other to my sense of what was right. The unease wouldn't leave, and I couldn't shake the urge to do something about it. I slowly rose from the couch, grabbing my purse from the ground. I hastily signed a cheque and grabbed my discarded jacket from the kitchen chair.

I slipped out of my apartment with a glance into the dark alley across the street, counting on my shadow to keep me safe wherever I went. The night was cool, and I shivered as I wandered the streets of Shard City, keeping my head down. I grabbed my phone, and the screen lit up my face.

Me: *We're on the news. Are you watching?*

The street lights cast ominous shadows, and the occasional police sirens in the distance caused me to clench my jaw. Ashar had always been safe for me, but I had never been so conscious of the sounds surrounding me until now. The tension in the air grew as I ventured further into the center. My unease deepened as I sensed the prying eyes of people trailing me from the shadows. I kept walking, my determination to do something, *anything*, growing with every step. I passed alleyways and deserted streets, refusing to let fear haunt me.

Z: *Don't worry. We have it under control.*

When I arrived at my destination, I hesitated outside the building they had shown on the news, reading Zade's response. Was he fucking serious?

Me: *I'm past the stage of worrying, Zade. It's a fucking obvious problem—one we're all tied to.*

Z: *You're clean. We should talk about the gala, Ley. Can I come over?*

The gala? What the hell had he been taking? Our interaction was the least of my concerns right now. Ambrosia was tearing down the city, and Zade acted like nothing was amiss—like they managed problems of this magnitude daily.

My father had bit off more than he could chew.

Me: *L.C. is clean. That is not me. I am his lightsdamned daughter!*

Z: *You know he's got you. I got you. You're good. We take care of our own.*

Me: *I don't fucking care. It's not me I'm worried about. What happens to the assignment if they start digging into X's life and they find out about his daughter? What if the Archangel finds out?*

It took some time for Zade to answer my text. The three little dots indicating he was typing a response seemed to go on for an eternity.

What *would* happen if Dominic found out? *When* he found

out? The man was already imposing, and he still liked me. I could only imagine how he would react if I were the one to cross him. *Nobody* wanted to be on the receiving end of that.

Z: *What do you need to feel at ease? I'll make sure you get it.*

Me: *Pull it off the streets.*

Z: *That is never gonna happen. Even if we wanted to, it's already out there.*

Me: *You're really okay being complicit?*

Z: *It's not my job to have an opinion.*

Me: *It is apparently also not your job to use your brain.*

Z: *Leyla...*

My blood was boiling. What did they want me to do? Look the other way and ignore it? I could not fathom how this drug would help anyone besides the organization's bottom line. My father said he had a plan, but was this carnage worth it? Did it truly benefit our cause? How did we expect the rest of Ashar ever to treat Ashrior the same if we kept showing them why they should distrust us? Sure, wealth and power had not been distributed equally, but those were not the only measures used to influence an outcome and force change.

Z: *Can I please come over and help set your mind at ease? We need to talk.*

Me: *No.*

I was fucking sick of it.

After several deep breaths, I silenced my buzzing phone and put it away. I finally mustered up enough courage to push the doors open. As soon as I stepped inside, the smell of despair hit me. Graffiti covered the walls, and broken furniture littered the floor. People lay or sat on stretchers, some sleeping, some just staring into nowhere. It was one of the many emergency havens Dominic had opened in Shard City today for anyone who needed help or a place to stay, because people couldn't remain on the streets any longer, not if they valued what little they had left.

Hesitating at the entrance, I suddenly felt overwhelmed, out of my depth. I wasn't like Dominic—wasn't the hero in these people's stories. I was the villain who worked against them, aiding in their demise.

Volunteers passed me in a blur, too busy to notice me, and another person trickled in, brushing past me through the doorway. Food and clothing were offered to those in need, and some healthcare professionals moved through the space to provide first aid. I watched from the shadows—like the shadows now watched me—as they moved between the makeshift beds, some talking quietly while others continued with a subtle nod or gesture of kindness. I stopped one nurse close by and forced the folded slip of paper from my pocket into her hands before slipping back into the night.

None of it made me feel any better. Then again, it was not supposed to.

This wasn't about me.

The next day, my father summoned me to Ashrior.

As I waded through the city, I once again sensed the foreboding atmosphere that had taken root in the streets. It seemed like everyone was on edge, waiting for the other shoe to drop.

Despite arriving in Ashrior at midday, the streets were quieter and the air less bright. Still, the Undercity was heating beneath the stifling sun. The lifts connecting to Ashium rose high, their grey metal reflecting some of the light. I made my way past one of the clubs my father frequented, and it was clear that the Lupines had blocked access to it.

I knew my father had invisible protections scattered through the streets surrounding his home. He always knew what was happening within his domain, but even from miles away, I could see the guards lining my father's estate, searching the streets like hawks. That was new.

The moment I entered their vicinity, all attention turned to me.

"State your business," the one in the center said as I approached, his voice cool and even.

Halting, I drew a sharp breath, my mind racing for the right words. "I have a meeting with Xanon."

"Name?"

The hell? I narrowed my eyes. "Leyla."

He walked back to check something, talking into the walky-talky attached to his suit. Eventually, the gates opened, and the guard stepped aside as he motioned for me to proceed. I walked into the courtyard I knew all too well. The moment I set foot on the terrain, two guards lined my sides, and although the quiet sound of birds chirping and the smell of freshly cut grass was soothing, I remained skeptical.

I followed them inside, but instead of entering the office next to the main door, they led me farther through the hallway. We eventually reached a room at the back of the house, where they opened heavy doors and urged me inside. I resisted rolling my eyes and huff in annoyance when my father spoke.

"Dismissed."

The guards stepped outside, closing the doors behind them. My father was standing in front of a large, empty desk with a look of impatience.

"I gather you saw the news last night?" I gestured back at the closed door. "Though this is a bit much, don't you think?"

My father sat down, still tall and imposing, and gestured for me to do so as well. My throat tightened when I had no objection ready to decline.

"Leyla," he said in a voice that was both a greeting and a reprimand—ignoring my comment altogether. "You have been busy, I hear."

"Did you or did you not?" I asked him again, my patience wearing thin. "See the news?"

"Yes, I did." My father's gaze was piercing. "Content?"

No, I don't think I am, lay on the tip of my tongue; *why has it frightened you so?*

"Was there anything you wanted to share with me? Thoughts, perhaps?" my father drawled. I bit my tongue as I noticed the warning in his eyes. I was surprised Zade hadn't told him. "No? Now, then, can we get back to business?"

I swallowed as my father sat down opposite me. "How close have you gotten to the Archangel?"

I forced myself to keep meeting his eyes, aware of their assessing heat. I struggled to keep my voice impartial as I said, "It's going well." Taking a breath, I willed my racing thoughts to still. What else was I supposed to tell him? *I am catching feelings for him; he makes my breath hitch?* "I'm still in the beginning stages of gaining his trust," I explained. "He has not yet… opened up to me fully, and I'm not sure if he ever will, but I am optimistic I'll find a way to obtain the sword."

My father nodded slowly. A twinkle of interest had entered his gaze. "You've been to his home again?" he asked.

"Since the first time? No."

"You need to speed things up, *Cara*, use every trick at your disposal."

"I'm doing my best."

"Do better. You don't have to cozy up to the Angeli," he spat. "It isn't like he's going to be my son-in-law. Stop talking and get to business."

Despite gritting my teeth, I managed a curt nod. My father stared at me with intent from across his desk. I looked out the large bay window, wishing I could be as still and unperturbed as the buildings outside.

"On another note," he said. "Large amounts of money have been withdrawn from your account this week."

I should have known I would get caught one way or another. My father had a knack for discovering what I wanted to keep hidden. "It isn't considered disappearing if I know where it went."

"Where is it, then?" my father asked, unbothered by my quick remark.

I looked at my nails, stretching my long fingers and raising my brows. "Clothing, among other things."

"Leyla, look at me."

I slowly lifted my gaze to meet my father's. He carefully examined my face. "You went outside several nights this week. Want to tell me why?"

"I have a feeling you're going to tell *me*," I said.

My father leaned back in his chair, his face filled with disappointment—and even some traces of disbelief. "I have humored this do-gooder side of you for years, looking the other way when you desired to help the weak, but this is outrageous. Pull yourself together." He shook his head. "I knew those posh friends of yours would rub off on you, but what spell did the Archangel cast on you to take his side in this?

Because it sure as hell isn't mine."

I fought the burning sensation in my rib cage. There was truth to some of what he was saying, but I couldn't stand by and let innocent people get hurt. "No one influenced me," I said finally, lifting my gaze to meet his again. "I'm going with my gut, doing what feels right."

My father opened his mouth to reply but then closed it again, looking away with a sigh. He pinched the bridge of his nose. "Doing what *feels right*? Spitting at your heritage, the cause you so desperately wanted to be part of? Turning your back on Ashrior—your people?" He clucked his tongue and shook his head. "You're a *Naan*, Leyla. Not a Fivaldor, not an Eden, and certainly not a Venetia. No matter what you may think or want. It's irrelevant. Blood does not lie. Blood does not betray."

"I've been a Cuprum for much longer than I ever was a Naan." I couldn't remember a time when I'd even been allowed to use that name.

"Want to say that again?"

I turned my head as I swallowed. The underground air pressed on me, and my body itched to return to Shard City. I needed to breathe in fresh air, see the sky, feel the sun on my face. I was tired of this back and forth. No matter what I did, I couldn't seem to please him.

Fuck it.

I stood. I could be professional—detached. "It's time for me to go. I'll keep you updated on the progress."

My father seemed like he had something else to say, but I didn't wait for his response. Without hesitation, I left his new office, slamming the heavy door shut behind me. He never saw me as anything other than his precious, weak-hearted daughter. Nothing more than a sheltered child.

But I had a job to do, and no matter what he said or what he thought of me—no matter how much I disagreed with him—I was going to prove him wrong.

CHAPTER THIRTY

Dominic

Things had both cooled down and overheated in the days that passed. Nathan was a no-show to the afternoon drinks with Inesa that Friday afternoon. He only showed up at the meeting with the representatives earlier that week but still didn't acknowledge me and acted distantly. Inesa told me some bullshit about him not feeling well, but I knew that meant he wasn't ready to see me.

My nights had been lonely, fingers itching to text Leyla and ask her to go out with me. Yet I refrained from doing so. After the kick-off gala, the ball was now in her court. We would reconnect at some point, but she had to be the one to reach out. It was only a matter of when. And when some clubbers had been attacked by someone under the influence of Ambrosia, I had immediately pulled some strings to find out who the victims were before I made a fool of myself by calling Leyla. She had promised to steer clear of those clubs for some time, but I couldn't help but imagine worst-case scenarios.

So, when she finally contacted me during another meeting with the representatives, it was a welcome surprise.

Leyla: *How are you?*

I tried focusing on the discussion between Serena and Rakelsh, who went back and forth in circles. Eventually, my mind wandered back to Leyla.

Me: *That depends…*

Leyla: *On what?*

Me: *Did you cut ties with Starball's golden boy?*

"Tighten the fucking leash. Your drug cartels are messing up my streets."

Rakelsh laughed. "*Please.* Tone down the drama, Serena. They are not my anything. How about you stop your pathetic humans from buying bad shit? They are the ones creating the mess."

Heller let out a loud sigh, and I met his gaze. None of us wanted to intervene because it got us nowhere. They were always at each other's throats. Why couldn't they cohabitate in peace and sit through one meager meeting? Was that too much to ask?

I glanced at my phone underneath the table.

Leyla: *You were serious about that?*

I shook my head as a smile tugged at me lips.

Me: *Did I look like I was joking?*

Leyla: *Now you mention it…*

Me: *I take that as a no.*

"I can't believe you." Serena let her head fall back in frustration, her auburn hair cascading over the chair she was sitting on. She closed her eyes, her tongue moving over her bottom lip.

"Fall reborn is a peak time for transactions. Ambrosia is no exception, but no one expected this," I said, trying to defuse the situation and dissolve the tension. I moved my attention to Rakelsh. "Are there any hoops for them to jump through, at the least?"

The Daemon's bright purple eyes focused on me. "I thought we decided on first approaching the problem with a focus on rehabilitation?" Her voice was dripping innocence.

"That doesn't mean giving the dealers free rein," Heller told her. "This week alone, Lupine forces have picked up twenty-four dealers. That's a fuck ton too many."

Rakelsh rolled her eyes, her dark purple-painted lips turning into a smirk. "Well, at least we're all pulling our weight in the ecosystem, right? Without addicts, there wouldn't be dealers, and without dealers—" she looked at Heller "—our precious law enforcement would be out of a job. Not to mention the economic benefits."

Paplos rubbed a hand over his eyes. "It almost sounds like you're siding with Xanon, Rakelsh."

"Glad to hear I am not the only one who sees the middle fingers pointed at us," Nathan said, his voice dripping with sarcasm.

Rakelsh was glaring daggers at Paplos. "Shut the fuck up about things you do not understand, fisherman."

"Get your lights damned domain together, *Rakelsh*," Inesa abruptly said from across the table. She had managed to remain remarkably quiet during the meeting.

The Daemon next to me chuckled. "If it isn't our pristine Angeli cursing. I never thought I'd see the day."

Inesa's eyes were cold. "There's a lot you haven't seen."

"Says the girl who has immunity because she's besties with the Archangel."

"Enough," I said to both of them.

Nathan arched a brow.

"Oh?" Rakelsh hissed, uncurling her long-nailed fingers. "She can dish it out but not take it?"

Our eyes met. "Seriously? You know better than this."

The room was quiet for a few moments, and I could feel the tension evaporate as glances were exchanged. Rakelsh's face hadn't softened, but the cold in her eyes melted a little as she looked at me. With a sliver of vulnerability, she swallowed, and her eyes steeled over as she sat back, her shoulders stiff. Rakelsh was an incredibly complicated character. Her life had started out rough, largely due to Xanon Naan. It had toughened her—made her more wary of people. And though she would never admit it, she was scared. Working against him was a challenge, especially being a Daemon.

Rakelsh crossed her arms and looked out of the windows, remaining silent as the conversation picked back up, shifting to the upcoming ACC tournament. We discussed the strengths and weaknesses of each team, some of us even placing bets on our favorites to emerge victorious.

I stood and cleared my throat, drawing everyone's attention. "I think it's time we wrapped this up for today and take some time to think about what we discussed," I said calmly. "We will reconvene soon with an action plan for the situation at hand."

Everyone murmured their agreement and began getting up from their seats, filing out of the room. Nathan was the first to leave. It was fine. Whatever. Heller gave me a nod before departing. The Lupine must be eager to return to his domain after spending so much time sitting here. As an active law enforcer, he was always ready to spring into action. He wanted to be out there with his units, especially during times like this.

Rakelsh slowly rose, retrieving her coat from the chair, and then met my gaze again, saying with her eyes what she could not get past her lips.

"I know," I said, nodding.

She merely clenched her jaw before turning away and heading towards the exit herself, ignoring Inesa altogether as she left us alone in the conference room. Thoughts piled up in my head, tangling into a giant knot as I took my phone from my pocket again.

"Give him some time, Dom." Inesa stood suddenly next to me.

"He can get all the time he needs." I forced a smile at her. "But it would've been really fucking mature of him to at least acknowledge me at work."

"You know that's not how he deals with his emotions." She rested a hand on my arm. "Call me if you need anything?"

I nodded at her as she left the room. Inesa was a great friend who didn't deserve to be on the receiving end of my frustration. Sighing, I finally looked at my phone to see if Leyla had texted back.

Leyla: *My life is complicated, Dominic.*

I knew the feeling. Hell, my own life was a complete headache.

Me: *That doesn't scare me.*

Leaving the conference room with my eyes glued to the small screen, I opted for the stairs leading to the roof.

Leyla: *It should.*

Me: *Why? Want me to leave you alone?*

Would I? If she asked? Would I leave her be, even though I knew there was something there?

Leyla: *That's not what I said.*

I grinned. Seems I wouldn't have to find out.

Me: *What do you want, then?*

Her reply took long enough for me to stash away my phone and fly back home before looking at it again.

Ashtior was beautiful in the setting sun; its surfaces reflected the bright rays down onto Shard City and the rest of Ashium. I bet Leyla would like this view despite her supposed fear of flying.

I let out a deep breath as I landed in my garden, the soft grass cushioning my feet and the warmth of the setting sun on my skin a pleasant change from the chill air. The flowers in my garden were wilting, their petals turning brown and stems drooping ever so slightly. Fall had barely begun, and the vibrant colors were fading and replaced with a softer palette of orange, red, and yellow.

I stalked through my garden, enjoying the view of the changing season, before heading inside and checking my phone again. Sure enough, there was a reply from Leyla waiting for me.

Leyla: *Something real.*

My throat dried up as I read her message. I opened the sliding doors and stepped inside my house as my eyes remained locked on the screen. Leyla was typing again, but no response came. There was no need for her to overthink this. She could say anything to me. I wanted her to know that. Whatever had happened to her in the past, whatever she feared, I would be different.

She would be different.

Me: *Come watch the ACC's opening game from my sky box.*

Leyla: *Dana and I received invitations to the Ethereal family and friends box.*

My eyes narrowed as I typed and retyped my response.

Me: *My view is better. Bring Fivaldor.*

Leyla: *I'll think about it.*

"What has gotten you into such a merry mood?" Amy looked at me like she'd seen a ghost—a nice one, for her smile stretched from ear to ear. She put groceries on the kitchen counter as I entered the living room.

I plunged onto the couch and draped my arm over the back, not meeting Amy's prying eyes. "Nothing."

"*Nothing* has you smiling at your phone?" she mused casually as I heard the paper bags rumple while she unloaded products and loaded them into the fridge.

I inhaled. "Just a good day, is all."

"Sure, Dominic," she answered, but I could hear the smile in her voice.

CHAPTER THIRTY-ONE

Leyla

Exhausted beyond belief, I climbed the stairs to my apartment. Running had proven a lousy distraction, even as I pushed myself to my limits. Staying up late watching Starball games of Dominic and researching the ACC wasn't weird, right? It counted as work.

My heart leaped when I noticed the large package barricading my front door. The item was protected by cloth and secured between two wooden panels. Who had brought this upstairs for me? I hadn't been informed about any package being delivered today. Carefully, I pulled it back from the wall and noticed a white envelope attached to the wooden panel at the back, reading *Leyla Cuprum*.

What the hell?

I opened my door and dragged the package with me, haphazardly slinging my bag and coat on the couch before unwrapping it to reveal what was inside. As soon as all protection fell away, I stepped back, covering my mouth with my hand in shock.

It was the painting I had seen—had adored at the fall reborn kick-off gala.

The painting was just as stunning as I remembered, depicting a night sky filled with stars and the grand backdrop of Shard City. The cityscape sparkled with bright lights as shooting stars streaked across the sky, each one intricately detailed. Its colors were vibrant and alive; a deep blue hue dominated the night sky, while lighter shades of purple and pink added to its beauty. Distant stars sparkled brilliantly against the canvas, adding even more depth to the painting's mesmerizing effect. I was so taken aback by the beauty I felt almost transported into it.

Breathtaking—a masterpiece in its own right. I felt a wave of emotion wash over me. I knew without a doubt who had bought it for me. Only one other person had seen me looking at it that night and had witnessed my awe from up close.

I opened the white envelope and read the card, which was written in hand. I didn't recognize that handwriting, but the strokes were determined.

Art belongs to those who know how to appreciate it.
D.V.

My reaction must have caught his eye. Dominic was an art collector; he recognized the sight of someone drawn to a piece. I looked at many pieces with awe that night, but he had noticed this spark was different. No doubt admiration had radiated off me as I looked at this painting. And the Archangel had been watching.

My phone buzzed, interrupting my thoughts. I blinked several times, wiping at my cheeks, and inhaled deeply.

Dana: *I'll be outside your house in fifteen.*

I stepped back from the painting, letting it lean against

the wall, still marveling at the fact that Dominic had bought this for me. It was such a touching present that it rendered me speechless.

Shaking my head, I snapped out of it.

I had a game to get ready for.

Ashar was buzzing. Since it was the cup's opening weekend, most people had this time off and partied all day long. Already, we passed drunk people in the streets who would never make the game. I maneuvered around their puking forms with rolling eyes.

Ambrosia dealings spiked during this time. People were betting more, using more, and spending more. The season heavily affected the Human Domain, the Daemon Domain, and especially Shard City. Police forces mainly comprised shifters from the Lupine domain, who were busy guarding the players and patrolling the city. Many lined the stadium, all outfitted with guns and other weapons. They looked as dangerous as they were. Living in Shard city, it was impossible not to have seen them take down people—and those Ashari did not beat around the bush.

However, the Lupine were stretched thin during the season. They barely had people left to station around the city or patrol for underground markets, which, according to what Zade once told me, was prime time for the organization. We never celebrated the ACC because my father thought it a waste of time and space—never minding business was booming. He despised nearly everything that occurred above ground, especially when it had something to do with the Trias Politica.

The main stadium in the Human Domain hosted all the official Ashar City Cup games. It starkly contrasted the domain's scenery: a shiny, hyper-modern mega stadium in the middle of a domain riddled with poverty. Although this part of the domain was fairly modern, the difference was staggering.

Despite not belonging, the humans had wanted the stadium in their domain because of its poverty. That way, they could draw on opportunities to make additional money. But every year since then, the humans complained. The domain became unbearable to live in during this time, and they regretted hosting the stadium, even though, economically speaking, their domain prospered during the fall—both legally and illegally.

A guy bumped into Dana, nearly spilling a drink over her white dress. "Hey!" she yelled. "Watch it."

The human was drunk out of his mind, belonging to the not-being-able-to-enter-the-stadium category. Security would never let him in like this, even if he reached the entrance. Snapping out of his stupor, he noticed Dana. "Damn," the guy said slowly, blinking. He stepped closer, eyeing her from head to toe. I blocked his vision, stopping in front of my friend as she was trying to get some droplets off her coat.

"Get lost," I told him.

The human's eyes moved to mine. "Ooh, you're both hot. Two for one?" He slurred.

Before I could respond, a set of hands grabbed the guy back and tore him away from us. The human who dragged him away looked from me to Dana apologetically, noticing our annoyance. "Sorry," he said. "Our friend has a rough night."

I cocked a brow. "Let him have a rough night somewhere else."

"Sure thing." The guy saluted.

"Don't worry about it," Dana said to him as she stood next to me. "He stopped before making any permanent damage."

The human looked from me to her. "I'm glad."

"Have a great night!" she called after them as she took my arm and dragged me after her. "Scaring them like that is really unnecessary. They might start thinking all Daemons are this unfriendly."

"Good riddance."

"Leyla…"

"Alright," I sighed. "Whatever." *They already do, anyway.*

Humans also took part in the competition, but, as expected, they never came in first. Genetically, they were at a disadvantage: less agile, fragile, had no wings, and were hurt easily. But humans were fighters—some with an ambition so ruthless it rivaled some of the top-Ashari players. Teams who desperately wanted to prove themselves made it far, with the human team even reaching the top three in certain years. But the best teams and players usually came from Ashari races, aside from the Pisces, for obvious reasons. This game wasn't designed for them.

This was my first time watching live in the stadium. Josiah and Tommy had promised us VIP tickets weeks ago, and the latter sent them over to Dana's apartment as a sort of peace offering with roses and everything. She took the tickets but didn't respond to him. It seemed his luck had finally worn out. Josiah had sent mine with a text, saying he hoped to see me there.

I hadn't told her Dominic had invited us to his sky box,

even though there was a high possibility of her parents being at the Ethereal one. I was nervous. His friends would be there, including other important people who didn't know who I was, and I wished to keep it that way.

Going over there felt like admitting something. And there was nothing to admit.

I looked at my reflection in the stadium's glass panels and surveyed my outfit. I'd chosen a tight red dress paired with strappy-heeled sandals. My long, dark hair fell in loose curls. Elegant yet comfortable.

"What do you think?" Dana asked, pointing to her freshly painted red lips.

Nodding, I said, "Looks great."

My best friend smoothed her white, flowy dress. She wore her now darker pink hair pulled back into a long ponytail.

"I hope it fucking blinds him." She sighed happily. "Maybe he'll get distracted by all the blowjobs he won't be getting from me."

Tommy had once again been spotted with someone else, and he had called Dana all weekend, begging for her forgiveness, until she had blocked his number. Dana had finally realized what a douche he was—at least, I hoped it had gotten through that thick skull of hers. I bet he wasn't expecting her to show up. He'd better not think she wanted him back.

"Excited?" I asked her.

"I hope the Ethereals lose their first match." Dana's eyes sparkled with excitement. "When are you going to break the bad news to Josiah?"

"There's nothing to tell," I murmured.

The other day, after a few too many drinks, I spilled my conflicted feelings about Dominic to her, recounting what he had said at the gala. She had squealed. *Squealed.*

We walked inside the stadium with our VIP badges and were led to the reserved seating area. It was already filled with the rest of the ACC Ethereal players families, friends, and sponsors. The sky was still clutching onto the last rays of the sun. Not too late yet to go to Dominic's sky box. I looked around to see if I could spot gold in the crowd.

"You're looking for him, aren't you?"

"By the light!" I said.

"Who are you kidding, Ley? I, for one, hope we run into the Archangel tonight. He won't know what hit him when he sees your outfit." Dana gazed up dreamily.

I shook my head, forcing my eyes to remain in the VIP area.

She just chuckled in response, looking around her. "They're not here," she said. "They would be here by now if they were coming."

Her parents' absence would not be missed. "Good," I said, squeezing her hand as the atmosphere buzzed with excitement. People of all ages filed into the stands, eager to watch the match. The more people entered, the more the crowd's cheer grew deafening. We made our way to our seats and settled in. Everything about the event was enticing, from the vibrant colors of the arena to the perfectly manicured grass. Sunlight was disappearing fast, and the first stars twinkled in the sky.

Music sounded, and a voice announced both teams. I recognized Josiah immediately, looking impressive in his full Starball uniform. The players ran onto the field in a formation, waving at the howling crowd. Dana looked at me, eyes rolling, as Tommy looked up to the box, clearly spotting her.

I focused on Josiah's frame, his number eight a beacon on the field. My internet research on Starball had mentioned his name a lot. I already knew he was good even though I didn't care for the game; I'd seen him move, play, and heard people talk about him. It was alluring, for sure.

Not only was Josiah Eden the hottest guy on the field—he was kind, too. And I didn't want to get his hopes up, thinking I was there solely for him. Because although I'd gotten in with his ticket and was curious to see him play live—I wasn't. Did that make me a bitch?

"Now," the announcer called, and the stadium quieted as if everyone knew what was coming. "Our Prime will officially open the season."

Dana looked at me, waggling her brows at me. "*Our Prime.*"

"He invited us to his sky box," I whispered.

Her jaw slackened, the smile dripping off her face. "And you tell me that now?"

People around us hissed at her to keep quiet. She turned back, but not without a fierce glance my way. I gnawed at my lip as a spotlight focused on the left of the stadium, at the same height as us—the middle ring—where Dominic's golden wings reflected the light. He was wearing all white and had his hands on the railing, casually looking at the field, the stadium, as if he ruled it all.

A lot happened at once. The music stilled, and people seemed to hold their breaths. Dana had often gushed about how fascinating and beautiful those falling stars were from up close, but I had never witnessed it.

Until now.

Dominic raised a hand, fingers slightly curled as if holding something, and looked to the sky. Being the Archangel of

Ashar, he controlled the weather. His powers held the city together with a magnetic field and protected it from the extreme weather of the rest of Celestia. Places that didn't have their own archangels usually had other ways of protecting themselves against meteorites.

He was opening a small part of the dome to the field for the game the teams had been training all year for. I had read online that they had banned him from playing when it had become apparent he would become the next archangel. His powers could influence the meteorites falling from the sky and thus the game.

For a moment, there was nothing. We all stared at the Archangel. Then—a flash. Blue, yellow, and orange, all at once.

Like the painting.

I had never seen it from this close. My father detested things like this: all the domains mingling and putting aside our differences and problems for a brief season. But I got it now—I understood why some people sold their souls to attend each one of these games.

It was magical.

Another star fell through the invisible hole in the barrier, and another, and then the entire stadium exploded. People yelled, clapped, hollered, and stood in their seats—every sound fueled by pure excitement. Adrenaline coursed through the stadium with a steady pulse as the players got ready to start the game. Some falling stars seared holes in the arena floor, and some burnt out before even hitting the ground. A transparent shield that protected everyone but the players dissolved falling stars that strayed from their course, moving towards the crowds.

I sat straighter and noticed my mouth had dropped open, but I couldn't be the only one. The night sky was filled with stars. There were so many of them.

All the while, Dominic stood there, not looking at the stars but at the field. The spotlight was gone from his balcony, but I caught sight of his wings flaring—as if he wanted to take flight. *Play*.

My heart ached a little, watching him, though the rest of me was in awe. What he did was nothing short of magical. The painting he had bought for me, the fall reborn depiction I had loved… It was the spitting image. Another manifestation of his magic, captured on canvas.

There were no words to describe it.

The starting signal sounded, and I forced my eyes away from the now-empty balcony and looked at the game. Both teams stormed onto the field. Transfixed, I tried to block out any intrusive thoughts of the man responsible for the falling stars.

Which was probably even harder than catching them.

CHAPTER THIRTY-TWO

Dominic

Every year, all domains came together to support their favorite teams during the Ashar City Cup. The best players were picked during the selections at the beginning of the year, and depending on how good you were and what team you played for, there was a lot of money to earn in this game. There were a lot of great teams, so first place alternated from year to year. Though, statistically speaking, the spot usually went to either the Angeli, Ethereals, or Lupine teams.

Starball didn't have many rules. The main goal was scoring points and preventing your opponents from doing the same. It usually came down to which team was the most powerful, strong, agile, and strategic. You needed all these types of players in your team, both defensive and offensive, a mix of brute force and swift attacks.

The ACC was held during fall reborn for a reason. Meteorite showers, which we called falling stars, occurred nearly every night. Thousand upon thousands of them crashed onto the city's protective walls, the shield invisible to the eye. Most of the rocks could survive the entire way down to the ground without the shield, but instead, they dissolved immediately. It was quite a sight by itself. When the game was first played, there had been no protective shield. People used to have their own magic to protect themselves and their homes. Our ancestors' magic was gone, leaving me solely responsible for protecting the city. Before every game, I opened part of the shield so the stars could enter the stadium.

I sat down next to Inesa, who had brought Leon. Nathan was there, too. We hadn't spoken to each other, but everything remained cordial as long as the other representatives were here. They always watched the first match from my sky box, and this season's first game kicked off with Nathan's domain, playing against the Lupine—the reigning champions. The Ethereals had a real chance of winning the competition this year. Their team was exceptionally talented.

I looked at the onslaught below. Nathan held onto the balcony railing and cursed loudly as the Lupine team scored points or reached a fallen meteorite faster than one of the Ethereals. To score points, you had to get the rocks to your side of the field, and until you got there, the other team was allowed to take it from you. The match had only been going for ten minutes, but uniforms were already singed and smeared with soot and sand. There were even a few brawls that referees had to stop.

When a meteorite entered the atmosphere and descended, it started burning. You didn't just 'catch' a falling star—well, most players didn't, as they lacked the power to slow or cool them on the way down. They had to grab them from the ground. But the players that did… they were fucking powerful and often the highest-scoring in the competition. Those players practically had free gain if not too many defensive opponents shadowed them.

It was a simple game, really. The team with the heaviest bucket won. Sometimes, there were many, creating absolute chaos. Other nights, especially later into the season, around the finale, fewer and fewer stars fell, which made every point to score a battle on its own. I preferred those. They were more intense and the most fun to watch. It was the point in the competition where it came down to the most talented team.

The field was the only place without protection during this time, and it often resulted in severe injuries. If players didn't watch out or made a wrong move at the wrong time, a ball of fire could hit them. While there were designated players who protected their teammates, there had been a couple of deaths over the decades. The competition was popular enough for people to keep coming back to watch, regardless of the circumstances—perhaps because the stakes were so high.

When I played, I was the best in the competition, bringing the Angeli team victories five years in a row. I could catch a falling star from the sky with my ability to fly and slow it down with my powers, even before my wings had turned golden. Many opponents had complained to the board of cheating but never succeeded. Only after my wings changed color was I politely asked to step down. By that point in my life, I hadn't felt like playing anymore.

A server refilled our glasses, and I stared into my drink, which reflected the blazing lights that entered the stadium. The other representatives were mixing, having brought their respective partners, but save for a few conversations beforehand, I mostly sat next to Inesa in silence.

I tapped the chair with my signet ring, eyes drifting away from the field and into the crowd on my right, where the

Ethereal players families sat. I could see her frame from the distance—sensed it was her. My eyes kept shifting between her and the game, and I took out my phone when we were just a few minutes from halftime.

Me: *Red suits you.*

My lips pulled into a smirk as she left the chat on read for a while.

Leyla: *You're too far away to know what color I am wearing.*

Me: *You're right, it is too far. Watch the game from my sky box. Bring Lodana.*

Leyla: *Dana wants me to let you know she wanted to come sooner.*

Me: *I like her.*

Leyla: *Not too much, I hope.*

Me: *Get over here, Leyla. We're on the same level, east wing. You have clearance to enter.*

When the teams pulled back from the field, the matted glass doors of the sky box opened and revealed Leyla Cuprum and Lodana Fivaldor. Leyla's high heels clicked on the marble floors as she entered the large space. Behind me, outside, Inesa and Nathan were watching us as their conversation came to a halt.

"Leyla." My voice was low, but I grinned at her, moving my gaze from her heeled feet to her eyes—which she rolled. Red really *did* suit her.

"Hey," she said, oozing confidence. She gestured to her friend, who was smiling at me like she could see straight through me. That girl was a handful. "You know Lodana."

I nodded and gestured to the bar on the side. "Can I get you both something to drink?"

"Wine?" they asked in unison, and I bit my cheek as they laughed at each other. Leyla's face completely lit up when she looked at her friend, her guard down. I made the order and turned around to see Nathan walking over to us. He shook Leyla's hand before turning his attention fully to Lodana. "I'm Nathanial, but friends call me Nathan."

"Am I?" she asked, raising a brow. "A friend?"

"I hope so." Nathan had already spoken more words to Lodana Fivaldor than he'd done to me all evening.

Lodana bit her lip. "I'm Lodana, but please call me Dana. My mother would die of a stroke if she knew. Which would be worth it."

A server brought two glasses of wine, one of which Lodana took from him without looking. Her gaze was locked with Nathan's, and he, in turn, was unable to keep a smile from his face.

Leyla and I shared a knowing look.

"What team is going to win, you think?" I asked her.

"Ethereals," Nathan and Lodana answered in unison instead, though Dana added, "Duh." Which made Nathan's chest rumble with laughter—a sound few people heard from him.

Leyla took a sip of her wine and brushed her thumb over the lipstick stain on the rim of her glass. She leveled a look at me. "Thank you for the painting."

My chest constricted, but I shrugged it off. "Your admiration for it was obvious."

"Still. You didn't have to." She grabbed her opposite arm, taking another sip.

"I'm pleased you came."

"Dana was very excited," she said, but her eyes told me something else. It wasn't hard to discern how she tried hiding her amusement and attraction to me. Those green eyes of her betrayed her every time.

I chuckled and stepped closer. "You don't have to pretend with me, Leyla."

Her throat bobbed, and her gaze moved to her glass again. I soaked in every detail of her reaction. "What do you mean?"

"I told you before; you already have my attention."

She was about to open her mouth as the teams returned to the stadium to resume the match. All the people who had gone inside to get a drink or stretch their legs walked back out.

I followed Leyla to the balcony while she looked out onto the field, and I noticed Ethereal's golden boy looking up at us. He greeted her with a wave, and she responded by raising her hand. Josiah Eden looked away as I stepped closer to the railing, and he huddled with his team to prepare for the second half. I gripped the railing next to her and rose to my full height, my arm brushing her bare shoulder. Looking out onto the field instead of at her, I said, "He's a good player."

"Yes," she responded, a tad too admiring to my liking. "He's also a good guy."

"Leyla," I purred, letting my fingers wander to hers. "He's an adult, he'll get over it."

Her lips parted, emerald eyes moving to where we were touching. "I know," she breathed as my little finger brushed hers, leaving a streak of burning hot skin behind in their wake.

She stepped back, cheeks flushed, putting distance between us as if I had crossed some invisible boundary by touching her, even though it had been just the slightest brush of my fingertips. I could feel my heart beating, and I knew she sensed it, too. The air around us buzzed with tension, and neither of us spoke as we continued to look out onto the field.

"Listen—"

Leyla spun around and brushed past me. "I have to use the restroom. Excuse me."

I watched her exit the balcony, charting the curves of her body through the fabric of her dress as she walked away from me. My eyes locked with Inesa's, who was trying to gauge my reaction to what happened. I kept my expression blank, glancing at Nathan and Lodana, who were still in deep conversation on the other side of the balcony—oblivious.

But not Inesa; Inesa noticed everything.

I only registered Nathan's presence when he dropped into the chair next to me and crossed an ankle over his knee. He leaned his arm casually over his bent leg, and I frowned at the peaceful expression on his face.

"Scared her off so soon?" Nathan asked, but I could see the gentle smile on his face for what it was: a peace offering. "That sets the bar low, even for you."

I wrapped a hand around my neck, leaning back in the chair, and smiled at him. "You're done now?"

"That depends," he drawled. "Will you get me Lodana Fivaldor's number?"

"That depends," I countered. "Will you stop talking shit about the person I have to get it from?"

He gave me a pointed look.

I laughed. "Couldn't get it yourself, *Farcroft?*"

Nathan sighed deeply. "Trust me, I tried. But she said she was coming out of a complicated relationship with some dipshit from the Ethereal team."

How unoriginal.

"And you want to pursue her because…?"

"She's special." He shook his head. "From the get-go, she understood my complicated family dynamic like no one I ever met. She gets the relationship with my father because she has an almost identical one with her mother. Lodana doesn't care about conservative Etherealism and has the brightest personality ever. Plus, have you seen her? She's stunning. Should I continue?"

That was a lot coming from Nathan, both in words and praise.

The falling stars were dropping in great numbers now, dispersing against the invisible shield, hitting the field below far too close to some players.

"Listen, Dom," he said. "I'm sorry about what I said. I still don't have... a good feeling about the girl, to be honest, but I should have said it in another way. And I should trust that you know what you're doing."

"I'm sorry, too."

Someone whooped behind us, making both of us turn. "I'm so happy to see my boys back together!" Inesa made a heart with her fingers. Leon, next to her, just looked at us with raised brows, warning us to never, *ever* put her through that again. As if we had hurt her on purpose.

Nathan looked at me with a question in his eyes, snorting, "Remind me to never get on his bad side."

"You remind *me*."

He smiled a little as he bumped my shoulder. "It's okay, you know. Families fight."

"Leon isn't family, though," I said.

Nathan's eyes crinkled. "Damn right he isn't."

CHAPTER THIRTY-THREE

Leyla

"Hold on. I still don't understand," Dana said, leaning back against the beige-tiled wall. "You're hiding in here because Dominic Venetia expressed his interest in you?"

I ran my hands through my hair and glared at her in the mirror. "What do you want me to say? The man is fucking overwhelming. I do not know how to behave when he talks to me like that."

"No shit." She placed her hands behind her back. "I've never seen you act like such a baby."

"He's too much. I am practically choking."

"Never had a problem with that before, huh?"

A laugh bubbled out of me despite myself.

"You aren't the type to scare easily, Ley."

"You're damn right I'm not."

"Then go back out there." Dana pointed to the door leading back into the sky box. "And stop whining."

I rinsed my hands with the lukewarm water. "Okay, mom." I took one last deep breath before walking through the door she held open for me.

My heart started racing again as soon as I stepped onto

the balcony. Dominic was seated near where I had left him earlier, seemingly unfazed by my abrupt departure. The Archangel must have heightened senses because his head turned my way as I neared. Our eyes met. He rose. The man next to him, Nathanial Farcroft, looked back and left without a word, making his way toward where Dana went to the bar. I reminded myself to ask her about him later.

I glanced at my phone and found a text from Zade, giving me something to do other than look at the imposing man waiting for me a few paces away.

Z: *I just spotted you on TV in the Archangel's box. Everything OK?*
Me: *Yes.*

Dominic smiled as I arrived, though his observing eyes moved to the phone I was putting back in my purse. "You returned," he said, voice suave. "For a moment there, I thought you wouldn't."

My face grew hot. "I wouldn't have left without saying goodbye."

He chuckled lightly and then held out his hand to me in an invitation. I looked up into his golden eyes and hesitated before taking his hand and letting him lead me back to the front of the box. I tried ignoring the prying eyes following us from every direction.

"What did I do to scare you off?" he asked softly as we settled into the seats, and I had to double-check if the words had actually left his mouth.

The fact that I don't want to like you, but I do.

I blinked. "Nothing."

He leveled a glance at me. "I clearly affected you."

"You don't affect me at all."

"And I think you're full of bullshit," he said.

I chuckled. "You have no idea."

Dominic Venetia smiled fully, teeth bared, eyes crinkling, and everything.

The Magnum Iter flashed before my eyes in bright neon lights, and acid burned through my veins. To get closer to the sword, I had to take action at some point. But how the hell was I supposed to bring it up without Dominic getting instantly suspicious?

"What's on your mind?" The Archangel had stepped closer and lowered his voice.

I swallowed, hesitating. "I was thinking about this book I read once… but it would definitely bore you."

A low chuckle sounded from his throat. "Okay, Leyla, try me."

"Alright. It was The Magnum Iter. You might've heard of it since you're such a know-it-all, not to mention older than me by a lot." Time stopped as I felt his full attention settle on me. "I was thinking about this supposed magical sword it mentions. Now, I know not to believe grand tales like this, but I caught a rumor the other day that the sword actually exists. The possibility seemed cool to me." It slipped out so damn easily.

Dominic looked at me for a long moment, so long that I started thinking he was on to me. "Found yourself in need of some light reading, did you?"

I shrugged, feigning indifference.

An incredulous laugh left him. "You read that thing?"

"Not entirely, but dim down the surprise, Dominic. Your superiority complex is showing." I rolled my eyes at him in emphasis. I really needed to play this off.

"You must be aware only a minority of people have read

that text or understand the references it makes. Where did you get a copy? There aren't that many going around."

He was right. I hadn't even heard about the book before my father told me about it. "My boss—the business side, not the pleasure." My smile was timed, and Dominic's eyes moved to my mouth as if I dragged them there. "He's a collector; art, books, whatever holds value. He was the one who told me about it."

His golden eyes turned back to mine, moving between them. He was a picture of casualness, but something simmered beneath the surface. "Your boss has a particular taste. Who is he?"

Dangerous territory.

"He wishes to remain anonymous."

Dominic moved his hand over his mouth, thumb and index finger brushing his lips. My brain scrambled, threw up, and somersaulted inside my skull, all while I tried to recollect my thoughts. I carefully kept my face blank. Did I cross the line? Was I wrong to mention the sword?

"So? What do you think?" I pressed, still with that joking smile on my lips. "Is it true?"

He pursed his mouth, but I could see his molars grinding.

"You know, don't you?" I narrowed my eyes at him playfully. "I would owe you one if I could tell my boss yes or no."

His expression was a carefully crafted mask of neutrality, eyes searching my face. The man didn't give me any hint of what he was thinking until he spoke again. "Where did you hear that rumor, anyway?"

"My boss."

"Hmm," Dominic murmured, brushing a finger over his lips.

"Well?" I pressed. "Do you have an answer for me, then?"

"I might have something better."

I smiled through the nerves, pushing them down as much as possible. "And what would that be?"

"Patience, Leyla." His head dipped low, an escaped curl dropping in front of his eyes as he perused my face. "First, we go on a date."

My throat was dry as I got lost in his eyes and whispered, "Okay."

I had just made the biggest mistake in my life or luck was on my side like never before. Either way, *I was fucked*.

At the end of the game, I said my goodbyes to Dominic, who had many guests lined up to speak with him. I felt he didn't want to let me go just yet, but that was precisely the moment I had to leave. Judging by the man I knew Dominic to be, the date he promised me would be soon.

I walked up to Dana, who was still chatting with Nathanial Farcroft. She had a hand on his arm as I approached them with a smile and asked, "Ready to go?"

"I am if you are," I said, giving her an opening. "I could go ahead if you—"

"No!" she said. "Let me go to the restroom one more time. Then we can go."

"Congrats," I told Nathanial once she left. His domain had won the first match of the season.

The Ethereal adjusted his stance, wrapping his arms together—so different from the lively person he'd been during the match. "Thanks." As soon as Dana was gone from view, he surprised me by saying, "Dominic seems enamored by you."

Quizzically, I turned my head to face him, my fingers weaving together in front of me. "You seem enamored by Lodana."

He wasn't smiling, just watching me—gaze penetrating. "Didn't she tell you? She wants her friends to call her Dana."

His sarcastic tone raised my hackles. "So you are friends now?"

The Ethereal licked his bottom lip. "I'd like to think we're going to be more than that."

I couldn't get a read on the guy. At least he was better than Tommy, though that set a low bar.

"And you and Dominic?" I asked. "You've been friends for long, right?"

"We have."

"You must know each other well." So many years. I felt like I had known Lodana all my life, which was a blip in time compared to their friendship.

"That depends."

"On what?" I turned to him more fully.

"On what you are going to ask me."

I smiled, close-lipped, but it didn't reach my eyes. The effort strained my cheeks. "I'm not going to ask you anything."

"Not even if he has mentioned you to me?" Nathanial looked unimpressed.

My cheeks heated with indignation. I didn't know what to do with my hands, so I searched for Dominic in the crowd. "No."

"You wouldn't be the first." Nathanial's voice had gone lower.

He didn't trust me.

"And I'm sure I wouldn't have been the last—but alas, I

have not." My breathing deepened, and I looked away from him, getting irked. "This isn't the way to go about getting in the good graces of the best friend of the girl you're interested in."

"Dominic is very important to me, Miss Cuprum."

I understood. I felt the same about Dana. "What are you insinuating?"

"Merely that you shouldn't play games you don't understand the rules of."

My composure wavered as I stared at him in astonishment.

"This city is filled with ambitious people," Nathanial mused.

"What makes you any different?" I hissed. "For all I know, your career exists only because of your 'supposed' friendship."

Nathanial Farcroft narrowed his eyes at me. Stupid, stupid, stupid! Making an enemy out of the friend he's had for decades was not the way to go about this, either. Shaking my head, I tried to swallow, but my throat had become dry as sandpaper from the anger that now inhabited me. Tearing my eyes away from the Ethereal representative, I noticed Dana coming back towards us.

"I'm ready," she sang as she gripped my arm. I was stiff as a board, but she didn't notice. Smiling at Nathanial, she said, "It was nice meeting you, Representative Farcroft."

His icy facade melted right off. "It's Nathan."

She just winked at him before tearing me away from the sky box.

I looked back to see if I could catch one last glimpse of Dominic, but all I saw was Nathanial Farcroft's stony gaze focused on me, eyeing me from head to toe like I was a problem.

303

Right back at you, pal.

I had only visited the Museum of Modern Art once. The gala had left me in awe of the vast array of art adorning the walls and the beautiful sculptures filling the hallways. Today, however, something in the air was different. I had been walking around, taking in the masterpieces and admiring the talent of those who had created them, when I suddenly felt a sharp stabbing pain in my head.

I froze in place, my breath catching as I turned around.

What I saw sent a chill down my spine. Dozens of people were lying on the ground, writhing in pain. I stumbled towards them, my heart racing as I watched helplessly, not knowing what to do.

And then I noticed her—Dana—lying motionless in the sea of people. I ran to her side, kneeling next to her. I tried wiping away the blood that was pooling from her eyes, but it was too late.

I was too late.

My best friend was gone. *Dead.*

How did this happen? I had just seen her, hadn't I?

Tears streamed down my cheeks as I whipped around in panic, now realizing that everyone in the museum was dead. I was the only one still breathing. My inhales and exhales were the sole sound in the room; the rest was filled with a sickening silence.

As I rose on trembling legs, I noticed a man stepping around the corner, seemingly unaffected by the chaos that had just ensued.

His golden wings were unmistakable.

Dominic stared at me like it was the first time he truly saw me—his face filled with sorrow that matched the feeling in my heart. Slowly, he moved towards me, stopping a few feet away. As he gently wiped away my tears, it seemed like he understood what had happened. His presence was calming. Comforting.

I looked down at my hands, which were still smeared with Lodana's blood. My tears kept falling, but Dominic raised my chin to meet his hardened gaze. "Don't cry, Leyla," he said softly, voice distorted. "Red suits you."

The room spun, and I was unable to move or speak as my vision blurred. My body slumped to the ground as I drifted into unconsciousness.

I awoke with a start, gasping for air as tears rolled down my face. It had been a dream—a horrible dream. I tried to orient myself and get my bearings. *My room. My bed. My home.* Everything was as it was supposed to be: no traces of Lodana's blood left on my hands, nor any sign of Dominic's haunting presence.

But the bad aftertaste still lingered. The sadness and guilt were still there, but so was something else.

I just couldn't put my finger on it.

"Hey, Leyla. How are you?"

Josiah had called me right after I sat down to eat breakfast. His voice on the other end of the phone was like an anvil, dragging me back to the present moment—away from last night's nightmare.

"I'm good." I scratched my neck. "Congratulations on the win."

"I hoped to catch you after the game. What did you think of it?"

"It was great," I said, swallowing. "You were great."

"Just great?" His soft chuckle sounded.

"You were amazing, Josiah." I tried sounding cheerier than I felt. "But you already know that." The amount of girls who would want to switch places with me right now was staggering.

"I wanted to hear it from you." After a slight pause, he said, "I liked seeing you there. Could get used to that."

My grip tightened on the phone. "Yeah," I said, my voice a little smaller now, "I enjoyed seeing you play for once after all the big talk." The silence that followed was thick and heavy with what felt like the calm before the storm.

"Go out with me after the tournament, Leyla. Give me a chance to show you where this could go."

I pinched one eye closed as I let myself fall back on my bed. "I can't date you, Josiah." Clearing my throat, I clarified, "I'm kind of seeing someone right now."

"Ah," Josiah said after a few moments, followed by a sigh. "Alright."

My heart sank in my chest, and I suddenly wanted to be anyone but me. "You're truly a great guy, and if I were anyone else, I would have given you a fair chance." I cringed internally.

"Don't worry about it."

"I'm sorry," I said, more affected than I thought. In another life... If I had been any other girl from a different family and wanted something else, Josiah and I could have been something. But we were not meant to be.

"Don't be," he said, and I could hear the smile in his voice.

"I'll be fine." The silence that followed was unbearable, and my palms turned clammy. "Make sure the Archangel treats you right, yeah?" Josiah said, his voice seeming to echo in the silence.

I felt myself wavering, the ache in my chest growing as I sighed.

"And if he won't—do not come to me because I don't think I can take him on." He chuckled.

My responding chuckle made me want to tear my hair out. "I'm a big girl, Eden."

"Hmm." The line cracked. "Hey, Ley?"

"Yes?"

"Call me if you need anything, okay?"

I nodded, even though I knew he couldn't see me, and I swallowed my dread. "You too," I said, my hoarse voice barely rising above a whisper.

The line went dead, but I kept lying on my bed as the rain outside splattered against the windows. And I never felt more like a piece of shit than I did at that moment.

CHAPTER THIRTY-FOUR

Dominic

Leyla left her apartment wearing a short black dress with a high neckline. The garment stressed her curves, highlighting the contours of her body without being too revealing. Every inch seemed designed to fit her.

She matched with my black, hand-tailored suit without even knowing it.

A look of amusement flashed on her face when she eyed me up and down, a small smile stretching her lips. I didn't give her any other info except the time and day—*be ready at 7*—and she followed without questioning.

We stood on the side curb, taking each other in. The street was silent, save for one person wearing headphones walking past us, completely indifferent to our presence.

"You look sensational," I said.

Leyla tucked her clutch underneath her arm. "How did you know where I lived again?" she teased, one eyebrow raised defiantly as she closed her apartment door.

How I would enjoy making that smart mouth scream my name.

I clenched my jaw and shook my head. "Let's save the

fighting for after dinner, Leyla," I said, holding open the car door for her. "You may even scratch my back."

We arrived at a secluded restaurant in Shard City, and I offered Leyla my arm as we stepped out of the car. She took it without hesitation, unleashing an unexpected warmth that filled my body. Walking inside with her was… I didn't know how to describe the feeling. Something about having her on my arm made my chest fucking swell with pride.

The restaurant was a small place without stature, tucked away from the hustle and bustle of the city—nothing like *Moby's* popularity. With its warm lighting, faint background music, and relaxed atmosphere, I knew it would be the perfect spot for us. Going by the way Leyla smiled up at me, I had been right.

The server led us to our table in a quiet corner of the restaurant. It was exactly what I had requested. I appreciated having privacy in public spaces, especially when I was there for pleasure. My wings were beacons in the night, easily recognized, and there usually were one or two nosy people who couldn't mind their own business.

As we settled into our seats, I watched Leyla take in the space. A low hum of conversation reached us from other tables and couples dining nearby, but this corner seemed another space altogether. It felt as if we were the only two people in the room. The candlelight cast dancing shadows on Leyla's face, dimming the brightness of her eyes as she gazed at me.

I ordered a bottle of champagne with two glasses and handed her one. Feeling intensity charge the air between us, I said, "Seems we're finally on a date."

She swallowed the drink. "You asked me once, and I said yes. What's *finally* about it?"

"Does it count if I thought about it a lot?" I put my glass back on the table to look at the menu, knowing I would order whatever the chef recommended.

"It counts." Leyla wrapped her arms underneath her chin and looked at me, blinking those dark lashes. I envied every man who went on a date with her before me. "How is life as the Prime of Ashar nowadays?"

"Same old, same old," I said, only half joking. "It is not nearly as impressive as it sounds."

"I won't lie. It sounds like shit to me. Though your relatives must have been very proud when you were appointed for the role."

I leaned back, my wings accommodated by the chair. "None of them lived long enough to witness it. My mother died at my birth, and my father passed away a century and a half ago."

Leyla reached out and put her hand on mine. "I'm sorry."

"Nothing to be sorry for," I said with a faint smile. "It has been a long time. I never knew my mother, but my father was strong and wise and taught me much about life. He had been old when he died. It was his time." My father had been powerful, which many think contributed to my status as the Archangel.

Leyla's grip on my hand tightened before letting go, and I already mourned her touch. "Did he witness your Starball career?" she asked.

I smirked at her. "You did some research on me, huh?"

She shrugged. "Everyone knows you were a great player."

"*Were?*"

Leyla rolled her eyes.

"I went pro shortly after his death. He knew I loved the game and that I was talented, but never watched me compete for the cup." I had never been this open about my personal life on a first date. If ever. No one asked me these types of questions, either. Conversations mostly revolved around flirting.

"Did your mate see you play?"

The question dragged me back to a filled arena, cheers filling my ears as I zoned in on one person in the stands, white-winged and blue eyes filled with tears as she watched me hold up the cup. My hand scratched at my stubble. "She was there when I won my last season."

Leyla wetted her lips, her green eyes cast down. "I can't imagine what you went through."

"I have great friends." I didn't want to dwell on the sadness of my past tonight. "What about your family?"

Leyla's expression froze, suddenly uncomfortable. "My family is… complicated," she said vaguely. "Like yours, my mother died early enough to have no active memories of her, but my father's still alive. No siblings." Kids were scarce for Ashari.

I got the feeling she didn't want to elaborate on it, so I dropped the topic for now. Sometimes, people had complicated histories or family dynamics, and it took time to open up. I was that way, and so were Nathan and Inesa. I wanted her to know she could trust me—that she didn't have to hurry opening up to me. We had all the time in the world. I respected her boundaries, but I wouldn't let it go; I'd just hold on to it for a little longer. Leyla couldn't hide from me forever.

The server eventually brought out the main course, which

looked amazing: meat glazed with hot honey crust, stuffed potatoes, and steamed vegetables. The smell alone made my mouth water—and so did Leyla. My body responded to every movement, every moan, every appreciative murmur that the food coaxed from her lips.

"Did you end it with that Ethereal?"

She cut the meat on her plate in neat bites. "You mean Josiah?"

I willed myself not to narrow my eyes. "Is there another?"

Shaking her head, Leyla said, "I did." She caught her glistening bottom lip between her teeth.

The admission affected me, but I kept my smile from fully seeing the light. She shouldn't be aware of the amount of power she held over me. I had a feeling she would exploit it, just like I did with my power over her.

Desserts arrived, and Leyla's attention was pulled away from me. She chuckled at something the server said, and all I could do was look at her—enthralled.

Something settled over me at the sight of her smile.

Acceptance.

Taking her cutlery, she started meticulously dissecting the food, having no clue what was happening inside me. "So," she said, those beautiful lips forming around the word. "What do you do when you're not being Prime of the city?"

"I love art, always have, and sometimes hire off an entire gallery to curate new pieces for my home," I said. "I also enjoy lounging on the couch, watching TV, and pretending to be a normal person."

"It must be hard to forget who you are."

"Only because people won't let me." I swallowed down a mouthful of food with wine. "And what do you do, *Leyla*

Cuprum, when you're not curating art for your boss or helping the homeless?"

She brushed of my comment by hiding her smile and glancing down, but I caught it as it reached her eyes. "Then I'm at home or with Dana, probably."

"Ethereals have their moments, for sure." I leaned my elbows back on the chair. "When they're not being too meddlesome."

"Or arrogant," she added. "Although Angeli are good at that, too."

I pulled a hand through my hair. "There are exceptions, of course."

Leyla snorted. "The terrible sense of humor is new to me. I have to add that to the list."

"What about Daemons?" I asked. "Are all of them scared of flying like you?"

Her face changed as a genuine smile broke free. I liked her unguarded. "I imagine they are. Anyone without wings, for that matter."

"So you fit right in with the masses?"

"Spoken like someone who doesn't know me."

"Perhaps." I took the last bite from my dessert. "But I'm starting to."

As we finished our plates, I put down a cheque that covered the bill. "Want to take a walk?"

"Please."

We left the restaurant and stepped out into the night air. The streetlights cast a soft glow on the sidewalk, and the stars glowed in the sky. We wandered for a while, speaking and laughing together, occasionally stealing glances that stretched into moments of silence charged with electricity. I found myself entranced by Leyla—the way her face lit up when she talked about college, Lodana, and what restaurants and food stalls she loved most in Shard City. I learned more about her, what she thought about specific political topics, and how she scrunched her nose whenever I said something she disagreed with.

By the time we stopped, the sky was turning dark blue, and even more stars had gathered on the canvas. The thought of leaving made me hesitate.

Leyla smiled a little reluctantly. "It's getting late," she said.

I nodded, not quite wanting this night to end. "It is."

We stood in the middle of the street as I called a cab for her. Even in the dim light, I could see the city reflected in her eyes, their brightness showing more than they had all night. I wanted nothing more than to lean in and touch her, but forced a smile instead. "I presume you still won't let me fly you?"

"Not a chance."

"Soon," I promised.

Leyla walked over to the car that had stopped near the sidewalk. "*I don't know*, Dominic. I don't do reckless things like that on first dates."

"Good thing then," I said as I followed her to the car and opened the door for her, "that our first date just ended."

She stepped into the car. "The plural was intentional, Prime Venetia."

My chuckle was hoarse. I put a hand in my pocket, unwilling to close the door yet. "When will I see you again?"

"You have my phone number. Don't be afraid to use it."

"Cruel woman," I muttered, closing the door after her.

Her laughter lingered in my ears as she waved goodbye

from the cab. I wanted her to stay longer but wasn't sure if I'd ever be ready for her to go.

It was unlikely.

CHAPTER THIRTY-FIVE

Leyla

I noticed a dark presence hovering in front of my building's entrance the moment I stepped out of the taxi. The driver did, too, because he turned down his window and asked, "Everything okay, miss?"

With a nod, I said, "Thank you."

The driver didn't bother asking twice and drove off as the man waiting in front of my door opened his mouth. "Were you with him?"

He sounded drunk.

"Go home, Zade."

Zade pushed away from the wall and stepped closer, towering over me. He pushed back the hood of his black hoodie, revealing his disheveled hair. "I can't stop thinking about you."

Sighing, I maneuvered around him, rummaging through my bag in search of my keys.

"Tell me you didn't see him tonight."

"I did see him."

"I'll fucking gut him if he put his hands on you."

I advanced, extending a finger toward his face. "Don't you fucking *dare* interfere!" I warned. Zade had to angle his head down. The dark circles underneath his blue eyes were visible in the soft light of the entrance, and they widened in surprise at whatever he saw on my face.

Zade pushed his hands in his hair, head shaking with disbelief. "You like him, don't you? You actually fucking like him." A manic laugh escaped him.

I turned my head in denial. "I swear, Zade, don't mess with this assignment."

"I know you, Ley—better than he does. I know what it looks like when you're falling." He grabbed the back of my neck and pulled me flush against him, his forehead touching mine. "Don't do this." His hands splayed over my cheeks, and he pulled me closer until our lips touched.

With a frustrated growl, I pushed him away. "Don't touch me," I hissed. "*Not like that. Not here. Not anywhere.* You seem to have misunderstood our relationship because you never had the right to have an opinion on this." My chest heaved. "You don't get to say what I do or don't do. *Ever.*"

"You don't mean that." His blue eyes were no longer sad. They looked broken.

"Oh, but I do. I'm going to accomplish this assignment, and then I'll never see him again." My throat clogged with emotion at the thought, but I forced them back down. My face crumpled from the pain it caused. "And by any chance, I won't have to see you either."

"Ley—Leyla, please."

"No." My chin quivered. "Leave me alone. Or we'll find out what my father does to people who try to cross him."

Then I slammed the door in his face.

A shuddering inhale forced its way inside my body. I wouldn't let myself break. Not tonight. I had pretended for so long I could pretend a while longer.

I took a bite of my chocolate cake when the TV in the coffee shop switched over to the news, covering the drug dealings surrounding the ACC in the Human Domain. I nearly groaned because I did not have the energy to be confronted with another of my shortcomings.

I'd been tossing and turning all night, but sleep hadn't found me. The conversation with Zade last night kept replaying in my mind, driving me insane.

I know what it looks like when you're falling.

Swallowing, I switched my attention back to Dana, who was sipping from her coffee without a care in the world. "How is your friend?" I asked her. "The one who was hospitalized?"

She put down the coffee cup and nodded. "Doing well. She was there soon enough to get the worst out of her system. None of us dared to do any drugs since then. We're all spooked."

"Good." I glanced back at the news, showing footage of another shooting in the Sanguis Domain late last night. "Can't be too careful."

Dana nodded, eating a chocolate bonbon from her plate. We loved coming here when we were younger. The coffee shop was close to our boarding school and sold the best homemade chocolate. We'd even tried our first cup of coffee here together, which Dana immediately switched back to hot chocolate. Unsurprisingly, I liked the bitter taste.

My friend's eyes widened as she moved closer. "On a lighter note, I've been dying to tell you something."

"What?"

"You remember Nathanial Farcroft, right? He was at Prime Venetia's sky—"

"*By the light*, Dana. I was there."

"Yeah, yeah—listen." She waved her hands at me. "He got my number, and we started texting, and now he has asked me out."

I grinned at her. "I was wondering what Dominic needed it for."

"What!" She shoved my arm. "Why didn't you tell me that, you traitor!"

I arched a brow as I raised my cup. "Don't you mean ally?"

Dominic asked if I was cool with it, and I sent it to him. The positive outweighed the negative. Nathanial Farcroft disliked me for some unknown (yet valid) reason, but he'd ask out my best friend. The guy didn't trust me around Dominic, but he wanted to be around Dana. It was ironic.

Obviously, I had my reservations about that. But I would've done her a disservice not to, both with the fierce way he looked after Dominic and Dana's crush on him. It was much better than her getting back together with fucking Tommy.

Dana's smile froze. "You're not excited."

I put a reassuring hand on her arm. "No, I am."

What kind of hypocrite would I be if I told her about my conversation with Nathanial? He was right, after all. It implied he was a decent guy.

She pushed her long fuchsia hair over her one shoulder, clad in a dark green leather jacket. "He's been messaging me every day. Even after I told him I was still sort of cutting things off with someone else."

I wiggled my eyebrows. "*Someone's interested.*"

"We went out earlier this week, and I pulled the final plug on Tommy right after. He gave me a hard time for about a night and then moved on. Which honestly says a lot—compared to someone being told the person they're interested in is hung up and not giving a shit." Her eyes crinkled.

"It was long overdue," I said. I'd been getting frustrated with the way Tommy seemed to shift on and off all the fucking time. Dana deserved better. Whether that was Nathanial Farcroft... That was yet to be determined. "And, how was it?"

Dana smiled immediately, a blush crawling up her cheeks—a rare sight.

"He got you good, huh?" I smirked.

She puckered her lips. "It wasn't even like that. We... we're just really similar."

"*Ugh*," I said, "Now you're making me nauseous, Dana."

"Believe me," she threw up her hands in defense, "that date was anything but boring."

I barked a laugh. "I'm really happy for you."

"Thanks," Dana said, eyes twinkling. "The only downside is that my parents would approve of him."

"Oh, most definitely. The representative of the Ethereals? Evelyn would probably want a relationship with him, herself. The guy is every mother-in-law's wet dream."

She chuckled. "I bet." Then she crossed her arms and bowed forward to me. "How was your date with Prime Venetia?"

"Stop calling him the Prime. It makes him sound old."

"Newsflash: he is old." Dana rolled her eyes. "So...?"

"I don't want to make it bigger than it was."

"You tell me about all your hook-ups, Leyla. I think the opposite is happening; you're actually serious about this one.

Nathan thinks he's serious about you, too. He asked me several questions about it."

I bet he did. Sighing, I brushed a strand of black hair out of my eye. "I don't know. I've never been in this situation." *Understatement.* I fixed my attention on a specific point on the wall. "It's getting complicated."

She put a comforting hand on my arm. "What's complicated about it? The feelings?"

"That too, but… I'm also afraid to fuck it up," I confessed. "I like him. He's funny and intelligent. He listens to me when I speak, you know? Not just waiting to say something but truly interested in what I have to say or think… I'm just not sure there's much of a future for us, and I don't want to invest in something that might not even last."

I caught the lie as soon as it left my mouth. My feelings for Dominic were real, and I *was* invested. But who was I kidding? This—*we*—were not meant to be. An Angeli like him and a Daemon like me? We were a natural disaster waiting to happen.

Dana stopped stirring her hot chocolate, the metal ringing against the ceramic mug. "What are you talking about? Nobody knows what will happen in the future. Relationships take time, and life doesn't work that way."

If only I could tell her the truth about how this relationship was doomed to end in flames. I forced a smile onto my face, ignoring the hollow pit in my stomach. "It's hard not to. He has a loaded past, and I'm not sure he's ready to move on. Not to mention, he is the Archangel and Prime, on top of everything. That's a lot."

"He's too much for you?"

My heart thudded in clear denial. I just shrugged at her,

the lie looping like a noose around my neck.

"Give it some time," Dana suggested. "I mean, it's only been a few weeks. He might need to adjust to being in a relationship just as much as you do."

I pulled on the ends of my hair. "Maybe."

Dana gave me a sympathetic look. "Keep an open mind, okay? He might surprise you."

"You're right," I said. "There's no rush." Bile crawled up my throat. What would Dana do if she found out I was deceiving him? Deceiving her? I needed some fucking time to think it through.

She smiled reassuringly. "I've got you."

I took her hand, biting my cheek. "Got you back."

Dana winked. "I know."

Just then, a figure outside caught our attention. An unfamiliar man pointed a camera our way through the window. He was standing on the sidewalk, framed against the backdrop of the city skyline, snapping pictures of the inside. At first, I thought he was taking photos of the shop, but I quickly realized he was pointing his camera at us.

My cheeks flushed with anger. I glanced around to see if anyone else had noticed, but nobody seemed to pay attention. I glanced back at Dana, hoping he would dissolve into thin air. "Tell me I'm not crazy," I said. "That guy's taking pictures of us, right?"

The man continued to take photos from different angles, as though we had paid him to capture every moment of our encounter. Dana looked from the window at me with revelation. "Oh, no. I think he's taking photos of *you*." She leaned closer, whispering now. "People must've noticed you and the Prime together. You know they are obsessed with his personal life."

I felt exposed, something I had never been a day in my life. Was this how Dominic felt every single day?

Around us, customers started noticing, too, and looked at our table with blatant curiosity. Dana became aware of my growing unease and went to the counter to settle the bill. "Let's go," she said upon her return.

I nodded absently as I watched the man continue snapping photos of me. Was that even legal? I scowled at him. Upon leaving, he continued following us, leading me to choose not to walk home that way. *I was taking a cab, damnit.*

Dana waited with me until the car arrived and hugged me goodbye. "My boss will demote me if I'm not back soon. I'll call you tomorrow, okay?"

"Thanks for waiting." I hugged her back. "Love you."

"Love you more." Dana waved as she left. I hoped that whatever happened, she wouldn't come to resent me too much. We had been through too much together, and my friendship with her was real. It had always been.

Before I opened the car, I looked at the photographer, still snapping away at it, drawing attention from people on the street.

They are obsessed with his personal life.

"How about you get a life instead of selling others?" I said to him.

He smirked from behind the lens. "Why don't you smile for me again, honey?"

"You're fucking pathetic!" I yelled, but smiled, raising my middle finger at him at the same time. Then I entered the taxi and closed the door, blocking my face from view by leaning my arm against the window.

So much for staying under the radar.

CHAPTER THIRTY-SIX

Dominic

I trudged through some of Ashrior's sinister alleyways to reach Nitas' home on this dark, chilly night, entering as I always did. He had once again invited me, saying it was urgent. I had no doubt it was about Xanon Naan.

"Where have you been?" Vaphoryn's voice drifted over to me the moment I stepped out of the elevator. She was pacing in front of the fireplace, close to where Nitas sat behind his desk.

"He's been a little absentminded," the Supreme said, leveling a bored look at me. "And I think I might have a clue why."

I ignored their comments. "What's going on?"

Nitas leaned back in his chair, his expression serious. "Xanon has been wreaking havoc in the Undercity," he said.

"Old news."

"Just listen, Dom," Vaphoryn snapped irritably. She was hardly ever in a bad mood.

Nitas' dark eyes were inscrutable. "We received information from our source about the whereabouts of the drug."

"The Cardinal wants to hold off," Vaphoryn clarified.

"So we've decided to take matters into our own hands. Heller already knows and is willing to bypass anything we do and even offered to send some of his forces to help."

"Hold on." I shook my head. "We're going to do what?" I looked at Vaphoryn. "If the Head Cardinal finds out you're going behind her back, you'll be dragged to court. And you—" I pointed at Nitas "—went to my representatives behind my back."

"And?" Nitas wove his fingers together, but his dark eyes flashed with impatience. "It's a powerful drug, Dominic. Xanon heightened the production, which lowers the price. Even addicts in the slums now have access to it. It's causing uncontrollable chaos. We need to find out if this lead points in the right direction and put a stop to it."

I wiped a hand over my scruff and looked at the ceiling. "There must be another way to do something—stop this."

"Then you should figure it out now because we've got no time to waste." Nitas rose from behind his desk, putting his hands in his pockets as he approached, his stance at odds with the tone of his voice. "Especially not on trivial shit like bureaucracy."

With my hands tucked under my suit jacket, I asked, "What are you thinking?"

"We need to raid the warehouses where, according to the source, Ambrosia is being stored," Nitas said. "If we can eliminate the stock, we can buy ourselves some time to find a way to stop Xanon from overturning the city. Time to do it *your* way."

"So, what's the plan?"

"We've mapped out the area," he said. "All possible locations based on the information our source gave us."

"How well do we even know the source? Can we trust them?"

"We can," Nitas said, looking at Vaphoryn, who nodded. Wait—they both knew? "Who the hell is it?"

"It doesn't matter," Vaphoryn said. "We can trust them."

"What's with the secrecy?" I asked Nitas.

The Daemon shook his head and continued, "We have the information needed to take action. Being more careful, we'll go in quietly to not alert anyone to our presence. Once we're in, we can search the warehouses and destroy everything we find, trying to make as few casualties as possible to reduce Heller's imminent headache. Though if it were up to me, we'd label them collateral damage."

"Nobody's past the point of damnation, *Divinitas*," Vaphoryn said.

With a glance her way, Nitas clucked his tongue. "I disagree."

She shifted her gaze to me, her red braid moving with her. "No casualties, okay?"

Nitas sighed. "Sure," he answered for the both of us. But I nodded at her, making some tension leave her shoulders. "Shall I put the plan in motion?"

Both Vaphoryn and I nodded in silence. We had to do something; hurt him while we had a chance. But something within me knew this was only the beginning of our fight against Xanon.

I was turning around to go back home when Nitas' voice filled the room once more. "Wait."

He grabbed something from his desk, a folder, and pushed it my way, his face a blank canvas. "This is about to go to press." His black eyes bore into me. "Thought you might like the heads-up."

I took it from his desk, clutching it as if it were a doom card.

Nitas leaned back, face unreadable as he said, "I know I would."

My flight back home from Ashrior was a silent one. The gentle wind whipped softly against my face, and the city below was quiet. Even my head had muted for once. No thoughts whatsoever—as if an invisible mental wall had risen that I could not bypass. As soon as I arrived home, I retreated into my office, the folder Nitas' had given me on the desk before me. I lit a cigarette, accepted Amy's offer to make me some coffee, and invited Leyla over.

When the doorbell rang an hour later, I left my office and stopped Amy before she could reach the hallway. "I got this," I said, and she nodded, but I saw the ghost of something akin to worry on her face before she turned around and disappeared back into the kitchen.

My steps were deliberate as I walked to the front of the house, discarding my suit jacket. I could see her silhouette through the side glass panels, but she came into full view when I opened the door. Leyla wore jeans and a turtleneck—looked stunning wearing it, too. Her hair was even pulled back into a high ponytail. It was as casual as I'd ever seen her.

She cocked her head, a smile playing on her lips. "Hey."

"Hey." My voice came out rougher than I'd intended. I pushed open the door farther and gestured for her to come inside, making sure my wings were out of the way as she entered.

"How are you?" Her scent reached my nose, and I grabbed the front door a little tighter as my clothing strained against my skin. A storm was brewing inside me, and I knew I was standing on a cliff regarding my emotions. It wouldn't take much to trigger me.

I closed the door with a bang, rattling the glass chandelier hanging in the hallway. "Fine. To your left." I walked behind her, following her to the staircase. It made me notice how much I towered over her. She wasn't wearing heels, the only type of shoe I had ever seen her wear, which made her noticeably shorter than usual. And all I could think about was grabbing her, burying my nose in her neck and hair, and inhaling her scent deeply. I'd tear off her clothing to get even closer to that intoxicating fragrance; wanted my mouth all over her body. Her mouth all over mine.

I blinked the thought away. "Thanks for coming on such short notice."

She slowed down on the stairs and turned to me. "How could I refuse? You were very insisting."

"That wasn't me being insisting." My gaze seared into her skin, carefully tearing down the walls she had built around herself. A single touch and it would crumble completely.

She was meant for me—to be seen, to be discovered.

"You truly have a beautiful home, Dominic," she said, pointing her hands both ways at the top of the staircase. "Where are we going?"

I took her right arm and redirected it to the left.

Her lips popped open in surprise. "Can't speak?"

A strained chuckle escaped me. "No, I can."

"Are you going to lock me up somewhere?" she teased.

"It's a surprise." My reply didn't match her tone. The

words came out stiff. Guarded. And she noticed—I could see it in her tense form.

"Are you alright?"

"I'm perfect," I lied. Her attempt at trying to dig her way under my skin was pointless. She was already there, and. It. *Itched*. The Ashari in me wanted to burst from my skin. He *did* want to lock her up, hide her from the world, far away from where others could ever reach her.

I passed her, opening the door to my bedroom, and she followed, albeit hesitantly.

Leyla looked around the dimly lit room. The emperor-sized bed was freshly made, as if I had never slept in it. The door to my walk-in closet was open, revealing my extensive collection of tailored suits, while a window overlooking the garden allowed the nightly breeze to sway the curtains.

It was the first time I brought someone in here. The sacred space was intended as my safe haven. I wished it had been under different circumstances, but here we fucking were.

"Dominic?" she asked, that velvet voice brushing a trail of goosebumps over my body. Her pull was unlike anything I had ever experienced.

"Patience, Leyla. Patience."

I went to the wall across from my bed and revealed a safe by moving a big painting out of the way. The door sprung open with a loud sigh as I unlocked it. When the contents were revealed to us, I didn't hear Leyla. Not even her breath. It was like she wasn't there at all.

Ignoring the voice in my head telling me to get my shit together, I took the clothbound bundle from the safe with care and unwrapped it in front of her. "Very few people know about this." I revealed the object to her. "But I am a man of my word."

She shook her head in confusion like she couldn't believe what she was seeing.

"It exists." I forced a smile, but all I managed was a twitch of my lips. It was supposed to come out as a joke, but her face shadowed, eyes latching onto the object I held as if in awe.

It made my heart fucking sink.

I took the sword in both hands, turning it around to reveal the intricate designs. I had no mental capacity to think about the consequences of what I was doing because my brain was exhausted.

I didn't care.

"You really *do* owe me one," I told her and watched as alarm seized hold of her.

CHAPTER THIRTY-SEVEN

Leyla

It felt like a bucket of ice-cold water poured over me as I stared at the sword.

It was bigger than I'd expected: it had a large metal heft bound in dark, worn leather and an oval chunk of stone between the grip and the long metal blade. The way Dominic held it between his hands made it seem lethal—a daunting combination.

Waves of power emanated from it, causing the hairs on my neck to rise. You could feel it was ancient just being near it. This had to be it: the sword my father was after. What all of this was for; the purpose of getting close to Dominic. Part of me wanted to look away and ignore why I was searching for it. The blade didn't matter to me; it could rot away in that safe for all I cared.

Dominic tipped up my chin with one hand, caressing my cheek, dragging me back into the present. "Relax, Leyla. You're looking at me like I've shown you a stash of bodies."

Why would he choose to show it to me now? If it was so important, why reveal it?

My throat dried up. "I'm just..." *Speechless*. "I hadn't

expected you to have a sword at home." A lie? I didn't know anymore; my thoughts were jumbled, truths and lies weaving together as if they were just as confused.

He smiled. "Not just any sword."

"How do you know it's the one?" Who else knew Dominic had the sword? Which of them had told my father? He somehow knew it had been in Dominic's possession—someone had passed that information along.

He turned the blade again, revealing a slit in the middle of the decorative stone. "It's in Ashtior for safekeeping. It was passed over to me because of my wards. They're the strongest."

"So, there's actual truth to the stories in that text?"

"There is truth to any story, Leyla, but you must look for it. With some deeper than others."

"Well." I cleared my throat and forced a smile on my face. "I'm impressed." My voice was hoarse. That was a lie. I didn't care about the sword; I worried about Dominic and my impending betrayal—how I wasn't sure I wanted to do it anymore.

"Shouldn't I be prohibited from seeing this?"

"That depends," he drawled. "Who are you going to share it with? Your boss?"

I swallowed, unsure of how to respond to that.

"Can you trust him to keep this to himself?"

"He's my *boss*. I don't tell him what to do."

"Then don't tell. Knowledge holds power in this world, Leyla."

"Not if it's just rumors."

Dominic angled his head. "Lots of them going around these days."

I didn't like the way he was looking at me. His eyes seemed too bitter. I averted my gaze to stop looking at the sword. I wanted him to put it away. Everything it represented nauseated me.

Dominic started binding the sword back in the cloth and put it back in the safe, hanging the painting back to cover it. It was beautiful: a dark green, serene meadow. The direct opposite image of how I felt inside.

"You often go down to Ashrior for your work?"

My head whipped back to him. I was getting really confused, and not in a good way. "Are you sure you're alright, Dominic?" There was something off about him.

He bared his teeth, cocking his head to the side as he leaned against the wall, ignoring my question completely. "Did you watch the news about Ambrosia?"

"Yes," I answered.

"Do you visit the poorer areas for your job?"

My breathing came in shallow bursts. "Not often."

"You should be careful."

"I am." I was getting dizzy.

His eyes flared. "And your *boss*? Does he care about your safety during times like these?"

Did he know? This side of him was new to me. "I'm on his payroll, Dominic. He cares as long as I do my job." My voice was steady, thank the light. "The question is, why do you?"

He pushed away from the wall with a sneer on his face. "Because you matter to me, Leyla!" he snapped, ammunition freely given. "Don't you fucking get that by now?"

I stepped back, pushing back the burning that was gathering behind my eyes. "You don't even know me." The words were soft.

Dominic smiled, a cruel smile, and he nodded. "You're right; I don't."

I was about to respond without knowing what to say when he approached me in two long strides. Dominic grabbed my head between his large hands and dragged me closer. "Let me in, Leyla."

With trembling hands, I grabbed his wrists. "I don't know how," I whispered.

His eyes darkened, roaming over my face. The gold in his eyes had darkened as they moved to my lips, the shadows on his face hollower than they had been moments before. His fingers buried into my hair, and I watched him shake his head, fighting an invisible battle.

"Dom—"

With a growl, he closed the gap between us. It was an ugly kiss, his mouth pressed firmly against mine like he would die if he didn't touch me.

I was frozen, eyes wide open as I stared at him.

The pressure of his hands on my face increased as he lowered until he was at the same height as me. His chest heaved as he whispered, "Tell me I am not the only one feeling this." His breath caressed my lips as I trembled, barely restraining myself. "Tell me you can't stop thinking about me, too."

I couldn't speak. I wasn't prepared for him to hear yet another thing that would haunt him in the wake of my deception.

Dominic didn't give me a chance either way, before he pressed his lips back to mine. His lips were insisting but soft, and his stubble chafing my chin in precisely the right way. At first, he was holding back, but he soon opened his mouth to deepen the kiss, stealing the air from my lungs.

The fear in my body dissipated beneath his touch.

His scent engulfed me in the most intoxicating way as he kissed me with conviction, deepening it with a plea. And *fuck*, did I kiss him back.

Our tongues clashed, the kiss turning frantic. We kissed as if we were fighting. When he shoved me back, I felt something hard prod against my hips, the pain a welcome surprise in the sea of bliss I was experiencing, reminding me I deserved to feel anything but this.

In a swift movement, he shoved me roughly onto the dresser, and things clattered to the floor as Dominic leaned into my body, opening my legs as I wrapped my arms around his neck to pull him even closer. The bulging muscles beneath his shirt sent tremors through me with each touch, igniting my core, and every stroke of his tongue ignited me. One of his hands moved to my hair, the other wrapped around me like a cord keeping me in place against him.

I cursed every woman he had ever touched with every last breath in my lungs.

My hands curled in his unbound hair, finding the silky curls wild and untamed. My throat was clogged with desire; I could only act.

His feathers brushed my legs as they wound around his hips, and I zoned in on the soft feeling against my bare skin. My fingers moved to the front as his lips moved a sloppy trail over my cheek, my neck—sucking, biting, licking. Everything else around us had disappeared. His body had become part of mine, and I wanted this moment to last an eternity. I started unbuttoning his shirt with deft movements, and the moment his warm skin was bared to me, I brushed my hands over his chest, touching his strong shoulders and pecks—touching everything I could get my hands on.

Dominic pushed away with a low growl, chest heaving, his shirt half unbuttoned, revealing the tan, muscular skin of his chest. He looked like a sculpture.

Unreal. Too good to be true.

I was shaking. My hands moved to my bruised lips. I felt more alive than ever. It felt so fucking right. This, us, *we*. My feelings had never been more polarized. It felt both wonderful and terrifying. I let myself drift off, and now I found myself in the middle of the sea with no way of returning.

I looked into his eyes and was shocked by their deep intensity, how the gold had molted and become a dark brown. His curls were mussed, and his lips red. I watched his throat bob.

"That was…" I trailed off hoarsely, my voice barely a whisper.

Incredible?

Overwhelming?

Too fucking much?

"I know," he said, stepping further away from the dresser, pulling a hand through his hair. I licked my lips, and his eyes followed the movement. "*I know.*"

We stared at each other, still catching our breath.

"You should leave," he said abruptly.

I understood. All too damned well. "Yes," I agreed as I slid off the dresser, the wood groaning as my feet reached the ground. I looked at him again, finding his eyes on me, dark with desire. I tried cementing it in my memory.

It wouldn't be a sight I'd see again. Everything was about to change. I felt it.

As if he had also come to that realization, he averted his

gaze and folded his wings stiffly. "Please go." His voice was void of emotion.

So I did. I backed away. This, whatever *this* was, was too real. Too much. He was still hung up on his great love, and I… I couldn't handle it anymore. The lies were suffocating. I was drowning in them, tied like an anvil to my feet, dragging me down, down, down.

It wasn't worth it.

Dazed, I pushed myself through the door opening, bracing my hand on the wall as I found my way back through the house. I let my hand slide over the railing, finding purchase as I made my way down the stairs in a hurry. Even Dominic's housekeeper, Amy, was kind to me as she stepped into the hallway and stopped me to ask if I was alright. I couldn't recall exactly what I said, but she nodded and stepped back.

I had no right to her kindness—to be seen as anything I wasn't. She should go to Dominic. He was the one deserving of compassion, because he wasn't the villain in this story.

I was.

CHAPTER THIRTY-EIGHT

Dominic

I lit a cigarette and inhaled deeply, taking a long drag. The smoke left my nostrils in tendrils, coiling around me like a blanket. The taste of her, the feel of her skin pressed against mine... I wished I could get intoxicated and forget she existed. Unsee that fucking face right after I'd kissed her; her swollen lips and dazed eyes, the black silk locks I never wanted to let go of.

Lightmother, give me a fucking reprieve. I sloshed down a gulp of whiskey, the alcohol granting me a temporary escape. The rope around my chest loosened, but it didn't last as long as I wanted.

"When will you quit that bad habit?" Inesa asked like a broken record, a hand braced on her hip as she looked down at me with a glass of whiskey in the other.

"The day it kills me, probably." I swallowed more of the liquid.

I hoped I drowned in it.

Inesa raised her brows, unimpressed.

"Or perhaps the day it kills one of us?" Nathan remarked from where he lounged in the seat across from me. "We're inhaling those toxic vapors every time you light one, so who knows?"

I had met my best friends for our usual end-of-week night at Inesa's place. Leon was often away for work. Leon was from a different generation, he didn't understand the phrase 'work hard, play hard', which could explain the differences in our sense of humor. As in, he probably didn't have any.

"Stop criticizing me," I said, and let my head fall back against the couch, the cigarette limp between my lips.

"You don't know the meaning of the word." Nathan sighed deeply. "My father has been persistent about me *procreating* and putting forth the family name. More and more, as of late."

"Let me guess; he found out you're dating Lodana Fivaldor?" I asked.

Nathan grimaced. "He did."

His father was one of the wealthiest Ethereals on the planet and very... traditional—close acquaintances with the Head Cardinal, Seraphim Kemalgda. The first time I met him had been before I was declared Archangel and Prime of Ashar and still played Starball. He'd shaken my hand but merely grunted in acknowledgment.

The man had only started speaking to me in full sentences after I received my titles. The second time I had seen him, as Prime, had been decades after that first time, and I had let him introduce himself again, pretending I didn't recognize him—causing Nathan to choke on his drink at the time and Inesa smothering a horrified laugh.

Nathan hadn't had it easy growing up, that was for sure. As his friend, I couldn't forget that fact.

I took another sip of my drink, slowly sinking back into

the whiskey's thrall. "You should tell him to back the fuck off and put a hidden camera somewhere so we can watch it back later."

Inesa nodded eagerly from me to him, her arms draped over her knee. "That's actually a great idea."

"This is really good, by the way," I told her, pointing to the drink in my hand.

She nodded. "Leon had it imported from the north."

"Let him bring some for me next time."

"I will ask him."

"Please do."

I definitely wouldn't get any.

Nathan stood from the chair and started pacing in front of it. "How would I go about telling him?"

Inesa snapped her fingers, pushing herself upright, wobbling a little. Even her usually crisp and perfect clothes were a little wrinkled. Leonardo Zemya would not be amused to find his mate drunk with the two of us. He'd said more than once that we didn't bring out her best side. *Indeed*, Inesa had responded, *they bring out my fun side.* Which had earned us a glare full of warning from him behind her back while she winked at us—intoxicated, then, too. "You could write him a song, accompanied on the piano, of course," she suggested.

"Of course, why hadn't I thought of that?" Nathan shook his head and massaged his temples.

Why was he always so serious? I straightened a little, sloshing whiskey down my throat in a big gulp. The warm liquid burned through my body, making my head swim in pure bliss for a few seconds. "You could finally show him how those forced piano lessons as a kid paid off."

Nathan closed his eyes. "Why am I friends with you?"

I barked a laugh as Inesa walked over to high-five me. It had been ages since I had felt this light, and it formed a sharp contrast with the week I'd had. Apparently, Leon's expensive whiskey had done its temporary damage. Thank the fucking light. I toasted my glass to his ghostly presence.

Inesa looked at Nathan, who'd sat back down. "To be frank, your father is not too old to conceive again if he wanted to. And he's attractive."

Nathan grimaced. "Don't make me sick." He looked at the ceiling. "Besides, I don't wish another kid the childhood I've had."

"Full of luxury?" I joked.

"Full of scorn," he said.

My head cleared, and I sobered up a little. "Sorry, brother. I didn't mean to imply that you had it easy. We know you didn't."

He waved a hand my way, meaning he understood.

"How are things going with the Fivaldor girl, anyway?" Inesa asked, blinking more than usual. Probably to keep her eyes open.

"Well," Nathan responded, smiling a little. "I can't complain."

She laughed. "I'm happy for you, Nathan."

I raised my glass his way, and we all took a sip in silence.

As I focused on the drink, I tried to push back the memory of green eyes blazing—the fire in them caused by me. The way she had clung to me as I pushed her on that dresser, as if she couldn't get close enough. An electric current had run between our bodies, everywhere we touched static. It had crackled in the air as if even the gods themselves willed us together. "Can Ashari have more than one mate?" I asked, leaning back on the couch.

Nathan's eye ticked, and Inesa's were focused on me, suddenly not blinking at all. Both of them seemed slightly taken aback by my question.

"If they do, I've never heard of such a thing," Inesa said carefully. "Why?"

"Just something I was wondering." I willed myself not to think about her tonight.

Inesa glanced around her living room. "Just because I haven't heard of it doesn't mean it couldn't be."

I ground my molars.

"You finally found someone who makes you feel an inkling of what *she* did. Of course, you want that to be true," Nathan said matter-of-factly. "But I think you're seeing things into existence with this one."

He really should learn when to stop. "You're one to talk."

Nathan sat back, irritation spilling from him. "I spoke with her, you know."

"Leyla?" My voice turned dangerously low. "When?"

He nodded, seemingly unaware of what those words did to me. Nathanial enjoyed testing me. Always had. "At the opening game."

"About what?" The alcohol was leaving my bloodstream in a steady trickle. Fuck. I could tell sober me wasn't in the right headspace for this conversation.

"Just gauging her intentions."

I pushed up from the couch, set down my glass on the side table, and smothered the cigarette in the ashtray. "Her intentions?" I asked carefully, too lucid. "I don't go talking to Lodana Fivaldor now, do I?"

Nathan raised his brows. "You know what I mean."

"I don't think I do."

Inesa jumped in, "I think he means—"

"I want to hear it from him," I cut her off, but put a hand on her shoulder in thanks.

Nathan gave both of us a dry look, acting like he was the only rational one, but he addressed me when he spoke. "You've had your fun, Dom. Don't go looking for pieces of her in other women. It's time to move on."

I snorted defensively, and this time, Inesa looked at me in warning. I humored Nathan only because I loved him like a brother. He could say what he wanted—I would never ignore him or shut him out of my life—but I had my limits. "Is that what you did?"

Nathan's face turned thunderous. "I want what's best for you, and I don't think she's it. You know that. Stop deflecting."

"Not this again. Shut the *fuck* up, both of you." Inesa suddenly stood, raising her hands. "*By the light!* Just agree to disagree and accept we all want what is best for each other."

"He knows better than to bring up Apolo," Nathan said.

My snort was cold. I clapped my hands in mock amusement. "Because bringing up Emiliana every time I mention Leyla works wonders for me?"

"All I'm saying is that you should be careful around that Daemon," Nathan said. "Something about her feels… *off*."

Wings bristling, I walked over to the drink cart to fill my glass again, looking for something even stronger—pure alcohol, for example. Or straight poison. I was past the point of giving a fuck. It could burn a hole through my throat for all I cared. Anything but feeling this—this emptiness. "I'm done talking about her."

Because I feared he was right. I poured a drink, making

sure some of the tension had left my body before turning back around. Inesa slumped back into the seat with a dramatic sigh, raising her arms to the ceiling in defeat. "Ever since that gods-awful day over a century ago, the both of you have become morons! Absolute morons!"

Nathan and I shared a look as I walked back with my drink in hand, and I nodded.

We were a mess. *Families fight.*

Honestly, Inesa was the only good person left in our friend group. She was probably tired of trying to fix our problems. Looking at her, I couldn't help but feel compassion for her. It was quite a challenge to tolerate us. "But that's why you have Leon, right?"

"How are you two?" Nathan asked Inesa, catching on to my effort to change the conversation. We shared a look of understanding.

After college, where the three of us had met, Inesa became an advocate for female Angeli rights. That is how she and Leon met. She had often frequented the Angeli consulate way before I did. By the time Leon first saw her, she had already pushed through radical changes—building a platform for female Angeli, underage females in particular, to have a voice. Even more so after what happened with Emiliana.

I had just been named Archangel of the city when I could give Inesa a role in the Angeli counsel. Leonardo Zemya had been known for his conservative ways, but from the first moment Inesa stepped into that room, Leonardo had fallen for her. I had never seen that man stunned before, but he had been silent for the entire conversation, clinging to her every word.

It had taken him a long time to win her over—to warm

her up to the idea of marriage. She was a lot younger, progressive, and stubbornly independent. Inesa had even become representative of the Angeli Domain during their courtship. And then their mating bond had clicked into place, and they'd become inevitable.

Not married, but mated.

They had remained deeply in love, even after all this time, and Leon hadn't tried to change a thing about her—adapting himself and his ideas, instead.

Inesa looked at us. She tried to remain angry, but at the mention of Leon, she couldn't help but break into a tiny smile. "We're doing fine."

"Nes?" The front door slammed shut, leaving a loud echo through the large mansion, and a low male voice sounded from the far hallway. We exchanged looks and straightened, brushing at our clothes, trying to get most of the wrinkles out. Inesa even had the decency to blush a little, already knowing she was intoxicated enough for him to notice.

The door opened, and Leon entered the room, taking in the three of us. But his gaze kept lingering on Inesa's pink cheeks—his eyes changing. His blonde hair had been pushed back behind his ears.

"Leon," I said in acknowledgment as I stood and nodded at the Angeli. I helped Inesa up from the couch with one hand, steadying her. "We were just leaving. Right, Nathan?"

"Definitely, yes."

Leonardo looked at where I held Inesa's arm and narrowed his gaze ever so slightly. He had never said it, but he didn't care I was the Archangel. Not one bit. All he cared about was Inesa. I looked at Nathan, and he mouthed something along the lines of, *he's going to kill you.* And despite our argument from earlier, I grinned at him.

I turned to Inesa. "Thank you, *Nes*."

She gave me a look. "You're pissing him off," she whispered loud enough for her mate to hear, but she couldn't mask her amusement.

"I know." I bent forward and kissed her on her cheek, noticing the room temperature dropping below zero. "Thank you," I told her softly, only for her ears. She squeezed my arm in response, her eyes soft.

Nathan was wise enough to only wink at Inesa as I let go of her. "Thanks for your hospitality, Leon," I told him. "You have excellent taste in drinks—and women."

Inesa groaned at the same time Leon drawled, "Get out."

Like I said, *no sense of humor*.

CHAPTER THIRTY-NINE

Leyla

It felt as if I was submerged, struggling to catch my breath.

There were two, no, *three* unfamiliar Angeli with me this time. They seemed to be speaking to me, but I couldn't hear anything besides the ringing in my ears. My vision blurred as if I was about to pass out. A painful lash cracked through my spine, and then the three Angeli were writhing on the ground, dying before my eyes. The familiar streaks of blood on their faces were reminiscent of previous dreams. I could hear the distant sound of nails scratching on the wood-paneled flooring, leaving markings carved into it. The wooden chips were probably still underneath their nails.

Tears streamed down my face as I tried to block out the chaos before me. I stumbled back, falling over something before I shoved myself against the wall, caging my body and shielding myself from what was happening. Every limb froze from the shock that coursed through my body.

The place, too, was different this time. The interior was opulent: white-painted walls, velvet drapes, ornate furniture and fixtures, and paintings on every wall. I brushed my hands over my face, and they came back wet. I drew back in horror, looking at them, but it was not blood—just tears. I pulled my legs closer to my body and wrapped my arms around them to create a safe cocoon. I was shaking, my chest heaving, but there was only a loud ringing in my ears.

Someone walked into the room. I sensed their presence before I heard them but didn't move, not even to look who it was. The person stepped farther inside, taking in the sight of the bodies on the ground, witnessing the havoc I had caused, and then they moved over to me, crouching low to the ground. Another Angeli with those large white wings. His hair was blonde, and he was tall. I couldn't feel his touch as he put his broad hands on my arms. Felt nothing. My gaze clouded and cleared, focusing and unfocusing. He moved his broad hands to my face, saying something to me—shaking me gently.

"Stay away from me," I croaked, pushing his hands off, panic rising like bile in my throat.

I couldn't hear him, didn't know him. I had no idea what to do.

He moved away and disappeared, leaving me alone once more. My eyes strayed back to the bodies on the floor, and an icy web of dread wove through me. I clamped my lips shut before giving them a chance to tremble again.

After an unclear amount of time had passed, the Angeli returned. He had brought someone else. I recognized the Angeli walking in after him—his golden eyes beacons of safety.

Dominic.

He looked the same, yet different, as his pain-filled eyes took me in, scanning frantically to see if I was hurt. Then he looked back into the room and exchanged a wordless glance with the blonde guy. They had a muffled conversation before the other Angeli left the room again. Dominic lowered to his haunches, blocking my view. He was the only one I could hear loud and clear.

"You're okay," he said as if from afar. "You're okay." His strong arms wrapped around me, lifting me from the ground, and he carried me out—away. Somewhere safe. In his arms, I was safe.

I wanted to tell him that nothing about me was okay. That he should stay the hell away.

The scene cut away, and I finally came up for air, gasping as I woke up, cheeks still wet with tears. I blinked up at the ceiling, processing the dream I just had. The void within me had trouble stitching back up.

I was so tired of pretending.

So, so tired.

I turned on my side, curling in on myself as my face contorted with pain. Sobs wracked my body in violent bursts as I held on to my sheets like they were a lifeline, and I let the tears flow freely, for once not masking my feelings.

I had pushed back the nightmare from last night, stuffed in a box with things that wouldn't ever see the light of day. My soul already had enough to process at the end of all this. There was no need to add to it.

That morning, I received a call from my father, asking me if I had time to meet him in Ashrior. It was the first time I hesitated; the desire to tell him *no, actually, I didn't,* had been overpowering. But after the last few nights, I knew I had to face him. Who knew what bullshit Zade had been spewing.

My father had ordered the guards to escort me to a room in the lower levels of the mansion, where I hadn't been allowed to come as a kid. Zade was already waiting inside. He wouldn't meet my eyes, just lounged against the dark walls, flicking a knife up and down, looking bored.

"Leyla, I'm glad you came," my father said as he walked in, dragging a jittering woman with him. He let her fall to the ground in the middle of the room like a sack of grain. Beneath a wan face and chattering teeth, she appeared to be in her late twenties. "Meet another one of my brave volunteering employees."

I frowned. "She looks unwell."

Zade snorted, appearing underwhelmed by the whole situation. "She's *addicted*."

"Well, she looks hardly able to stand because of her 'addiction'. Seems pointless if customers can't even buy the next supply without being on life-support."

There had been many questionable things my father had done over the years, but Ambrosia topped them all.

"Is it true you have feelings for the Archangel, *Cara*?"

His question surprised me. My eyes moved to Zade, but he had the good sense to look away. "Did he also tell you he has approached me in public—twice? Or did he forget to mention that?"

I got my answer from the look on my father's face as he studied Zade, his stance thunderous. "What is she talking about?" he barked.

Zade had the audacity to shrug.

"He approached me at the gala and in front of my house."

"Is that so?" my father drawled, not done with him.

If Zade were willing to throw me to the wolves, I would sacrifice him right back.

"You haven't answered my question, though."

My eyes snapped back to my father's. His eyes had dimmed, becoming pools of darkness. His black hair seemed to move in an invisible breeze. "*Of course* I don't have feelings for him," I scoffed.

Breath lodged in my throat as he moved his hand to his pocket, getting something from it. "Come here," he said after a long moment.

I didn't move, was rooted to the spot when I noticed the syringe in his hands. The woman in the middle of the room whimpered at the sight of it, the metal chains rattling against the floor as she advanced. I knew immediately what he wanted me to do—and I didn't want to do it. That wasn't the way I'd prove my loyalty to him. This wasn't the job I'd taken on. "I thought it was a powder?"

"Products develop. We're adding this to the market after we complete the testing stage."

"Why?" I asked, my voice barely louder than a whisper. I wasn't asking about the new product.

"If you want power in this world, you must take it—force it." His eyes turned to me, his gaze intense. "This is how," he said, his voice full of conviction. "*Come.*"

I moved forward against my will and without knowing how to get out of it. When I was close enough, he grabbed my hand and pushed the syringe into it. "Actions have consequences, *Cara*. Are you strong enough to face them?"

A chill ran through me. The coppery liquid was undoubtedly Ambrosia, the drug that had caused so much harm in the short period it had been in circulation. I'd seen the results with my own two eyes, and yet here he was, asking me to inject another person with it. A wave of nausea hit me, and I had to stop myself from turning away, moving out of his grasp and dropping the syringe. It felt dirty. *I* felt dirty.

"It changes nothing," I said, but I understood it wasn't about Ambrosia. It was a power play. He wanted me to understand who was in charge.

My father's gaze softened, and he took a step toward me. "I understand your reluctance," he said, "but nothing can harm you here."

I focused on the syringe in my hand, recoiling at the sight. Slowly, his hand closed over mine and moved me over to where the woman crouched on the floor, her dilated pupils focusing on the liquid inside, and she licked her cracked lips as if relishing the taste of a meal to come.

Part of me wanted to obey him blindly, but another part resisted. That part wanted to break free and tell my father to stop. But I knew he would never listen. His sole focus was on reaching his end goal, and he wouldn't let anyone hinder him. Not even me. I was powerless.

Zade regarded us with a guarded look, his face as void as the emptiness within me. He wouldn't help me, either.

If I declined, he could remove me from the assignment or the organization entirely. I couldn't bear any disappointment I would see in his eyes. His respect and admiration were like a dopamine hit: hard to come by, but once it hit you, it hit hard. Fear overshadowed shock and hate as I moved. It felt like I wasn't really there as I pushed the needle inside the woman's arm, pressing my thumb down and injecting the drug into her bloodstream.

Her body went rigid, and I felt my stomach clench. I watched, heart pounding, as my father walked to the other side of the woman with a satisfied expression. I dropped the syringe to the ground—wanted to scream about how wrong this was, that he was spreading a fire he couldn't contain—but my words were trapped inside. Time stilled as we watched the woman's body tense and tremble. Then, after what seemed like an eternity, she relaxed, her breathing deepening and evening out. She opened her eyes and scanned the room, looking dazed.

"You see?" my father said, clasping the woman's shoulder. "You did her a favor." He looked at me with an indecipherable expression.

The employee looked confused, then rose from the ground and shuffled through the room a little.

"Don't you agree?" my father asked.

My eyes shifted back to his dark form, trying to ignore my clammy hands. "Right."

He turned fully to me. "The Prime and the Supreme have ordered raids to find out where the Ambrosia warehouses are, so we moved underground whatever we could save in time."

"How did they find out?"

Zade pushed from the wall. "That's what we like to know."

I turned to my father in a flash. "I didn't—"

"I know." He looked at me with a stone-faced expression. "*I know*," he said again, his eyes softening ever so slightly. "You don't even know where these places are."

That softness was gone in a blink as footsteps approached us from the side. My father moved out of nowhere, his eyes closed, jaw clenched, and his muscles straining. Zade flinched, backing away and warning me to do the same with the first genuine emotion in his blue eyes.

One of my father's arms reached out in the way the woman had approached, and she was suddenly gasping for air, a dark cloud obscuring her throat that she tried to grab with her hands many paces away. Too far for my father to touch.

"I. DARE. YOU!" he bellowed. His eyes had opened again and seemed almost entirely taken by darkness. The vessels in his face and neck started bulging, and he clenched his fingers like he was squeezing a ball with all his might, making the woman choke.

The dark spot on her neck looked like a hand made of shadows.

My throat dried up at the sight of it.

What the hell?

My brain couldn't compute what I was seeing. "You…" I stammered, walking forward to… I didn't know, do something? But my father pulled me back with one arm and clenched his hand into a fist, the woman on the other side collapsing against the wall.

Her lifeless eyes were open, the dark spot around her throat gone.

With horror, I stared at my father's hand, tendrils of black smoke curling around his fingers before dissipating. I took a trembling breath as I stared on in horror, from the dead woman slumped against the wall to Zade—who didn't seem nearly as shocked—and back to my father.

"You have magic?" I asked him, and it seemed like the stupidest question. Why did it feel like I had just watched him rearrange the insides of my body?

"I do." He seemed pleased with himself.

Shaking my head, I tried to compute the information I was getting. "You have—*What?* Since when?"

He raised a dark brow. I ignored the chasm opening inside me and the feelings that sank into it. "It seems like something I should've known."

His eyes clouded with something I couldn't identify. "Are you questioning my choices, daughter?"

The word sounded sweet coming from him, but I recognized the quiet warning in his tone. I turned my body, willing myself to keep looking his way and not glance back at the dead woman in the corner. Or Zade. "Tell me, and I'll tell you what the sword looks like."

My father's face changed in a blink. Even the shadows in his eyes faded. "You have seen it? Are you certain?"

I nodded.

"I've had magic for much longer than you're alive, *Cara*. But I have decided to stop hiding it from you—hiding myself."

The realization that my father was dangerous struck me, perhaps for the first time in my life. I'd known he was powerful; how could I not? But after today... He had kept his powers from me all this time, which meant he was capable of so much more than he had let on. I wondered what else he could do and how far he would go to protect it. How far he would go to get what he wanted.

My mind raced as I tried to wrap my head around this new information. The image of him I had created as a kid morphed into something new, and I wasn't sure if I liked it. The thought made me uneasy, but I reminded myself I could still trust him. No matter what kind of power he possessed, he wouldn't use it to hurt me.

I wasn't sure what else to say, so I started describing the sword to him. I zoned out as I rehashed what I'd seen—the first of many betrayals pouring from my lips.

As much as this new side of him frightened me, no matter how much I despised Ambrosia, it didn't negate the fact that he'd taken care of me all my life. He did what he thought was right for us and always ensured I had everything I wanted, even if it was diametrically opposed to his interest.

Because my father cherished me. *Loved* me. And that was enough.

It had to be.

CHAPTER FORTY

Dominic

I remembered the first Starball game I ever saw. My father had brought me to the stadium when I was old enough to be allowed inside. It had been a spectacle unlike anything I'd ever witnessed before. The stadium had been buzzing with life, the stands full of fans from all domains. There had been an electric current in the air, pulsing through the large crowd gathered to watch the match.

After witnessing that, I started practicing the sport and dreamt of turning pro. I wanted to be on the receiving end of that energy.

I watched as the players ran around the large field, the thrill of the game still palpable within my body, desperate to answer its call. The game had never lost its appeal to me, and the desire to play never ceased. But now it was my job to attend, to just *be* there, a spectator drawing eyes from every corner of the stadium—and not in the way I wanted.

Before the game started and the warming-ups drew to an end, my attention was pulled by Nathan as he entered the balcony with Lodana Fivaldor. She whispered something in his ear, and he gave her a genuine smile as he nodded. My gaze moved further behind them, looking for the woman I knew wouldn't be there.

Nathan put a hand on my shoulder. "I'm sorry we're late. Traffic was hectic."

I brushed off the comment. That was the least of my concerns.

"Too bad Leyla couldn't come, huh?" Lodana said as she popped into view again, grinning.

"Yeah," I muttered, though my voice was tight. Immediately, my thoughts turned to her, thinking of our kiss. It was the last time we had spoken, except for the text I'd sent her to invite her to tonight's game. I didn't know what had possessed me to ask her, but the pang of jealousy I felt as she texted back that she couldn't make it had no business being there. It made my blood run hot. So fucking hot I could combust in mere moments.

Nathan had his eyes on the game as he asked, "She had other plans?"

I ignored the undercurrent of his question. I didn't have the energy to deal with it today. He didn't even know.

Lodana shrugged. "She mentioned something about work in Ashrior. Her schedule is very inconsistent."

Right. Ashrior. Work. Her mysterious boss.

I cleared my throat, forcing down the caveman trying to take control within me as I thought of Leyla not being here—but *there*. That feeling wasn't welcome either. I forced my attention back to the game, but the emotions remained like an insistent rash.

Nathan and Lodana were immersed in each other, and I was glad. I wasn't in a chatty mood tonight. The teams raced up and down the field, catching falling stars wherever they landed. Lots of them descended tonight, but not enough to distract my thoughts. They kept circling back to Leyla, looping and looping until I was sure my sanity was on the line.

Everything in my life had toned down after I'd lost Emiliana. I had bled dry until all that had been left was monochrome. The only point of life was to continue and make it as bearable as possible—with a few bright lights from my friends. But ever since meeting Leyla, my life had regained some color. It started small; she had been a beacon in the night when I first saw her, so bright I realized I'd forgotten what true color looked like. Her presence had been infectious, leaking her palette everywhere. She equipped me to paint in polychrome—it was the only way I could now.

But I didn't see the point. Not anymore.

The game's halftime rushed by, and it was clear the Lupine team would win. They were crushing the Pisces team, to no one's surprise, but this win had even Paplos shaking his head with embarrassment, and he didn't even care for the sport. On the other hand, Heller was hollering like I'd never seen him before. He was always in control of his emotions, never betraying what he thought, but he was cheering for his team like he'd never seen them play. They had a shot at winning this year's cup.

I looked beyond the Lupine representative. Cloaked and with her long, silvery-white hair bound back, Head Cardinal Kemalgda was watching the game with a look of stoic boredom on her face. She somehow sensed my attention and caught me looking—her face betraying nothing as she studied me for a heartbeat. When I turned away, I noticed the Head Cardinal walk toward me through the sky box. She moved with authority, her robes flowing behind her. I gave her a quick look as she stopped beside me to show I acknowledged her. It seemed like an eternity before she spoke.

"Prime Venetia," she said, bobbing her head.

I mimicked the gesture with nonchalance. "Head Cardinal."

The Lupine team scored another two points in quick succession, and the stadium erupted, along with Heller. The other representatives did their best to remain impartial, but even Paplos was laughing behind his hand.

"This year's City Cup is a success."

I gripped the balcony's railing. "It appears so."

"Ambrosia sales have also decreased significantly in the last couple of days."

My nostrils flared. "I heard. Good news." Nitas' intervention had helped slow down the production, though we couldn't get all of the drug destroyed.

Head Cardinal Kemalgda stepped closer. "Any ideas on why that could be? I am very curious. It's a learning opportunity, after all."

I wetted my lips and leaned down on one foot, crossing my ankles. "You are intelligent, Head Cardinal. I think you already know the answer."

She seemed to hold something back for a second, but she had been alive for a long time, and if time taught people anything, it was how to keep their composure. "You know that you could have destroyed more than you did good by going rogue."

"It seemed like a better solution than doing nothing."

The old Seraphim turned fully to me. "Sorting out and managing situations like these take time, Prime Venetia."

"Well," I said with a breathy laugh. "Let that just be the

one thing we don't have. Look around, Head Cardinal—this is the third time you've gone down to Ashium this year. You do not see what we see. The Upper City is spared from the misery, but down here, in the city, there's turmoil, unrest, poverty." I was shaking my head as I nearly hissed the last word. "Open your eyes."

Head Cardinal Kemalgda was silent, and her stance was passive, but her eyes scanned my face while she clamped her lips shut. Then, she inhaled and said, "Let's hope, for both our sakes, that your actions haven't done any permanent damage."

"Yes," I hissed. "Let's focus on my actions instead of Xanon's and see how that works out. Gods forbid we actually find a solution to this problem."

"Dominic," she said as she touched my arm. "I know you want what's best for Ashar, but I do, too. The only thing we've bought with this action can be measured in time. The Undercity's hackles are rising; they've added protection everywhere—probably moved this practice further down, making it nearly unreachable."

There was a point to what she said, but my priority wasn't taking down the Undercity right now. My priority was damage control for Ashar, getting the drug back off the street with haste. Xanon Naan was nearly impossible to catch, but his product—the physical proof of his business—was not.

Seraphim Kemalgda walked off as calmly as she'd come, which infuriated me. The woman had no idea of the situation's severity. How could she, holed up in the *Curia* all day?

I tried to put my mind back to the game, even attempted to redirect my thoughts to Ambrosia and the conversation I'd had with the Head Cardinal—anything to keep it from drifting back to Leyla. I watched as the teams ran back and forth, catching meteorite after meteorite, but the memories of her skin, lips, and presence dragged me down. My thoughts obsessed over the Daemon with bright green eyes.

The sick and twisted part of me somehow relished the pain from the knife she had twisted in my back.

The final whistle blew, signaling the game was over, but I hardly registered it. It was only when Nathan nudged my arm that I finally stepped forward and raised my hand to close the city's wards back up again.

My thoughts were elsewhere.

I had hoped for the game to clear my mind and distract me, to no avail. With a deep sigh, I got up and walked to the exit, my mind still on her.

Only her.

CHAPTER FORTY-ONE

Leyla

I cringed at Dana's message from last night.

Dana: *Missed you at the game yesterday. A certain Archangel did too!*

The whole situation made me sick; my blurry feelings for Dominic, my shaking loyalties. I was still reeling from what had happened in Ashrior. The way my father had killed that woman like she had been nothing. What he had made me do.

What I had done—because I sure as hell hadn't pulled back when the syringe went into that woman's arm.

I needed help. But what if I got it? Tell the psychiatrist about my family? My father? The things I was involved in? There was patient confidentiality, sure, but to what extent? I assumed committing and confessing crimes was something they had to report. Perhaps only a lawyer could withhold information like that from the authorities. Maybe I needed to think about getting one of those.

I couldn't make up my mind. All I managed instead was to take a run. It helped me cope; jogging had always helped me get my thoughts straight.

My eyes caught on something when I ran past a news

stall on the street in the Ethereal domain, but I ignored it. My brain couldn't possibly process any more information. Ashar City was facing a crisis, and my knowledge about it was already extensive.

The music blasting in my ears suddenly stopped as I rounded a corner. I did not check who was calling me before I answered with a breathy, "Hey."

"What the fuck, Ley!" a voice yelled through my earbuds, and I slowed down. My best friend wasn't calling to chit-chat.

"Dana?"

"Yes, Dana," she said. "Didn't you see?"

"See what?"

"That article about you! It's going fucking viral."

My heart skipped a beat at the same time I stopped moving altogether. I grabbed my phone and searched for my name. Several sources popped up, and I opened the first one—from *A-sham*, one of the most popular tabloids in the city. It was posted a half hour ago.

Black spots danced in my vision as I read the title.

LIVING PROOF YOU CAN('T) HAVE IT ALL

The pretty girl, the dark stranger, the pro-baller, and the eligible prime—a love rect-angle for the ages, or a glorified mess?

My neck itched. Part of me wanted to shrivel up and die on the spot. It wanted the ground to swallow me whole and never let me come back up. I wanted—

"Is it true?" Dana asked.

"Wait." I continued reading.

The girl, known as Leyla Cuprum, was first spotted with pro-Starballer Josiah Eden on several occasions. The athlete had expressed sincere interest in Miss Cuprum, according to sources close to the Ethereal team captain. He was heartbroken to hear of her ties with the Archangel not much later.

And we all know him. Our Prime, Dominic Venetia, was seen with her frequently. The two seem inseparable in accompanying photos: in a nightclub in Ashrior, at the famous kick-off gala, and on an intimate date in the city. We haven't seen the Archangel this interested in anyone for a long time.

The look on his face speaks volumes. Is the Archangel in love? For real, this time?

The photos showed me and Dominic close together in the club while we were talking; I was smiling, and he looked captivated by me. He and I from a distance on the street after our date, before I stepped into a cab. A blurry photo of us standing to the side at the ACC team presentation—him leaning close to me.

There was also a picture of us at the gala. It was blurry, but only because we were moving. It was a photo of us on the dance floor, our faces close together, genuine smiles overtaking our lips. My eyes were closed, and Dominic looked at me like I was the only woman in the room.

Like he had feelings for me.

> **But there is a third player in the mix. A mysterious Daemon from Ashrior. They were seen kissing on the street in front of Miss Cuprum's apartment but quickly broke it off before anyone could see. Or at least, they thought they did. You don't get to be sneaky in Shard City, Dear. But I think you've learned your lesson.**
>
> **Here is the real kicker, though: that little tryst was on the night of her date with the Archangel.**
>
> **Whether Prime Venetia is aware of her other beau is unknown, but knowing his track record, he prefers monogamy. According to one of his ex-lovers, he is persistent and possessive. The Archangel demanded exclusivity, even though they weren't 'together'.**
>
> **Says it all, don't you think?**

What the fuck?

My heart thudded in my throat.

"Leyla!" Dana practically yelled over the phone.

"Wait!" I snapped back, panicking. "*Fuck.*"

"Oh my god," she said. "It's true, isn't it?"

I was shaking my head and tried to swallow. The photo of me raising my middle finger was added next to a photo of Dominic waving at the camera with a smile.

I closed the article.

"I can't talk right now, Dana," I choked out.

"No! Wai—" But I had already broken the connection.

Had he read it? He had people on this, had he not? Dominic must've seen the article by now. Even one from a tabloid.

Just as Dana called me back, another caller showed up. I looked at my phone, foot tapping on the concrete as I bit back the pressure behind my eyes. I ignored my father's and Dana's calls and turned off my phone entirely before the missed calls could accumulate.

I was unable to speak—could barely think.

I started running again, this time straight back home. Anger and anxiety made me go faster than I'd ever done, and I was home in a heartbeat.

Spending time with Dominic had made people curious about my past, my life, and who I was. I hadn't understood the scope of his fame; I had been singularly focused on getting what I needed, which was my father's praise—the sword.

At home, I nearly tore off my clothes and stepped into the shower, turning the water hot and steamy. I focused on my breathing, but my lungs stopped working properly from the minute I read the article's title.

I was calmer and clear-headed when I got out of the shower sometime later, though my entire body was still shaking. Turning my phone back on, I returned my father's call instead of looking at my notifications.

He answered on the first ring. "Leyla."

"I want out."

"You can't, *Cara*."

"Did you read that fucking article? I need to move to the other side of the world, and even that wouldn't be enough."

He would never forgive me.

"Zade fucked up with that public display. That is not your fault."

"I don't care about—"

"Listen to me. We're working on getting the article down in most places, so you will have time to go to the Archangel's house and retrieve the sword."

I bit back a groan. "I can't. It's protected."

My father grunted something. "Go now, get the sword for me. I know you can do this. You're a Naan—my daughter. All will be well. I won't let anything happen to you. I promise."

I felt the knot in my chest tighten. If I did nothing, my father would be so disappointed. I would prove what he was thinking: that I couldn't do it—that I'd choke on the last stretch. If I did do it, anything I'd ever build with Dominic would be destroyed irreparably.

If it wasn't already; my secret was out, and my reputation was in shambles.

"There is no time to waste. Don't let it all be for nothing."

My father's message was clear: get the sword, whatever means necessary.

But I was not thinking about the sword at all. I could only think about Dominic's reaction when he read the article. When he realized I betrayed him.

I looked in the mirror and wished I wouldn't come to hate what I'd see the next time I looked at my reflection.

I stood before the gates leading to Dominic's residence, a daunting sight. Trepidation was such a different emotion from anger, which had spurred me to get over here the last time. It had made me barge through the gates. Now, I hesitated.

I took a step forward, passing the borders of Dominic's estate. A tremor went through me, meaning I was still allowed to enter. The relief I felt was short-lived. If he let me enter and hadn't changed the access to his wards, it probably meant he hadn't read the article yet. This privilege would have been the first thing to go.

What would happen if I told him the truth? Did he have room in his heart to forgive me? The heart that was already bruised?

When I reached his front door, I knocked on it with more force than I'd intended and was greeted by Amy a few seconds later. "Leyla," she said, smiling. She hadn't read it either, or her voice betrayed nothing.

"Hey," I responded awkwardly, stepping inside as she held the door open. "Is Dominic home?"

"Not at the moment, but he'll be back soon." Amy didn't feel like the person who read gossip sites or sat around on her phone all day.

"Can I maybe wait for him inside?"

The Angeli nodded. "As you wish. If you need anything, you know where to find me."

Part of me didn't want her to be nice to me. Her smile made me feel so much worse. She looked at me like I was worth something. As if she actually liked me.

I sat on the living room sofa, my feet tapping against the

carpet. The thudding sound was the only thing I could hear in the otherwise empty house. Frantically, I wiped my clammy hands on my trousers, legs rocking. My eyes kept darting back to the hallway, to the door Amy disappeared through, as if, at any moment, she was about to burst out of there and point a finger at me in accusation.

The more time that passed, the more likely it became. What was she doing in that room? Was she calling someone? Searching online? How long until she came across the article or someone pointed it out to her? Dana had mentioned it was going viral. Many people must know by now.

Knowing Dominic, his reaction would be catastrophic. We had often spoken about the unrest on the streets, and now I had been inexplicably tied to the enforcer of the distress. I had been captured kissing someone else—no matter if I didn't want it or if my feelings for Dominic were real. That wasn't how it appeared, and there was no way for me to explain without betraying him, anyway.

What would he think if he found out I was with him for ulterior motives, like all the others?

It was the truth, wasn't it? At the start, at least. But I knew he would never believe another word I said after he found out I was Xanon's daughter. There would be no going back from that. Ever.

The ticking clock on the wall kept me on my toes. Every second that passed increased my growing headache.

I needed to do something.

Anything.

No more hiding.

No one was here; the home was silent. I had waited around for fifteen minutes, and it had felt like an eternity already. There was an opening—just the slightest. My reputation was already in shambles. There was no way out for me. It was between choosing my father or losing them both.

I stood and headed towards the stairs. Part of my mind screamed at me to stay put in my spot on the sofa, wait until Dominic came home, and try to explain. But that would inevitably result in him kicking me out of his home—in the best-case scenario—and my father not wanting anything to do with me. He hated rats. And where would I be going? What did I have left, then?

It would have all been for nothing.

My father had always given me everything I wanted. And now he wanted one thing in return—something I had practically begged for. Dominic had only been in my life a fraction of the time my father had taken care of me.

And then there was *Bohrod*… The way Dominic had taken his body and deprived him of a decent burial made me see red. It was the last straw before I soundlessly made my way up the stairs, tracing my steps from a couple of days ago.

I entered Dominic's dark bedroom and walked over to the painting that hid the vault where he kept the sword. I looked at the art, its beauty striking me again. It truly was a marvelous piece, so much like the painting still lounging against the wall of my apartment. Thinking of the thoughtful gift he'd bought me made my heart clench involuntarily.

No matter now—that ship had sailed. It had never been allowed to dock. *There was no going back*, I repeated in my head. *No explanation that would ever fix this.*

I stepped forward and took the painting down, setting it carefully on the ground next to the dresser, and dialed my father's number. There had to be a way to open the safe. He would know what to do.

As my phone rang, I steeled my emotions, locking away my feelings for Dominic in a vault of my own where no oxygen could reach them. I left them there to suffocate, burying their remains so deep I could never touch them again.

Even if I were desperate enough to try, I would never have the chance.

CHAPTER FORTY-TWO

Dominic

Something about life felt like it was always laughing in my face. Whenever I found a shred of positivity, hope, or light, it had the habit of spitting at me in return.

I sensed someone entering my home's wards and received a text from Amy saying Leyla was waiting for me inside. I instructed Amy to leave for a bit, assuring her I would arrive shortly, and told her not to say a word. Leyla had seen the article, just like me. It was why she had come.

Now, she would get one chance.

One out.

Because that kiss between us had been honest, there was no way of faking something like that. I would know, which is why her deceit cut me so deeply.

I stood on the threshold of my dark bedroom, leaning against the door frame. Leyla had already carefully put the painting on the ground, and I watched as she tried to open the vault. She kept reaching for her phone, but her calls would never go through. I made sure the signal didn't cross the ward. "Whoever you're trying to reach can't help you."

Leyla froze, her whole body locking at the sound of my voice.

"Did you honestly think you could steal from me and get away with it?" My voice was soft, but she recognized the undercurrent. I flicked on the lights.

Leyla whirled around like a deer caught in headlights. Her chest was heaving a hundred miles an hour as she looked at me, straightening. "Dom—" she stammered, sounding so unlike the woman I had gotten to know. "I—" She tried to get a grip on herself but failed. "I came over to talk, and—"

"And yet," I interrupted firmly. "I find you *here*, trying to break into my vault."

Her jaw snapped shut, and she averted her green eyes in shame. It was appropriate. She ought to feel humiliated.

"I read that article days ago." It was inside the file Nitas had given me. The article had been weeks in the making. It outlined everywhere she'd been, including the timelines. She had gone to Ashrior often on or after days we'd been together. I had been a fool to turn my eye, blinded by the picture she painted me. I wished I had listened to Nathan. He had been right about her from the start.

"That kiss—you have to know it meant nothing. I didn't even want it. And Josiah—"

My stomach twisted, listening to more of her godsdamned lies. "I don't fucking care," I snapped. "Nor do I want your excuses." It wasn't about the light-forsaken men. The article had just been a device to open my eyes. "I am not stupid, Leyla. Though the press couldn't figure out the Daemon you spread your legs for is one of Xanon's cronies, doesn't mean I am the same. I know about every piece of vermin that crawls through the Undercity."

Her green eyes flicked up at me, fear swirling in their depths.

"What is it you want?" I should have known, put two and two together the moment I had seen her. I knew she would fuck me over; the woman was too good to be true. "It's the sword you're after, isn't it?" Alarm bells should have rung when she asked me about it at the stadium.

She blinked and folded her lips.

"Of course it is," I hissed, baring my teeth at her. "It was the only reason you popped up everywhere, attempting to get close to me, wasn't it?"

Leyla remained silent, but her eyebrows furrowed, throat bobbing.

"*Tell me I am wrong!*" I roared, and she winced, taking a step back, eyes blinking rapidly. She swallowed and had the gall to look shocked. "You must think I'm stupid," I said, voice still raised. "But I've lived for over a century, Leyla. People don't cross me and walk away from that."

"It's complicated, but I can explain." She wrapped a hand around her opposite arm, making herself smaller. It made the gall rise in my fucking throat.

"It's extremely simple, actually," I said, wrapping my arms over my chest. "You lied." *I had asked her if I could trust her.* "You lied about everything and inserted yourself into my life. I had never seen you before, but you were suddenly everywhere. I should've known. Fate really had nothing to do with it." I clucked my tongue. "It was *all* you."

There's a sense of fatis surrounding her.

"And then you mentioned the sword—strange, because no one ever does. At first, I had written it off as a coincidence, but after I read the article, I understood."

Silence settled over the room as she didn't contradict my words. I could see the truth in her eyes.

"Tell me his name."

Her chin started trembling. "I thought you didn't care."

My chuckle was low and hollow. "Do you fuck him *nice* and *good*, Leyla? Follow his every command like the good girl you are?"

"Dominic," she pleaded, shaking her head, her expression definitive. "I told you, it isn't like that. Not anymore. He—"

"But you do what he tells you to? He's your 'boss'?" I cut her off. She didn't respond, hesitating, and I nodded. "That's what I thought." If her fucking boyfriend worked for Xanon Naan, she did so, too.

Leyla remained silent, not even a single hair out of place. The jeans and shirt she was wearing looked good on her, too. Too good to be real. *How ironic.*

"Did you know about Ambrosia before it hit the streets?"

There was agony in her eyes as she moved her jaw and nodded—quickly. A truth, then.

"I thought you were smarter than that." I was shaking my head. Pacing back and forth across my bedroom floor, I was acting erratic. Her eyes trailed me every step of the way. The homeless people she helped, the things she did… All a farce. What a disappointment she had proven to be.

"Why didn't you confront me when you found out?" she asked.

I leveled a stare at her. "What difference would it have made?"

Leyla looked away, grabbed the hem of her shirt, and smoothed the fabric. I could see her jaw working, her eyes blinking, and her chest rising and falling. She was nervous. And she had the good sense to be.

I suddenly stepped forward and opened the safe with ease

while she backed away toward the door, swapping places with me. I unlocked it, retrieved the clothbound bundle, and stepped forward with the sword in my hands. "Why do you think I would show you this, Leyla?" I asked her as I looked around, a manic chuckle escaping me. "I don't know you. You never proved I could trust you."

Her lip trembled. "You knew?"

"That's godsdamned right."

"Dominic, you need to know that our connection was genuine. I hadn't planned on feeling this way about you, but I did."

She twisted her knife deeper with every plea and word laced with feeling. Her lies made me sick. I stepped forward, but she retreated, eyeing the door. "I am giving you an opportunity to do the right thing." Shoving the bundle in her arms, she stumbled back a step or two. "Tell me everything. Leave the sword. And start over—somewhere else, in another city far away from here."

I honestly didn't care about the fucking sword. The object held no meaning to me. Only the gods knew why they wanted it.

Without giving her the object, I would never know the outcome. It was easy for her to tell me what I wanted to hear when she was trapped. And I needed to know. She had crafted her lies so perfectly that I couldn't discern them from the truth. Now, she had a chance to show me who she really was. How honest her feelings for me had been, or if they had all been lies, too.

She decided her fate.

Leyla's chin quivered again, but her fingers curled around the bundle in her hands. "I can't."

"Oh, darling," I said. "Don't you understand? It isn't a choice." I stalked closer to her, making her chin rise to follow me. "When you go, you will find yourself knee-deep in legal problems. Either way, you'll have to leave—to another town or prison, you decide. Look at it like a loss or a bigger loss."

She didn't look away. She was pleading with those green eyes. "Dominic, I—" But again, her lips snapped shut.

How I longed to pry them open and drag all the bullshit out. "What would you give to return to the beginning and start all over?" I whispered. "Would you do the same? Or would you want the thing between us to be real?"

At the last word, the look on her face had me wanting to turn around and never look at her again, but she quickly steeled her gaze. "I'm not that desperate," she said, but the words were gruff.

Once a liar, always a liar.

"Yet you are that desperate to please your masters?"

Leyla narrowed her eyes. "I don't have a master."

Ah—there she was, finally showing her true face. "What does that boy have on you to whore yourself out? What did Xanon Naan do that makes you willing to squander your life for his gains?"

I'll make it go away.

Look who was desperate now. *No more*, I scolded myself. *No fucking more.*

"I owe him," she just said.

Not-fucking-good-enough. "What does he want with it?" I gestured to the bundle in her arms.

"I don't know."

"You never asked him before you came here?"

"He wouldn't tell me."

"I don't presume he wants to do much good with it."

Leyla looked at the sword in her arms, and I saw a flash of doubt on her face. The barest flash, enough to tell me she didn't entirely want to do this. A spark of hope ignited in my chest at the sight of the girl beneath the mask—the girl I'd gotten to know.

Then her head snapped up, and her face was impassively blank. "I don't care."

There, and gone in a blink.

CHAPTER FORTY-THREE

Leyla

"Bullshit," he said, shaking his head with conviction.

I shrugged, steeling my muscles to keep from trembling. Why had I become so weak for this man?

Dominic stepped closer. "You don't want to do this."

"What I want is irrelevant."

The comment struck. I watched his belief waver—and then unravel. The clothed sword in my hands was burning into my skin.

He narrowed his eyes and brushed a hand over his face. Wings bristling, he looked suddenly tired, as if the weight of the world was leaning on him. I knew it wasn't far from the truth. "So, this is who you truly are, Leyla? A coward?"

Years ago, I had not taken action when I needed to, but I would not choke again. I would make it up to Bohrod—make things right. This time, I wouldn't hide.

"It isn't even about the sword, you know?" Dominic said. "It's the lying."

Part of me shriveled, seeing the betrayal on his face, the hurt I caused. I had the sword in my arms, and he had been the one to put it there. He was done with me, with us—something that never even existed or was viable in the first place. We had been doomed from the very start.

"All people ever want from me is something to advance them," he said, looking me up and down with disgust on his handsome face. "And you're not any different."

"I'm not leaving without the sword." *I'm sorry.*

Dominic smiled, every bit the predator lurking beneath his skin. "I won't fight you for it, Leyla." The bite had left his voice. He closed his eyes and pinched the bridge of his nose. "You know your options: run back to your master, give him the sword, and deal with the consequences. Or give me the sword back right now and tell him you couldn't do it. Tell him it was too hard."

His offer was tempting, but where would that leave me? I'd be alone. Why throw away the one chance I had to show my father what I was capable of? I had succeeded. Why would I trade that for a life back in the shadows? This thing that had just begun between Dominic and me was broken, as he'd made abundantly clear. And me being Xanon's daughter... I didn't see how that would ever work.

My loyalty lay with the man I'd known my entire life; who had cared for me and given me everything I ever needed. There was only one logical choice to make. I took a step back. "I'll deal with the consequences."

Dominic's eyes flared, and then he took a step forward, eyes darkening and brows creasing. Even his wings flared dangerously. "*No.*"

The soft prattle of rain had become loud and insisting, and I could hear thunder roaring in the distance. It was storming outside, and I had an idea why. I clutched the bundle in my arms. "You gave me a choice."

"Yes," he said, "but there was only one good answer."

"I know." I took another step back and looked on as Dominic stopped moving.

"You're so young. So naïve."

My hands tightened on the sword. *So close.* "Perhaps."

I received a perplexed look from him, as if my loyalty was beyond his grasp. Unfortunately, revealing I was Xanon's daughter would not bide well for me. Dominic let go of a breath as he cocked his head to the side.

"You'll let me leave?" I asked, my voice dead.

Something snapped between us, and he waved me away with a hand, informing me with one gesture he was sick of the sight of me—that he never wanted to see me again. "I will give you a head start."

I nodded, casting my eyes down, my hair falling in front of my face, and turned around to walk out of the room before he changed his mind, biting on the inside of my cheek until I tasted blood. I focused on the pain.

"Leyla," he said, making me pause in the doorway. I turned to him halfway, not all the way back. Looking at him hurt. I stared at the floor instead.

"Was it worth it?"

For a moment, I closed my eyes and clenched my jaw. I bit my tongue, fighting for dominance as tears threatened to cross a boundary.

I left without answering his question.

CHAPTER FORTY-FOUR

Dominic

Bang.

The front door closed, its sound echoing in my house. Coldness spread to the cracks in my facade.

Leyla had made her choice. She had left. And she had taken the sword. She could drop it in the ocean for all I cared. It was just a piece of metal. Any powers it had were long gone. The gods had made sure of it.

Numbly, I discarded my suit jacket and opened the top buttons of my dress shirt. I sat down on the foot of the bed, my hands braced on my knees, pushing into my hair. Her loyalty shouldn't be with that garbage working for Naan.

Who says she's not just as perverted? A voice in my head whispered. *Who says she did not relish hurting you just like he would?*

I doubted everything but one thing: I was a fool. I was a damned fool to trust her and fall for her lies.

I looked out of the window. The sun had disappeared, clouds blocking its rays, making room for yet another night of my too-long, miserable life.

Overwhelmed by conflicting emotions, I became numb and found myself stepping into my garden. Rain drizzled on my face, latching onto my hair and lashes, but I didn't blink. I looked up at the dark clouds hanging high above, mocking me.

The rain started pouring down faster, obscuring my sight as if taunting me. My breathing came in bigger and bigger gulps, expressing the rage that seemed to coil deep within me. I arched my back and stretched my wings.

Leyla's scent lingered on my skin. I loathed it.

What it meant.

What it *made* me.

I bent my knees, and with a mighty push, I took off from the ground, giving my wings the head start they needed as I thrust into the sky—drops of water trickling from my feathers. Another burst of my wings sent me off. Their unwavering strength unleashed something as I kept looking up, jaw clenching, fists balled, and continued to thrust myself upwards.

Soaring higher and higher into the taunting sky, I left Ashtior behind. I flew through clouds, the temperature decreasing with every powerful beat of my wings, but I couldn't feel the cold's sharp bite. I'd taken all the lashings I could muster for one day. Pain was just another emotion I was numb to.

The second layer of clouds came into view, but I knew I couldn't reach them. Metaphorically speaking, I, as Archangel, was bound to this place to maintain the city's magnetic shield to keep the three layers of the city intact.

How often I hadn't dreamed of letting it all collapse.

Thunder boomed, but it did not hit me. A web of electricity formed and disappeared again, its vibrant blue veins colliding with the invisible barrier through which it couldn't reach me.

My wings thrust again, and I soared even closer, forcing myself to stay in the raging storm. "STRIKE!" I bellowed at the thunder. "I DARE YOU!"

The thunder roared back, an embodiment of my anger, the sound of its hard clasp against the barrier resounding again—*taunting* me.

"HERE I AM," I roared again. "*OBEY ME.*" The wind swept through my hair and feathers, trying to shove me back down. I tried harder, my wings beating faster, mightier, trying to get closer, but the storm wouldn't let me.

Rain soaked me to the core as I was pushed farther down. "HIT ME, *DAMNIT!*" I urged, wanting to feel anything other than the storm brewing within me. To forget all about those green eyes, the betrayal that they represented.

"Please," I whispered, the sound drowned out by the wind cutting against my body.

Closing my eyes, I swallowed, regaining my composure.

I was tired.

So tired.

My wings clasped together, and with one last look at the thunder above, I let myself fall back into the sky and dove for Ashtior, the glinting disc hovering in the air. The roof of my mansion quickly came back into view, and I let myself land on the pavement with a loud bang, cracking the expensive stone beneath my feet. I walked to the front door, opened it, and stepped inside, water dripping on the tiles with every step.

A door opened, and Amy walked into the hall, eyes wide. The older Angeli looked at me. Not at my disheveled appearance but at my eyes. She knew me. She understood.

"Dominic—"

I shook my head, drops of water falling from the movement. "I'm sorry I've woken you," I breathed, my voice hoarse.

"I waited up," she said, closing her robe with determination. "I will set some tea."

I tried to ignore the worry in her eyes. The pity. It seemed to follow me wherever I went, no matter how badly I wanted to escape it.

"That won't be necessary," I said mechanically. "I'll take a shower and go to bed. But thank you."

Amy frowned but nodded—a sharp, unhesitating nod. She knew better than to push me at moments like this. "Don't let the shadows of your past win, Dominic. There's so much left to live for."

I looked ahead of me to the large staircase but didn't want to go to that room, *my room*, where I would only be greeted with a deafening silence. I moved over to the living room, where I sat on the couch, not caring that I was soaking wet. My dress shirt clung to my chest, and my pants were fully black instead of dark grey. I brushed my hair back, looking at the ground.

Despite my earlier declination, Amy walked into the living room with some hot tea and fresh towels. "Do you need fresh clothes?" she asked me.

Once again, I shook my head. "Thank you."

She seemed to hesitate. "People do questionable things and make poor decisions. Especially when they grew up not knowing right from wrong."

"I don't want to hear it right now, Amy."

With a nod, she left.

Sometime later, after the tea had turned cold and night

had crawled over Ashar, I had somehow found the strength to go upstairs and dress in some dry clothes before going back down—shunning my bedroom. The sound of the front door opening pulled me from my thoughts, and the outline of two people appeared in my hall.

Inesa and Nathan walked into the living room, both wearing fierce expressions.

"Oh, Dominic," Inesa said immediately as she rushed forward and pressed herself to my side, her warmth seeping into me. "We were worried sick after Amy called us! We couldn't get a hold of you. And your wards kept refusing us to enter."

Nathan approached silently and sat on the hocker opposite us. "What happened? You saw her?"

"Yes," I croaked.

"And it did not go well?" he guessed.

I exhaled. "You must be having a field day."

Nathan shook his head, sincere compassion in those dark eyes. "Of course not. What sort of friend would I be if I relished in your pain? Do you think I expected *this*? That she's in bed with *Xanon Naan*, of all people?"

"Is it true?" Inesa asked. "All of it?"

I shrugged. "The parts that matter."

"Maybe she's in trouble. Something about it is off. They might have leverage on her."

"Inesa," I warned her. "Not now." That thought had been running through my mind, too. Leyla said she owed them, *him*, and—"I don't care. I gave her an out. She didn't take it."

"What does that mean?" Nathan asked.

"She was here for the sword. Naan wants it, and he had tasked her with getting it from me."

Nathan stopped breathing. "But she didn't get it, right?"

he asked carefully, bracing himself for my answer. "It's locked away in your vault."

I looked at the ceiling.

Nathan swallowed. "What did you do, Dominic?"

"Dom?" Inesa asked with a tremble in her voice.

"I gave her the option to take the sword or leave it here."

"*You did what?*" Nathan bellowed at the same time as Inesa said, "And?" She was brushing her thumbs over my arm in soothing circles.

"There was no other way in my head for her to prove herself."

"*Prove* herself?" Nathan was shaking his head, a frantic laugh escaping him. He rose and paced through the living room with his hands planted on his sides.

"She took it," I said. Leyla had been showing her real face to me the entire time. I just hadn't wanted to see it, especially after I had given her the sword.

I was a fool.

"*Fuck*," Nathan cursed. "Xanon Naan has the Wielder's sword?"

"It's been hours. I assume she went straight to him."

My friend was shaking his head at me, the white of his eyes starkly contrasting with his brown irises. "Why, Dom? Why would you give it to her? Why would you *ever* let her leave with it—knowing it was going to Naan?"

"*I don't know!*" I snapped. "My head is fucked. I. Don't. Know." I had no idea whatsoever—not even about myself.

"What does he want with the sword?" Inesa asked.

I rubbed a hand over my forehead. "It's an ancient artifact. Worth as much as a small country, probably."

"Xanon Naan doesn't want it for the price it could fetch,"

Nathan cut in. "It has *power*."

"Not anymore, it doesn't."

"*Dominic*, I did my master's thesis in history on the topic. All sources agree it's in slumber—not dead."

Inesa cleared her throat. "So, what does that mean? Would he be able to use it?"

Both of us looked at Nathan. I had a sinking feeling in my gut that I fucked up, big time. I had let emotions—the disappointment, anger and hurt of Leyla's betrayal—cloud my judgment, and now others would have to pay for it.

"Let's pray to the fucking gods he does not know how."

CHAPTER FORTY-FIVE

Leyla

I had no recollection of how I ended up in Ashrior. Everything happened in a haze. Once I exited the aircab, I phoned my father to arrange a private meeting spot. Being out in the city made me anxious. I hadn't checked the article to see how many people had read it, but I knew it would be enough to get recognized.

The location he had sent me was in a poorer neighborhood of Ashrior—one of the areas Dominic had warned me away from. I understood why; I passed several people that seemed out of it or too fucked up to realize what was going on. The irony of the situation didn't escape me. I knew my part in it.

And now Dominic did, too. Dominic—who had been *so* angry. *So* disappointed in me.

Drops of water splashed onto my face, and I looked up. Rain seeped through cracks and holes in the ground above, reaching the Undercity. The weather had taken a turn for the worse since I had left Ashtior.

Reaching the building, I entered it with trepidation. It was dark, the ground wet, and the space made me feel instantly claustrophobic. My father was already waiting inside, together with Ulverin and Zade. They spoke to each other, but their conversation stalled as I entered, all eyes going to the clothbound item in my hands.

"You didn't hide it?" Ulverin asked, grimacing.

"It is concealed."

My father stepped forward after silencing Ulverin's next comment with a hand on her shoulder. "Show me, *Cara*."

My grip on the bundle tightened. "What are your plans for it?"

His eyes, which had been glued to the item in my hands, moved to mine. "We've gone over this, Leyla. You will see. Don't worry. Nothing will harm you."

It was all fucked either way. Too late to back down now. I stalked forward and laid the bundle on the table. I debated dumping it on it, but throwing a tantrum would only cement their opinions of me. Those emotions had no right to be there or to be experienced by me. My actions had been voluntary. No one had forced me.

My father deftly unwrapped the clothed exterior to reveal the sword—still the same as when Dominic first showed it to me. He had already known about the article, then. I hadn't even thought about the possibility of Dominic swapping it.

I hoped he did—wished he had expected me to take it.

"You did so well," my father said breathlessly. Even Zade stepped closer to look at the sword—*no*—he didn't look at the blade at all. He was watching me, stepping closer to *me*, his blue eyes worried as they roamed over my face.

He mouthed, *are you okay?*

My nostrils flared, and I looked away, blinking furiously.

Ulverin also stepped closer, looking at the ancient weapon.

"How do you know this is it?"

My father didn't look up as he grabbed the hilt of the sword and raised it in the dim lighting of the room, reflecting it on the metal surface of the blade. "I can feel it. Its power is faint, but I can sense the ripples."

The red-haired Daemon merely raised a skeptic brow as she looked at the blade.

"You have no idea what you've accomplished," my father told me, still looking at the sword, letting his hand glide over the rounded ornament, as if he was caressing a lover. "I knew you had it in you." With this, his eyes moved back to me.

I could only swallow and give him a weak nod in response. "Can I go now?" I asked.

He nodded, attention moving back to the sword. "Get some sleep, I will get in touch. I am proud of you, daughter."

Here they were, all the words I had ever wanted to hear spilling from my father's mouth. I didn't feel euphoric like I'd imagined. All it did was dig my agony deeper, shoving it down with such force that the realization of the situation sank in—an anchor rooting me in place, one I'd never be able to lift.

I nodded and turned around. I wasn't proud of myself. Not in the slightest.

All I felt was disgust.

"Leyla?" Zade called after me, the first thing he'd said since I arrived. I halted, facing them once more.

My father looked from the table to Zade, who had walked closer to me.

"Leave her alone," my father barked. "You've done enough, don't you think?"

Ulverin looked from me to Zade, to Xanon beside her, with a bored look.

"She is not well." This came from Zade. He was gesturing with his hand to me. Anger had replaced the sadness in his blue eyes.

"Leyla is tired," my father said. "Let her go."

Inhaling, I tried to force a smile on my lips to tell Zade I was doing *fine*—that going against my father wasn't worth it—but the gesture didn't stick. When I turned on my heel again, nearing the exit, my chin started trembling from the effort it took me not to cry.

Zade had been right; I wasn't well. Far from it.

I pulled the hood of my jacket further over my head, shielding myself from the rain and unwanted attention. No one had recognized me yet, but the time of night and weather had probably helped with that.

There was no way I could go home tonight. Selfish as I was, I didn't want to be alone. I'd even prefer wandering the streets over sitting in that apartment, surrounded by reminders of Dominic, of the life that was now over.

Zade had been calling me non-stop after I left Ashrior, but I didn't want to talk to him. He couldn't help me, and there was nothing I had to say. He had cared for me in his own way, but things happened. Our relationship had changed. He was no longer that person for me.

I arrived at Dana's apartment building in the Ethereal Domain. On the first ring, nobody answered. On the second, I was growing afraid Dana somehow knew it was me and intentionally ignored me. By the third, my resolve was hanging by a thread. I tried reaching Dana by calling her, but the amount of rain that was pouring down made it hard to touch my phone's screen.

I let out a frustrated cry and threw my phone against the wall with all the strength I could muster. A loud crack followed, and the fractured screen flashed a few times until it turned black. Taking the phone from the ground, it was clear I had ruined it—yet another thing.

There was too much pent-up energy, rage, frustration, and sadness inside of me. And I didn't know how to get it out.

I dropped my hands in defeat and looked up at the sky. The large disc of Ashtior did nothing to shield the rain pouring on my face. Everything about this *lightdamned* city made me think of Dominic, being up there, doing the gods knew what.

How deep did my betrayal cut him? Was his wound as deep as mine? Worse?

I didn't know when I started crying, but tears were streaming down my cheeks, mingling with the rain. I stepped back, bumping into a wall, and sagged to the ground, letting the storm swallow my sobs.

After what felt like hours, a car pulled up to the sidewalk. The rain had stopped, and I was way past shivering. My body, for once, was completely still.

"Ley?" a worried voice reached me.

Suddenly, Dana crouched in front of me, and two warm hands smoothed my hair and grabbed my face. "*Damn it, Ley.*" She helped me stand and hugged me tightly. "I've searched everywhere for you."

I tried swallowing.

"I was worried *sick*!" she shrieked into my hair, a sob breaking free from her.

Why would she be worried about me? Backstabbers and liars were alone in this world, for good reason.

My stiff lips opened. "I'm sorry." *About everything. For having to worry about someone who is not even worth thinking about.*

Dana took her keys from her pockets and hauled me inside. "Let's warm you up."

The way into her apartment was a blur, but she never let go of me. She had her arm around me the entire time. I was so fucking grateful to her.

She stepped away, and I heard a bath running in the distance. I just kept standing in the hallway.

"What happened, Ley? Where were you?"

"I'll explain," I said, voice hoarse. "Everything. And if you want me to leave at any point, I will. Just say the words."

Dana huffed an indignant breath. "Are you crazy? I'm not throwing you out."

"Just—know you can, alright?"

"Yes, well, thanks for the green light regarding my *own* home." She rolled her eyes and started helping me out of the wet clothes before handing me a steaming cup of tea and ushering me into the bathroom.

When my body had thawed in the steaming bathtub, Dana eventually knocked on the door and pulled over a chair, sitting down beside me. "So," she said. "Why don't you start at the beginning?"

"I fucked up so badly." I had pulled my legs close to my body in the warm bath and pressed my eyes to my knees. "You must hate me," I mumbled into my skin. Everything I told her added up: the Ambrosia, deceiving Dominic, who my father was, Bohrod, Zade... And I probably hadn't even covered every little lie in between.

Dana still hadn't said a thing. She was chewing on her lip with a conflicted look. "Well, you aren't wrong about that."

Another tear escaped me, and my hands grabbed my legs in a bruising grip.

"I don't know this part of you, but I don't hate you, Ley. I could never. Yeah, you have a father who's the fucking devil incarnate—I mean, *shit*, I'm sorry, though he is currently public enemy number one. And you've made some fucked up decisions. But you're still you. I love you. You were there for me through it all."

I looked up, and Dana offered me a tight smile. "I only wished you had told me. That you felt like you could trust me enough."

"It wasn't about trust," I said immediately. "For my father, yes. But in the end... I didn't want you involved. I think it was a way of protecting you—and myself."

Dana pulled her hands through her pink hair. "Family is complicated. Yours especially."

I leaned my head back against the tub, rubbing at my chest to get the pressure to ease. It felt like my heart was beating through sludge.

"We'll figure it out." My best friend's voice was filled with resolve. "You stay here for as long as necessary. Your apartment was flooded with press this afternoon anyway, and I'd bet they'll be back today, too."

"Thank you." *What had I done to deserve a friend like her?*

Dana took the empty tea mug from the edge of the bath and just nodded. "You don't have to thank me, Ley. You'd do the same for me. We're family."

CHAPTER FORTY-SIX

Leyla

A few days passed, and I only went outside when most people were asleep. My phone was officially dead, so I hadn't been in touch with Zade or my father. I didn't plan on fixing it or getting a new one soon. Being unavailable, alone with my miserable thoughts, suited me just fine.

I also had no idea how bad the fallout from the article was, but Dana had promised not to inform me. Although she clearly had to get a little readjusted to me after my confessions, everything between us quickly returned to normal. Sort of.

While she was at work, working even longer hours than I realized, I spent my days binge-watching reality TV like a waste of space. There was no way for her to let me know when she came home, which differed each night. We ate together every time, talking things through—which was the most peaceful moment of my day. And despite her bringing back delicious food every time, I couldn't get much past my throat.

Dana sat opposite me, her plate empty, as she took the bottle of wine and poured herself a glass. "Tell me more about Zade."

The first night we discussed the article, I tried explaining the published photos, including the one of me and him, but I hadn't told her more than a name, and that we had been sleeping together for years.

"What do you want to know?"

"How did that work? Did you have feelings for him?"

Swallowing, I pulled one of my legs up on the chair and close to my body. "I used to when I was younger. I still care for him now, but it's complicated."

She arched a brow. "Because of Dominic?"

"Because of everything." I combed a hand through my hair. "Zade had never wanted my father to know we were seeing each other—which suited me just fine, we weren't in a committed relationship. But when my father asked me to get close to Dominic, he did not object and naturally, we took a step back."

"Because you had to use whatever means necessary?"

Nodding, I said, "Don't get me wrong, I wasn't pressured into anything. And although at first, Zade appeared to be fine with it, later on, as time progressed and Dom and I grew closer, he did not take it as well as I thought. Our... relationship changed. Things turned darker, and he was a mess."

"So what, he kept harassing you?"

"It's not like that."

"But that kiss in the newspaper was against your will? You told him no."

I had told him no on several occasions.

When I didn't respond, she sighed. "I think it's pretty simple, Ley. If a guy's into you, and I mean, really fucking obsessively into you, he would show you off to the world so unabashedly you'd practically be wearing his name as a tattoo on your forehead." Her eyes were piercing, conveying something. "Someone who wants to keep you a secret does not care about you enough. Those boys should be proud, but instead they're just plain narcissistic."

The unspoken meaning echoed through my skull as if she had said it. I pushed down the regret I should not be feeling.

"On the night of the photo, Zade came to my apartment, drunk, and told me to end things with Dominic. By then... I don't know. I'd just been done with it all. The whole situation had fucked with my head. I wasn't sure of anything, least of all my feelings for Dominic." I poured my own glass of wine. "And in the end, I still betrayed him—for some sort of misplaced revenge."

We were both silent.

"Life is complicated, Ley. Families in particular." Dana sighed and sipped from her wine before glancing back at me. "Nathan asked me if I knew where you were."

"When?"

"Today."

Anxiety zipped through my body. No search warrants were given out for me, but I was sick of counting down the days till they would. It would harm Dana when they found out she was protecting me. "You don't have to lie to him."

She smiled. "I know."

I didn't know if my father had reached out. He was aware of where I was, though. He had to be; my shadow had probably traced me back from Ashrior to the Ethereal Domain. Yet no one had come to get me. I was used to being out of touch with my father for weeks at a time. Maybe he was too busy with his new toy. Maybe he was the one who held off any warrants. Maybe he was giving me time to come to terms with what I'd done. *Accomplished.*

It didn't matter.

"I thought avenging Bohrod by taking something from Dominic would make me feel better. I thought getting my father's pride and approval would give me everything I desired."

The little girl who froze when her uncle was brutally killed had been hurt a long time ago, but it was too easy to blame either the Archangel or the system. People sometimes did horrible things, and I had not known how to grieve or give it a place—how to live in an unfair world without wanting to even the scales.

I had lashed out because I had been hurting, yet all it did was bring more destruction into this world. It took more from me, making me feel emptier.

I swallowed the last bite of food with some wine and put down my utensils. "I'm going to turn myself in tonight."

Dana set her glass down forcefully. "What?"

Putting a strand of my black hair behind my ear, I wetted my lips. "I can't do this anymore." Guilt had been chipping away at me. I wanted to be punished, needed the reprimand—needed to feel like my actions were met with an equal reaction.

"Dominic pressed the sword into your hands, right? You told me he gave it to you. Something like that might hold up in court."

"Dana…"

My best friend looked at her plate.

"Before I do, I want to go by my apartment and change into fresh clothes, okay?" In truth, I wanted her to have some of my valuable things: the paintings, jewelry—anything that could sustain her business if she wanted to start.

Dana swallowed. "I don't know, Ley. Maybe Dominic

decides not to prosecute?"

"If he won't, someone else will. That sword didn't belong to him."

I would be honest about betraying the Archangel's trust by going through his home. That I only got close to him so I could steal the sword. I wouldn't tell anyone Dominic had handed it to me; I'd explain the Archangel hadn't even been *there* when I took it. However, I wouldn't tell them about my father. I'd say I sold it to an anonymous buyer in the Undercity.

"Is there still press at my apartment?"

She sighed. "Last I checked, most of them had given up."

"Will you wait up for me?" I asked her.

Dana grabbed my hand on the table. "If you thought I was going to let you do this alone, you're out of your damned mind."

My shadow was nowhere to be seen, but I knew he must be around. Had he reported back to my father yet? Had he told him his daughter was weak and had been holed up at her friend's apartment? Would he report back to my father quickly enough to prevent me from handing myself in?

We stepped out of the taxi on the sidewalk, and I rummaged through my bag, searching for my keys. The street was deserted, back to normal. The entrance to my home looked like I hoped it would. There was no graffiti telling me I was a liar or a whore, or any signs of breaking in.

As we stood in front of the door, I was still searching for the keys I should've had in my hand by now. Dana leaned on the frame, gazing out into the street. Suddenly, bright lights lit up her face, and she squinted her eyes, hovering her hand above them, looking at whatever douchebag put on his high-beam car lights.

The light expanded, and the street filled with the sound of slipping tires. Dana's eyes widened, and she straightened, pushing away from the door frame. "What the—"

I turned back the moment I pushed the keys into the keyhole and watched as five dark figures jumped out of a large black van that had stopped in the middle of the street. They were concealed from head to toe. My body locked up as I noticed the white skeletal smile painted on the mask they wore.

They were *not* cops.

I jerked open the door and pushed Dana roughly inside, slamming it shut behind me. I barricaded the door and locked it for the first time. "FUCK!"

Dana was already running upstairs, and I followed her, dropping my keys on the way there. I rushed down and quickly swept them off the step just as I heard the door downstairs creak in protest. Muffled voices sounded from beyond the only barricade between them and us. My fingers tightened on the keychain, and I ran upstairs, sifting through them to get the right key to open my door.

"Call the cops, Dana!" I hissed. My phone was gone. I couldn't do anything. All the blood had drained from my face. Breathing was hard as I unlocked my front door. Who the hell were these people? What were they doing here? And where the fuck was my shadow? He'd better be running to my dad to tell him what was happening so he could send backup.

My best friend held the phone to her ear and looked wide-eyed as we both heard a loud crash downstairs and banging footsteps vibrating on the stairs, running through the hall.

Not knowing what else to do, I pressed my back against the door.

"I can't get through," she whimpered. "All operators are busy." Her hands were shaking as she tried another number, pacing back and forth through my living room, pushing her hand to her forehead.

The door shuddered, the hinges groaning, and my back ached from the force they used.

Dana whined as that call didn't go through either.

A loud bang busted against the door again, and my whole body shook as I stood against it, pushing back. Dana was typing on her phone, wiping away the tears clouding her vision.

"*Fuck. Fuck. Fuck,*" I muttered, praying to the gods—whoever was listening—that we would get out of this situation unharmed. That help would come on time.

"I texted Nathan." Dana typed something on her phone and put it back to her ear, still calling. "He will come," she told me. "*He will.*" She sounded like she was trying to convince herself.

I shook my head, warding off any invading thoughts. They would not get here in time. They couldn't. Where the hell was my father? My shadow?

"*Godsdamned police!* Fucking answer!" Dana growled.

Curses and muffled voices rang from the other side of the door when the banging stopped.

A ping sounded, and Dana lowered her phone from her ear, looking at the screen, her eyes widening. "He is coming!" she practically yelled, adrenaline taking over.

At that moment, the door took a significant hit, and I felt a sting of pain shoot down my spine. I clenched my teeth to keep from screaming out. "Get out of here," I hissed at Dana. "Through the window!" I added, whisper-shouting and pointing to the windows in my kitchen accessible from other roofs.

"No!" she shot back, eyes still wide. "I'm not leaving you, you idiot."

"They're here for me, Dana. *Get the fuck out!*"

The door burst open against my back, and I tumbled forward, pulling Dana to the windows. I opened one and tried to get Dana on the kitchen counter, out of the apartment, but hands dragged me back before I could push her through.

"Don't touch me!" I screamed, kicking my legs, but to no avail.

If my shadow would ever show themselves, this would be the perfect time. They had to be skilled if my father assigned them to me or at least capable of getting help quickly. But—*nothing*. There was no one barging through the door.

Dana was pulled away from the window, thrashing like a banshee. Her hands were pried from the counter, and she collapsed on the floor, screaming in pain before her assailant kicked her between the ribs. She wheezed, sobs wreaking her body.

I screamed from the top of my lungs, nearly foaming at the mouth at the sight of my best friend curling in on herself and one of the dark-clad figures taking the phone from her hands and destroying it with the back of a knife on the kitchen counter.

The person behind me twisted my arms back painfully, and the other kicked Dana again as she tried to get up.

"Don't fucking touch her!" I screamed.

The hold on my arms tightened, and my body screamed

out in protest. As the other person made another move to hurt Dana, time stopped.

Instinct took over, and I erupted.

It felt as if my head split apart, a loud ringing sound vibrating through my skull. Suddenly, the arms holding me let go, and the person who had kicked Dana slumped to the floor, both of them clutching at their throats.

Anger rolled off me in waves as I took the opening to help Dana up. She was still trying to catch her breath, her face wet with tears as she clutched a hand against her rib cage. In this state, I couldn't get her through the window—I couldn't even get her to stand on her own. I brushed a hand over her hair and promised to wait with her until help arrived. I looked through the apartment and noticed a third guy, also on the ground, face-down. Whatever was happening, my brain couldn't compute, but I wouldn't stick around to see what happened next. Help would come; it had to—

I felt a sharp sting in my neck and smacked at whatever it was. Without delay, Dana and I were forcefully torn apart, our bodies separated.

"The bitch killed them," an unrecognizable voice sounded from behind. "They're fucking dead!"

I was still clutching at my neck as I started blinking and wobbled on my legs, panting. Another sting in my upper arm, and I looked at whatever was the cause, seeing a black-gloved hand pushing a needle into me.

"No," I gasped, panicking as I looked at the leftover coppery sustenance that was still inside the syringe. "No!"

With this second wave of product flowing into my veins, I sagged through my legs.

Dana cried out for me. "Leyla!" She was being hauled

from the ground by another of those figures. "*Leyla!*" she called again as she tried to get close to me, but then they pushed a needle into her neck as well. Dana shrieked as they dragged her from the apartment, out of sight.

I tried to speak, but my tongue felt too thick. My world tilted, and after a few loud beats of my heart, they were moving me, too.

Then, nothing.

EPILOGUE

Dominic

I was the first to arrive at Leyla's apartment.

My bones groaned with effort as I landed from my flight with such a loud bang that the entire street seemed to shake on its foundations. I didn't bother pulling in my wings, my feathers brushing against the remains of the destroyed doorway. The sight of it made my blood boil.

Being in the shower, I had missed Nathan's calls, but his one text had been enough. *Dana and Leyla are in trouble at Leyla's apartment. They need help ASAP. I'm on my way.* I had thrown on the suit I had worn today, still lying discarded on the bed. All I'd send back was, *OMW*.

There was nothing to hear—no voices pleading for help or movements indicating anyone was here. Leyla's apartment door had also been destroyed, the brunt force of the attack visible on the abused frame.

Inside, the first thing I noticed were the bodies, three of them. I searched the entire place, but neither Dana nor Leyla were anywhere to be seen. They had been here, though. That much was clear.

I wanted to turn back and scour the city for them, but I

knew it would be pointless if I didn't know which direction to look in.

My feet continued, and my eyes found the painting I bought her at the gala, leaning against the wall with my written note on the dresser next to it. I continued into her bedroom, my eyes raking every inch of space, but stalled as I noticed the smaller painting hanging above her bedside table. It was the storm canvas—the one she'd bought for her 'client' at the auction.

I had forgotten about that one.

Outside, I heard a car pull up with squeaking tires and a speeding set of footsteps on the stairs not much later. Nathan rushed into the apartment behind me.

"They're gone," I exclaimed from the bedroom but didn't avert my eyes as I kept staring at the storm painting. It perfectly captured the conflicting feelings brewing inside of me.

Nathan cursed, his eyes feral as he breathed in and out in deep gulps. "*Shit!*" he roared as he slammed his fist against the wall.

I walked back into the living room as Nathan picked up a broken phone, his hand curling around the device, before he crouched in front of one of the bodies, tipping the guy's head back to show the mask. "A Sanguis gang," he muttered. "Rival?" He looked at me, and I pushed a hand through my hair. They had to have been in a hurry if they hadn't taken their deaths with them or cleaned up the evidence. "Guess they also found out she is his daughter," Nathan said.

My anger spiked as my palms started sweating. I felt restless. Nathan and I both knew these people were ruthless.

Nitas had told me he had looked into Leyla after he'd learned about the article because he had his suspicions when he met her at the club and had sensed something about her. When I saw him yesterday, he told me her name wasn't *Cuprum* but *Naan*—Xanon Naan's *daughter*.

It made sense. It brought another perspective to the whole picture I had conjured of Leyla. I thought I'd seen her do good with Lodana and the homeless people; it had all looked so sincere. But it wasn't; it had been a performance to benefit Xanon. She *owed* him because she was loyal to him.

Her father.

She had tried to tell me. *You don't understand.*

I hadn't been able to sleep in fucking days thinking about it all on a loop. She really messed me up, just like she intended.

"*Dom*—" Nathan said, his voice hitching.

Shaking the thoughts from my head, I walked over to where he was still crouching on the floor. Nathan stood slowly, walking backward, shaking his head. He was holding one of the masks in his hands.

I frowned. "What?"

Nathan looked like he was going in shock.

I got closer to one of the bodies he had unmasked, looking at their exposed face. What I saw made me recoil, reel back, blinking in slow motion. As if time sped up again, I examined the other corpses, yanking off their masks with aggression. Their faces, the three of them—

Blue veins bulged from their skin, and red blood had dried in streaks beneath their eyes, oozing to the side, some of it staining the floor beneath them.

All. The. Fucking. Same.

"*I killed them,*" Emiliana said.

I took her face between my hands, brushing the blonde strands of hair behind her ears, averting her gaze from the bodies and onto me. "What happened, Coranima?"

Tears were streaming down her face, and she clutched my wrists and started moving frantically—as if she were in pain. "I killed them," *she repeated.*

"You're okay, Emiliana. You're okay."

She shook her head and tried pushing me away from her. "Stay away from me," *she said with a loud sob.*

"Calm down," *I muttered against her skin as I pulled her closer, and she leaned her head on my shoulder.* "You won't hurt me."

Another sob wracked her body. She was having a panic attack. With a hand on her head, I rose from the floor, carrying her with me, and turned around, looking at the bodies on the ground one last time before I left the room. Their blood-streaked eyes, the blueish tint of their skin, and the open mouths—as if they'd suffocated.

"I'll take her home," *I told Apolo. Right now, I trusted no one else to care for Emiliana—I didn't trust her around anyone else either.* "I'll come back when she's asleep. Tell Inesa and Nathan to come too."

Apolo nodded. He stepped closer, kissing Emiliana's head before looking at me again. His blue eyes were filled with barely restrained agony. We understood the severity of the situation, but that didn't matter now. Both of us had the same priority.

The girl in my arms.

I stared at the bodies—nearly identical. Their cause of death was one that I knew all too well.

Nathan cursed. "What does this mean?"

A wave of questions overwhelmed me, but at the same time, clarity emerged. I knew there had been something about Leyla—something familiar.

Fatis.

Now I understood.

"It means I'm going to get her back."

END OF BOOK 1

READ THE BONUS SCENE

Read about Dominic Venetia's final Ashar City Cup win.

Download the newsletter-exclusive bonus scene and subsribe to my author newsletter (cancel anytime).

Or find out more about the New Dam Universe:

CONTINUE READING
BOOK 2

ACKNOWLEDGMENTS

The more you do something, the better you get, and I hadn't realized how much I had grown as an author until I reread parts of Battle Heat, my first book. Sentence after sentence, I noticed things I wanted to change or would have written differently if I had written the book now. It was not a pleasant discovery; being a perfectionist made the realization itch. Part of me wanted to rewrite the book and republish a new and improved version.

But it would be a shame if I got stuck on improving my earlier work and did not work on new stories. There are so many left within me that I can't afford it. Another, more relaxed part of me also really likes the idea of having a chronological portfolio of my writing evolution.

The only book you can judge my skill by is the last book I published, and then again, it's all about personal preferences. *Oh*, how I sometimes wish for writing to be more binary: yes or no, right or wrong, good or bad.

Having said that... Leyla and Dominic's story is far from done. I want to thank you from the bottom of my heart for reading the first book in this trilogy, and I hope you join me with book 2, where we will continue this epic adventure about right vs. wrong, magic, and above all... *Love*.

BRITT VAN DEN ELZEN ALWAYS WANTED TO EXPLORE OUR SOLAR SYSTEM BUT INSTEAD DECIDED TO CREATE HER OWN UNIVERSES. WHEN SHE'S NOT TRAVELING, SHE RESIDES IN THE NETHERLANDS, WHERE SHE LIVES WITH HER FAMILY.

WWW.BRITTVANDENELZEN.COM
INSTAGRAM @BRITTVANDENELZEN
FACEBOOK & TIKTOK
@BRITTVDELZEN

www.ingramcontent.com/pod-product-compliance
Lightning Source LLC
LaVergne TN
LVHW091655070526
838199LV00050B/2175